Madly Deeply Wildly

Madly Deeply Wildly

katherine turner

This is a work of fiction. Names, characters, places, and incidents either are the product of the author's imagination or are used fictitiously. Any resemblance to actual persons, living or dead, events, or locales is entirely coincidental.

First edition: June 2023

Editing by Kayli Baker
Cover design by Murphy Rae
Print formatting by Shanna Hammerbacher
E-book formatting by Jo Harrison

Library of Congress Control Number: 2023902945
Library of Congress Cataloging-in-Publication Data available upon request.

ISBN 978-1-955735-10-0 (ebook)
ISBN 978-1-955735-11-7 (paperback)

Josha Publishing, LLC
Independent Publisher
www.joshapublishing.com
Haymarket, VA

Printed in the United States of America

for the one who taught me what is it to love

madly, deeply, and wildly

NOTES FOR THE READER

Content

This novel contains references to and some description of physical and sexual violence in a domestic setting. While not intended to be unnecessarily graphic, the content may be triggering for some.

Music

Music plays a role in this novel. For an enhanced reading experience if you enjoy listening to music, refer to the playlist on page 367 for a recommended soundtrack while reading.

ONE

The blinking cursor on the screen mocked me. It always mocked me. Not that I could blame it; I wanted to be a writer again, but I couldn't write anything. I *used* to be able to write. Not that it was any good, but at least it was *something*. Now, though?

Nothing. Except for a damn blinking cursor, that is.

I shut my laptop with more force than was necessary, but at least I didn't pick it up and chuck it through the window like I really wanted to do. Eyeing the closed lid, I blew out a sharp breath upward, knocking some of my hair out of my face. No matter what I did, my long, wavy, light brown hair was always slipping in front of my face.

Too bad words don't just slip out like that for me anymore.

I pushed away from my desk, pulled on a sweatshirt, and found my tennis shoes, deciding to go for a run rathen than stare at a blank screen any longer. The same thing I decided every day after spending hours doing just that. Before stepping through my door, I reached over and touched the photo of my dad and me hanging on the wall next to the doorway. In the photo, I was fifteen and we were sitting on the porch of the house I grew up in. Well, one of the houses, but this was the one that was home to me—the one I'd lived in with him. We'd just finished a naming battle I lost to him. I always lost to him, although I'd been getting closer to tying him, maybe even winning one day. We were getting ready to leave for my cross-country meet, so I was wearing my uniform, and Dad was wearing the same t-shirt he always wore to my meets or anything else where it could embarrass me. It said "Awesome Like My Daughter." It was supposed to be a gag gift for his birthday when I was twelve, but then he started wearing it because it embarrassed me. We had an agreement that if I won the naming challenge, he'd wear a normal t-shirt. If I lost, he'd take a photo and wear the embarrassing shirt. At one point, I had a box full of those photos, but this one—the only one I had left—was different. It was the last photo we ever took together. It was on the way to that meet that we were hit by a semi that ran a red light. I'd happily have worn that shirt myself every day for the rest of my life if I could have had him back for just five more minutes.

"I promise to make you proud," I whispered.

However, I wasn't sure how that was going to happen when I couldn't seem to write anything.

With a sigh and a forced smile in an attempt to change my sullen mood, I locked the door and tucked the key into the pocket of my gray sweatpants. As I headed down the stairs from my fifth-floor apartment, I pulled out my ponytail and redid it to capture all my flyaways, which would last all of about five seconds flat before they'd be escaping again.

I couldn't remember when I first started running. In my memories, it was just something I'd always done. It wasn't that I was competitive about it, really, but it was an activity I enjoyed that I could also do with my dad. He loved it, too. Rain or shine, even when he was sick, he never missed a run. He said he didn't feel like himself if he didn't get in at least a few miles. When he died, I began running more often—it was all I did in my spare time. I wanted to feel close to him and so I ran, searching for even a few seconds of his presence. When I couldn't find it, I kept thinking if I could just run a little further, I would. I never *did* find it, though, until I moved back to the town where I'd grown up with Dad until he died.

Renata, you must always follow your heart. Trust it—if you listen, it will never lead you astray.

My dad's voice was clear in my mind—as clear as it was when he told me that only moments before I lost him. But when he'd said that, he'd had no idea what my life would turn into. He'd worked hard to make sure I'd always be able to follow my dreams of being a writer, and I was letting him down every day I closed a blank word document. Who was I kidding? I'd already let him down a long time ago when I first lost my words.

I gave a sharp shake of my head to clear the direction of my thoughts and headed toward the local nature preserve where Dad and I used to spend all our free time together when I was growing up, trying to sift through to find my first memory of being there with him. But, like running, I couldn't remember a time when I didn't feel at home in the preserve. I felt an urge to call Connie, but I couldn't do that anymore. I hadn't been able to in a long time. She had been my best friend since preschool, but we hadn't spoken at all in years. It wasn't her fault—it was mine—but an apology wouldn't be enough to fix the destruction of our friendship.

As I jogged past a woman, my lips curved slightly and I tilted my head in greeting, then shifted my eyes past her. I used to study people—their expressions, the way they moved and held themselves, their eyes, the way they dressed, what they were doing—to learn something about them. Then I'd use that information to guess their names. It was the game Dad introduced me to when I was young, and we got competitive about it. I was good, but Dad was better. For years after he was gone, I would play with myself, though I never really asked anyone their names to see if I was right like he always did when we were competing. And studying people enough to get a sense of them to guess their name wasn't something I did anymore, either.

Not since Damien.

I should have walked away the instant he told me his name. Damien means, among other things, one who subdues others. It had been a warning. My chest tightened with conflicted feelings, just as it did every time I thought about my ex. Even now, doubt was clawing its way in; maybe I was being too harsh and a bit unfair. It was the same doubt that kept me in a relationship with him for as long as I had been. Seven years of anger that turned to confusion before morphing into self-blame. A constant cycle that made me feel like I was always losing my mind. But it didn't matter—none of that was the reason I left him. *That* was for something unforgiveable.

Was that really the only unforgiveable thing he ever did to me?

I gritted my teeth and pushed myself to run harder so thoughts of Damien would slip away, but it didn't work. Instead, my thoughts drifted to a time when I used to push myself hard regularly. I had no specific end goal except to run the marathon Dad and I were supposed to run together the year I turned thirty, but I'd always found it rewarding to push myself to improve. I never became obsessive about it and never pushed myself to the point of injury—

Dad had taught me to listen to what my body was trying to tell me—I simply liked to work hard. But I hadn't run more than two miles or sprinted at all in years. Not since Damien and I had been dating for a few months.

"Babe," Damien said, his arms crossed over his bare chest as I laced up my running shoes. Like most nights now, we'd spent the night together. "Are you sure about running this much?"

I laughed, glancing over and drinking in his exposed torso. He said crossfit was to thank for his chiseled physique the first time I gawked at him shirtless. "I love running—you know that."

"Yeah, but are you sure you should be running this much?"

I shrugged, cocking my head at him, confused by his question. "I love it. And it makes me strong."

He stepped over and ran his hands down my legs, nuzzling into my neck. "You're strong enough, babe." He kissed under my ear. "You don't want to look like a bodybuilder, do you?"

I laughed again, stepping away from him, my confusion growing. "A bodybuilder?"

"Yeah. Do you really need to be that strong? Those women look like men. They must all be lesbians."

My eyes rounded and my jaw was slack. "Are you serious right now?"

He huffed out a laugh. "No, of course not, babe. I just don't know why you need any more muscle than you already have."

He stepped up and wrapped his arms around me again, pressing himself into my backside, pulling my earlobe into his mouth. Despite my confusion and aggravation, my body responded, arousal beginning to buzz through my veins.

"You're hot enough as you are," he whispered into my ear.

He spun me around, pulling my shirt off and distracting me from my intent to remind him that I didn't run to look a certain way. His hands slid down to grasp my buttocks, squeezing hard—just hard enough to hurt.

"You don't need a hard body," he whispered again, his lips against my throat. "You're soft and perfect like this. I can be strong

for both of us." He lifted me from the ground by my backside, smirking. "See?"

I rolled my eyes at his unnecessary display of strength. "Showoff," I laughed.

"I'll show you a showoff," he growled, turning and tossing me onto the couch.

Giggling, I said, "I'm sure you would, but I really want to go for a run."

He kissed me, his body lowering over mine and pressing me into the cushions as his hands slipped around to unhook my bra. I broke our kiss, breathing hard and my body warm, but still wanting to go for my daily run while I had the time.

"Seriously, Damien—"

"Shh," he said, cutting me off. "Don't tell me you'd rather run than have me service your every sexual need?" His eyebrow was lifted as if he were joking, but he sounded serious.

"That's not what I mean. It's—"

"Good," he said, cutting me off again and beginning to peel off my pants. "Now that that's settled... I have some showing off to do."

I hated that I was simultaneously disgusted by that memory and self-conscious about looking too muscular. *Screw him. In fact, screw men. I'll be as muscular as I want, and I don't care if I repulse them because I'm not interested in them anyway.* My legs pumped harder, and soon I was gasping in air as fast as I could. Up ahead, I could see a bench and made that my goal; once I reached it, I could stop sprinting and walk. I used to be able to sprint much further, but the years of little exercise and even less food had taken their toll. Less than a minute later, I reached my goal, but barely. As soon as I stopped, my legs collapsed and I tumbled down onto the bench, hunched over my knees and trying to stop the vomit tracking up my throat. Between the exertion and the oppressive, humid heat, I was close to passing out.

Okay, so maybe I'd ignored the signals my body was sending me this time. I wasn't even sure how to listen to them anymore because it had been so long. But this was definitely too much. At least in this heat. Looking around, everything was blurry and dim the way it would be if I were looking through a long, dark tunnel. Closing my eyes, my focus shifted to slowing my heart, and I became more and more aware of how badly my lungs burned. Shit, I was out of shape—more so than I'd realized. It would take a while to build it back up, but I'd do it.

As my breathing slowed, I allowed my eyes to open and was relieved my vision was mostly back to normal. Sitting back against the backrest with a thump, I glanced around at the familiar trees, the same ones I'd watched grow since I was little. As I studied them, I began to feel it—to feel *him*.

"I miss you, Dad," I whispered, my eyes filling with tears. "I need you."

As hard as I listened, all I heard was the breeze in the trees.

I sighed. "I don't know what I'm doing, Dad. I thought I could be a writer and I promised you I'd follow my heart, but... I just keep failing." Tears streamed down my cheeks, and I used my sweaty forearm to swipe them away. "I don't know if my heart knows what it's talking about. I just... I wish you were here. You'd know what to do."

The wind picked up in preparation for an early summer thunderstorm, and the leaves that had been hiding under trees and bushes since fall blew noisily along the paved path in front of me. I watched them go, wondering what it would be like to be a leaf. To be born in the spring and grow and work hard to feed my tree until one day I began to change color and dry out. Then I'd fall and blow wherever the wind took me, the end of my life revealing an entire world I'd been unable to see while still attached to my tree. Was that what all of life was like? Was I just in the summer of my life, where I was working hard but without reward? And then, maybe, in another twenty or thirty years, I would be rewarded?

A flash of white caught my eye just before something plastered itself to my face with a gust of wind. Just as swiftly, the wind shifted, and it fell into my lap. It was a flyer. It had probably blown free of the staples holding it to a telephone pole or one of the several info boards in the preserve. I could drop it in a recycling bin on the way back to my apartment. I scanned the flyer, stopping short, my heart racing all over again.

"Dad?"

I looked around as if he would materialize in the erratic wind that was growing in intensity. Which of course couldn't happen. But no way it was a coincidence; the flyer was advertising a writing conference in mid-June, only one month away.

TWO

Less than two hours after leaving my apartment, I was clean and working on my second glass of water. I'd booted my computer back up and typed in the web address from the bottom of the flyer I'd carried home with me. Reading through all the information on the conference, I stared at the sign-up sheet for long minutes. To sign up or not to sign up was the question.

Sign up.

I typed in my name, address, reason for interest in the conference, and my credit card information, then moved the cursor over the "submit" button and… just stared at it.

The next morning, after staring at the blinking cursor on the same blank page for an hour, I found myself back on the conference website. It was expensive. And while technically I could afford it, it wasn't that simple. All of my money was Dad's money. Money from his life insurance policy and that he'd worked hard to save so I'd have financial support to follow my heart and my dreams one day. After I turned eighteen, I'd invested it and refused to touch it unless I needed to. I'd also worked hard and saved a lot of my own money up until Damien; while he insisted on paying for everything as a matter of pride, I'd also become unemployed. But now I was twenty-eight and hadn't had a job in six years; I didn't even know how to go about getting one, let alone why anyone would want to hire a failed writer with no marketable skills. I'd decided to live off my savings while trying writing again, but I was just about out of the money I'd earned and saved myself, and this conference would mean using the money from Dad. But what if I used it and still failed? That was the fear that kept me from signing up, even as the window to do so was rapidly closing; registration was only open for another week.

I read through the conference information again, lingering on the recommended reading section. While not required, it was suggested that participants read the books in advance as a sort of prep for several of the conference sessions. Maybe I could read the books—or at least one of them—to gauge the usefulness of the conference? But even if it was good, could I justify shelling out that much of Dad's money? My forehead dropped to the desk in front of my laptop with a thunk and I took a deep breath. I wanted to scream with frustration... but I didn't. Instead, I tried to listen to my heart. All I heard was it thumping, however. I sat up and blew my hair out of my face with a huff. I'd give it two more days. If I was still thinking about it, maybe I'd do it.

Two days later, the conference was all I could think about. I couldn't get past the thought that somehow it had been a message from Dad. But I also couldn't get on board with the idea of using Dad's money. Which was why I was now standing in front of a local café trying to find the nerve to apply for the job advertised in the window: cashier. With my heart in my throat, I pushed through the door and walked up to the counter.

"Welcome to Café Brew and Chew," a friendly young woman I guessed was around my age called out. She was taller than me—most people were—with dirty blonde hair pulled into a high ponytail. Her slim figure sported faded blue jeans and a pink company-branded t-shirt.

I smiled, projecting a confidence I didn't feel. "Hello."

"How can I help you?" she asked with a bright answering smile.

The nametag on her chest revealed I was speaking to Fern. It was an adorable name and one whose meaning I wasn't already familiar with; I'd have to look it up later. "I'd like to apply for the open cashier position. Do you have any applications?"

She watched me, one hand on her hip, her eyes narrowing slightly and her lips pulling into a thin line after taking in my appearance from head to toe. "What's your name?"

"Renata Hayden," I replied, hoping I wasn't betraying how unnerving her behavior was. I fought against the urge to shove my hands into the pockets of my baggy jeans or pull down the hem of my t-shirt closer to my knees.

"Ooo, I like that," she said, smiling again and reaching out a hand, her eyes flicking over me once more. "I'm Fern Connelly."

I shook her hand. "Pleased to meet you, Fern."

"I have a thing for unusual names," she said, wriggling her eyebrows and laughing. She gestured around her. "This is my place," she said, her eyes glowing with pride. "Do you have any experience?"

I looked down and could feel some heat rising into my cheeks. "No, I've never been a cashier before."

"Any experience baking or with a latte machine?"

I gave a small headshake, forcing myself to look her in the eye. "I'm sorry, no. But I promise you I can learn whatever you need me to, and I'll be reliable."

She gave a thoughtful nod. "When could you start?"

"Whenever you would need me to."

"You're hired," she said. "Welcome to the team," she added, pulling me in for a hug.

"Th-thank you," I stammered out, stiffly hugging her back and wondering how we'd already moved beyond a handshake.

"You can start the day after tomorrow," she said after she stepped away. "I'll be right back."

She disappeared through a doorway into a small kitchen area, and I took the opportunity to look around. In addition to the tables and chairs and service counters, there were quite a few paintings on the walls in a mix of styles; some abstract, others almost realistic but with lines and dots of gold added to flower stems and petals or the edges of clouds. They were beautiful, and I wondered if they were done by local artists and if they were for sale. Before I had a chance to walk over to see, Fern reappeared with several sheets of paper and a couple of t-shirts in her hands.

"Fill all this in and bring it in with ID at five fifteen on Thursday morning. We open the doors at six. Jeans or shorts or whatever's comfortable and well-fitting is fine, and one of these. Any questions?"

I shook my head, accepting what she was holding out to me. "No. Thank you. I'll see you Thursday morning."

"Sounds good, Renata. I'm looking forward to it!"

Just then, I remembered I had no idea what the pay was—not that it would matter, I'd accept anything—but the bell on the door jangled as a customer walked in, and I decided to wait to ask her until my first day. So I returned her smile, gave a small wave, and headed out the door. Once outside, I let out a loud sigh, my shoulders falling with it; I felt lighter than I had in years.

I'd done it—I'd gotten myself a job.

Screw you, Damien.

I wished for a brief moment to see him again just so I could tell him I'd gotten hired at the first job I applied to and see what he had to say since he'd been so sure I'd never be able to get another job. In fact, he had told me I was "unemployable." Of course, he would deny it if I reminded him of having said that to me. And he might even be able to convince *me* that I was imagining it.

It was definitely better that I just never see him again.

Shaking off my thoughts of my ex, I turned my attention to my next stop: the bookstores on the other side of town to see if I could find the books on the conference reading list.

It wasn't until the third bookstore that I found even one of the books on the list, but I figured that was fine—now that I had an actual job to go to on top of my daily runs and staring contests with my laptop, I might not have enough time to read them all before the registration deadline anyway; I'd know for sure once I knew what my work hours were like.

Heal Your Heart, Heal Your Art by Alan Edwards. The cover was the most interesting one in the list, the one that kept drawing my eye when I was on the website. It was rich, purply-red and indigo with a texture reminiscent of concrete and had an abstract broken heart painted on it. It was sad and beautiful with a bittersweet quality to it. I stroked my fingers over the heart and flipped the book over to read the back cover.

The short blurb talked about finding the source of your broken art, whatever form that took, and healing that in order to find your creativity. *I wonder, will it tell me how to find words when I'm staring at a blank page?* My eyes traveled through several testimonials, then down to the next block of text, the author bio:

> Alan Edwards is the best-selling author of *Heal Your Heart, Heal Your Art*. He is passionate about learning how to unlock creativity to find deeper meaning in life and sharing that knowledge with other creatives. He founded the renowned Pacific Coast Writers group and teaches courses on breaking through creativity blocks. You can learn more about him on his website or connect with him on social media.

I finished the bio then shifted my attention to the author photo next to it. Full-color, it revealed eyes the color of milk chocolate and medium brown hair, a definite shadow on his face from whenever he'd last shaved. He was smiling, but it was a real smile—not one formed just for the sake of a photo. I could tell because his eyes matched his mouth, and there were the tiniest dimples on either side of his lips. He looked like he was caught mid-laugh, perhaps about something I'd said, and the candidness of it was alluring.

Alan Edwards. Alan, handsome and cheerful. Edwards, wealthy guardian.

Well, he's certainly handsome. Appears cheerful. I guess it's fitting he seems to be watching me; maybe a guardian of my creativity, if I had any anymore?

I looked at his photo again, my fingers tracing around the outside of it. He was really attractive—even more so with a name that didn't scream danger. With a shrug, I turned to head toward the checkout with the book in hand.

THREE

"This won't be easy... it'll be downright painful. But in the end, it'll be worth it," I read aloud. I was hunkered down on my sofa with my new book, a glass of water on the table next to me. "Well, Alan, if it's going to hurt, it damn well better be worth it," I muttered, feeling some reservations. What the hell was the book going to have me doing that was painful? And since when did a book recommended for a writing conference even talk about causing you pain? Shouldn't it have been giving me tips to trick my brain into bypassing my writer's block? Giving me an outline of when and how much I should write and a list of various writing prompts?

Was that really what I wanted, though? I'd read books like that before... back when I was first losing my words. I'd bought dozens of books on ideal schedules and prompts sure to blast away writer's block, how to find your writing style, and more. And none of them had helped at all—not even one, not even a little bit. But surely there were so many of them out there for a reason. Surely they *should* have helped me and simply hadn't because there was something wrong with *me*.

But from the first paragraph, this book was different. I could tell the whole thing would be different. And if nothing else, maybe different would be the key to getting my words flowing again; none of the others had been successful.

"Okay, Alan," I said aloud again, as if he were sitting right next to me. "I'll bite. But it better work."

The first few chapters laid the foundation for what the rest of the book would contain, the first exercise appearing in the fourth chapter. But this wasn't your standard exercise. It instructed the reader to recall a specific memory, calling upon the use of all senses. The memory? When you first realized you were a creator.

"What are you looking for, Renata?" Dad asked, turning his head to peer at me from the stove in the kitchen where he was making dinner.

"My pencil," I replied. "I can't find it. Do you know where it is, Daddy?"

I ducked my head under the small table in our eat-in kitchen. We had pencils everywhere, but this was a specific pencil I was looking for: my special writing pencil. I had my writing notebook, but now I needed my pencil so my story would come. It was different from the other pencils—it was fancier. It was a real writer's pencil. As soon as I'd seen it, I'd wanted it. That and the notebook in my hands. They were exactly what I needed. Daddy had hesitated when I asked for the pencil—it came in a pack of twelve, and they were the most expensive pencils we'd ever seen at twenty-five dollars—but while I passionately made my case, he listened to me, just as serious as he was when I saw him talking to adults about work. He always treated me like an equal in that way and never like a child who couldn't possibly have something worthwhile to say. In the end, I had persuaded him with a promise to be very careful with them and use them only for writing in my new notebook. Both items would only be used for writing the things I always had in my head: details about the people around me, then stories about them.

"Ah. I picked it up earlier. Look on my desk in my pen cup."

Sure enough, my pencil was nestled in with his pen collection. He preferred ink to graphite, but not me. He said that would likely change as I got older—I was only eight—but I knew it wouldn't. I loved the way pencils smelled and the way they contacted the paper, simultaneously gliding and catching on its texture. No pen I'd ever tried came close to comparing. Especially since I'd gotten my new pencils.

"Thank you, Daddy," I said as I returned to the table, now with both my notebook and my pencil in tow.

"You're welcome, sweetie," he said, glancing over his shoulder to smile.

I smiled back, then sat. A thrill ran through me as I turned the pages to reach the one where I'd left off. I'd always loved the physical act of writing; since I could hold a pencil, I wrote. First, I wrote nonsense gibberish, then when I learned letters, I wrote those, then words. I would sit and copy down the words from books or boxes of cereal or junk mail my dad hadn't thrown out yet, whatever happened to be close by and gave me reason to put a pencil to paper. But this was different—this notebook was filled entirely with my own words. I'd been working on it for two weeks, and instead of my interest waning, it had only grown with each word, each page, each day. I dreamed about my story at night, then wrote it down when I had time around school and homework and reading club and running with my dad.

"What chapter are you on?" Dad asked without turning around.

I reached the page I was on and smoothed the notebook open, beaming. I could smell the mixture of graphite and paper rising from the pages, and it made my heart race with excitement. "Almost done with chapter six," I said, sitting up taller in my chair with pride. I didn't know anyone else who'd written a chapter book.

"You're making good progress. That takes persistence and dedication to keep working on something for this long," he mused.

I laughed. "It's easy, Daddy."

"How so?"

"It doesn't feel like I'm doing 'work' when I'm working on it like it does when I'm doing math or social studies. It's fun. It's like... um..." I tried to think of a way to explain. "You know when you take me to Twisties to get an ice cream cone after we go for a long run on the trail and it's hot?"

"Yes. That's a special treat."

"Exactly. When I work on it, it's a special treat. I might even choose this over ice cream cones if I had to pick one or the other."

There was a loud tapping—the sound of the side of a wooden spoon on the saucepan Daddy was making spaghetti sauce in—then *he turned to me fully. He was smiling, but his eyes looked full like he might cry.*

"What's wrong, Daddy?"

"Nothing's wrong, Renata—I'm happy."

I eyed him, trying to decide if I believed him. "You look happy and sad."

He chuckled. "You are so observant," he said so that I could barely hear him. Then he added more loudly, "That's because I am. I'm both happy that you enjoy writing so much and sad that your mother isn't here to see this. She always wanted to be a writer, too."

I watched the emotion on his face as I listened. I loved when he talked about my mom, even if it always made him sad. Usually, it was things I already knew, but this was something he'd never told me before. He laughed, but then had to wipe a few tears from his cheeks. Happy and sad together... I learned a word for that the other day. What was it? I was reading and didn't know the word and had to look it up in the dictionary. What did it start with? A? B? Yes—B! That was it.

"Bittersweet," I said.

He shook his head, his eyes rounded as he grinned wide at me. "Yes, bittersweet. Exactly."

As soon as he said it, I had a new story start forming in my mind where I could use my dad's words. It would be a book all about bittersweet. It was different because you felt different things at the same time. I'd always hated having to pick one feeling because I usually didn't feel just one. Maybe the characters could find or create new words for those mixed emotions like bittersweet was.

Jumping up from the table, I ran to grab a piece of paper from the printer on Daddy's desk. When I returned to the table, I wrote down my new idea, then folded the paper and slid it into my notebook. When I finished the story I was on, I would start on the new story, and because I wrote down my idea, I knew I wouldn't forget.

I breathed deeply, barely containing my exhilaration at having another story idea. I was going to be a writer one day... I already was.

My cheeks were wet, the moisture running down my throat and soaking the neck of my t-shirt and the top of my bra, when I opened my eyes at last and allowed the memory to dissipate. The next day, I'd declared to Dad what I'd decided about being a writer, and he'd regarded me with gravity, then given a definitive nod of his head. "You absolutely will," he replied. "I have no doubt." And for many years after he said that, I had none, either.

But then, at some point, things had changed. The words receded into shadow, the ideas no more than nebulous wisps I couldn't quite grasp. Now, I was filled with doubt and would have abandoned it entirely, except that I'd promised my dad I'd never give up. I already had for a while, but I wasn't going to do it again. I'd never broken a promise to him before and couldn't bear the thought of doing so now, even if I still didn't know how I was going to keep it.

My eyes fell and landed on the open book in my lap. I'd forgotten it was there. Setting it aside, I rose and went to the bathroom to blow my nose and splash cold water on my face. I pulled out my ponytail holder, poised to tie my hair back again using the mirror, when a different memory washed over me... an entirely different memory in every way.

I'd been crying then and didn't want Damien to know. When I heard him come through the front door, I'd slipped into the bathroom and locked the door, trying desperately to will the tears away as I dug through the bathroom drawer for my eyedrops. I'd gotten them from the eye doctor to clear redness. They worked like magic—a few drops, and within a minute, the redness was gone. She'd warned me not to use them too often and I'd assured her I wouldn't, but I had to do something to keep my eyes clear for Damien. If he knew I'd been crying, it always made things worse.

"Babe? Where are you?" he called, his voice muffled.

"I'm in the bathroom," I called back, trying to sound cheerful.

Seconds later, his footsteps stopped outside the door, but my eyes weren't yet clear. The handle twitched but didn't turn.

"Why's the door locked?" he asked, an edge to his voice.

My heart raced as my mind spun to come up with a reason that didn't involve telling him I'd been crying again.

"Renata, open the door now," he commanded before I found my voice.

"Just a minute," I said, still trying to force cheerfulness into my voice. "I'm using the bathroom."

The knob jiggled violently, and I began to cry harder. Shit.

"Who's in there with you?" he shouted as something slammed against the door.

I jumped backward and almost tripped over the edge of the tub. "No one," I replied. "It's just me." Swallowing, I leaned forward and flushed the toilet as the slamming repeated, growing louder, Damien's curses and threats of killing whoever was in there with me filling the air. My tears dried up and my body trembled. He was trying to break the door down. I needed to unlock it before he succeeded, but I couldn't move. I was frozen.

The doorframe splintered and Damien barreled in. What happened next was a blur; I went flying backward over the edge of the tub, taking down the shower curtain with me. I landed on my back as my face exploded with pain. I was dazed and shrank away as Damien peered down at me, his face screwed up in rage before most of it slipped away.

"Renata?" he asked, his voice holding a note of near-panic. "Are you okay?"

I stared at him, trying to understand what had just happened, but it was so hard to see through the pain. I didn't respond, lifting my hand and cradling the side of my face. It felt like everything had been crushed by a sledgehammer. I tried to replay my fall in my mind to figure out what I'd hit my face on, but there was nothing. My face hadn't hit anything—it had been hit by *something... a fist.*

Damien had punched me.

The horror of my realization must have shown on my face because Damien was now shaking his head rapidly back and forth, already denying what I hadn't even said aloud yet. He reached for me, and I flattened myself against the back wall of the tub. His face tightened in anger and he grabbed my wrists, pulling me until I was sitting up. Then he grabbed me by my biceps and yanked me to my feet. He was pulling so forcefully I almost fell again trying to step over the edge of the tub on my shaky legs. Once I'd cleared the tub, he pushed me down until I was sitting on the toilet lid and crossed his arms, his jaw ticking. He turned and looked toward the wall.

"You hit me?" I whispered.

He rolled his eyes and turned back to me. "Do I look like someone who would hit their fiancée?"

I gave a small shake of my head. "No. But—"

"You fell, Renata, and hit your face on the side of the tub on the way down."

I shook my head more forcefully, and it made the throbbing in my face worse. "No, I didn't."

"Yes, you did. I saw it. Are you calling me a liar?"

I looked down at my lap and began to replay what happened again, but I wasn't sure I remembered correctly. "N-no," I said quietly. "It's just..."

"It's just what, Renata?"

"I don't remember hitting anything—"

"Of course you don't," he cut me off, "you probably have a concussion."

"And why would I have fallen backward like I did?"

He clenched his jaw. "How the hell should I know? I wasn't in here—because you'd locked me out."

I knew he'd hit me... or was I imagining it? Had I startled when he came through the door and fallen backward and hit my face, and it all just happened so fast I didn't register what was happening? I glanced back up at him, tears streaming down my throbbing face. Damien's eyes softened and his mouth pressed into a thin line that meant he was worried.

"We should go to the doctor, babe," he said, reaching out and cupping my jaw on the side that hurt with a sudden gentleness. "You hit your face pretty hard. It's split open and might need stitches."

He lifted his hand and pushed his fingertips into my cheekbone. Something shifted and excruciating pain spread through the entire side of my face. I cried out and pulled away sharply.

"I'm not trying to hurt you," he said, his voice still calm and soft. "I think you broke your cheekbone when you landed, too."

I moved my head absently, my mind grasping and caught in a repeating loop of the few minutes since Damien had gotten home. He reached under my biceps again and pulled me up, gently this time, and I was sore from when he'd grabbed me the first time. Or maybe from my fall? I wasn't sure which anymore. He carefully folded me into his arms and pressed the uninjured side of my face into his chest, then kissed the top of my head.

"I hate seeing you hurt," he said, kissing the top of my head again.

His hands smoothed up and down my back, and the fear that had filled me began to dissipate to some extent. It was Damien. He got pissed off sometimes, but he'd never actually hurt me. I'd been so miserable before he got home that I must have just imagined it to make myself feel better or something.

"Next time, don't lock the door," he added with yet another kiss. "I imagined the worst and you know I lose my mind when that happens."

I nodded, more tears sliding down my cheeks. "I won't."

He pulled away and surveyed the damage in the bathroom. "We need a new shower curtain—we can stop so you can buy one on the way home from the doctor. And you'll need to find a carpenter or something to fix the door."

I nodded again, understanding that none of it would have happened if I hadn't locked the door when I knew he wouldn't like it. I'd need to dip into my savings to pay for it since I'd just lost my job—it was the reason I'd been crying to begin with. I didn't want to tell him until I could do it without emotion. He'd been telling me to quit for months, because it was only a matter of time before I'd be let go, and didn't understand why I cared so much about keeping my job writing articles for a creative writing journal. He'd have been annoyed that I was so upset about what he saw as inevitable. And I knew he wouldn't let me get another job—he didn't want me working at all. He said he worked hard to make sure I could just hang out at home and do whatever I liked, and that I didn't appreciate what he was doing for me when I insisted on working.

But it wasn't that. It was just that I wanted to be financially independent, and I really liked my job. At least, I had at one point, before everything I turned in started getting rejected. It didn't matter now, though, because they'd fired me today. Damien had been right. Just as he'd been right about so many other things we'd argued about before. Maybe I should listen to him and stop trying to figure things out myself... it did seem he knew better than I did.

It was a rough night. I tried to fall asleep thinking about my new job at the café and the memory of my dad, but I still ended up with dreams—nightmares, really—of Damien, a mixture of reality and fiction... at least I thought it was a mix. It was easy to get myself into the same confused state I'd spent years in. I'd learned to question my memory because it was often remarkably unreliable, something Damien had pointed out often. However, it hadn't always been that way. When I was growing up, Dad was always amazed by my memory. He called me a walking dictionary because my memory was strongest with words. But things had certainly changed since then.

On the bright side, there was nothing better to do after giving up on sleep except pick up my new book and start working through it, one exercise at a time. My hand ached and I had a stack of printer paper filled with notes and completed exercises by mid-morning. And while I was exhausted, I still felt more optimistic than I had in a long time. I wasn't able to write yet, but it felt like the words were nearing the surface. Something about the probing questions in the book had loosened something within me. I couldn't find a single memory from my childhood in which my confidence in my writing had been damaged, yet I had a renewed sense of passion to make this work somehow. Wading through my long-ago past had revived my love for the written word and returned my sense of excitement; I was even beginning to hear my heart speaking again. It was too faint to make out, but it was there nonetheless. That's more than I'd been able to hear it in over ten years.

I flipped the book over and looked down at the author photo as I'd already done dozens of times since buying the book the day before. *Yes, Alan, I think I like your book. I didn't find any writing traumas like you assured me I would, but does it matter if it's helped me?* I hugged the book to my chest. *Thank you for helping me.* Then I turned to my computer; I had a writing conference to register for.

After registering, I decided to take my last day before starting my job and venture out to some other bookstores further away to see if I could find the other books from the recommended reading list. Considering how helpful the first one had been already, I couldn't wait to get my hands on more like it.

FOUR

Despite my body not being accustomed to rising anywhere near that early in the morning, I woke thirty-six minutes before my alarm was due to go off at four thirty for my first day at my new job. Anxiety over potentially sleeping through my alarm and being late made it impossible to sleep any longer. Normally, being up that early in the morning would guarantee grogginess, but my nerves were buzzing. I desperately wanted to make a good impression and didn't want Fern to regret having hired me.

Fern... she'd liked my name because it was unusual, but so was hers. She was the first Fern I'd ever met. Based on my first impression of her, I'd guessed her name meant something about vibrancy and maybe having an old soul. I typed in my phone password and searched her name to see if I was right and discovered I'd been close; it symbolized new life or beginnings, humility, sincerity, and sometimes magic. So far, it was the perfect name for the lively, down-to-earth woman I'd met.

Even moving leisurely, it was closer to five than five fifteen when I approached the front entrance to the café. I wasn't the first person there, however. The lights were on beyond a swinging door with a window; someone in there baking? I'd assumed the food sold was pre-packaged like most cafés in the area. If this one actually sold homemade food, it would soon be the most popular one around. I felt a small measure of pride that I'd be working somewhere with real food—somewhere that was doing something different.

"Good morning, Renata," Fern said from behind, startling me. She sounded as perky as she had the day she hired me.

"Good morning, Fern," I replied, my hand on my chest. "You startled me."

"Sorry about that. I saw you when I was pulling in. Follow me, we go in through the back door when the café's closed."

Fern led me around to the back of the building as she talked about what she expected business to be like when we opened the doors, assuring me it would slow down after a while and urging me not to feel overwhelmed by the rush. Early morning and lunchtime were the busiest times of day, she explained, especially during the workweek. As we neared the back door, something smelled delicious... it was like a cloud with the aroma of fresh-baked pastries.

"Oh my god," I said, raising my voice to be heard over the music that blasted from the door along with the aroma when Fern opened it. "It smells amazing."

Fern turned and threw a smile over her shoulder. "Doesn't it?" she shouted. Using a knob in the wall next to the back door, she dialed down the hypnotic, beat-heavy music to a more reasonable volume. I followed her deeper into the kitchen and jumped out of my skin when someone appeared from nowhere between two long metal tables covered in flour and dough. My hand flew to my chest again as I gasped.

"You scare easy, don't you?" Fern asked with a friendly laugh.

I shrugged, my face heating up, then glanced to the stranger whose brows were drawn in as his eyes scanned me from head to toe. My arms crossed over my chest after brushing some hair back from my face. The stranger was tall and broad, with hair the color of roasted chestnuts, matching neatly-maintained facial hair with what appeared to be maybe a month or two's worth of growth. His most striking feature was a pair of piercing eyes unlike any I'd ever seen—both grayish-blue and light golden-brown, and they sparkled.

"Renata, this is Chad. He and the other bakers make all our pastries and breads here overnight. Chad, this is Renata, the new cashier."

He inclined his head, his lips quirked liked he was amused, his brows still drawn in slightly. "Nice to meet you, Renata."

"Nice to meet you, too," I said, stepping forward and reaching out a hand.

Chad looked down with a soft snort, the corners of his mouth now twitching, then raised both of his hands in front of him. "I would, but I think you'd rather I didn't."

I laughed, my face heating again; he was covered in flour from fingertips to elbows, where the sleeves of his black chef's coat were rolled up to. I watched as he lowered his hands back down to the table in front of him and began kneading some type of dough, the muscles in his forearms flexing. He handled the dough deftly, naturally, and it was mesmerizing to watch. There was an incongruous tenderness in the way he folded and pinched the corners when taking in his large, muscular frame. A hmph-ing sound interrupted my study of his hands, and I glanced up to find Chad smirking. He opened his mouth, but Fern began firing off questions about what was in the oven and what was left to make.

I stood by, awkwardly trying to follow Fern's questions and Chad's responses while *not* staring at Chad's hands again, then followed Fern as she gave a quick tour of the kitchen before leading me to the front of the store. I stole a last glance at Chad's back as we passed through the swinging door, wondering if I'd see him again before he left. I kind of hoped so.

"Renata?" Fern's voice cut into my thoughts.

I shook my head to clear it, embarrassed about where my thoughts had been. "Sorry," I said.

"Everything okay?"

"Yes, sorry. There's just a lot to take in."

She smiled kindly. "I promise it's not that bad once you get used to it."

"I'm sure."

She gave me a rundown of how the register worked and provided me with a sign-in number. When she was finished, her eyes fell to my pants and lingered, her brow creasing, before she looked back up. I looked down, afraid there was some big stain I hadn't noticed, but there wasn't. My jeans looked the same as they always did.

"We open in about twenty minutes. Do you have any more questions on the register before we start getting all the pastries into the case?"

“No, thank you,” I replied, my voice trailing off at the end as the kitchen door swung open.

“Pastry delivery,” Chad called out as he headed toward us carrying a large tray full of pastries.

“We were getting ready to grab them,” Fern said with a small headshake.

“Well, other than cleanup and the last pan of turnovers in the oven, I’m all done and figured you could use the extra time to get your new cashier up to speed.”

Chad winked, looking at me as he’d been the entire time. My face heated up yet again. Fern’s gaze darted to me and back to Chad, her lips turning under and her cheeks pulling in. “Well,” she said with a hint of laughter, “that was certainly thoughtful of you.”

“Just looking out for my boss and my new coworker,” he replied.

Fern rolled her eyes, and I suddenly felt panicked. Chad was too close to me, and he was looking at me again as he passed, his arm nearly brushing mine. If Damien saw, he would lose it. I’d already scanned the empty café and the area in front twice before I remembered: I wasn’t with Damien anymore. Besides, I’d moved away and hadn’t told him where I was going. Of course, he could figure it out if he wanted to—I’d mentioned to him before where I grew up, and while he never wanted to hear anything about my life before meeting him, he could remember the name of the town if he wanted. But it had been eight months—surely, if he was going to come after me, he’d have done it by now.

I excused myself to the bathroom before anyone could notice that I was shaking and splashed cold water on my face while forcing my breathing to even out. When I left the bathroom, there was a new person chatting with Chad by the pastry case. She had long, curly, light blonde hair, was a few inches taller than me, and was leaning back against the counter as she described her bad luck with red lights on the way in. Before she noticed me, Chad did. The friendly smile he’d been wearing while listening tightened, and the twitch at the corners of his mouth returned. He tipped his head toward me, and the blonde woman turned.

“You must be Renata!” she called out loudly, smiling.

Everyone here smiles a lot. It's weird... but I kind of like it, too. I smiled back and held out my hand after shifting some hair back from my face. "I am."

She gave me a firm handshake, pronounced dimples in her cheeks. "I'm Caroline."

"Nice to meet you, Caroline."

"Chad," Chad said, holding out his hand, his eyes dancing.

His eyes appeared to have changed color, so subtlely I couldn't quite put my finger on how. Regardless, they were beautiful.

"You guys haven't met yet?" Caroline asked.

I startled, realizing I was still staring at Chad's eyes.

"Well, not officially, because I was covered in flour," Chad said.

"Still are," Caroline replied.

"No—I washed my hands," he said, a hint of laughter in his voice as he wiggled his fingers.

I snorted but held my hand out and shook Chad's. His handshake was also firm, but pleasantly so. I'd expected with how strong he was that my hand would be crushed. Damien had been strong and often hurt me doing even mundane things; he'd said it was something that couldn't be helped when you were as strong as he was. But this man looked to be as strong as Damien, and he hadn't hurt me at all.

Rather than letting go, Chad pulled my hand up and brushed his lips over the back of my fingers. "Nice to meet you... again... Renata."

Caroline and I both broke into laughter, but it didn't seem to bother Chad. Instead, he grinned and winked at me, then strode off back toward the kitchen, humming.

"What a flirt," Caroline said as he disappeared behind the swinging door, then turned to me. Her eyes fell and paused around my legs just as Fern's had... and Chad's, now that I was thinking about it. "Laundry day?" she asked.

The skin on my face felt tight and I had an urge to cross my arms over my legs. "What do you mean?"

She pointed. "I'm not sure how you're keeping those pants up."

"What?"

Holding up her hands in a gesture of surrender, she said, "Everyone has their own taste, and I'm not knocking the wide-leg trend that's coming back, but you'd have to gain, I'd guess, at least thirty pounds for those pants to fit you properly."

I cocked my head. "You think they're too big?"

"*Way* too big—it's almost comical."

She paused, eyebrows falling in and smile fading. Silence stretched between us as I tried to figure out how to respond. I used to wear skinny jeans like she did, I supposed, but it was hard to remember that time. Over the first year I was with Damien, he'd gradually replaced all my clothes, explaining why mine were inappropriate. "Begging for attention," he'd said—attention I shouldn't be getting from anyone but him. If we were going to date, I needed to dress more modestly. And I definitely noticed that once I was wearing baggier clothes all the time, men generally ignored me. Until I met Chad, but that was probably because the shirts Fern had given me were too small.

Or were they? If my jeans really were too big, maybe my shirt *wasn't* too small. It wasn't tight across my chest, although you could make out the rise and fall where my breasts were instead of just folds of fabric, not to mention some skin at my neck since it was a v-neck cut. I hadn't worn something like it in how many years? Five? More?

"I didn't mean to offend you," Caroline said, laying a hand on my shoulder. "Really. I had no idea that you..." She closed her eyes and scrunched up her face. "I suck at being politically correct, I might as well warn you now." She opened her eyes and looked at me again. "You look like you might be homeless. Fern didn't mention that, but... are you?"

I laughed a little in surprise and discomfort. "No."

She exhaled sharply. "Okay, good, I was afraid for a second you were going to say yes, and then I would have been the biggest asshole on the planet. But you look like it."

"Lovely," I mumbled.

She flipped her hand. "Don't worry about it—the customers can't really see below the height of the counter when you're at the register anyway, so no one will notice besides us."

"Okay," I said, my voice barely a whisper as I turned away, pretending to fuss with my purse under the counter.

"I upset you," she said. "I'm sorry. Really. I swear I'm actually a nice person. Let me make it up to you?"

Again, my head bobbed forward. "Sure."

She let out a breath. "Great. We're on the same shift today—if you don't have any plans, let's go shopping together after work."

By the time Caroline and I walked out the door, I was exhausted. The café had had a long line for most of the day, and there'd barely been enough time to use the bathroom. At the same time, it had been almost energizing. Most of the clientele was friendly, albeit rushed, and Fern and Caroline had been patient and helpful as I learned the point-of-sale system and where to find the various items we offered. Luckily, I hadn't needed to make any of the coffee confections—that was something I'd be learning later.

Before leaving, all three of us had taken a few minutes to eat a bagel, sitting together at a table in the dining area while the next rotation of staff handled the couple of straggling customers that came in. I sat quietly, listening to Fern and Caroline chat about how things had gone that morning, what regulars had come in and how they were doing, and comparing to volume on other days. They had an easy, comfortable manner with one another, like they'd known each other for a long time.

I'd once had that kind of closeness with Connie, and listening to Fern and Caroline made me miss her intensely. I wanted to call her and apologize, but knew she'd never even answer a call from me. And I couldn't blame her. I was the one who destroyed our friendship when I was dating Damien... the one who said things I could never take back. The reason I'd even said them was a mystery—I didn't mean them. Damien had assured me that I'd done the right thing and that she wasn't the kind of friend I wanted in my life, but as hard as I'd tried, I'd never believed that.

"Ready?" Caroline asked, breaking into my thoughts.

I swallowed the last of my flavored seltzer. "Ready."

We headed out on foot, then caught a bus to the shopping district, another place I hadn't been in years, and not just in Amestown. Anything I'd needed that I didn't have, Damien bought and brought home for me—so I wouldn't have to waste time doing it, he'd said. I'd missed going out and doing things like that for myself, but had chosen to focus on how thoughtful he was.

As soon as we walked into the first store, Caroline beelined for the jeans section. She glanced at me with narrowed eyes, then looked back to the shelves of jeans. She pulled out a pair and held it up to me, tipped her head from side to side in contemplation, then turned back and began pulling from different stacks so quickly I lost count of how many she'd grabbed. Then she moved from hanging rack to hanging rack, combing through and pulling out a shirt here and there. I followed, equal parts amused and alarmed, sure none of what she'd pulled out was going to fit me. At long last, she wove expertly between clothing racks to a half-hidden dressing room and dumped the pile inside.

"There you go," she said. "Let's start with this."

My eyes wide, I stepped inside, closing the door behind me. As I changed, Caroline picked up conversation where we'd left off when we'd walked into the store. She'd begun with questions about my first day of work, but the questions were gradually becoming more personal.

"Why haven't you had a job in a few years?" she asked, then immediately continued. "Are you still changing into the first outfit?"

I decided to ignore her first question. "No, I'm on the third," I replied.

"No!" she cried dramatically. "I need to see! Start over and show me."

I groaned inwardly. I'd been afraid she'd say that. I wasn't sure I was comfortable with anyone—even her—seeing me in these clothes. They were nothing like the baggy jeans or sweats and baggy t-shirts I always wore now. My hand trembled as I opened the door to the fitting room and stepped out, my eyes darting over my shoulder toward the entrance. Again, I wasn't sure why I was afraid of seeing Damien here, but I was.

Caroline noticed and glanced behind me to see what I was looking at, but then she gave a shrug and returned her attention to me. She stood up and walked around me, making thoughtful sounds.

"Jeans are perfect. Not the shirt, however," she said.

If I'd had to guess, I'd have assumed the opposite. While not baggy, the shirt had some space in it. The pants... not so much. "I think the jeans are too small."

"They don't look it." She reached out and lifted up the front of my shirt to look at the waistband. "They look perfect. Are they uncomfortable? Can you move in them?"

I thought about her question—*were* they uncomfortable? I could feel them touching me everywhere, but I wouldn't call them uncomfortable. And could I move in them? I dropped to a lunge like I would if I were stretching after a run, and the jeans moved with me. Holding the stretch to assess, I could confidently say nothing was digging in anywhere; they felt as comfortable as leggings were when I used to wear them. Caroline's eyebrows raised in question as I stood back up.

"They're comfortable," I said. "They're just so... *fitted*."

She laughed and flicked a hand. "They're skinny jeans. They're supposed to be fitted. But they're comfortable?"

I nodded. "Yeah... they are. Surprisingly."

"I only buy my jeans from here," she said. "They're the *best*. I've yet to find jeans anywhere else that are this comfortable, and trust me—I've looked. I love shopping."

I smiled but didn't say anything.

"Try some of the others, but definitely get these. They look great on you. Can actually see that you've got some shape now."

My face heated and I glanced over my shoulder again.

"Who are you looking for?" Caroline asked, cocking her head. "You keep checking the entrance like you're expecting someone."

My head moved side to side as I turned to walk back into the dressing room. "No one."

Hours flew by, and the exhaustion I'd already felt when we arrived at the first store was nothing compared to what I felt now. But much like when my shift had ended, there was also a strange excitement and optimism. I'd spent enough money to turn my stomach in several stores and had an entire new wardrobe now, bags full of clothes like I used to wear, new running clothes, and my first haircut in over two years, but I'd somehow had fun. Caroline was endlessly energetic, friendly, direct, and funny; my sides hurt from laughing. It felt like the beginning of something, like a new me. A new, Damien-free me—one with a new job and a new friend and new clothes.

I'd learned about Caroline, too. She and Fern had met during their first year in college and had been close ever since. Caroline had studied fine arts and moved to Los Angeles after they graduated, but found herself working three jobs to afford her tiny apartment and having no time to paint, which was her true passion. Fern had moved to Amestown and opened the café. Caroline became depressed and suicidal and stopped talking to Fern until, one day, Fern showed up at her apartment door with a stack of empty boxes and a suitcase. She'd refused to leave without Caroline, so they'd packed up the tiny apartment and Caroline had come to Amestown. The plan had been for her to live with Fern and work at the café for a few months to save some money and get back to painting.

After a few months, however, Caroline discovered she really enjoyed working at the café and decided to just stay. Now she worked whenever Fern needed her and spent most of the rest of her days painting—in fact, all the paintings I'd seen on the café walls had been painted by her.

"I didn't think for a while it was possible to ever be happy," she said, her eyes faraway. "I couldn't see a way out of the way life was then... except one." Her eyes focused intently on mine for a few minutes. "There's always a way to find happiness, though, Renata. Fern taught me that. It's just that sometimes you're not looking in the best places for it."

FIVE

After showering and falling into bed as soon as I got home from my first day at the café and the impromptu shopping excursion, I woke the next morning refreshed and ready for work; I'd liked the people I'd met and was looking forward to spending another day around them. The only problem was that I'd forgotten to set my alarm in my eagerness to get to sleep the night before, so I barely had time to get dressed before I needed to leave. Eating would have to wait. I didn't usually eat breakfast, but I felt like my stomach was gnawing a hole in itself... I'd only eaten a bagel the day before because of nerves earlier in the day and being so tired I simply forgot when I got home.

Fern, Caroline, and I reached the back door within seconds of each other. We exchanged good mornings, Caroline commented on how good my new jeans looked, and we walked in together. As the day before, a cloud of the heavenly aroma of baked goods and yeast enveloped me. I could get used to that smell, as well as the music that was playing again. It made me want to close my eyes and just move to it. Fern and Caroline exchanged greetings with Chad after turning the music down, then he gave a quick rundown of baking status, inclining his head in different directions to indicate where things were as he talked, though his eyes kept darting toward me. He was confident and assured, but didn't seem arrogant, which made sense considering he didn't have a name like Jacob or Gulliver, which would mean greedy or supplanter. On the contrary, Chad meant protector or defender. *And it suits—he definitely seems like a Chad.*

I headed toward the front, not wanting to interrupt their routine, and situated my purse under the register. It was also making me self-conscious that he kept looking at me; I was already unsure about wearing my new jeans, aware of how they highlighted the curves of my body in lieu of hiding them. Especially after they'd drawn the attention of both Caroline and now Chad. After making sure the napkins, stirrers, and other self-serve items were stocked, I checked the time just as Caroline emerged from the back.

"I stocked out front," I called, tucking rogue hair behind my ear for what felt like the millionth time already that morning.

"Great," she replied. "I'll grab the cash drawers from Fern, then we can bring everything up. And we need to make sure we've got the coolers out here filled with milks, creamers, cream cheese—you get the idea. We can pull the chairs down last."

"I'll start on the coolers now," I said.

She grabbed an apron and tied it around her waist as she headed toward the back again. I flitted between the front and the large cooler just through the swinging door into the kitchen, ferrying refrigerated items until the front coolers were stocked. After placing the last of the items inside the below-counter cooler, I stood, turning to find Chad behind me with a tray of pastries. I squealed and my hand flew to my chest.

"I didn't see you." *Or hear you.*

"I didn't mean to startle you," he said, his eyes studying my face. "I was just bringing the pastries up."

My heart still racing, my hand still on my chest, I replied, "I was just going to come back for those."

"I know." He winked, the corners of his mouth twitching.

A gurgling sound interrupted the silence as he slid the pastries into the case, and my whole body leapt into flames; it was my stomach growling. *Loudly*. Chad's eyes widened and fell to my midsection before he burst out laughing.

"Was that—" he started.

"Don't," I said, mortified as I stared at the ground. "Please. Can we just pretend you didn't hear anything?"

"Absolutely not," he replied, still chuckling. "That's the most interesting thing I've heard since I arrived for my shift."

My mouth wanted to grin. I bit the corner of my lip to stop it. My gaze rose to find Chad watching me, his eyes dancing with good humor. He stood maybe a foot away, a hand resting on the back of the pastry tray. His lips twitched again, and we both dissolved into laughter. I threw up my hands in surrender.

"I overslept this morning and didn't have time for breakfast."

His eyebrows lifted. "That happens less than an hour after missing a meal?"

I tried hard not to laugh. "No. I also forgot to eat dinner yesterday."

Chad's eyes narrowed, and his arms crossed over his chest. Were his muscular biceps and forearms solely from kneading dough or did he work out, too? While I was still pondering this question, he turned and went back to the kitchen without a word.

O-kay.

With a shrug, I turned, but paused since Caroline was returning with the cash drawers.

"I already counted mine, but you still need to count yours."

"Will do."

As I counted, she headed back into the kitchen and ferried the rest of the pastries out while I finished with my drawer. I guessed something about my growling stomach had put Chad off, and he'd decided not to bring anything else out. My eyes darted to the swinging kitchen door, but I couldn't see anything. He'd probably already left anyway.

A dismayed Caroline rushed through the door. "Do you have any tampons or pads?" she asked with a hopeful lift of her brows.

I checked my purse, then shook my head. "No, I'm sorry, I don't have any on me."

"Damn. I didn't bring any either, and neither did Fern, and I just got my period. I need to run out to grab some. I should make it back before we open."

"I hope so," I said with a nervous titter.

She flicked a hand, already disappearing toward the back. "You'll be fine if I'm not."

With a deep, calming breath, I walked around the counter into the dining area to pull down all the chairs. I was on my third chair when Chad came through the swinging door with a plate in his hand and that same almost-smile he was always wearing. I paused, curious, and watched him, surprised he wasn't gone. He strode toward me and used one hand to flip down the last chair at that table, keeping it scooted back maybe two feet, then set the plate down on the table.

"Dinnfast," he said, pointing to the plate with a smirk.

I looked down at the croissant with egg, cheese, spinach, and bacon and my mouth watered. "Dinnfast?" I asked, meeting his eyes.

"Dinnfast," he said again. He stared at me for a second, widening his eyes like I should have already understood. "Dinner and breakfast. Dinnfast."

I burst out laughing. "That is *so* cheesy."

"Actually," he said, his eyes bright. "It's only a little cheesy—but I can go cheesier if you like."

He quirked an eyebrow as he waited for me to respond, and I completely forgot how to speak, my face warming. "N-no," I stuttered. "I'm... that's okay."

He laughed and gestured at the chair. "Go on and eat. It's gonna be busy today—you don't want to start with an empty stomach."

I glanced around the dining room, but before I had a chance to speak, he did.

"I've got it," he said. "You can eat."

"O-okay," I stuttered again. I was so embarrassed I thought I might implode, but sank down into the chair. As I did, he scooted it in for me. "Thank you," I said. "But maybe I should check with Fern first."

"Don't worry about that. I've got an in with the boss," he said with a wink. "Besides," he added, smirking, "I can do the chairs in half the time."

I almost choked on my food, and he smirked, turning and starting on the remaining chairs in the dining room. I chewed sluggishly, watching him flip chairs at *least* twice as fast as I had a few minutes ago. So, he wasn't just cocky. I wasn't sure I could ever get good enough to beat the speed of someone who could do it one-handed, but I was going to try. I wasn't usually competitive, but something about him was bringing the playfulness out in me this morning.

When I was finished with the breakfast sandwich, I walked my plate to the kitchen and was surprised to find that Chad still hadn't left; he was in the office, sitting on the desk and chatting with Fern.

I wondered what they were saying, but they were speaking too quietly for me to hear them. I washed the plate, found a clean towel, dried it, and put it away. Just before returning to the front, I looked over and found both of them watching me.

"Was it cheesy enough?" Chad called, grinning.

I bit my cheeks and laughed, noting that Fern was eyeing Chad in contemplation, much like she'd looked at him the day before when he'd brought out the pastries. Like when Caroline interacted with her, Chad also had a familiarity with Fern. *Oh my god, is he her boyfriend?* I didn't have any interest in dating to begin with, but I certainly didn't want to cause any issues with my boss' relationship. I wished I hadn't tossed out all my old jeans into the dumpster the day before... I'd promised Caroline, but it wasn't like she would have known whether I did or not. And if I hadn't, then I would have had them to wear from then on in place of these new jeans that seemed to be attracting attention from someone off-limits.

Apparently, Damien had been right—about that, at least. Even so, I still didn't really agree with him that anyone who wore clothes like what I was currently wearing was doing so only for attention. I certainly wasn't. It didn't seem Caroline or Fern did. And I knew Connie didn't... she never had, even if he'd convinced me otherwise for a while.

My first day off came both fast and slow. I was tired and ready for a break, but also had a twinge of sadness at taking two days off; the more time I spent with them, the more I liked Fern and Caroline. I got along with everyone I'd met so far, with the exception of James, the baker who worked on Chad's days off. Not that I *didn't* get along with him, exactly. It was more that he only cared about finishing up and getting out the door as quickly as possible. And despite my concerns about getting between Chad and Fern, I'd been disappointed not to see him when I came in the next three days after he'd made me breakfast.

The day before, I'd had a panic attack at the register when someone came in who looked like Damien. I'd been so sure for a few seconds that it was him that, even after I realized it wasn't, I couldn't breathe. Luckily, we were slow and Caroline was easily able to handle things until I'd managed to get myself under control. Of course, I'd been embarrassed and mumbled something about needing more sleep, and while neither Fern nor Caroline looked like they believed me, they didn't push the issue. They also hadn't been upset with me like I'd been afraid of; quite the opposite. They appeared to be worried more than anything. But they shouldn't have been worrying about me, either; they needed to feel they could rely on me so I wouldn't end up losing this job, too.

I hadn't slept well, waking repeatedly after dreams about Damien showing up in the café and getting me so confused and disoriented about why I'd left him that I ended up taking him back. They weren't exactly nightmares in the strict sense of the word, since nothing bad happened in them, but each left me awake, drenched in sweat, and my heart racing. Despite that, however, I was feeling upbeat and ready to tackle the next book from the conference's recommended reading list—*Bird by Bird* by Anne Lamott—after a run and a shower. It had helped to receive a text from Caroline that she and Fern weren't sure they were ever going to let me have days off again because everything was so much easier when I was there.

It wasn't until it was too dark to make out the text on the page that I noticed how much time had passed. The book was absorbing, funny, and enlightening, and I felt a little more of that loosening that had begun with *Heal Your Heart, Heal Your Art*. I still wasn't ready to face a blank page again, but the ability to do so with success felt closer than ever. With a sigh, I rose, stealing a last, longing glance back at the book, and headed to the kitchen to make something for dinner. Once I was moving around, I felt like I hadn't eaten in days; I was *hungry*. I'd spent most of the day sitting, but my appetite was always a bit excessive after running; at least that was Damien's word for it.

But screw Damien; I was going to eat what I was craving. I was going to make myself a bowl of spaghetti bolognese just like my dad used to make, and I was going to enjoy every bite of it knowing it didn't matter if it all went to my hips because there was no one there to care.

SIX

It didn't occur to me until I was on my way to work the next morning that I would need time off to attend the writing conference. I wasn't used to having a job to consider and had completely forgotten; it should have been mentioned on my first day at the latest. Hopefully it would be okay; missing the conference would suck as much as getting fired would.

"Good morning, Renata," Chad called with a broad grin, waving a flour-covered hand, as I walked in.

"Good morning," I called back, feeling my cheeks warm. What was it about him that instantly got to me?

He tipped his head to his right. "For you. Breakfast."

I stopped in my tracks, my heart refusing to beat. "How did you know I didn't eat this morning?" I asked sharply.

His hands slowed in the dough he was shaping. "I didn't," he said, drawing in his brows. "I just had some extra dough, so I made you guys pan-fried donuts." He tipped his head toward the office. "They already grabbed theirs."

My mouth hung open for a second. I'd snapped at him without thinking. *Why did I do that?* I didn't know what to say because I didn't know how to explain to someone I barely knew why I'd reacted the way I did, so I just turned and headed toward the office to let Fern and Caroline know I was there. I didn't even remember that I needed to request time off until I was walking out of the office. Stepping back around, I took a deep breath.

"Fern? I'm sorry I didn't ask you when you hired me, but can I request a few days off in mid-June?"

"Sure," she replied, looking up. "Everything alright?"

"Yes," I affirmed. "Everything's fine. I'm attending a five-day conference out of town, that's all."

"Five days? Holy shit, that's a long time," Caroline said.

"It's fine," Fern said, shooting Caroline a sharp look. "You can have it off. Just give me the dates."

"Oh, god!" Caroline laughed. "Yeah, definitely, I just meant that sounds like a long time to be in a conference."

"Yeah," I agreed. "It does. I have no idea how this'll go. It's my first conference."

Caroline grabbed two cash drawers from Fern and we headed toward the front of the café together.

"What's the conference on?" she asked, holding the swinging door open after I passed so Chad could come through with the first tray of pastries.

I kept my eyes averted from Chad's. "Writing."

"You're a writer?" she exclaimed. "That's so cool, I mean—"

"I *want* to be a writer," I clarified, feeling my face heat up. "That's why I'm going to this conference."

"What kinds of things do you want to write? Have you written anything before?"

I laughed at her enthusiasm. In the short time I'd known her, it was already apparent that Caroline loved getting to know people. "Honestly? I want to write anything at this point. I used to write all the time. When I was a kid, you couldn't get a pencil out of my hand. Then, when I finished college, I worked for a while at a regional publication—"

"Which one? Have I heard of it?"

"I don't know. It's called *Including the Kitchen Sink*."

"Yes! I love that journal. It's so much fun to read. They talk about *everything* in there. I love that it isn't just about health or just about politics or just fiction or any other one thing."

I smiled, thinking back to when I first applied to work there. "Yeah. That's exactly what drew me to it."

"Okay, so what did you write in there? I'm sure I've read something and just didn't pay attention to who wrote it."

I shook my head, my gut sinking. "You wouldn't have. I haven't worked there in years."

"Really? What happened? Was there some scandal or is it run by a douchebag? I'll boycott it if so, just tell me, I don't want to support—"

I shook my head again, holding up a hand. "Nothing like that. When I was there, everyone who worked there was great to work with. They were all amazing, talented people. I loved that job."

"Then why'd you leave?"

I was fired, I thought. *I didn't leave—not willingly, anyway*. I was embarrassed and didn't want to tell her that, but I'd had to put it on my job application, so Fern already knew. Surely Caroline would find out sooner or later, so it might as well come from me.

"I... um... I was let go."

"What? Why?"

I glanced away, trying to find words to explain what I didn't fully understand myself. My eyes caught Chad quietly pulling down chairs in the dining room. I hadn't even noticed that he'd begun doing that after sliding the pastries into the case. It meant now he also knew I'd been fired from my dream job.

"I lost my words," I said, looking back to Caroline. I shrugged. "And you can't work for a journal if you can't write anything. Or if nothing you write is worth reading."

I expected her to laugh or change the subject, but she didn't. "I'm sorry, Renata. That sounds awful. Do you know what happened?"

I gave a small headshake, then tucked back wisps of hair that had escaped my ponytail. I wished I did know, but I didn't. Damien thought I wasn't meant to be a writer, that it had been a fluke that I'd been hired to begin with. Any maybe he'd been right. Though Dad had always told me that we were meant to do whatever it was that we were passionate about, and I'd never been as passionate about something as I was about writing. "They just started slipping away until one day I couldn't find any."

"Well, maybe this conference will help you get them back," Caroline said after a pause.

"That's what I'm hoping," I replied.

"It'll happen. I know it."

I smiled politely, wishing I felt the confidence in me that she did.

"She's right, you know," Chad chimed in, heading toward us from the dining area. I hadn't been aware that he was paying any attention to the rest of our conversation.

I quirked an eyebrow. "And how would you know that?"

He leaned back against the counter across from me and crossed his ankles. Time stretched out as he studied me, a seriousness settling into his features. "First, you're determined. You applied for a job you had no experience in and were up front about it—you didn't try to play it off like you did when you didn't. Second, you're obviously smart. While it's not rocket science to learn the ropes here, you picked it up in record time. And you have a sense of humor, which happens to be a marker of intelligence. Third, you're tenacious. You just said you were fired from a job doing what you want to be doing. Regardless of reason, that's a rejection that hurts. Most people would turn their backs on whatever it was they were doing. But instead of giving up, you're doing something that can help you get it back."

Shifting, he lifted a hand, raising his index finger. "Determination." He raised his middle finger. "Intelligence." Ring finger. "Tenacity." He waggled the three fingers he was holding up. "As long as you have those three things, you'll achieve whatever it is that you set out to do."

"I never knew you were a closet motivational speaker," Caroline joked.

Chad chuckled, shrugging. "If you don't believe me, ask Fern how she opened this café. She'll tell you the same thing." His face sobered and his eyes bored into mine. "You'll do it."

My lips tipped up on one side and I tucked my escape-artist hair behind my ear. "Thank you," I said ruefully.

Still serious, Chad replied, "You're welcome."

After a moment, Caroline spoke, and I realized the last minute or so Chad and I had been eying each other. I looked down.

"So what kinds of things did you write?" she asked.

"Um, short stories, mostly. For the journal, anyway."

"What did you write not for the journal?" Chad asked.

Caroline looked at him, smirking. I blushed.

"Well, I wrote short stories. And also some poetry. I wrote some chapter books when I was growing up, but nothing that long after high school."

"What kinds of things did you write about?"

Again, it was Chad asking the question. My blush darkened and I glanced up at him. His eyes were intensely focused on me, his muscular forearms crossed. My eyes strayed to study them before I replied.

"Well, it just depended. I wrote about all kinds of things. My chapter books were about kids my age making it through life with only one parent mostly. One was about a girl who wrote a dictionary with new words for mixed emotions."

"Mixed emotions?"

"Yeah, like the word bittersweet, for example. It's a word that represents a complex emotion, a combination of two emotions, really. But we don't have a lot of words like that in English, so this girl set out to create new words for complex emotions like that."

"That sounds neat, Renata," Caroline said.

Chad nodded in agreement. "What's one of them?"

"One of what?" I asked.

"One of the girl's words."

"Oh... well, anxcitement for anxiety and excitement was one."

Chad nodded again. "So, would my new word have made it into her dictionary?"

I cocked my head at him in question.

His lips twitched; I knew he was trying not to laugh now. "Dinnfast."

I snorted and Caroline rolled her eyes, laughing.

"Dinnfast isn't a complex emotion."

"But it *is* a complex word, right?"

He was ridiculous, but I couldn't help giggling, then biting the corner of my lip to stop myself. "It is, I suppose."

His face split into a cheesy grin. "Does this mean I get credit when you write a new book about collecting complex words that aren't emotions?"

My lip biting failed, and I burst out laughing.

With his grin in place, Chad said, "You're welcome." He winked. "And it's opening time."

Caroline and I glanced at the computer register as he sauntered back to the kitchen. It was in fact exactly time to unlock the front doors.

"He's got an annoyingly good sense of time," she said. "Ready?"

I dropped my chin in affirmation. With a start like this, I was ready for *anything* the day could throw at me.

SEVEN

My heart thumped in my chest as I walked from the curb into the airport after giving a final wave to Caroline. She'd offered to drive me and insisted on helping me pack. Despite my assurances that I was terrible, she still thought it was really cool that I wanted to write. She kept calling me a writer, and while it wasn't true—a writer needed to actually write something—I was starting to like the way it sounded.

Renata the writer.

Renata, writer.

Writer Renata.

But first, I needed to attend this writer's conference.

Going through the airport was an exercise in patience. Wait... wait... wait some more... then rush. Repeat a few times, and then, *finally*, sit and wait again to board. My mind was bouncing all over the place, worry to worry, from ways the plane could crash to falling asleep during a lecture after arriving. My purse buzzed and I pulled my phone out, grateful for the distraction. It was a message from Caroline. Or, more accurately, Caroline had sent it, but it was a photo of her, Fern, and Chad with comically downturned mouths and a message that they all missed me already.

I laughed, my thumb moving over the photo. They'd become like a family of sorts over the last month, especially Caroline. The three of them were already close, and it felt like I was being welcomed into their close-knit group. Chad's arm was draped over Fern's shoulder, her head resting back against his shoulder in the photo. There were days I thought I was wrong and they must not be in a relationship, but then there were days I saw them just like they were in this photo, or hugging, and I wasn't sure. I'd thought about asking Caroline just so I'd know, but what did it matter? I wasn't interested in dating him. Or anyone, for that matter.

I now steadfastly avoided eye contact with Chad at work, and yet even without it, my body warmed when he was around, which was constantly from the time I arrived until the doors opened, and sometimes even for a while after. Just feeling that attraction to him seemed like a betrayal of Fern's trust, though. For his part, Chad continued to bring the pastries to the front every morning and always engaged me in conversation, usually leaving me laughing when he sauntered back toward the kitchen at opening time, the corners of his mouth twitching, his multicolored eyes dancing when I inevitably forgot I wasn't supposed to be looking at him.

Just as there was with Fern and Caroline, there was something about Chad I'd liked from the first time we'd met. I couldn't put my finger on what, but it was something. And that like for him was growing stronger as time passed, despite the fact that the way he flirted with me when he appeared to have a girlfriend painted a different picture of his character than the one I sensed. It was just hard to remember that when I was around him.

I refocused on my phone and zoomed in on the picture until Chad filled the screen. His eyes were a golden, caramel brown in the center with a bluish-gray around them, much like the first day I met him and noticed his eyes. It felt like he was looking at me—not a camera—those unusual eyes crinkled slightly at the corners and betraying that same good humor his mouth was always trying to hide, his lips ever ready to break into a full grin at a moment's notice. My body warmed as if he were actually in front of me, and I bit the corner of my lip, trying not to smile. He was so handsome and laid-back and friendly and cute.

Oh my god, Renata—stop looking at someone else's boyfriend.

With a flick of my finger, my screen was black, and I shoved my phone into my purse. I owed Caroline a response, but it would have to wait until I had enough self-control to open her text message without staring at my boss' boyfriend.

The flight had, thankfully, been uneventful. I'd never flown before and nearly panicked when we began to move. I'd clutched the armrests so tightly I was surprised I hadn't crushed them. But I hadn't. And we hadn't crashed, either. We hadn't even hit any turbulence. Even so, I was glad to be off the plane, my relief overshadowing my nerves about the conference until I was sitting in a cab on the way to the hotel.

Checking my phone from the car, there was another text from Caroline that had been waiting for me when I landed, asking how the flight had been. I responded, also admitting that I was nervous about the conference. After hitting send, I had a wave of doubt, Damien's voice loud in my mind, telling me I was too needy. But then Caroline replied, setting me at ease with a reminder that at least there wouldn't be any exams like in college. Laughing out loud in the back of the cab, I continued to text with her until the cab driver ushered me out of the car in front of the hotel. Once checked in, there was just enough time to unpack and get cleaned up for the first session.

By the time I walked into the "Healing Your Art" session on the third day, I felt oddly energized while simultaneously at my mental capacity. I'd attended lectures on everything from story structure to effective book marketing thus far. Much of it hadn't felt particularly relevant for me, either because it focused on topics I wouldn't ever write about or because it prescribed a process I'd already tried before without success, but at least as many resonated and could be indispensable as I worked on finding words again. I was most excited about this next session since it would be taught by Alan Edwards; I was eager for anything he might have to offer beyond what was included in his book and had high expectations.

What *wasn't* expected, however, was for him to be just inside the doors greeting attendees as they entered. So, rushing into the room, wanting to secure a seat near the front before they were gone, I practically ran into him.

"Alan!" I exclaimed, coming to an abrupt halt before realizing I'd said that like I knew him. He smiled the same smile that was on the back of the book. "I-I'm sorry," I stuttered out, mortified by the way I'd called out his name and tongue-tied by the focus emanating from this rather attractive man who'd also written a book I found helpful... a focus that was entirely on me.

Luckily, someone else approached just then who *did* seem to actually know him, allowing me to slip away and hope he wouldn't remember what I looked like. After reaching a seat, I flipped my head and watched him interacting with the woman who'd entered and relieved me from what was possibly the most embarrassing interaction of my life. Like he'd been with me, he was focused on her as they chatted and laughed. I could see a lanyard around her neck that revealed she was a lecturer, and I wondered what she would be speaking on. After a minute or two, they embraced, then she slipped back out through the doors as Alan headed toward the front of the room.

My heart was still racing from my encounter with him, mild nausea in my gut as he reached a podium to the left of the big projector screen on the wall behind him. I couldn't believe it was him in real life—the man who'd written the book that helped me remember what it felt like to love to write. The same book that was the reason I'd decided to attend this conference in the first place and gave me hope that I might be able to find my words again one day. Starstruck wasn't a strong enough word for how I felt.

His eyes swept around the room, deliberate and unrushed, pausing for a second or so on each face. He began in the back, and I knew at some point he would reach the front row and see me. *Please, please, please don't let him recognize me as the strange woman who acted like she knows him,* I begged the universe. His eyes found mine and his lips pursed together, the dimples on the sides going from mere hints to two prominent crescents, his eyes glittering with amusement as they lingered on me for two seconds... three... four. By the time he continued down the row and I could breathe again, passing out was a distinct possibility. A few heads turned in my direction, looking at me with curiosity.

I should have taken a seat nearer the middle of the room.

When Alan began to speak, all eyes returned to him. The first while was devoted to who he was and what the lecture was about, what we could expect from our time there, and what we shouldn't. He told the story he'd included in his book about when he was young and a teacher gave him brutally harsh criticism on his writing, and then he asked if anyone else had a similar story in their past, looking around as hands shot up all over the room. Mine was the only one that wasn't up. Alan's brows drew in a bit when his eyes passed me.

As several attendees shared their stories, it became apparent I didn't belong in this lecture, either; it was about healing from events in your childhood that were creating blocks in your creativity as an adult, but I didn't have anything in my childhood blocking me. I'd never had a teacher or family member criticize my writing ability in the way Alan's teacher had. I'd never been ridiculed by my grade school peers like one woman or told writing wasn't a real occupation by my parents like another. In contrast, my father had always believed in me and supported me, and anyone I'd shared my writing with was enthusiastic and encouraging.

And yet, when I'd had my dream writing job, my ability slipped through my fingers like sand that then blew away on a stiff breeze. My pieces had started coming back to me from my editor with more and more significant edits, then were being rejected altogether. Someone else had to start writing last minute content when I couldn't come up with something that could pass muster. Then I'd been fired after several weeks of not even writing enough to turn in to begin with. After that, I didn't even try to write. At Damien's suggestion and encouragement, I burned everything I'd ever written by hand and deleted everything on my hard drive. It wasn't until I'd left Damien that I regretted having done that and decided to try again. But by then it was much too late; all I'd done in the last nine months since I'd been on my own was stare at a blank screen.

Even so, I took copious notes on everything Alan said, barely raising my head until the lecture was over. My hand was cramped, and I'd filled pages upon pages in my new spiral notebook for notetaking during the conference. Much of it was essentially the same as what was in Alan's book, simply presented in a somewhat different way. I'd go back through my notes on my own when there was time to pause and consider what I'd written and see if it brought something to the surface that could help me move forward.

I reluctantly packed up my notebook and pen in my bag after flexing my hand a few times to relieve the tension, my mind wandering to times when I'd spent hours scribbling stories in my writing notebooks, something I'd done until things began to go downhill with my column. I'd always preferred writing by hand, even though I'd avoided it for the last year or so that I was writing for the journal. Even with my hand cramped, I longed to continue now; it didn't matter that it was only notetaking and nothing creative. Just the act of moving my hand across the paper, the feel of a writing implement between my fingers, gave me this strangely wonderful feeling of nostalgia, and I didn't want to let it go. I'd always hated writing with pens, but even that didn't bother me right then.

When I eventually looked up, Alan was standing near the podium speaking with another attendee. I debated leaving, but it was my last lecture of the day; I had nowhere I needed to be, and I had questions for him. With my bag slung over my shoulder, I made my way over, leaving a respectable distance between us as I waited my turn. It wasn't long before they were shaking hands and the man who'd been speaking with Alan turned, giving me a friendly smile as his eyes flicked over me. Instantly, I was even more self-conscious. After a month, I was getting used to wearing the clothes I'd bought when shopping with Caroline, but there were times I was acutely aware of them, and this was one of them. It didn't help that Alan also gave me a once-over.

Your clothes are asking for it.

I let out a loud exhale, trying to clear my mind, and stepped up to Alan without acknowledging the stranger.

"Hi," I said, still trying to shake off the stubborn and persistent whisper of Damien's words.

"Hello," he said, holding out his hand. "Have we met before?"

My mortification from earlier grew, and I couldn't speak without stuttering as I took his hand and we shook. "N-no, we haven't. I'm s-sorry about that. I'm Renata. Renata Hayden. I was just caught by surprise when I walked in and you were standing there and I've read your book and been working on the exercises for the last month and just felt like I knew you after that and it came out before I could stop myself," I rushed out in a long, run-on sentence. If only I could have put the words back into my mouth.

Alan's dimples appeared again. He really was cute, though now that I'd had a little time to study him up close, it was nothing compared to how good-looking Chad was. "I'm happy to hear you've been working on the exercises. There are people who think they can read about them and expect something to happen, but you have to put in the work. It's not easy—work never is, but healing from painful experiences is especially difficult. I commend you."

I bobbed my head, brushing aside his comment. "I'm struggling, though. I've been doing everything, but I've gotten nowhere. When I picked up your book, I couldn't do more than stare at my cursor on a blank screen, and that hasn't changed."

His face softened in thought as he rested an arm on the podium next to him. "I noticed you were the only person who didn't raise your hand when I asked about negative experiences that impacted your confidence in your writing."

I gave a miniscule nod. "Yeah."

"We're alone now," he stated, inclining his head toward the other side of the room.

When I glanced around, I confirmed we were indeed the last two people present. My heart sped up a little, but I was comforted that all six doors across the back of the room were wide open, and I could see people milling about in the hall.

"Would you be comfortable sharing your experiences now, without the large audience?" he continued.

The skin on my face tightened. What I was about to say made me feel like a fraud for having attended his lecture, for standing there taking up his time right then. "It's not that I didn't want to share earlier... it's that I don't have any."

He lips pulled up on one side. "Everyone here has at least one."

I eyed the floor. "Not me. But I can't write. Not a single word. I haven't been able to for a really long time. There's something wrong, but I don't know what it is. And what you teach resonates with me, but I just don't have a single bad writing memory, let alone several, that are responsible for my inability to write anything. Everyone in my life was really supportive." I raised my eyes and they abruptly filled with tears, so I glanced away. "I'm stuck and feel like there's no way out."

"Renata, you're on the right path. There's something in your past to heal, even if you haven't found it yet. Sometimes, discovering what it is can take time. Don't give up."

EIGHT

Five days after I entered the airport, I stood at the exit, scanning the cars at the pick-up area for Caroline's little red sedan. Despite my assurances that a taxi would suffice, she'd insisted on picking me up. And right then, I was relieved; I was *exhausted*. Maybe even more so than after my first day of work at the café. It had been five days with lectures starting right after breakfast and running until dinnertime. Five days of being around hundreds of strangers and making small talk at meals. Five days of new concepts and suggestions for writing swirling around in my mind like a tornado of words and ideas. The thought of sitting in the back of a stranger's car for the next hour was almost enough to make me cry.

Despite having checked in regularly via text while I was gone, Caroline was eager for all the details as she drove us toward Amestown. What had exhausted *me* excited *her*; she loved meeting new people and could spend all day mingling in a social situation. Just the thought of mingling all day made my inner introvert start looking for rocks to hide under.

"What are you doing for dinner?" she asked as we neared Amestown.

"Bed," I replied with a yawn.

She laughed. "You have to eat dinner first, and you should have some real food, not that crap they serve at conferences."

"The food wasn't bad, actually. I was surprised."

"It's still not real food," she countered. "Why don't you come over? Dinner's almost ready, and there's plenty for you."

I gave her a tired smile. "Thank you, but raincheck?"

"No!" she exclaimed. "You can't raincheck dinner tonight!"

I laughed at her exuberant response. "I'm really tired, Caroline."

"I know, and I swear you can go home right after, but you can't skip out on dinner. You need to eat, and this way you don't have to cook *or* clean up. Please?"

Again, I laughed, this time at the comical pout on her face when she glanced over at me at a red light. "Fine, fine," I said. "But I should shower and wash off the travel first."

"You're fine, I promise. So, you're coming?"

"Yes, I'll come for dinner," I replied, yawning. "But then bed."

"Absolutely. I'll drive you home as soon as we're done eating. Deal?"

"Deal."

She parked in the garage at the apartment she shared with Fern, and we made our way inside. Hopefully my appearance wasn't as disheveled as it felt; at least we weren't going anywhere public. It would just be us and Fern at their place.

"We're here!" Caroline called into the apartment as she closed the door behind us and the aroma of herbs and onions filled my nostrils.

When I looked over, she gave me a falsely-innocent, sweet smile, and I narrowed my eyes at her.

"Surprise!" called a chorus of voices. Fern and Chad walked in, followed closely by three more of my coworkers who I didn't know as well.

It was then that I remembered: it was my birthday. I hadn't intended to do anything to celebrate it, but in the chaos of the conference, I'd forgotten about it entirely. I also hadn't told anyone... Fern must have noticed it in my employment paperwork. When my eyes darted to hers, she winked, and it was all the confirmation I needed.

"We wanted to surprise you when you walked in the door," Caroline said, "like a normal surprise party, but Chad wouldn't let us."

My eyes rested on Chad for the first time; I'd been avoiding looking at him to minimize the warming sensation he caused. Aside from it being unwanted in general, I felt guilty knowing I was having that reaction to my boss' boyfriend.

"You'd have scared the hell out of me," I said.

Chad shrugged, his mesmerizing eyes darting toward Caroline only briefly before refocusing on me. "Told you," he said to her.

I could feel my jaw drop, unable to stop it. I'd always been the one kid who didn't like being scared or startled by people popping out unexpectedly. I hated it, and it didn't take much to get me. Damien had thought it was funny and "surprised" me often, as if I hadn't asked him not to more times than I could count. But someone I barely knew had figured it out after seeing me for only a handful of hours a week... and then had made sure I wasn't scared by the surprise.

In another timeline, one where I didn't have the history I did with Damien and Chad wasn't dating my boss... I'd have been deeply interested in the man whose gaze had trapped mine. Who wouldn't be? In the midst of using his hands to create culinary works of art and teasing me as he ferried pastries from the kitchen to the pastry case, he'd also been attentively taking in everything else around him. And he was disconcertingly attractive with those gorgeous eyes, lips that were always about to smile, and a perfectly muscular physique—no grossly bulging muscles on him. Against my will, my eyes dropped from his and took in his navy blue t-shirt branded with the café's name and logo, snug across his chest and biceps, and his jeans that were just fitted enough to provide an outline of his thighs. When I looked back up, his lips twitched, his eyes sparkling with something I couldn't quite identify.

Caroline linked her arm through mine and pulled me along, breaking the spell Chad held over me, and I resolved not to look him in the eye anymore. It was dangerous. It made me forget things... things like how to breathe, and what men were capable of when you trusted them, and that this one was taken.

Everyone except Chad squeezed around the small dining table that was set with placemats, napkins, flatware, plates, and white wine. Conversation returned to whatever they'd been talking about before I arrived, and I was content to sit quietly and listen, unnoticed. I learned in the few minutes we waited that Leslie and Drake, two of my coworkers who'd come for the surprise party, were going to a concert the next day with a large group of friends who were all country-music lovers, that Fern had hired two more cashiers and a new baker, and that Caroline was cutting back to three days a week once the new cashiers were trained so she could spend more time painting.

The chatter tapered off as Chad walked in carrying something cradled between two oven mitt-covered hands. Whatever it was, it smelled heavenly; like the apartment already smelled but stronger. My mouth watered as I watched him near me.

"For the birthday girl," he said, beaming.

I remembered I wasn't supposed to be looking at him and glanced away. He leaned over and carefully placed a personal pot pie in a small maroon-colored dish in front of me.

"That's the cutest little dish I've ever seen," I mused, tipping my head this way and that to look at it. "It looks just like a miniature dutch oven."

"It won't be so cute if it takes your skin off, so don't touch it," Chad said. "It just came out of the oven. And it's called a cocotte."

I nodded, repeating the word in my mind a few times so I'd remember it. I hadn't heard that one before. Surely, I'd read it at some point—I *had* read the dictionary when I was a child—but I couldn't remember it. I would this time, though.

Chad brought the rest of the cocottes of pot pie in one at a time, then sat down in the empty seat between Fern and me, urging everyone to start eating while it was still hot. I lifted my spoon but hesitated before touching the crust; it was golden and beautiful, and I didn't want to destroy it.

"So," Chad said, leaning in near me like we were sharing a secret. "Right there?" He inclined his head toward my hand. "That's called a spoon. You eat with it. Watch—like this."

I snorted as he used his own spoon to scoop up a bite and raised it to his mouth. "I know, it's just too pretty to eat."

He set his spoon down and held up a finger before reaching under the table. A second later, he raised his cell phone. "Smile, Renata," he said, his lips twitching again.

I tried to deadpan but failed miserably, breaking into a laugh when he raised his eyebrows at me.

The corners of his mouth curled up while gazing at his phone screen. "Perfect," he murmured. Then he tapped the screen a few times. "Your number?"

His eyes watched mine expectantly, and I noticed they looked darker than usual, almost entirely bluish-gray and only the tiniest bit of golden brown ringing his pupils. "My number?" I asked, my heart thumping in my chest.

"Yeah, so I can send you a picture of your dinner, so you'll finally eat it."

That's right... dinner. He just wants to send me the picture. My eyes darted to Fern on the other side of Chad, but she wasn't paying any attention to us. In fact, no one was; they were all oohing and aahing over the food. If Fern wasn't concerned, I wouldn't be either, I decided. I gave him my number, steadfastly looking at my dinner to avoid looking at him, and when I was done, I used my spoon to break into the crust as Fern commented to Chad on how tasty it was and everyone echoed her sentiments.

The crust was flaky and light, not at all hard, and below it was a rich, creamy gravy filled with large chunks of vegetables and chicken. I scooped a spoonful with chicken, carrot, and potato. After blowing on it to keep from burning my tongue, I popped the spoon into my mouth. A soft, involuntary moan came from somewhere deep in my chest. It was delicious. No—*better* than delicious. It was luscious, delectable, scrumptious, and more. I hadn't tasted something that rich and flavorful in so long. No—*ever*. It was so good, I wanted to stop eating it and take it home so I could have a few bites every day for as long as I could make it last, but I also wanted to eat every last bite, every flake of crust and every drop of gravy.

"How is it?" Chad asked as I went in for my second spoonful.

"Terrible," I joked. "Worst I've ever had."

His face fell. "Seriously?"

I stared at him for a second, shocked he'd thought I was serious; I was sure he'd heard my moan of appreciation. "No, of course not," I said with a short laugh. "I was kidding."

Everyone burst out laughing. "You need to work on your sarcasm comprehension," Caroline said to Chad.

"No shit," Chad grumbled, the corners of his mouth pulling up reluctantly.

"I'm sorry," I said, laughing as well, though I still felt bad that he'd believed me. "I... I don't know why I said that, but I wasn't serious. It's honestly the best pot pie I've ever had."

Brightness transformed his features right there in front of me; his eyes softened, and his mouth pulled into a grin. It was incredible to watch, and I found myself wondering what else would make it happen.

"It had better be," Fern said. "He spent most of the day making it."

"What? Really?"

"Mm-hm," Caroline replied around a mouthful. "He's been in our hair *all day*."

Chad chuckled. "Hardly *all* day. You guys spent at least *half* the day making out."

His words registered mid-swallow and I choked. Everyone's attention was on me as I coughed and sputtered for a minute, smacking my chest with my hand as my eyes watered.

"You okay?" Caroline asked, her brow creased as she patted my back.

I opened my mouth to reply, then coughed some more. When that subsided, I tried again. "Fine. I just thought he said you and Fern were making out," I explained, feeling my face heat up.

Caroline and Fern laughed. "We were," Caroline replied.

"What?" I asked. My mind raced, trying to figure out what they were saying. How could they be serious? Were they in a polyamorous relationship? Were the three of them together a couple—no, a *throuple*?

For the first time since I met her, Caroline's expression became guarded. She withdrew her hand and glanced at Fern before looking back to me. "Fern and I are in a relationship together—we have been for several years."

My eyes darted between her and Fern and Chad. Fern and Caroline looked uncertain, and Chad had lost any trace of humor. I got the impression he was... angry.

"If you have a problem—" he started, before Fern cut him off.

"Chad! Stop—she didn't—"

"I don't," I said quickly, shaking my head, interrupting them before things escalated any further. "I just... I thought..." I swallowed, wishing I could fall through the floor and disappear. "I thought you two—" I pointed at Fern, then Chad, "—were together."

After about a second, maybe two, Fern was laughing hysterically. I'd obviously been wrong, but I didn't understand why it was *that* funny. Soon, laughter from Leslie, Drake, Jessie, and Caroline joined in. Chad never laughed, but the anger was fading from his eyes. He sighed and sat back in his chair.

"Fern's my sister," he said.

"Oh my god, I'm an idiot," I muttered. It explained their closeness, the way they interacted, why I'd never seen any non-platonic displays of affection between them, all of it. It made so much sense. If Fern and Chad had any shared features, I probably would have figured it out myself, but they looked nothing alike. "I'm so sorry," I added.

Caroline waved away my apology, looking between Fern and Chad, laughing some more.

"This is why I should have just gone home and gone to bed," I said, intimating that tiredness was the reason I'd made such an embarrassing mistake. "I didn't mean to upset anyone."

"You didn't," Fern replied. "Chad's just a little overprotective sometimes. When we were growing up, people could be really mean. It still happens sometimes, and my brother thinks he still needs to swoop in and save the day."

"Screw you, Fern," Chad said without malice. "I'm not trying to swoop in and save the day, as you put it."

"We didn't know for a long time, either," Leslie chimed in. "Don't feel bad."

"I've just seen more affection between Fern and Chad than Fern and Caroline," I explained.

"There's a reason for that," Fern said, holding up a finger as she slid another spoonful of pot pie into her mouth. It reminded me that there was more pot pie in my own cocotte, and I returned my attention to it. "So," she continued after she'd swallowed. "When Caroline and I were first dating, we were *very* affectionate. Not inappropriately—at least not at the café—but affectionate. But we had a few customers who thought it was disgusting because one of us wasn't a man, and they made a big scene."

"Screw those assholes," Chad bit out.

Fern rested a hand on his arm and kept talking. "They *were* assholes, and I was happy they were never going to come back into my café. I'm not going to pretend to be something I'm not to make people like them happy. But, it was disruptive to all my other customers, and reviews were rolling in that said food and service was great, but that there were regular altercations, and business began to suffer. So, Caroline and I decided we would not bring our relationship into the building at all; when we're there, it's like we're friends who happen to work together. That's it."

"You guys shouldn't have to do that," Chad said. "It's bullshit."

"Should or shouldn't—it's how it is, and we do. Maybe one day we won't have to, but for now?" Fern shrugged. "We'll survive, won't we, Caroline?"

I'd watched Fern as she spoke and tried to imagine being in her shoes. I couldn't. The closest were things I'd tried to change about myself for Damien. My eyes filled as I watched Caroline nod in agreement, watched them exchange a quick kiss across the table, watched them look at each other with a tenderness born from going through harrowing experiences together. Chad was right—they shouldn't have needed to hide their relationship because of narrow-minded prejudice. It wasn't fair.

More than ever, I wished I still worked for the journal; I could use my section to open people's minds, maybe with a short story about Fern and Caroline's romance. Words could be incredibly powerful when they were arranged in the right way and made their way in front of the right people. Maybe one day, if I ever found my words again, I could still do something.

I was the last to finish my pot pie after spending so much time lost in thought and savoring the flavors and textures, and as soon as I finished, Chad rose and started collecting everyone's cocottes.

"I can help," I said, uncomfortable with being waited on and starting to stand. I had to use the bathroom anyway.

Chad rested his hand on my shoulder. "I've got it."

I halted and forgot what I was going to do; the buzzing of my skin under Chad's hand was all I could think about. My breath hitched, and I tried to disguise it as a cough. "Bathroom?" I asked. It was the only word I could get out while he was touching me.

Caroline heard me and responded before Chad did, pointing behind me. "It's in the hall just before the kitchen, first door on the right."

Air rushed into my lungs as Chad lifted his hand. If he had kept it there any longer I might have passed out. *Holy shit.*

Laughter at something Drake had been saying followed me from the dining room as I walked out. I used the bathroom, took my time washing my hands, then splashed cold water over my face. It didn't help. My body was still too warm and buzzing, and I felt wide awake, even though I knew I was tired. Hell, I *looked* tired; my eyes were a bit puffy and had the beginnings of circles ringing them. It had been a long five days. Worth it, but long. And now all of this here. It was the most social I'd been since I was fifteen... god, half my life ago, almost.

Twenty-nine. The last year of my twenties. And what did I have to show for it? Not much. But for the first time in years, there was hope of having a different response to that question soon. Closing my eyes, I grasped onto that feeling of optimism and let it spread, then headed out.

Rather than returning straight to the dining room, I detoured into the kitchen to see if I could help. Chad was alone, carefully icing a cake. I stopped and leaned against the doorway, stifling a yawn, and watched him. He was fully engaged in what he was doing, smoothing the sides and top, his hands so much more precise than it appeared they could be, something I already knew after watching him working with dough at the café. It was just as mesmerizing to watch, too; so much so that I didn't notice when he looked up and saw me.

"Voyeurs typically like to be hidden," he said, his voice full of laughter.

The skin on my cheeks tightened. "I was coming in to help," I said.

"I can see that," he replied, smirking. "I'm sure that wall is grateful."

I bit the corner of my lip after making a rather unladylike sound trying not to laugh. He noticed and wriggled his eyebrows. I lost the battle and laughed. "I got... distracted... but I really did come in here to help."

"Distracted—that's one way to put it," he laughed. "And now you've ruined your surprise."

"Since it's already ruined... what kind of cake is it?" I asked, walking toward the island countertop and leaning on the side perpendicular to where he was working, tucking wayward strands of hair behind my ear.

Chad paused with the icing, and his colorful eyes strayed down to my feet and back up. When they returned to my face, they'd changed color—they were mostly gray-blue now. I simultaneously wished I was wearing something nicer than jean shorts and a sleeveless top, and that I was in baggy sweats and an oversized t-shirt.

"Your favorite," he replied, the corners of his mouth twitching again as he resumed smoothing the icing.

"I don't have a favorite," I laughed. I'd never been that big on desserts in general.

"You will after you taste *this*," he retorted.

It felt like my face was under a heat lamp; more time had been spent blushing than not since I'd arrived. The sensation only intensified when he used a finger to wipe icing from the spatula and held his finger toward me, his eyebrows raised. I shook my head and he shrugged, popping his finger into his mouth. I turned away and walked to the sink, at long last heading to do the task that had led me into the kitchen to begin with.

"Don't even think about it," he said, his voice closer than I'd expected. He reached in front of me and dropped the spatula in the sink. "If you so much as touch a single dirty dish, I'll toss you over my shoulder and carry you out of the kitchen."

His voice was low and deep, and the teasing tone mildly subdued. When I rotated to face him, his eyes were close to mine. They were dark, all grayish-blue now, and seemed to be daring me to do what he'd just warned me against. More shocking, however, was that some part of me wanted to do it and see what happened. I looked back toward the sink.

"Try me," he challenged.

NINE

"Damien, that's ridiculous," I said, standing just inside my front door. "They're my coworkers. You know that—you've met them before."

"Were, Renata. They were your coworkers. They aren't anymore. You were fired, remember?"

My face leapt into flames and my stomach turned. "Yeah, I know I was fired," I replied, the shame sucking the volume from my voice. "But they were my coworkers and my friends. You've barely let me talk to them in weeks, and maybe they can help me get my job back."

"You were fired, Renata. I'm protecting you from more rejection. You're never getting your job back. They don't want you. And you can't even write—what would you do for them anyway?"

"I-I don't know, but—"

"Exactly—nothing. Which means there's no reason for you to see those assholes anymore."

"They're not assholes."

"You're telling me that someone who told me to fuck off isn't an asshole?"

"You accused him of trying to get into my pants, Damien."

"He was."

"No, he wasn't."

"Fuck if he wasn't, Renata. I could see how he looked at you."

My temples throbbed and I felt like I was neck-deep in mud, trying to wade to shore. "I don't want to fight."

"Me, either."

"Okay," I said uncertainly. He'd never been so complacent during an argument before. I readjusted my purse on my shoulder.

"But you're not going." He folded his arms across his chest and pulled his head back, making him tower even further over me. I barely reached his shoulder and had to crane my neck to look at him.

"Yes, I am," I practically growled in frustration. These were the only friends I had left after I'd cut everyone else—including Connie—out of my life.

"No. You aren't. I won't let you."

"You can't stop me from going," I said.

"Try me," he responded.

But he didn't move, and after a few tense seconds, I turned and reached out to open the door. My hand didn't make it, though. Sharp pain shot through my other wrist as something clamped down and yanked me back, the momentum sending me stumbling toward the living area and down to my knees. Damien now stood with his back leaning against the door and his arms crossed over his chest again. I knew he had grabbed and pulled me, but... it had happened so fast.

"It's not my fault you're a klutz," he said, glaring at me. "And I warned you. I'm not going to let you destroy our relationship by cheating on me with some douchebag you used to work with who wants to get into your pants. I love you too much to let you do that to us, Renata. Do you understand? I love you, and I'm doing this for us."

"Renata?"

My eyes sluggishly lifted from where they'd been staring ahead, unseeing. My hand caressed my wrist, despite the fact that it didn't hurt anymore—that had happened years ago.

"Renata?"

That voice again. Chad's voice, I realized. The brown was back in his eyes as I studied him, more of it than I'd ever seen before. I wondered what caused that. I'd thought the colors around him, but that wouldn't explain the last few changes.

"Are you okay?" he asked, his voice tinged with something that was normally absent.

I suddenly remembered where I was. It was as if I were coming out of a dream, the flashback leaving me feeling foggy and emotional. "Yeah... yeah... I'm fine," I replied, blinking back tears. "I'm... I'm fine." I attempted a smile, shame weighing heavily upon me.

Instead of the worry leaving Chad's face, his frown deepened. He reached toward me, but I jumped backward, slamming my back into the sink.

"Ow!"

"I'm sorry," he rushed out, holding his hands up and stepping back. "I didn't mean to... whatever I did."

I couldn't look at him anymore, and I examined the tiles under my feet as I tried to catch the breath that had been knocked out of me. "You're fine."

"Is your back okay?"

"What happened to your back?" Caroline asked from the edge of the kitchen. "And what are you doing in here, Renata? The cake was supposed to be a surprise!"

"I scared her and she hit her back," Chad answered.

"Let me see," Caroline said, heading toward me. "What did you do to scare her?"

I rested my hand protectively over my lower back. "I just smacked it a bit; I'm fine, really."

Caroline was so fast that she'd turned me around, moved my hand out of the way, and lifted my shirt before I knew what was happening. The sound of sharp inhales filled the air, and I yanked my shirt back down and turned.

"I'm fine," I said, unable to look either of them in the eye. "Cake time?"

Before they answered, I rushed to the dining room. I couldn't wait to leave. Chad and Caroline followed soon after with the cake, and I was grateful they appeared willing to let the kitchen incident go. I intended to practically inhale my slice of cake, but when it landed on my tongue, my body refused to cooperate. There was an explosion of flavor and texture that insisted on being savored. That same soft moan came out of nowhere again and my face leapt into flames.

"Good, isn't it?" Fern asked, her voice muffled by the cake she was eating.

I nodded. I had no idea what it was, but was convinced it qualified as the best cake I'd ever tasted. "What is it?"

"Carrot cake," she replied. "Chad's special recipe for it."

"With secret recipe cream cheese icing," he added. "So what's the verdict, Renata?"

"Verdict?"

"Yeah," he replied, a hint of laughter having returned to his voice. "It's your favorite, isn't it?"

I hmphed. I didn't want to admit it, but he was right. And he didn't have to say anything; I could *feel* his smirk even without looking at him. I pushed my plate back in lieu of responding and moved to stand.

"Thank you guys so much for this, but I'm exhausted. I need to get home and get some sleep."

"Not yet!" Caroline exclaimed. "Have another piece of cake first. Or glass of wine. Don't go so soon!"

I eyed my untouched wine glass. What I really wanted was some water, but I didn't want someone else getting it for me; I'd wait until I got home. "No, thank you. I'm really tired."

"Okay," she pouted. "Let me box this up for you and we can go."

"I got it," Chad said, snapping up the cake.

"You guys don't have to do that," I said. "I don't need to take any cake home—you guys should enjoy it. And I can just get a cab—you don't have to drive me."

"You're not getting a cab," Caroline said.

"Caroline, you can't drive," Fern said. "You're on your third glass of wine. And so am I, so I can't do it, either."

"I've got that, too," Chad shouted from the kitchen.

"Seriously, I can call a cab," I said, looking between Fern and Caroline.

Fern lifted a shoulder. "Why would you do that? Chad's got it. He has to drive himself home anyway."

No matter what I said, it appeared I was getting a ride home. From Chad. Who reappeared carrying a large paper bag with handles. It looked heavy and I wondered how much less than half a cake weighed.

"You really should leave it for them," I said as he followed me to the front door.

"No. I didn't make it for them," he replied.

It felt like something slammed into my chest, and I couldn't find words to respond. Of course I knew he'd made the cake, but I hadn't thought about the fact that he'd made it for *me*. Surely, that was only because Fern and Caroline wanted him to.

"You didn't have to do that," I said. Walking down the hall, it felt like everything was closer than it was.

He let out a laugh. "Unless I'm getting paid, I don't do things because I have to."

"So, the cake?"

"I wanted to make it."

"And dinner?"

"That, too."

"Driving me home?" *Why the hell did I ask that question? I don't really want to hear him say that's different, or that when his sister needs something it's an exception, or—*

He chuckled, then opened the front door to the apartment building, holding it for me to pass through. "I kept the wine glasses full tonight."

What did that mean? I risked a glance, and Chad's eyes were dancing again, his mouth fighting against breaking into a smile.

As we passed from the brightly lit area in front of the apartment complex entrance into the more dimly lit visitor parking area, my awareness heightened and my eyes scanned the area, finding no one there.

"Dessert or appetizer?"

I turned, my brow creasing. "What?"

"Dessert or appetizer?" Chad repeated. "If you had to pick one, which one would you pick?"

I let out a small laugh at the unexpected question as we walked, moving hair from my face again. "That depends."

"That's cheating, you have to pick one."

"But it really does depend."

"On what?" he asked.

"On what's being served. Typically, I'd say appetizer, hands down. I've never cared about dessert. But that cake you're carrying is making me hesitate. I think I'd rather have that over an appetizer."

He bumped my shoulder with his, looking pleased with himself. "Breakfast or dinner?"

"Dinner," I answered immediately. "There are so many more options."

"Is that why you skip breakfast all the time?"

I turned and stared at him. We reached an SUV, and he lifted an arm and leaned against it, quirking an eyebrow at me. As so often with him, there was a rush of conflicting emotions. On the one hand, I wanted to be as far away from him as possible; I didn't like how much he seemed to know about me. On the other, I felt more seen and understood than I ever had. But the real question was *how* did he know these things about me?

"How the hell would you know if I eat breakfast or not?" I asked, my voice with a slight edge.

"You could call it an educated guess," he replied. His playfulness had disappeared again, his forehead creased, although he was still smiling.

I looked away, not answering and hoping he'd let the question drop. After a beat, he straightened up and unlocked his car. I gave him my address, then silence thickened between us until he broke it.

"Early bird or night owl?"

"Neither—I prefer going to bed and waking up at a reasonable hour. What about you?"

"Early bird."

"That makes sense with your hours at the café."

"I was an early bird before that. And my hours at the café were shit hours—that's not an early shift, it's a shit shift."

I yawned, using a hand to smooth more rogue hairs back out of my face. "Were?"

"Yeah. The new baker is my replacement. I'll still help out on occasion if needed, but I'm now full-time at The Bakery Scene."

"Really?" I asked, infusing enthusiasm into my voice to mask my disappointment. I should have realized when Fern said she'd hired a baker that Chad would be leaving, but I hadn't. And I didn't want him to. The few days a week he was there were my favorite days to come to work.

"Yeah—finally. I'll be baking some, but mostly teaching classes through their school. I've always wanted to teach, and it's one of the best baking schools in the country. And I'll have freedom to experiment and improve upon existing recipes with them."

"You sound really excited."

He turned to me, his whole face lit up even in the dark. So, when I complimented his food, and when he talked about baking, both transformed his features.

"I am. It's what I've dreamed of doing since I was a kid. I've been there baking part-time for years, but couldn't give them the time needed for teaching because Fern needed help with the café. But now she's got enough good employees to keep things running smoothly without me, and the school actually had a need for a new teacher, so it worked out."

I couldn't help grinning; his passion and enthusiasm were palpable and infectious. "That's wonderful."

"Thank you."

Breaking eye contact as he pulled to the curb in front of my apartment building, I reached for the door handle. "Thank you for the ride." He leaned into the back seat, grabbing the paper bag. "And dinner. And the cake."

"You're welcome. It was my pleasure."

He moved to exit his car.

"I've got it," I said, not wanting to bother him more. "I'll take the bag."

"I can at least walk you to the front door," he said.

"No need. It's late and it's right there. But thank you."

Reaching over, I grabbed the bag from him, noticing when I peeked in that it had not only the cake, but more pot pie, and stepped out of the car. I could feel his eyes on me, and my body was warm under his scrutiny until I froze only a few steps away. Every hair on my body stood on end and I couldn't breathe; it felt like someone was watching me. Someone *other than* Chad. I turned slowly from side to side, trying to make out shapes in the darkness beyond the reach of the building lights, but couldn't see anything except varying shades of black in indecipherable shapes.

"Renata? Is everything okay?"

It was Chad. I hadn't heard his car door open, but he was now standing next to me.

"Y-yeah," I stuttered out. There was nothing there, but fear gripped my body the same way it would if there were some mortal danger mere seconds away.

Chad lifted the bag from me after staring at my arms. I looked down and saw what he had: goosebumps all over my skin and a profound trembling in my hands. "I'll walk you to your door."

His car chirped as he locked it, and he rested a hand on the small of my back. It wasn't pushy, but a gesture of reassurance. At least, that's what it felt like. Air rushed into my lungs, and I walked on shaky legs toward the door to my building as I tried to locate my voice.

"You don't have to walk me in," I said, my located voice wavering. "I'm fine."

"I can see that," he replied. "The most fine I've ever seen someone who's shaking like you are. I'm sure a puff of wind wouldn't knock you over right now."

I laughed, the sound awkward. "I just... I thought someone was there, but obviously no one is. You don't have to walk me in just because I was scared for no reason."

"Are," he said. "You *are* scared. Not were. You know, I'd expect a writer to choose the correct words," he teased. I smiled and he continued, his voice lower this time. "And it doesn't matter if it's something or not—the only thing that matters is that you're uncomfortable."

I didn't know how to respond. His perspective was so different and unexpected. Damien would have made fun of me for getting scared. *You're a grown woman,* he'd say. *Act like it*. But Chad's response made me feel like maybe it wasn't childish for me to feel the way I did. And while I still felt unsettled, his presence definitely helped. Whatever felt dangerous out there, it wasn't him.

"Are you nervous about teaching?" I asked as we climbed the stairs. There was an elevator in the building, but I didn't like elevators.

"Yeah. I am. Not because of *what* I'm teaching, though. I just want to make sure the students are learning something from me. It's why they're there, you know?"

We turned from the stairwell at the fifth floor, and I led the way down the hall. "When's your first class?"

"Two months. I need to have the course outline ready for approval in a couple of weeks, but I don't start teaching until the end of August."

I stopped in front of my door and spoke while I opened it. "Why don't you practice, then? You've got plenty of time."

He narrowed his eyes at me. "That's a great idea," he replied, his words filling the air as a smirk spread across his face. "You can help me."

"Me? No, I couldn't—I have no aptitude when it comes to baking. Or cooking at all, really. I mean, I cook well enough to keep myself alive, but that's about the extent of my talents in the kitchen. I'd be a horrible student."

"No, that would make you the ideal student to have because if I can teach someone with no aptitude, then I can teach anyone."

"That's not what I meant."

His eyes danced. "But it's perfect. Tomorrow?"

"I work tomorrow," I replied hastily.

"Afterward."

"But... I..." I was scrambling for some reason to say no, but came up with nothing.

"Are you busy?"

"Well, no, but—"

"Perfect. I'll pick you up at the café when your shift is over, then."

"But you don't want to teach me to bake, I promise you."

He reached out and tucked my escaped hair behind my ear, smiling, focusing intently on me. My ear burned and tingled where he'd touched it. "I promise *you* that I do. I'll see you tomorrow, Renata."

TEN

"Hello, old woman," Caroline greeted me the next morning when we walked up to the back door of the café at the same time.

"Good morning," I responded cheerily.

She pointed back over her shoulder. "You forgot your suitcase last night. I have it in my car. Don't forget to grab it this afternoon."

"I'll try not to." *We'll see how distracted I am when Chad shows up. Assuming he does show up.*

She ushered me inside ahead of her. "So, how did it go last night?"

"How did what go?"

"Good morning," she called to the new baker. "Lester, this is Renata. Renata, this is Lester, our new baker."

"Nice to meet you," I said.

He inclined his head. "Likewise."

His attention returned to his dough, and I watched him work as we passed by. I waited for that same feeling of warmth that came over me every morning I'd come in and watched Chad's hands as he worked, but it never came. It was still somewhat absorbing to watch, but it didn't have the same effect on me when it wasn't him.

"I'm still waiting to hear how it went last night," Caroline said. "It must have been good if you're keeping it to yourself."

I flushed, replaying him walking me to my door. Before he'd even had enough time to get down the hall afterward, he'd texted me, too. Right below the photo he'd sent me earlier was the new message that read: Sleep well tonight... you'll need to do more in the kitchen tomorrow than hold up the wall.

"How what went?"

"With Chad!" she exclaimed, rolling her eyes and gesturing toward the dining area. I followed her and we started pulling down chairs. "He drove you home." She snickered. "And I'm sure that's not all that happened since you found out he's not dating Fern."

I was speechless for a beat. "Nothing happened, Caroline," I said, avoiding eye contact.

"Come on—I don't buy it. The sexual tension between you guys is *insane*."

"Seriously," I said. My heart fluttered in my chest and hormones rushed through my body. "He drove me home. He left. That's it."

"If he just kicked you onto the curb, he's gonna hear it from Fern and me."

"He didn't—he walked me to my door. But that's it," I added hastily when Caroline wriggled her eyebrows at me. "We're just friends." *I guess. Is that what we are? We definitely aren't more, but do we even know each other enough to call ourselves friends? I don't know anything about him.*

"He likes you, you know," she said, oblivious that her words were a bombshell to drop on me.

"You called him a flirt when I met him," I countered.

"Oh, he totally *was* being a flirt with you, but he's not like that with everyone. And he doesn't cook for just anyone."

"That doesn't mean anything—he cooked for me because you guys asked him to."

"Renata," Caroline said, resting a hand on my arm. "Fern and I were going to take you out, but Chad insisted on cooking for you. That wasn't *our* idea—it was *his*."

My breath was so shallow I felt a little dizzy. My mind raced back over every interaction with him, finding different interpretations than I had before. I wasn't interested in dating, I reminded myself, but I didn't believe it anymore. I'd decided to steer clear of relationships after Damien, not sure how I could ever trust again, but something about Chad weakened that resolve.

"He's a good guy, Renata."

"I believe you, but I don't really know anything about him."

"What do you want to know?"

"What does he do in his spare time?"

"You think he does something other than bake?" she asked, laughing. "I'm kidding. He does bake a lot, but he also cooks other stuff and likes to spend time outside, like hiking and stuff. He has a thing for plants."

"What kinds of plants?"

"All of them. You should see his apartment. It's like a jungle inside."

"Really?" I wouldn't have guessed.

"Yeah. It's crazy. And it gets worse every year because he cuts back anything that's gotten too big and... ack, what's the word? He grows roots on the parts he cuts off."

"Propagates."

"Yes! That's it—he propagates those until his plant babies have enough roots to be planted in soil, then they get their own pots."

"Plant babies?"

She shrugged, giggling. "Yeah, it's what he calls them. Isn't that adorable?"

It was. Actually, it was more than that... it was charming, endearing. I loved knowing that about him.

"What else?"

"He's a coffee snob and is always trying different roasts and methods of preparing it. He doesn't drink a lot of coffee, but he's picky about what he does drink."

"Okay."

"He's a neat freak. It's really annoying. He lived with us for a while when he and his last girlfriend broke up a few years ago, and it made us insane."

I could see that; his car was spotless, not even a gum wrapper or a gas receipt floating around in it.

"But my favorite thing about him," she continued as we headed to the kitchen to start bringing up the pastries, "is how much he adores Fern."

"I still can't believe I thought they were dating," I muttered, laughing.

"*That* was funny," she agreed.

"Which one's older?" I asked, grabbing a tray.

"Chad, by six years. Fern turned twenty-seven in April. Chad will be thirty-three in October."

"I'm surprised they're so close when their ages are so far apart."

We slid our trays into the bakery case and headed back for more. "They always have been—as long as *I've* known them, anyway. Their parents were both sick a lot when they were growing up—both of them died of cancer within months of each other when Fern was sixteen—Chad was already taking care of Fern because they hadn't really been able to for a long time before that. After they died, Chad became her legal guardian and supported them. They have a special bond."

I sniffled, my eyes filling with tears. "Losing your parents is hard. My mom died from a hemorrhage a few weeks after I was born, and my dad died when I was fifteen."

"Cancer?"

"No, car accident. We were hit by a semi that ran a red light on the way to my cross-country meet."

"That's awful," Caroline said softly. She closed the bakery case after I slid the last tray in before turning and wrapping her arms around me. "I'm so sorry. Do you have any siblings?"

My head moved side to side. "No. I was an only child. I ended up living with a distant great-aunt until I was eighteen. She wasn't unkind, but she'd never wanted kids... she was just kind of uninterested. She passed away right after I left for college." I wished I'd had someone the way Fern had Chad. Maybe if I had... I gave a sharp shake of my head to clear my thoughts. No point in dwelling on what ifs.

I heard a buzzing sound from the shelf where I stored my purse and pulled out my phone, curious what I might be getting a notification for; Caroline was the only person who texted me, and I was there with her. I tapped the screen to light it up and couldn't help grinning at the notification: it was a text from Chad. I unlocked the screen and read the message asking if I'd eaten breakfast yet.

I laughed, feeling a little uneasy as I thought about his comment the evening before about my eating habits. Damien had scrutinized my eating habits, and I didn't want to end up in another situation like that one. Even so, I replied honestly that I hadn't, then dropped my phone into the pocket of my apron so I wouldn't miss it if he sent another message.

The self-serve area was almost fully stocked, and the only thing left to do was count the cash drawers before we opened. As usual, there was time to spare. Caroline and I usually chatted over a cup of coffee with our extra time, and I was looking forward to learning more about Chad.

"You have a visitor, Renata!" Caroline called in a sing-song voice from the entrance to the kitchen.

I spun around and Chad's frame filled the doorway. Instantly, I was too hot for the jean shorts and t-shirt I wore. In place of an air-conditioned café, it felt like I was in a sauna. What was he doing there?

"Chad." The word slipped out with my breath in my shock at seeing him there.

"Renata," he replied, the twitch in the corners of his mouth betraying his amusement.

"Why are you here?" I blurted out.

He lifted a hand and I noticed for the first time that he was carrying a container of some kind. "Breakfast. Not to be confused with dinnfast, which you don't need since I know you had dinner last night."

I huffed out a soft laugh, watching eagerly for him to get close enough for me to see his eyes; I wondered what they looked like this morning. "I just texted you less than five minutes ago."

He shrugged. "I had a hunch what your answer would be before I even asked, so I'd already made you something."

"Then why'd you ask?" I laughed.

"So I'd know whether or not to bring it inside." He handed me the container, including a fork he was holding on the lid, then leaned against the counter opposite me. "And because it gave me an excuse to text you again."

"Why weren't you sleeping? I know you said you're an early bird, but it's not even six, and you must have been cooking by what? Five thirty?"

"Four thirty. To get the right texture on the potatoes is a process. Texture that will be ruined by the steam if you don't get that lid off in the next sixty seconds or so."

I set the container on the counter and unlatched the lid as I spoke. "Why on earth would you get up at four thirty?"

"I didn't."

"But you just said you did to make breakfast."

His eyes twinkled and his lips twitched at the corners; he was trying not to laugh. "I said I started cooking at four thirty. I've actually been awake since about three thirty."

"Oh my god," I groaned. "Why?" I lifted the lid and melted. "What is this?"

"A breakfast hash. Bacon, potatoes, onions, garlic, bell peppers, parsley, eggs."

"It smells amazing." I took a bite and stifled another moan. I needed to stop doing that every time I ate something he made. "It tastes even better."

He waggled his eyebrows. "I know."

"So," I asked between bites. "Why were you up at three thirty?"

"I was thinking."

"Thinking about what?"

He didn't answer right away, his eyes exploring my face in earnest, drifting from my eyes to my nose to my mouth, up to my hair, back to my eyes. "There are so many things I want to know."

"About what?"

"About you."

I swallowed slowly and stared back at him. His eyes looked like they usually did, with only a small ring of golden brown around his pupils, but they were brighter than normal, almost as if the central rings were lit with flames from behind.

"Okay," I whispered.

He was so direct. I felt a bit off-balance, like the ground under my feet was tilting when he did that, but I liked that he didn't hide what he was thinking from me or say one thing while meaning another and expect me to know that. Several long minutes passed in silence, everything around us fading into the background until I could only hear my own breath and heartbeat.

"Aren't you going to ask me something?" I asked.

"I'm going to ask you *everything*," he replied, still watching me intently. "But later." He glanced pointedly at the register, and I followed his gaze. It was almost six o'clock. "You guys open in five minutes."

"Shit," I muttered.

I shoveled the last few bites of breakfast hash into my mouth. "I'll wash it and give it back to you later."

He smirked. "I'll let you."

I narrowed my eyes, surprised by his response after his insistence that I not touch a single dirty dish the evening before. He leaned forward and swept my hair behind my ear, then spoke close enough that I could feel his breath on my skin.

"That way, I know you won't decide to run off before I pick you up later."

ELEVEN

"Your date's here," Caroline whispered loudly into my ear, bumping my hip with hers as Chad walked in the front door to the café.

"It's not a date," I hissed. *Or is it?* "We're friends. Like you and I are friends."

"You guys are certainly *not* friends like you and I are friends, woman."

"Whatever," I mumbled.

My cheeks ached from smiling all day, and I was choosing to think it had more to do with Fern and Caroline's bubbly personalities rubbing off on me than with anticipation over my plans for the afternoon. Even so, I couldn't tame it. Chad wore his trademark suppressed grin with the corners of his mouth pressed to hold it in. The only customer in the store was now waiting at the end of the counter for Caroline to finish making her latte. For all intents and purposes, it was just Chad and me.

I took him in as he neared the counter. He was wearing blue jeans, a black button up shirt, untucked, with the top couple of buttons undone and the sleeves rolled up halfway to his elbows. Brown leather shoes matched the belt I saw a flash of when he slid a hand into his pocket. Looking down, my eyes scanned my blue jean shorts and café shirt. My shorts might have been unscathed since I'd had on an apron most of the day, but there was fresh coffee on my shirt from when I incorrectly attempted to remove the old grounds from one of the fancy coffee machines.

"I might be overdressed," I teased. "I mean, since you're such a hot mess."

"At least I'm not just a mess," he replied without a missing a beat.

My attempt to hold in my laugh was unsuccessful, and it earned me a full-on grin. "You are so cheesy."

He smirked, but didn't reply.

The bell on the door chimed and Leslie walked in after holding the door for our customer to walk out. The new cashier she was training had already arrived, and I told her that she was in the back.

"That means your shift's over," Chad said after Leslie disappeared into the kitchen.

My stomach fluttered. The day had dragged by in a way it hadn't since I'd begun my job, but now that it was over and Chad was standing in front of me, I felt overwhelmed with nerves. I worried about my clothes and my hair. I worried about running out of things to talk about or saying something that would make him regret spending time with me. I worried that I was reading too much into everything, despite what Caroline had said about him liking me—she was making an assumption, after all. She could be wrong.

Perhaps most of all, I worried that he wasn't the good guy Caroline assured me he was... the good guy my gut had been telling me he was since the first day I met him. I'd been wrong before. So very wrong. And because of that error, I'd nearly died more than once.

Don't be so dramatic, Renata. Except, it was Damien's voice I heard in my head—not my own... wasn't it? It was hard to know for sure sometimes. His voice had replaced mine for so long that they'd become one. This process of separating them again was hard. And confusing.

What if Chad was like Damien? What if he was charming now, but then that gradually disappeared, and I ended up in another relationship like I had before? What if I only felt drawn to Chad because he was showing interest in me? That's what Connie said about Damien, and I'd always secretly wondered if she'd been right. And Damien had always told me I was desperate for attention. Were they both right? I was dressing like I used to before Damien again—in the types of clothes he'd said were asking for attention. And now I had attention from Chad... Did that mean he was only interested in me because of the way I was dressed? Except he'd acted the same way toward me from the first day... the day I wore clothes Caroline said made me look homeless. That said something, didn't it?

Sensation drew my attention and I looked down, my eyes refocusing on my environment in lieu of my thoughts and memories. Chad had a finger on the back of my hand.

"Renata."

"Hm?" My eyes were still seeing through him, unable to focus.

"Are you okay?" he asked.

I forced my head up and my lips to pull out of my frown, still trying to shake off the direction my thoughts had been headed. "Yeah. I'm fine."

He let out a soft huff and cocked his head a few degrees. "I want to change my question."

"Sure."

"What's wrong?"

I was going to say "nothing" but the word died on my lips. He was so intently focused on me, I couldn't lie. As he waited, the v deepened between his eyes, which now had a thick brown ring in the center. I sighed and gave him a small smile. This one wasn't forced. I didn't lie or answer his question, though; I said something else that I believed to be true.

"I *will* be fine." Before he replied, I pulled my hand out from under his and turned toward the kitchen. "I'll be back in a minute."

We'd gone to Chad's apartment since he had everything needed for the baking lesson I was going to receive. When he first mentioned it on the way to his car, my step had faltered; for some reason, I'd expected to be at my place where I would feel more in control. He'd noticed, just as he noticed everything, and offered to just gather up everything we needed and bring it to my apartment if I was more comfortable with that. There hadn't been a hint of irritation, no attempt to persuade me, just what sounded like a genuine offer. That response, coupled with Caroline's words "he's a good guy" echoing in my ears, was enough that I declined the offer and agreed to go to his apartment.

Caroline hadn't been exaggerating—his apartment was spotless *and* he had plants everywhere. There were tables and shelves and stands filled with plants of various types; my favorites had large, almost heart-shaped leaves and grew on long stems like a vine. They draped so beautifully over whatever furniture they'd been set on. I gently fingered the leaves of one of them.

"It's a pothos," Chad said from right next to me.

"It's lovely," I murmured.

He tipped his head toward the left. "I've got some babies in the den if you'd like some."

I shook my head, smiling at his reference to his plant babies. "I'd kill it, I'm sure. I have even less aptitude for keeping plants alive than I do for baking. I've never owned a plant before."

"Well, you've picked the right one to start with. They're practically indestructible. I guarantee that not even *you* can kill it."

"Not even me?"

He smirked. "You're the one who said you had no aptitude for keeping a plant alive."

I laughed and followed him through his living room to his kitchen. What I'd seen of his apartment thus far, I'd have described as cozy, but his kitchen was something else entirely. It was enormous. There were three walls with rich, dark cabinets and a pale, linen-colored countertop, and a large island with the same creamy countertops and dark cabinetry. There were two sinks, a large one along a side wall and smaller one in the island, a faucet over the cooktop, and four wall ovens.

"Wow," I said, looking around and trying to take it all in. "I didn't know apartments came with kitchens like this."

"They don't," he replied. "This is custom."

"You're allowed to do that?"

His lips twitched. "Considering I own this place—yes."

Oh. Of course he owns it. Why didn't I think of that?

"What would you like to drink?"

"What would you like to drink, babe?" Damien asked once he'd closed the front door behind him.

I eyed him, but he was waiting expectantly, his expression blank. It struck me as strange that he was acting so normal when things hadn't been normal between us in so long, but I longed to believe that things would go back to how they used to be in the beginning, that the last couple of years had been some dark test of our relationship or something.

"I have a water. I'm good, thank you," I replied.

"I'll pour you a champagne with a touch of cranberry juice," he said.

"Champagne?" And cranberry juice?

"Yes. I picked it up on my way home. We're celebrating."

I waited until he'd sat next to me on the sofa. "What are we celebrating?" I almost hadn't asked; if there was some occasion I'd forgotten, he'd be angry again, but after wracking my brain, I couldn't come up with anything we could have to celebrate.

He smiled, but it didn't reach his eyes. He tipped his head toward my glass, downed his, and waited until I'd done the same. "The resurrection of our relationship, babe." He leaned forward, wrapping his arm around the back of my neck and pulling me into him.

"Damien," I said, turning my head to the side and ducking out from under his arm.

My mind raced to find a way to tell him—again—that I didn't want to have sex. It had gotten harder and harder to go through with it for months, but for the last several weeks, I hadn't been able to at all. He'd accused me of not being interested in him because I was cheating on him. It wasn't true, but he didn't believe me and hadn't allowed me to leave the apartment in eighteen days. He checked my phone every day when he got home. And while he found nothing—because there was nothing to be found—he was determined he would.

He stood and went to the kitchen, taking our glasses. When he returned, the glasses were full again. I didn't want to drink; I wanted to stay clear-headed. When I was drinking, I wasn't as careful as I should be and ended up saying or doing something to anger him, and I always ended up getting hurt somehow. But if I refused... that would anger him, too. And so, I accepted the glass without a word and drank it when he told me to after clinking our glasses together. I held the empty glass on my leg and thought how incongruous it was to have such a delicate, sophisticated piece of glassware in my hand while I was wearing baggy sweatpants and an oversized t-shirt. I set it down on the coffee table—I wasn't good enough for a glass that fancy.

Damien again reached an arm behind my neck and pulled me toward him, but when I tried to slip away, he wouldn't let me. He held me in place and smashed his mouth painfully against mine. He bit down on my bottom lip, and I opened my mouth; if I didn't, he'd end up drawing blood. His breath and tongue tasted strongly of alcohol—whiskey.

He held me against him and kissed me for so long I was becoming dizzy. I tried to push away from him, but he didn't budge. I felt strangely weak and confused. Even not drinking often, I shouldn't have been drunk off two glasses of champagne. Let alone that quickly. I managed to twist my face away from his.

"Damien," I said weakly. "I don't... I don't feel right." I was hot and cold and having trouble thinking clearly.

I woke up the next day, nearly twenty-four hours later, naked in our bed. My head was splitting and I felt sick. As hard as I tried, I couldn't remember anything after Damien's whiskey-saturated kissing and feeling like I was having hot flashes and being unable to make my body cooperate or my mind clear. I slipped out of bed as carefully as possible, so as not to wake him, and found a t-shirt to pull on to cover my nakedness and the bruises I saw all over my body. There looked to be more than I remembered, not that it mattered—all of them made me feel ashamed and disgusted with myself. Each one was another lie I'd told others, hoping if I told it enough times I'd believe it myself.

I rummaged around in the bathroom, my entire body hurting, especially between my legs, squinting against the sunlight coming through the blinds, until I'd found the bottle of ibuprofen. I tapped three into my hand and padded quietly to the kitchen to get a glass of water. When I reached up into the cabinet, something caught my eye. It was on a shelf out of my reach, something poking over the edge. It looked like the corner of a snack baggie. I grabbed the tongs from the utensil caddy next to the stove and pulled the bag down. It was a snack baggie, and inside it were several green, oblong pills.

What the hell were those? I turned the baggie over, inspecting them closer; they had a number on them. I'd never seen them before and wasn't sure why they were in the kitchen instead of the medicine cabinet or why they were in a baggie instead of a box or bottle. Using the tongs, I replaced them carefully where I'd found them and hunted for my phone after taking my ibuprofen.

My hands shook and my headache nearly prevented my ability to see my screen as I opened a secret browsing tab; I didn't want to risk Damien seeing that I'd found whatever drug was in our kitchen cabinet. I knew better than to confront him about it, but I wanted to know what it was. But if he saw that I'd been searching, he'd accuse me of not trusting him enough to just ask him to tell me. The thing was, though... I didn't *trust him. Not really. Not anymore. I hadn't in a long time.*

I typed in the description and the number and waited for the search results to load, glancing nervously toward the bedroom every half-second, afraid Damien would walk in before I was finished. When the results loaded, though, I wished I'd never searched. Ignorance truly was bliss sometimes. But I was no longer ignorant; I knew exactly what was in that baggie.

It was Rohypnol... the date rape drug.

I turned and lunged for the closest sink, but I wasn't quite fast enough; vomit landed on the countertop and the floor and dripped down the cabinets. My body wasn't content with only one wave, though; everything in my stomach exited my body over the next few minutes until I was left shaking violently and dry-heaving. I wasn't sure how I was still standing until the dry-heaving stopped and I realized Chad had an arm around my waist, the other holding my hair back. Tears streamed down my face as I turned, mortified, to see that he was covered in vomit as well.

"I'm sorry. I'm so sorry," I cried.

If this really was a date as Caroline insisted, it was going to go down in history as the worst first date ever. I wasn't sure I'd even be able to show my face at work again; as soon as I left, I was sure he'd be telling Fern and Caroline that I threw up all over him and his kitchen.

"I'll clean up in here and call a cab," I whispered, grateful that we'd grabbed my suitcase from Caroline's car.

Chad didn't say anything, keeping his arm around my waist as he opened a drawer and pulled out two kitchen towels. He handed one to me, then used the other to wipe his face.

"There's a bathroom through there—on the left, far side of the spare bedroom," he said quietly, pointing toward a hallway. "There's shampoo and soap and all that, and there are towels in there, too. Go ahead—take your time. I'll get your suitcase from the car and set it inside the door for you."

"Thank you. I'll have a cab come get me."

"I'll take you home, Renata—if that's what you want. You don't need to call a cab."

I nodded without looking up, then turned and headed toward the bathroom. I'd considered just rinsing my face and changing once I had my suitcase, but the mess wasn't confined to my clothes, or even my skin—it was also in my hair. *Chad's hand must have touched it when he pulled my hair back,* I realized. I could never look at him again.

Once the water was warm, I stepped into the shower and let the water beat down over my head. As mortified as I was about throwing up all over Chad's kitchen, my thoughts kept straying back to the day I realized Damien had drugged me. At least once; however, I suspected more. It wasn't the first time I couldn't remember drinking enough to get blackout drunk and waking up like I had that day, sore and with bruises I didn't remember having before. Damien swore I had a drinking problem, that I was drinking so much it was destroying my memory, and for a long time I believed him. But that day I found those little green pills, I wasn't sure how much of that was true.

TWELVE

The water was no longer warm as it beat down on me. I didn't recall moving, but I was sitting on the shower floor, crying, when the water temperature shocked me out of my memories. Standing, I scrubbed down and shampooed my hair as quickly as I could so I wouldn't stink. Pulling the curtain back revealed my suitcase sitting in the attached bedroom near the door, like Chad had just slipped it inside far enough to be able to close the door again. I dried and slipped into the sweatpants and baggy t-shirt I had packed for pajamas while I was at the conference and brushed my teeth.

I tip-toed from the spare bedroom toward the kitchen and living room, not sure where I'd find Chad. I wanted to disrupt him as little as possible, and despite what he'd said before I went to get cleaned up, there was no way I *wasn't* calling a cab. I couldn't possibly let him drive me home after what happened. And while I waited for the cab, I would clean up his kitchen.

But when I walked into the kitchen to find my phone, the mess was gone—there was nothing to indicate someone had thrown up everywhere. The counter and cabinets and tile floor were as pristine as they'd been when I first saw them. The stove, however, now had a pot on it with steam rising. I couldn't smell what it was—my nose was stuffy from crying in the shower. Chad had changed into sweats—light gray, like mine—and a black t-shirt. He was leaning back against the island countertop across from the stove, focused on his phone screen as he slowly scrolled.

I stood back and watched him as he read. After about a minute, maybe a little longer, he raised his eyes from the screen and stared ahead of him. Shifting his weight, he lifted his other hand from the counter and slid it across his mouth, then down over his jaw. The scratchy sound of his palm scraping the hair under it joined the sound of water beginning to simmer. He was deep in thought, and I felt like I was intruding on his privacy, but I wasn't sure how to make my presence known after what I'd done. He sniffed loudly, then looked back down at his phone, a hand still on the side of his jaw, tapping the screen a few times before he was scrolling again. Abruptly, he looked up, then turned his head to the side. In the moment before he registered my presence, I could see clearly the glassiness in his eyes. He paused for a second, then, sniffing loudly again, cleared his throat and set his phone face down on the counter. He stepped forward and looked down at the pot on the stove.

"I was going to clean up," I said, my voice fading near the end.

He didn't say anything, stealing sideways glances as the silence stretched out, his jaw working like he was struggling with something.

"And I'll get that cab now."

His head bobbed up and down absently, and I willed back the tears in my eyes as I turned to continue my search for my purse, which I found on a barstool on the far side of the island. After pulling out my phone, I unlocked the screen and swiped to find my app for cab service. Just as I tapped to open it, Chad stepped over and placed a hand over mine, barely touching me.

"Do you have seizures?" he asked.

I was so surprised by his question that I looked up. The gray-blue of the outside ring of his iris reminded me of a rainy day—one that was a steady rainfall all day—and the brown inner ring was wide. There was a pronounced groove between his eyebrows as he watched me closely.

I moved my head deliberately from one side to the other, trying to figure out why he'd ask me a question like that. "No. I've never had a seizure."

He gave the distinct impression that he'd expected that answer, but it wasn't the one he wanted. He inhaled sharply, loudly, held it as he considered me a little longer, then let it out in a rush. I wanted to look away, but I couldn't. There was something about his eyes that tethered me whenever I looked at them. Very abruptly, he turned away and walked back to the stove, his hand moving toward his face like he were wiping it. He cleared his throat again.

"I'm making soup," he said. "Vegetable soup. It's gentle on the stomach. And I have some dough rising for bread." He tipped his head toward a large bowl covered with a towel. "I'm not sure... I mean, you probably want to go. I can take you home." He gave a sharp head nod as if he'd decided something, his eyes staring somewhere on the other side of the wall again. "Yeah, I'll take you home. I don't know why... of course you won't want to eat. Right?"

He circled around and looked to me, waiting for a response. I had no idea what to say; I felt off-kilter by the way he was acting. He was always so self-assured and confident and decisive, but he was now indecisive and hesitant and seemed almost lost. Words slipped from my lips without my permission.

"I'm not hungry, but... I don't really want to go home right now, either." It was true—I'd be alone with memories I didn't want, but I couldn't believe I'd said that to the person whose kitchen I had thrown up all over.

His head moved up and down sluggishly, his eyes roaming over my face as he considered my response. "Okay," he finally said. Turning back to the stove, he stirred the contents of the pot, then adjusted the flame under it to be lower, and the newly boiling water calmed back into a light simmer. "This needs to simmer for a while. It won't be ready to eat for another hour or so. Wanna watch a movie while we wait?"

"Sure," I replied, wrapping my arms around myself. I didn't want to be home alone, but I wasn't sure this was the best alternative.

I followed him to the living room after watching him fill two glasses with water. I sat at one end of the small sofa; he sat at the other end, turned to half face me.

"I'm sorry about earlier," I said. "One hell of a first date, huh?"

"Who said it was a date?" he replied.

My stomach bottomed out and I felt sick all over again. I couldn't believe I'd made that assumption. *Damn it, Caroline.*

He leaned forward and rested his fingertips on the back of my hand. "Renata, I was kidding. It *was*—no, *is*—a date."

The air rushed out of my lungs and I let out a small laugh. Then an awkward silence began to thicken the air until Chad broke it.

"Do you want to talk about it?"

My heart pounded. "Talk about what?"

He swallowed loudly and his fingertips whispered over the back of my hand. "I, um... I Googled what happened in the kitchen while you were in the shower. And what happened earlier today when I picked you up, and yesterday at Fern's, and what's happened a few times at the café." His fingers left my skin, and he scrubbed his hand over his noticeably red face. "It sounds like it's one of two things: a type of seizure, or a PTSD episode."

That's why he asked if I had seizures. I couldn't move for several seconds—not to breathe or blink or look away.

"Do you want to talk about it?" he asked again, his focus on me intense. "I don't... I don't know what would be helpful. I haven't had time to research yet, but I can listen. If you want me to, that is. I want to know. But I don't mean that you have to tell me, just that..." His voice trailed off and he scrubbed his face again, then glanced out the window on the far wall. "Fuck," he breathed out. He looked back to me. "I have no idea what the hell I'm doing right now. And I'm nervous—*really* nervous—about doing or saying the wrong thing. I'm not used to feeling this way. I just... I want to help. I want to be whatever you need right now. I just don't know what that is."

No one had ever said something like that to me before and my eyes flooded. I exhaled with measured slowness, trying to keep the emotion inside from building and spilling over. No one had ever done something like he just had to try to understand me. No one had ever asked me point blank what I needed or if I wanted to talk about it. Well, Connie had, before I destroyed our friendship. And Damien had, but he hadn't meant it. Chad *did*—I could tell. We barely knew each other, really, and yet it felt like we did in some way—that *he* somehow knew *me*.

"It was a flashback," I whispered. "Something..." I exhaled carefully when my voice cracked. "Something I don't like to remember."

"And yesterday, at Fern's, when we were in the kitchen and I teased you about doing the dishes? Was that a flashback, too?"

I squeezed my eyes closed, lowering and raising my chin, feeling the hot tears slipping out, and my breath felt trapped in my lungs. I was embarrassed and upset and grateful and angry and so many other contradictory emotions that couldn't be accurately described with the words we already had. I startled when something touched my hand, but almost immediately after, the trapped air found its way out. His fingertips traveled patiently over the back of my hand, and my shoulders began to drop, some of the tension leaving. I opened my eyes.

He was watching me with his familiar, intense focus. "Is this okay?"

I blinked, not sure what he was asking.

His head tipped down toward our hands. "When I touch you like this—is that okay?"

"More than okay." In fact, it helped in some way I couldn't find words to explain.

His fingertips smoothed outward until his entire palm rested over the back of my hand. The situation was less than ideal. It sucked, actually. And I was drained, physically and emotionally, but there was something almost painfully wonderful about the moment at the same time... it was *bittersweet*. A warm rush of gratitude filled my chest, and I turned my hand under his until we were palm to palm.

"Thank you," I whispered.

He sucked in a breath and slid his fingers between mine. "Rena," he breathed out.

My head turned sharply, and I scrutinized his face. He'd called me Rena. Not Renata, but Rena.

"What is it?" he asked.

"You called me Rena," I replied.

"Is that okay? I won't if you don't like it."

"I mean, yes, it's okay, but—it's just that—" I stopped abruptly, not sure if I should tell him what he'd just called me.

"It's what?"

"Names are words—they have meaning just as any other word does."

"That makes sense. What does your name mean?"

I paused; his question caught me off-guard, like so much about him. Every other person I'd ever talked to about names having meaning had first asked me what their own name meant. No one had ever asked me about my name first.

No one.

Until Chad.

"Renata means reborn. Together with my last name, Hayden, which means fire, my name means 'reborn from fire.'"

"Like a phoenix. That's powerful. Did you parents realize that when they named you?"

I smiled. "Absolutely—my dad had a thing about names. My mom had a really hard life—my grandparents abused her, and she lived in extreme poverty. My dad's life wasn't much better. They saw me as a chance to break that cycle of the hell they experienced when they were growing up, a kind of rebirth for them out of the fire their lives had previously been. And when my mom died, my dad said my name was even more fitting because I was so much like her."

"I'm sorry you lost her."

"It's okay. She hemorrhaged when I was a few weeks old, so I never really knew her. And my dad was amazing while I had him."

"He passed away, too?"

"Car accident when I was fifteen, on the way to my cross-country meet."

"Oh my god," he breathed out. "I'm so sorry. Is that where the scars on your back came from?"

His question set up the perfect opportunity to lie, to tell him yes and let it drop. He had no reason not to believe me, and he'd never ask me about it again. Not to mention that the truth was something I could never share with anyone. I gave a slight nod, avoiding eye contact.

He sucked in a breath. "Jesus. Is that..." He swallowed. "Is that where the PTSD comes from?"

I gave another nod, filled with shame for lying. But I couldn't even untangle my past with Damien in my own mind—how could I possibly explain it to someone else? Any time I'd ever tried, most people had thought I was crazy or exaggerating or making things up, especially once they met him. Damien was so personable and funny and good-looking; the things I thought he'd done were unimaginable for someone like him. The only person who'd ever believed me was Connie; she'd not only believed me, but tried to convince me things were worse than I thought they were at the time. She'd never trusted

Damien. But she was one of few, and I'd learned to keep my thoughts and suspicions to myself because they always wound up backfiring in some way, and I'd end up more confused than I'd started. And I didn't want to make Chad or his sister or Caroline think I was crazy. I needed to keep my job, but even more than that, I liked them. They were the only friends I'd had in years, and I didn't want to do anything to jeopardize that.

"I'm sorry about the loss of your parents as well," I said quietly, hoping he wouldn't be upset that Caroline had told me.

"Me, too," he replied. "Did Fern tell you?"

"No. Caroline did."

"She did?"

"Yeah," I replied, my cheeks warming. "I, uh... I was asking her questions."

"About my parents?"

"Well, no, not your parents exactly—just about you."

"Really?" he asked, his lips starting to pull into a smile. "What kinds of questions?"

The heat in my face increased tenfold. "Just questions. You know, trying to learn a little more about you."

"You know," he said. "I've asked her questions about you, too."

We watched *Pitch Perfect,* which I'd never seen before but Caroline had insisted we watch, then Chad finished up the soup and baked the bread. When all was finished, he served it on a tray in the living room, and we ate together while watching *Pitch Perfect 2*; we'd both laughed so hard at the first movie that we decided to watch the second as well. By the time the movie was over, aside from my eyes burning and feeling dry from crying earlier in the day, the fiasco with my flashback in the kitchen felt far away. Sitting on the sofa with Chad, laughing with a movie, had been exactly the balm I needed to soothe the broken pieces inside me. And when he returned from taking our dishes to the kitchen and sat down right next to me rather than the other side of the sofa, it had somehow felt natural. Just as it had when he slid his fingers between mine and tightly clasped my hand.

After the second movie was over, a heaviness settled onto my shoulders; I didn't want to go home and be alone with my thoughts. I wanted to stay there with Chad where everything that was normally right under the surface felt distant. Based on how reluctantly he rose after turning off the television, I got the feeling he felt the same way. But there was no way I was spending the night with him, as much as I thought it was something I wanted to do. People could change when you spent too much time with them, especially behind closed doors.

When we arrived at my apartment, Chad parked in the visitor lot instead of pulling up to the curb in front of the building like he'd done the night before. We talked about some of our favorite parts of the movies we'd watched as we meandered hand-in-hand. The hair on the back of my neck rose like it had the night before, but I tried to ignore it. I wasn't sure what I was afraid of, exactly, and it didn't matter anyway—Chad was with me.

At my apartment, I unlocked the door and stepped inside after setting my suitcase out of the way of the door. Part of me wanted to invite Chad in, but I didn't do it. Earlier, I'd been unsettled by going to his apartment in lieu of my own, but now I was glad that was how it happened; the thought of him being inside my apartment made me anxious. It was my safe place inside those walls, and I wanted to keep it that way. He leaned a hand against the door frame, and we studied each other's faces. The brown ring in his iris was narrow and had darkened, more like I most often saw his eyes.

"Can I see you again?" he asked.

I let out a sharp breath and my eyes darted to the floor. "I can't believe you'd want to," I said, half under my breath. I looked up when he moved my hair behind my ear.

"I definitely want to, Rena."

My knees wobbled slightly. I loved him calling me Rena, even if he had no idea what it meant. If he had, he probably wouldn't have been doing it.

His eyes flitted over me. "Either exhaustion is making your legs weak or you like it when I call you that," he said, taking my hand tenderly in his. "Tell me it isn't exhaustion."

My heart hammered in my chest. He was the most observant person I'd ever met. "It isn't."

His smile appeared and his eyes flicked downward from mine, then back up. He leaned forward, slowly, and I swallowed, trying to make my breathing sound more normal and less disjointed and loud. He stopped, so close I could feel the warmth from his lips hovering over mine. The anticipation was almost too much.

Please kiss me. Please kiss me. PLEASE kiss me.

"Is this okay?" he whispered.

"Yes," I breathed out.

His fingertips whispered along my jawline, pressed ever so gently into my skin, and then his lips touched mine at last. My whole body tightened like a spring and unfurled like a flower at the same time. My heart both raced and slowed. Every inch of me buzzed and was warm and alive. The hand I still had wrapping the door tightened as I tried to process all the different sensations his touch was creating; I'd never felt this way before. There was a shiver, and I realized it was his—not mine.

When he pulled away, I beamed—I couldn't help it. It was gratifying to see his expression mirroring mine when I found the courage to look up.

"I work until three tomorrow," he said, his voice low, his thumb moving from my jaw along my cheek to my temple and back. "But after that..." He swallowed.

"Yes," I interrupted, answering his unspoken question. "Maybe you can teach me to bake this time."

"Perfect," he murmured, then touched his lips faintly against my temple. "Good night, my Rena."

THIRTEEN

Chad's last words to me had been echoing in my ears since he'd spoken them the night before. *Good night, my Rena*. My Rena... my joy. He had no idea that's what he was saying, but it gave me a thrill anyway. I'd fallen asleep smiling and my cheeks felt they had a permanent ache as I neared the end of my shift. Caroline had overslept and I'd opened without her, then we were slammed. It had finally quieted down, and the two of us headed to the dining area to wipe down tables and collect trash.

"Sooooo, how did it go?" Caroline asked in a sing-song voice.

I glanced up at her, my face heating at the memory of getting sick all over Chad's kitchen. Surely, he'd told them—Fern, at least, and she would have told Caroline. "You know how it went, I'm sure."

She shook her head. "I mean, I know how Chad thinks it went, but I want to hear from you."

Bingo. I knew it. The heat on my face intensified. "I'm so embarrassed."

She stopped wiping and drew her head back. "Embarrassed? What happened?"

"Chad already told you."

"No," she said, the word drawn out. "He texted to ask me what questions you'd asked about him and I asked how it went. He said it was amazing and that he was seeing you again today. That's it."

"Amazing?" I gaped at her. Then I couldn't help grinning. I'd thought it was amazing, too, in spite of how it had begun.

"Yeah," she said, eying me like I was losing my mind. "So what was embarrassing?"

"I, um... I threw up."

"What?"

"All over him and his kitchen."

"*What?*" she asked, louder.

I was grateful we had no customers in the dining room.

"Yep. It was awful."

"What the hell did he make that made you sick?"

"Nothing—I threw up right after we got to his apartment. I... I had a bad memory and it made me unwell for a while."

"Jeez, Renata. What memory is so awful it makes you throw up? I can't even imagine. What happened?"

I knew she was asking about the flashback, but I chose to misinterpret her question; I didn't want to answer what she wanted to know. "I showered, he showered. He cleaned the kitchen before I was finished. He made soup and we watched movies. *Pitch Perfect* one and two. Great recommendation, by the way. They were hilarious."

She beamed. "Aren't they good?"

"Yeah, they really are. I don't remember the last time I laughed that much."

"What are you guys doing today?"

"I think he's going to give me a baking lesson since we didn't do that yesterday. He wants to practice teaching before he has to do it in a room full of students."

"That's a great idea! And good luck—I *suck* at baking. Like seriously suck at it. I'm not too bad with cooking in general, but baking? Let's just say Fern has asked me to never try again."

We both laughed. "I'm afraid that's what's going to happen with Chad and me, honestly," I said. "I'm not great with anything in the kitchen, though."

"I'm willing to bet that Chad would spend every day teaching you even if you did suck as badly as I do. Just a hunch."

She winked.

I blushed and beamed uncontrollably.

I hoped she was right.

"How's your writing since the conference?" she asked as we meandered back behind the counter.

"I've barely even gotten back," I laughed.

She shrugged. "And?"

"Honestly? I haven't even tried. I was beat last night and the night before when I got home. But since I'm off tomorrow, I'll see what happens."

"My fingers are crossed that words pour onto the page like... like... coffee from a carafe," she finished.

I snorted, she giggled, then we both doubled over with laughter.

"That was..." I trailed off, searching for the right word.

"Fabulous? The best metaphor you've ever heard?"

I snorted again. "Simile, and sure."

"And that, my friend, is why I'm not a writer."

"What is? Not knowing the difference between a simile and a metaphor or your singular ability to use them?"

"Both, of course," she giggled again. "Oh-oh-oh! That reminds me! There's a bookstore we should go to. I forgot about it. It's a hike—like forty-five minute drive—but it's the coolest bookstore I've ever seen. It's called Literal As A Simile. And actually, now that makes sense," she added with a chuckle. "Anyway, it's got a pretty good selection of new and used books, but it's also got all kinds of quirky writing paraphernalia, stuff I've never seen anywhere else. It's really cool."

"Sounds like it. Where is it?"

"Jacksonville. Wanna go Sunday? I think we're both off then. We could go early so you can still write after?"

"Sunday works. But how about going later? Then I can run and try to write in the morning."

"Works for me—then I can sleep in. But stop saying 'try.'"

"What?"

"You keep saying try to write or try to be a writer... stop saying try. It's like you're setting yourself up to not succeed or something. Say you're going to write, you're going to be a writer or are a writer." She shrugged. "I double majored in psychology in college, and small things like that can make a big difference in your confidence and performance. What you say to yourself is what you begin to believe will happen, and what we believe shapes what we do. It's actually pretty fascinating."

I looked at her, processing what she'd said. "Yeah, it is." But it was going to be easier said than done.

Twenty minutes later, I clocked out to head home. There should be just enough time to shower and get myself dressed and ready before Chad would be there to pick me up.

"Make good choices!" Caroline called as I neared the front door.

I laughed at her *Pitch Perfect* reference and she winked at me. I waved and stepped outside. For some reason, it felt like the most beautiful day in years.

I was agonizing over what to wear and felt so incapable of deciding that I texted Caroline with photos and asked her to just tell me which outfit to put on. She instead told me to grab one of the dresses I'd bought when I went shopping with her. None of the three dresses had been worn yet. I eyed them in my closet. She'd specifically said to wear the dress that was a dark denim blue with tiny cream-colored flowers. It had a sweetheart neckline, cap sleeves, a fitted waist, and a full skirt that fell an inch or two above my knees. While longer than my jean shorts that I'd gotten used to wearing, it felt more revealing. And the bodice definitely showed more skin than my t-shirts or blouses. But Caroline was insistent on that dress, so I put it on.

With my hair brushed again, I flipped my head upside down a few times to add some volume. While I had thick hair, it was fine enough that it had a tendency to sit closer to my scalp than I liked. Lastly, I rubbed my lips together with some pressure to give them color; I didn't wear lipstick or lip gloss. A basic beeswax lip balm was as close to makeup as it got for me. A glance at my phone revealed that Chad would already be downstairs waiting; he'd texted when he was five minutes away, but that had been nearly fifteen minutes earlier. I snatched my purse off the hook on the wall and flung the door open, barreling into a solid body.

"Oof," I said, jumping back. I wasn't sure if I was more relieved or embarrassed that the person I'd run into was Chad.

"I was just about to knock," he said, amusement tinging his voice.

"I'm sorry, I was rushing."

"You mean that's not how you always exit your apartment?" he replied, the corners of his mouth twitching, his beautiful eyes dancing.

I bit my lip, trying not to laugh. He leaned forward and my breath hitched. He place a very soft kiss on the corner of my mouth. "Hi," he breathed out as he straightened back up.

"Hi," I replied, my breathy tone matching his.

He grinned, his eyes scanning over me then returning to mine, only the tiniest hint of brown remaining. "You look beautiful."

The skin on my face felt tight and I looked down. "Thank you."

His fingertips skimmed down my palm and my fingers, and the sensation reverberated throughout my body. Who knew how that was even possible, but it was, and it was incredible. We held hands and walked down the hall as he asked me about work. I stole sideways glances, studying the way his rolled shirtsleeves pulled tight against the most muscular forearms I'd ever seen—bakers' arms, he'd called them. I tried to memorize the way his eyes looked right then as he listened attentively, the way his lips were relaxed. Everything about him fascinated me; he was so different from what you'd expect from just looking at him. He was muscular, but gentle—tender, even. He was tall, but he didn't tower. He was sexy and cute, but he wasn't arrogant. He was self-assured, but wasn't afraid to be vulnerable. I adored his contradictions.

"Wheat or white?" he asked as he shifted into drive once we were in his SUV.

"Wheat," I replied.

"Crusty or soft?"

"Crusty."

"Fruit or vegetables?"

"Both."

"That's not an answer," he laughed.

I shrugged and giggled. "I know, but I love them both. I couldn't pick one or the other."

"Okay. What are your favorites?"

I sighed, trying to narrow it down. "Peaches, bananas, melon—any kind of melon, carrots, kale, leeks, peppers, grapes, apples, green beans, peas, broccoli, sprouts, plums, potatoes, cherries—fresh only. I can't stand artificial cherry flavor."

"So basically the produce section."

I shrugged again. "I can't help it. I know it's weird."

He scrunched up his face. "There's nothing weird about it. You like what you like."

"What about you? How would you answer all those questions?"

"Wheat, crusty, fruit if I'm eating it raw, vegetables otherwise. I especially love mangoes and parsnips."

"What do you put parsnips in?"

"Lots of things. They were in the pot pie I made for your birthday."

"I thought the potatoes were a little sweet!" I exclaimed.

"That'd be because they weren't potatoes," he laughed, parking. He opened my car door and took my hand after closing it. "Run or lift weights?"

"Run. Absolutely run."

He groaned. "I only run for my cardiovascular system—I wouldn't do it otherwise. I can't stand running."

"Not me—I love running. I've always loved running."

"That's right—you ran track."

I nodded. "Cross-country. I prefer longer runs at a steady pace over short sprints. I used to run every day, but then..." My voice faltered, but I swallowed and pushed on. "Well, I didn't for a while, but I'm running again now. Not every day yet—it's taking a while to work back up to it, but I'm getting there. I want to run a marathon next year when I turn thirty."

"A marathon! Holy cow. That's like..." He trailed off, and his eyes squinted as he thought.

"Twenty-six point two miles," I offered.

"I could never do something like that. I think that's incredible."

"You could, if you wanted to," I said. "But you have to want to. Training for something like that isn't easy."

"Have you ever done it before?"

I paused before responding, thinking of the past. "No. It's something my dad and I were going to do together the year I turned thirty. I know he'd be proud that I'm doing it without him." I sniffled, blinking back the tears in my eyes.

"I think he'd be proud of so many things, Rena," Chad said.

"What about you?" I asked, shifting the topic before I cried. It was hard to think about my dad without the emotion taking over sometimes. "What do you do aside from run occasionally for health reasons?"

"I didn't say occasionally," he replied, quirking an eyebrow.

"Oh, I just assumed that's what you meant."

He laughed. "It was. I'm just giving you a hard time. So, I run *occasionally* and I lift weights a few days per week, I hike when I can get away to. I used to do crossfit, too, and I really liked the physical aspect of it, but I didn't like the environment. There was a lot of pressure to be there every day and spend all your free time training even if you had injuries, and a lot of the people had this idea they were better than people who didn't do crossfit, and that all bothered me. I don't know if it's like that everywhere, but it is in the local box, and after a while, I realized I was paying a ridiculous amount of money to do something I dreaded, so I stopped. I added some of the exercises into my lifting routine and that works for me."

I made a sound of sympathy. Damien had been into crossfit, and he was one of those people Chad was describing whose life revolved around it and who thought he was better than people who didn't live that way. That had always bothered me about him. Connie had called it a red flag. I'd thought at the time that she was unfairly judging him.

We walked the rest of the way to his apartment in a comfortable silence. When we stepped inside, it looked like it had the day before, nothing out of place, except that there was a large paper bag from Home Depot on the island countertop. Chad dropped my hand and swiped it off the counter, rolling the top down before placing it in the pantry.

"For later," he said with a wink.

What the hell could we be using from Home Depot for a baking lesson?

Chad laughed and walked over, stopping in front of me. He reached out and pressed his fingertips gently against the right corner of my mouth. "When you're perplexed, this side of your mouth raises just a little higher than the other. It's adorable."

My body buzzed. I very suddenly wished it was his mouth and not his fingertips touching me. I cleared my throat and took a step back out of his reach. My head was starting to spin, and I was having trouble thinking and breathing. "Okay, Chef Chad." I swallowed. "Wait, is that what you're called? Or is there another word when it's baking?"

"Chef is what my students will call me."

"Okay, then. Chef Chad. Are you ready?"

"Depends."

"On what?"

"On what you're asking if I'm ready for," he said with a smirk. "You didn't specify."

My face heated and I rolled my eyes at him. "Teaching me to bake."

He inclined his head. "Okay." He turned and headed toward the wall next to his pantry, lifting two aprons. He stepped back over to me and handed me one. It was black and covered in white script. "It was the most writerly one I could find on short notice," he said.

"You bought me an apron?" I asked.

He gave a single head nod.

"I could have gotten one," I said.

"I could have let you use one of mine, too," he replied. "But I wanted to get you one that would be yours when you're here."

"That sounds an awful lot like you think this isn't a one-time deal," I teased.

The brown disappeared from his eyes. "It isn't, Rena. It definitely isn't."

Chad interspersed instructions with questions, mostly the type where I had to choose between two alternatives. When I tired out before the dough had been kneaded sufficiently, he took over as I stood to the side and watched, mesmerized. I couldn't get over how deftly he manipulated the dough, how he made it move the way he wanted it to, and yet there was still a care and gentleness in his movements. I was taken by the way his forearms flexed as he moved, spattered with flour. I never would have guessed how content I could feel watching someone bake, but Chad made it sexy.

Once the dough was covered and set aside to rise, we washed up side-by-side in the sink. I dried my hands first, then Chad dried his, chuckling when he looked at me. He flipped the towel over his shoulder and reached up, swiping his thumb over my forehead.

"You had some flour up there," he said.

"Thank you," I replied.

He didn't respond, his eyes following his hand as it feathered down my cheek. "I very much want to kiss you again," he said, barely above a whisper.

Oh, god, yes. Please, yes. I nodded.

He pulled the towel from his shoulder, tossing it on the counter, and moved that hand to the small of my back, pressing subtly as he stepped closer. His hand glided from my cheek into my hair and cradled my head. My eyes fell closed as he neared me, and his nose brushed the side of mine so softly it gave me goosebumps and I shivered. I lifted my hands and rested them against his chest, stepping the rest of the way into him. Feeling the bulge of an erection pressing against me made my breath catch just as his did, and for the first time in years, my body ached with want. It felt so exquisitely sweet that emotion swelled into my chest, rising into my eyes behind my closed lids. I didn't want to do anything about it right then… I just wanted to savor feeling a desire for sex again after so long feeling nothing but dread and hatred. How Chad could do that after so little time amazed me; something about him disarmed me at the most fundamental level.

The chime of the doorbell sounded like it came from far away, the rushing of the blood through my ears drowning it out. And I thought maybe it did when Chad didn't move, but then it rang a second time, and there was no doubt it was coming from his door. He brushed his lips across mine and then stepped back, his hands reluctant to leave me. I gulped in lungfuls of air, realizing all of a sudden that I wasn't getting enough. He smiled apologetically. "I'll be right back."

As soon as he turned around, I slumped back against his refrigerator. Holy hell. I wasn't sure if I was glad or irritated to be interrupted. A strange mixture of both. I heard hushed voices coming from his entry and couldn't make out any of the words; I just knew it was another male voice. Then, the voices ceased and Chad walked in carrying a bouquet with a collection of yellow, orange, red, and purple flowers. I recognized some roses and sunflowers, but I wasn't sure what the others were. The bouquet was wrapped in burlap and tied with raffia. It looked like it came from a cart in a market in some charming European town.

"These are for you," he said. "I didn't have enough time to pick them up after they were ready, so I had them delivered, but they were supposed to arrive while I was picking you up. They're a little late."

"Chad," I breathed out, accepting the bouquet from him. "They're beautiful."

No one had ever given me flowers like that before. Damien used to give me roses, at the beginning, then again after every fight in which I'd ended up hurt, but they were always the same: a dozen identical, flawless red roses. I'd never particularly liked red roses, and I grew to hate them over the years. But this bouquet was different, filled with so many different kinds of flowers, and the roses in it were a beautiful peachy orange. They were perfect.

"I love them. And sunflowers are my favorite." I lowered my nose into the center of the bouquet and inhaled deeply. "They smell lovely."

He bent where I'd just been and breathed in. "Yeah, they do." He straightened up and tucked my hair behind my ear. "Let me get you a vase."

"I wish I didn't have to," I lamented. "I love the way they're arranged in the burlap. It's such a romantic look, and it won't be the same in a vase."

"Then don't," he said. "You don't have to. You can dry them."

"But they'll turn brown and wilt and look awful."

"No, they don't have to. Yes, they'll brown some, but they'll keep a lot of the color if you hang them. You can tie some twine or something around where the raffia is and hang it upside down. Leave it that way for a month or so until there's no moisture left. Then you can lay them out or hang them however you like."

"I didn't know that," I said, gazing at the flowers. "I'll try it. It'll really work?"

"Yeah," he replied. "I've done it before."

I inhaled their fragrance again. "Thank you," I said, lifting just my eyes.

His eyes warmed and his face softened. "You're welcome."

Even with Chad's help, I'd half expected to mess something up with the bread, but he'd been a great teacher and it had turned out wonderfully. We paired it with the soup he'd made the day before, and everything was just as delicious. As we ate dinner and talked, I felt at ease. I'd gotten used to his frequent questions, charmed by his thirst to learn about me, and was falling for him more with every new thing I learned about *him*. Too soon, it was time for me to leave; we both had to work early the next morning. When I asked about whatever was in the Home Depot bag, he said he would save it for another day.

"I'm wrapping the bread in paper because it'll keep it fresh without ruining this perfect crust you made," he said as he tore paper off a roll and began carefully folding it around the bread.

"You have given me at least a thousand compliments on that bread tonight. I'm beginning to think you're trying to win me over."

"Is it working?" he asked with a wink.

I giggled. "Maybe."

"I can work with 'maybe.'" He finished tucking the paper around the remainder of the loaf. "You can warm it for a few minutes in the oven, then have bread and cheese, even a little slice of apple and some jam on it in the morning. A quick and delicious breakfast."

"Is that your way of telling me to eat breakfast?"

"Requesting, but yes," he replied, serious.

"You're very concerned with my eating habits."

He sighed, turning away briefly. When he returned, he spoke quietly. "You remind me of Fern when she had an eating disorder."

My body froze, stiff. I hadn't expected him to say something like that. How the hell was I supposed to respond?

"She routinely skipped breakfast, but then would skip other meals, too. She was thin, but very self-conscious about how she looked; she had body dysmorphia. You're sometimes uncomfortable around food the way she was. And you skip a lot of meals. And you're... you're the most beautiful woman I've ever seen, Rena, but you seem to be most comfortable when you're wearing oversized clothes, like you're hiding in them or something. I just..." He let out a loud breath. "I don't want to see what happened to Fern happen to you, that's all."

My mind raced, conflicted. He'd called me beautiful, but he thought I had an eating disorder and I reminded him of his sister. Was that what all this was about? Was he inviting me over and making food for me and complimenting my looks just because he thought I wasn't eating? Was that all it was to him—helping some woman he thought needed help because she reminded him of his sister? I wasn't sure what to believe; my feelings were all jumbled and confused.

He scrubbed his hand down his face. "I upset you," he said. "I didn't mean to, I swear." He swallowed. "I like you, Rena. I like you a lot. And when I care about people, I can be a little... overprotective, Fern would say. I'm sorry. I shouldn't have said anything."

"Do you?" I asked, shocked by my ability to speak up.

He gave a slight shake of his head. "Do I what?"

"Do you actually like me or am I a project to you?"

His brow furrowed. "You're a *person*, Rena. A human being. You're not a project."

The words were perfect, but I just wasn't sure. I wasn't sure of anything anymore. I *had* been—I'd been sure he was different, but just now he'd sounded like Damien had a thousand times about my career, about fitness, about my clothes, about my diet... Damien was the reason I ate the way I did now.

Maybe Chad is right... maybe it is *a problem.*

Except that I wasn't sick, I was eating enough to run, and I'd even put on quite a bit of weight since leaving Damien. But what right did Chad have to control when I ate? I swore when I left Damien no one would ever tell me what to eat or when again...

Isn't he still, in a way? What Chad said is different—he's not telling me what to do.

He might as well have been. And who knew if he was telling me the truth, if I was anything more than someone he thought needed saving or could be molded into what he was looking for like I was for Damien.

"Rena?"

His voice was plaintive, his face pleading, but was it real? This was why I'd decided not to date again after Damien. It was too hard to know when people were telling you the truth. I never should have allowed myself to lose sight of that.

"I should go now. I'll get a cab."

I turned away from him but stopped abruptly when he touched me. His hand was on mine, but it was gentle. He wasn't yanking me or grasping so hard I couldn't easily pull away.

"Rena... please." His voice was slow and quiet. "Maybe I shouldn't have said anything, but I'm being completely honest with you. I'm worried because of the similarities I see, and because I care. But that has nothing to do with why you're here right now. It has nothing to do with why I found every excuse I could to hang around in the front every morning I worked with you just so I could be near you, so I could hear your voice and learn something about you from your conversations with Caroline. It has nothing to do with why I wanted to cook for you on your birthday and why I asked you out. It has nothing to do with why I can't stop thinking about you. It has nothing to do with the way I feel when I'm around you, like we've always known each other and just fit, the way I feel when I touch you or when you laugh at something I say or moan when you're eating my food. It has nothing to do with why I looked up what Rena means last night, so I'd know what I was calling you, since you told me how much names mean to you. It has nothing to do with the fact that finding out that Rena means joy just made me want to call you it even more because that's what I feel when I'm around you."

"Do you promise?" I breathed out, lifting my gaze to search his eyes, his face, for any sign he was disingenuous.

"I promise," he said, no hesitation and no flickering in his eyes or his body. He was steady.

No, not just steady. *Steadfast*.

FOURTEEN

The café door chimed with someone's entry. I looked up and broke into a grin before pulling my cheeks in and biting my lip, trying to temper my reaction to seeing Chad. The sight of him made me feel giddy and inordinately happy, but I didn't want to scare him off by being too enthusiastic this early in whatever this thing was between us. However, that worry was lost when his eyes found mine and his whole face lit up. It reminded me of what happened when I told him how good his pot pie was on my birthday. So, complimenting his food, talking about baking, and seeing me made his face light up that way.

"Hi," I breathed out when he reached the counter.

He reached out and ran a finger down the back of my hand that was resting on the countertop. "Hello, my Rena."

My knees weakened and my breath was heavy. His Rena... his joy. It was the second time he'd said that, but he hadn't known what he was saying the first time. He did now, though, which gave so much more meaning to it.

"You're early," I murmured. We were supposed to see each other after my shift, but that ended in another hour.

"I know—I couldn't wait any longer to see you, though. I know I need to amuse myself for an hour and I don't mind."

I laughed; I felt the same way he did. It had only been two days since I last saw him—the day we baked and he got me flowers—but it felt longer. Something had shifted between us that night when he'd bared how much he liked me, and I'd chosen to trust him. I could even feel the difference in the text messages we'd been exchanging since, and I could feel it now as his eyes, those ever-changing eyes, focused on me. It felt like he was seeing me in a way I wasn't used to being seen, as if he knew me more than I knew myself almost. It was terrifying, but I loved it, too.

He glanced around, then turned back to me. "There's no one here."

"Nope—it's been slow for a while."

His finger moved back and forth across my hand, and each pass made my breath shallower. His eyes were changing color before me, the brown disappearing little by little, leaving only a gray-blue that appeared to become darker as he looked down to my lips. I bit them together, trying to hide that they wanted to be touching his right then.

"Holy shit, the sexual tension in here," Caroline's voice rang out, followed by her laughter.

Chad's face was as flushed as mine felt. "Hi, Caroline," he said, his eyes still on me. He lifted my hand and kissed where his finger had been smoothing.

"Oh, yeah, this is uncomfortable," Fern chimed in as she came through the swinging door.

Chad hmphed, reluctantly turning in her direction. "Me talking to a woman is uncomfortable for you?"

"No, what you *aren't* saying is uncomfortable. You're my brother!"

"And yet, you and Caroline make out in front of me all the time."

"Not all the time," Caroline said. "That's only happened a few times."

"But it's happened," Chad said, a slight edge in his voice.

"Chad," Fern cut in, "I was kidding." She glanced at me. "I was just teasing you guys." She looked back to Chad. "Seriously. I'm just happy you finally like someone."

"You act like I've never dated before."

Fern shrugged. "It's been long enough you might as well not have."

I looked back and forth between them, listening to their conversation, not sure what to make of it. Was Fern actually upset or not? And then Chad... I felt embarrassed by what Fern said about him liking me, but he was unphased, completely *un*-embarrassed. He was the most straightforward person I'd ever met.

Fern tilted her head toward the front where several people were approaching. "Customers coming."

Chad gave me a half-smile. "That's my cue to make myself scarce."

He settled into a corner of the café with a magazine he'd been carrying under his arm; something about baking, based on the breads on the cover. I turned to our customers and the next hour passed quickly. When it was time for me to turn in my cash drawer and clock out, Fern called out as I was turning to leave.

"Renata?"

I turned back around. "Yeah?"

"I was just giving Chad a hard time earlier."

My face heated and I looked down. She'd said as much to Chad, but I was still worried about upsetting my boss if she thought I was too distracted to work or something.

"I'm fine with you guys dating. More than fine—I'm happy he's interested in someone. His last girlfriend did a number on him, and he's barely even flirted with someone since. He smiles more now, like he used to before Lilith. I've never seen him quite like he is now, and it makes me happy. He's given up a lot for me over the years—most of our lives, really. Anyway, he was worried you'd think I was actually upset about you guys dating or him coming to see you here, but I'm not. At all. I think it's great. If it was anyone else, I'd be worried about it interfering with work, but not with him, and not with you."

My face was now on fire. "Okay."

"Good," she said. "Now go—I know he's waiting on you."

"I need you to pick a place," Chad said as we left the café, his fingertips pressing faintly into my lower back.

"What kind of place?"

"The kind of place you'd choose," he laughed.

I rolled my eyes. "What are we doing there?"

He waggled his eyebrows and leaned in toward my ear. "Lunch," he whispered.

I giggled. "Okay, so what you're asking is my place or yours."

He gave a small headshake. "No. I mean, you can choose one of those places if you want to, but it's not limited to our apartments. The food is already cooked. Anywhere you want to go is an option."

If he wanted to go somewhere other than his apartment, it was an easy choice for me, even in the midsummer heat. "Let's go to the preserve."

"As you wish," he replied, his lips twitching.

"You've read *The Princess Bride*?" I asked, shocked.

"No—watched the movie."

"Of course—most people watch the movies. I read the books."

"You don't watch the movies for books you've read?"

"I mean... I have, of course, but it's always so disappointing. Books are just so much better."

"Okay, I know what we're doing tonight. We're watching *The Princess Bride*."

I groaned.

"No—trust me. It's really good. I promise you won't be disappointed this time."

"Okay," I said, unsure if I believed him.

"You'll see," he said.

We arrived at the parking for the preserve a few minutes later and set out on foot. Chad had never been there before, but I knew it as well as I knew the inside of my apartment and guided us along the trails to the perfect spot for a picnic. It wasn't the only clearing in the preserve, but this one was hidden, so it usually didn't get crowded like the others did. And because it was smaller, the towering trees overhead provided a wonderful shade from the midday sun.

"Wow," Chad said, looking around as we stepped through from a short, narrow trail into the intimate clearing. "This is really cool." He pointed upward. "Those trees are poplars. They've got to be a hundred and fifty years old, maybe older. It's amazing."

"I can't believe you've never been here."

He shrugged, still looking around. "I didn't realize it was this big and didn't think something in the middle of an urban area could look like this. I figured it was just another park that was billed as a preserve for marketing reasons. But now that I know it's like this? I'll definitely be coming here again."

"This is where I run," I said, taking a seat on the grass in the sun-dappled shade. Leaning back on my arms, I closed my eyes, feeling my body relax. "I learned these trails when I was little—I knew them all by heart before I was ten. My dad and I came here almost every day. I knew every nook and cranny in here. It was as much home to me as my house was growing up. Some things have changed since then—all those benches we passed are new, as are the message boards, and a few of the trails have been extended or closed—but it's still like home to me."

I inhaled the unique scent of the preserve down into the recesses of my lungs; it didn't smell like any other forested area.

"Did you know this preserve was created when the town was founded in the late seventeen hundreds? It was bigger then, but not by all that much, really. The town grew around it, but the preserve remained. Back in the early nineteen eighties, the town was going to clear the land and build a planned community. Houses, condos, a strip mall. Technically, the land was protected, but they made some adjustments to the law to get around it—they were going to carve out a four-acre space next to the highway and plant some trees and said that would make up for building on the preserve. But the residents revolted. My mom and dad, among others, organized protests and got thousands of signatures on petitions to keep the preserve. They staged a sit-in and strikes. It took a toll on the town's economy, and eventually the town decided to put up condos by the interstate instead and leave the preserve alone."

"I had no idea," Chad replied, his voice close.

"Mm-hm. My dad always said that's why the preserve was so lush and beautiful—because it fed off the love of the townspeople who'd fought so hard to keep it. He said that all life around us needs more than just food and water to survive, and that with enough love, anything can be vibrant and thrive... especially people."

"Your dad sounds amazing," he said, his voice barely more than a murmur.

"He was."

I opened my eyes to find Chad studying my face. Out of the blue, I felt self-conscious about having gone into a history lesson about the preserve. It wasn't that I was all that interested in history, but I loved the preserve. I plopped backward so I was lying in the grass and crossed my arms over my face.

"I'm sorry—you didn't want to know all that. It's boring, I know."

The hair on my forearm tingled just before his soft touch met my skin. He gave a gentle nudge to my arms so they fell on the ground above my head. "Nothing that interests you could ever bore me, Rena," he said. "When you talk about them, I can feel your excitement and your passion like it's mine."

My eyelids lifted and Chad grew closer, his fingers whispering over my cheek and jaw. My breathing became disjointed and my chest rose and fell noticeably. His eyes were bright and intense, the ring of brown just a sliver in width that disappeared.

"Your eyes," I whispered. "They're changing."

He nodded, swallowing, and then he kissed me. It was like the first time, but somehow the sensations throughout my body felt more intense. He pulled back marginally, then pressed his lips to mine again, his body shifting and some of his weight resting on me. He took my top lip between his in a soft, nibbling kiss, and my mouth fell open—I couldn't get enough oxygen otherwise. I felt everything throughout my whole body, and the same desire I'd felt in his kitchen returned. His tongue was soft against mine as we continued to kiss, and I lifted my hands to his shoulders. As he had once before, he shivered and something in the air shifted. My hands clutched at him and pulled him closer, and his hand snaked under my lower back. My body arched up against him.

Seconds later, voices wafted into the air around us—there were people approaching. Chad rested his forehead on mine with a small chuckle, then, with a deep breath, he sat up. I opened my eyes and followed him, grinning uncontrollably. His eyes were the darkest gray-blue I'd ever seen them.

He cleared his throat and, flushed, turned to the bag he'd carried in with us. "Lunch," he said, glancing up as the group we'd heard walked into the clearing, heading to the opposite side before sitting.

I avoided eye contact now, feeling embarrassed about nearly having people walk in on us making out. Or kissing, rather. Or was that making out? Did it qualify? I wracked my brain for the definition of making out: kissing or caressing amorously. *Yes, we were definitely making out, then.*

"Your eyes change color a lot," I said, when I couldn't think clearly enough to come up with something else to say. All I could think about was the way his mouth felt on mine. And that I wanted to feel it again. "Sometimes they're gray-blue, sometimes they also have some brown, sometimes a lot of brown. I've never seen eyes with more than one color, let alone that change the way yours do."

He beamed at me, that same lighting up of his face happening. "They're called hazel. They're multicolored. The gray-blue on the outside appears to change based on what's around me—the more blue, the more my eyes look blue. They probably look almost green right now."

"Actually, they're more dark gray. And I meant with the brown that comes and goes."

His lips pulled up on one side. "It doesn't actually go anywhere. It's always there, it's just that you can't always see it."

"How is that?"

"Changes in my pupils," he replied, his eyes now showing me that sliver of brown again, the blue lightening just a bit. "When they dilate enough, the brown disappears and the gray-blue seems to be darker. It isn't actually darker, but it looks that way. And when my pupils shrink, you see more of the brown and my eyes look lighter in color."

"Your pupils change often," I observed.

He shrugged. "Everyone's pupils do. Aside from light, they dilate and contract based on emotion. So if you're angry for instance, they shrink."

"And what makes them dilate?"

A breath passed between us while he considered me. "Pleasure and arousal."

His words felt as if he'd touched me, and I watched the brown disappearing in his eyes as he held my gaze intently.

"Your eyes just darkened," I whispered.

"So did yours."

After we ate the chicken marsala Chad had made for us, complete with a loaf of bread still warm from the oven—the fanciest picnic lunch I'd ever had—he pulled out a small package from the bag and handed it to me.

"What's this?" I turned the item over in my hands. It was wrapped in brown paper and tied with twine.

"For you," he said, his cheeks tinged with pink. "I got it for your birthday, but I was too nervous to give it to you the other day."

"You didn't have to get me something. You didn't have to do that or cook for me—any of it."

"I know," he replied. "But I wanted to. Open it."

I carefully untied the twine and lifted the edges of the paper, then folded it open. Inside was a book: *The Dictionary of Lost Words*. I turned it over and read the back.

"This sounds really good," I murmured.

"I hope it is. I wasn't sure what to get, but when I saw the title, I thought of you and your lost words and had to get it."

My chest warmed. It was the most thoughtful gift I'd ever received—at least since my dad had died. I held it to my chest. "I love it."

"I wouldn't go that far," he laughed. "You haven't read it yet—it might totally suck."

"Even if it's the worst book I ever read, I'll love it anyway." *Because you gave it to me.*

We stood and decided to walk around the park for a bit before heading back to his apartment; he said he had another surprise for me. I was enjoying the anticipation of not knowing what it was. We meandered through the heat, hand in hand. It was a new thing for me. I hadn't dated in high school because I'd withdrawn into myself for several years after my dad died, and then there was Damien. He didn't like holding hands. He thought it was juvenile. He liked to hang his hand over the top of my shoulder or hold the back of my neck when we walked. I'd never liked it and grew to hate it. Like a lot of things with him.

But holding hands, I liked. A lot. Especially when Chad would tug on my hand without warning, and when I moved toward him, he'd kiss my cheek. Was that something he did with all his girlfriends, or was it just with me?

"So," I said, my heart beating faster. "Fern kept me in the office after I clocked out today to make sure I knew she was only joking about... us."

"Good. I asked her to because I could see it was worrying you."

"She said she was glad you liked me."

"She did?" he asked, the corners of his mouth twitching. "I don't know what on earth made her think I like you."

I hmphed. "And she also said your last girlfriend did a number on you."

His playfulness fell away, but he didn't say anything for a long time. When he did speak, his voice was quiet. "She did. She was cheating on me with her ex. For a year. I ignored all the signs because I didn't want to believe them, but I couldn't ignore finding them in her bed."

"Oh, Chad... I'm so sorry."

He gave me a soft smile. "It sucked. But it's okay. That's been over for more than three years now. Besides, I feel happier with you right now than I ever did with her."

I didn't know how to respond to that, so I didn't, my heart flipping over in my chest and my stomach fluttering. Being talked to that way was new to me.

"What about you?" he asked after a while, on our way back to the entrance to the preserve.

"My last boyfriend?" I asked, feeling a chill pass through me. I shivered and the hair raised on my arms.

"Yeah."

"Damien..." I wanted to tell him the truth, that Damien had done a number on me as well. I wanted to tell him that I spent years afraid all the time, but I always thought I was crazy. I wanted to tell him that sometimes he hurt me, and that even after I discovered he was drugging me, I almost didn't leave. I wanted to tell him I was still afraid... afraid he'd come after me one day like he'd said he would if I left him the last time I ever saw him. But that was a lot of baggage for anyone, let alone so early in a relationship. And I'd already lied about the source of my flashbacks... I'd have to tell him I lied to him, and he'd never trust me again—not with what happened with his last girlfriend. "We just weren't compatible," I eventually said.

He was quiet for a while as we walked. "I'm glad. That means he didn't hurt you."

FIFTEEN

It had been a month since the writing conference, and for most of it, not much had changed; I was still staring at a blank page every day, unable to write a single word. I'd broken down and emailed Alan in desperation the night before, hoping he'd remember our conversations from the conference. He had, and suggested I stop trying for a while and start a journaling practice. He encouraged me to give it at least a few weeks before I tried anything else. So, now Chad and I were en route to Literal As A Simile, the same book and writing supply shop Caroline had introduced me to.

He pressed his fingertips against my lower back and kissed my temple once we were inside. "Take your time. I'm going to look around."

"Okay," I said, smiling. I loved the way he touched me, that gentle pressure against my back, his lips against my temple, the whisper-soft caress of a single finger down the back of my hand when I told him about my day. I'd never been touched the way he touched me, and I now couldn't imagine being without it. It was gentle and caring and reverent and respectful. It was sometimes full of desire, but inviting and never pushy or demanding.

I watched his back as he meandered down an aisle, still smiling. I couldn't help it. I felt things with him I'd had no idea existed before we met. Remembering what I was there for, I tore my eyes away and headed toward the journals. My eyes roamed the shelves, my hand lifting to touch several books before I found it.

It was bound in leather that was embossed with leaves and had textured, hand-pressed paper. It was beautiful and I longed to fill the pages. Near the register with my find, Chad sidled up next to me from wandering around and touched his fingertips to my lower back.

"I found something," he said. "For you."

I looked down, but he was holding a hand behind his back.

"It's a surprise."

A warming sensation flooded my body. "Okay."

After paying, I waited just outside the door while Chad checked out. When he walked outside, he handed me something long and square wrapped in brown paper and tied with twine—the same paper and twine my birthday present had been wrapped in.

"To use with your journal," he said, then kissed my cheek.

I gingerly pulled on the twine and peeled the paper off to find a box of the very same pencils I used to use before I gave them up after Damien insisted; pens were more adult and wouldn't leave gray smudges on my fingers. I pulled the top of the box off and held the fresh pencils to my nose. The smell of cedar and graphite gave me a thrill that ran all the way down to my toes. When my eyes rose, Chad was watching me with a giddiness in his, the corners of his mouth twitching.

"I can't believe you got me pencils! These are perfect. Thank you."

"What else would I give my writer girlfriend who's stolen my heart?"

"Stolen your heart?" I teased, loving hearing him say that as much as I loved hearing him call me his girlfriend.

He laughed and slid his arms around me, his fingertips urging me closer to him. He touched his lips to mine. "That's right. I'm falling madly in love with you."

I blushed furiously and leaned into him. "I'm falling in love with you, too, boyfriend," I whispered back.

With my new journal and pencils in tow, we headed back to Chad's apartment. Today I was making him my dad's spaghetti bolognese. I'd told him it would be the best he'd ever had, but now that it was time for action, I was nervous. He was a professional in the kitchen, after all. He, on the other hand, was giddy about it.

He perched on the kitchen counter where he could watch, his eyes dancing in amusement as I began pulling out ingredients and utensils, directing me where to find things as needed. After filling a large pot with water from the faucet over his cooktop, I placed it on the largest burner.

"You're not salting the water?" he asked.

I turned and narrowed my eyes. "I *am*, I just haven't gotten there yet."

His chest shook with a silent chuckle.

Turning back around, my cheeks burning as I tried not to laugh, I dropped a pinch of salt into the pot, then sprinkled some into his preheated cast iron skillet and tossed in the ground beef.

"You're seasoning the pan instead of your meat?" he questioned.

I let out a small growl when I turned. "Who's cooking today?"

He burst out laughing and held up his hands. "I'll keep my questions to myself."

"Or you can observe from somewhere else," I said as sternly as I could manage when it was a fight not to laugh with him.

He didn't end up observing from anywhere else, and he also didn't entirely stop asking me obnoxious questions, which amused me as much as they worried me that I was doing something wrong. But, right or wrong, this was how Dad made spaghetti and how I liked it, so I continued.

Chad hopped off the counter when everything was almost done to dump the pasta and boiling water into a colander, despite the fact that I'd assured him I could handle it, saying he wanted to help—he wasn't used to other people doing the cooking. He stood right behind me and watched as I mixed the sauce and noodles together in the cast iron skillet.

"That looks and smells amazing, Rena," he said, pulling my hair over my shoulder.

My breath hitched and I lifted a forkful up for him to taste. He opened his mouth and I slid the fork inside. Watching his mouth pull the food off it, my body flooded with hormones, sending my temperature skyrocketing. I swallowed loudly.

"How is it?"

"Freaking delicious," he said, his eyes widening.

I blushed for the millionth time. "Really?" I tasted it and *I* thought so—it tasted just like Dad's—but Chad had probably had better.

"Really. I wasn't expecting that much flavor. That's really good—*really* good."

"You're not just saying that?"

He shook his head. "No. I'm not going to lie to you. If it sucked, I'd tell you, though I'd probably find a nicer way to say it." He paused. "Probably."

I rolled my eyes, but I felt like I was glowing. Chad actually liked it. It was as good as I thought it was.

His eyes darkened. "You're so beautiful, Rena. You know that?"

Rather than answering, I leaned forward and pressed my lips to his. We kissed feverishly and he lifted me to the counter, stepping between my legs, his hands squeezing my hips. I practically convulsed, feeling him against me, his hands touching me with so much want. I pulled him into me and kissed him harder, tasting my spaghetti on his tongue. His lips moved along my jaw, down my neck, to the v in my sleeveless button up top. Kissing just below my throat, his fingers started to unbutton my shirt, unhurried.

My breath stalled and I shifted my hips against him. He groaned against my skin and his fingers moved to the second button. I wanted him to continue—I wanted things I hadn't wanted in years—but it was making my head spin. It was too much and I wasn't ready. I swallowed and lifted a hand to still his.

He stopped, moving his hands to the counter on either side of my hips, and rested his forehead to mine. His breath was choppy against my face.

"I'm sorry," I whispered, feeling embarrassed that, after a month of dating, I wasn't ready to do much more than kissing.

He brushed a tender kiss across my lips. "Don't be."

"It's—I just—I want to move slow. If that's alright."

"More than alright, my Rena." He placed a kiss to my cheekbone. Another just below that one. Yet another to my lips. "Is this okay?" His voice was low and soft and barely loud enough to hear.

I nodded, trying to breathe. "Yes." Kissing was definitely okay. Especially when he was kissing me like I was something fragile and cherished.

By the time we could pull ourselves away from kissing, our spaghetti was cold.

I savored the deliciously cool air entering my lungs as I stretched out my quad in front of my apartment building. I only got to run in the morning on my days off from the café, which didn't come often. While I still ran in the afternoons most days, there was just something about running early that I preferred.

I pushed off and set a challenging but manageable pace, aiming for eight miles this morning. I hadn't run that far since before Damien, but it was time to start pushing it if I wanted to complete the marathon in May; it was only ten months away.

My feet landed and lifted off the path carved through the preserve with a rhythm I'd always found comforting. My breath and even my thoughts would begin to match it, and I'd fall into a meditative state in which the running itself was nearly effortless. It was the well-known runner's high, and I could often extend my runs like this. It was in this state on my tenth mile that I ran past him, not even registering who it was until I was around the next bend in the path.

Damien.

When recognition kicked in, the ripple of tension and anxiety that flowed through my body made my knees weaken and I fell. Scrambling to my feet, my heart hammered against my chest cavity, and the area around me felt like it was closing in. It couldn't be. I had to have been imagining it. I tip-toed back along the path until I could see around the curve. There was no one there. My mind must have been playing tricks on me. With shaky legs, I walked along the path, heading back toward the entrance. By the time I'd reached it, I was sure I'd imagined seeing Damien. There was no reason he would be in Amestown. And even if he was, he wouldn't know where to find me. He'd have no idea where I lived or worked or that I ran in the preserve—that was something I'd never told him about.

My knees were achy by the time I made it back into my apartment, and when I looked down, I found that I was missing most of the skin there, as well as some on my shins. The raw areas were filled with bits of gravel and dirt, and blood dripped down my legs into my socks, staining my shoes. *Shit*. I sighed, blowing escaped hair out of my face, my hands on my waist as I scanned my apartment. I'd been getting that feeling that I was being watched more often, and now this? I needed to get a grip. It was probably just because things had become serious with Chad so quickly that I was seeing danger everywhere. But Damien wasn't here—I was safe in this city, safe with Chad, I reminded myself. Chad was nothing like Damien; if anything, they were completely opposite people.

Thinking of Chad, my heartrate slowed and I began to feel better. Even today, Damien would have laughed at me for tripping over my own feet the way I did when I was more or less hallucinating. I couldn't tell Chad about it, but if I could have, he certainly wouldn't have laughed. He'd have used his fingers to move my hair from my face and wanted to know why what I thought I saw had that effect on me. I walked into my living room near the window and fingered the leaves of my pothos plant.

The day I showed Chad the preserve, we'd gone back to his apartment, and he'd pulled out his Home Depot bag. Inside was potting soil and a pot. It looked like hammered copper with distressed navy paint. Something about it energized me and gave me an urge to write. He'd said the pot made him think of me and that he hoped I liked it. I hesitated before telling him it's what I'd have chosen for myself; it was a bit unsettling to be seen in the way Chad saw me. Together, we'd potted his pothos plant babies in the new pot, and he'd taught me how to properly water it, how to tell if I was giving it too much or not enough. Much like when I watched him working with dough, I was mesmerized by his fingers in the dirt, carefully filling and pressing around the tender roots of the pothos babies. And then we'd made out right there in the kitchen. The intimacy of our fingers moving around each other in the dirt as he showed me how to properly fill in around the new plants set my body awash with want for him. When he'd looked at me with those dark, gray-blue eyes, his pupils wide, we'd knocked over the bag of soil and both ended up with smears of dirt all over our clothes and faces and arms. It had stained my white shirt, but I didn't toss it—I kept it and wore it around the apartment often when we weren't seeing each other because it brought back everything I'd felt that day.

Now, my happily growing pothos was giving me a sense of peace and safety. The memories of Chad filled me with warmth and security that intensified when I touched the plant we'd potted together; a plant that came from him. One that he'd cultivated from one of his older plants and cared for until it was ready to be planted on its own. I had no idea why I found that so sexy and reassuring, but I did. And right then, it was grounding me, much like Chad always did when I was with him.

Okay, Renata. You're fine. You were imagining things. You have a new life now, and Damien is somewhere far enough away you wouldn't ever cross paths again.

After a shower and some lunch—a leftover savory tart assortment that Chad had made us for dinner the day before—I felt somewhat refreshed. I was worried for no reason. But when I sat down with my brand new journal and a freshly sharpened new pencil, my thoughts strayed back to my relationship with Damien. While I didn't really want to give Damien anything else from me—not even space on my paper—journaling was for writing down your thoughts. Maybe if I could write them down, they'd decide to leave me alone.

Rising from the sofa, I moved my pothos to the table closest to me, then sat back down. Reaching out an arm, I confirmed I could easily reach out and touch it. Then, with a deep breath, I put my pencil to the page and began to write, taking breaks as needed to touch my plant in order to feel safe and grounded again.

When I first met Damien, I'd just graduated from college with a degree in creative writing and gotten a job writing for Including the Kitchen Sink. I was sitting on a bench outside the publication's building, eating the sandwich I'd packed for lunch. I watched the people around me and tried to figure out their names. If I was lucky, someone they were with would say their name so I could confirm if I'd gotten it right; I never asked people. My dad had done that, but I didn't do it without him.

A man walked up to the food truck across the street, and I watched as he moved. He was confident; his shoulders were back, his chin high. Even with his sunglasses—aviators—I could see him assessing everything around him. He was attractive—really attractive, especially when I saw him smile at someone who waved as they walked past. Then someone else, and yet another person... it was like he knew everyone going down the street in either direction. Either that, or he grew up in a smaller town kind of like I did and still greeted everyone who passed by. So he was personable—possibly even kind.

He stood to the side of the order window, one leg propped up on the curb, and I added muscular to the list. With his leg bent like that, I could see the outline of muscle through his pants, and when he crossed his arms, his biceps looked like they were about to tear their way out of his shirt sleeves.

Bodybuilder? Something like that, I thought. He must also be vain. I'd never met one who wasn't. So he was probably also arrogant. He accepted his food and turned, heading across the street in my general direction instead of back up Third Street the way he'd come; so he walked on his breaks. And oh my god, he didn't just walk—he swaggered. Literally swaggered. I also noticed he had one more button undone than most men, showing a lot of his chest. Definitely vain and arrogant. Ugh. He was probably a Michael. The name meant gift from god, and Michaels often thought they were.

I saw the man's eyebrows raise, and a small smile played around his lips. It occurred to me for a second before I dismissed the thought that he was walking toward me, that he was watching me behind his mirrored sunglasses. But that couldn't be; I was the kind of person who blended into the background; there was nothing exceptional about me. But then he walked up and sat down right next to me. Rude—there was an empty bench a few feet away.

He tipped his sunglasses down his nose and looked at me. I couldn't help but roll my eyes; he probably thought he was irresistible and that the sunglasses move was cute or hot or something. But it was stupid and he looked stupid doing it.

"I'm not used to offending people I haven't even met yet," he said, pulling his sunglasses off and hanging them over his chest on his ridiculously unbuttoned shirt.

"What?" I asked, thrown off by both his comment and the unexpectedly smooth, magnetic quality to his voice.

"That look on your face—it was disgust, wasn't it?"

My face leapt into flames; I hadn't meant to be that obvious in my facial expressions.

"You seem like I've personally insulted you, but I'm fairly certain I've never met you before."

I had no idea what to say. "I..."

He casually took a bite of the wrap he held, then slung an arm across the back of the bench behind me. "So tell me," he said, swallowing his food. "What's lacking?"

"Lacking?" I wasn't sure I'd ever met someone who made me feel so unstable. It was as if the world were flipping around and I didn't know which way was up.

"Mm-hm," he said around chewing another bite before swallowing that one. "I was over there for approximately eight and a half minutes, and you were studying me the whole time. But you obviously found something lacking. I'm curious what it was."

Oh my god, I thought. What an egotistical, self-important, condescending ass.

He raised his eyebrows, waiting, that same small, annoying smile on his lips. I didn't like it. I didn't like that he'd noticed me watching him, and I didn't like that he was over here making me feel confused and poking fun at me. I stood up.

"You're obviously arrogant, shallow, and self-absorbed, none of which are admirable qualities. I was simply shocked anyone would bother to say hello to someone who so obviously thinks they're better than the rest of the world. Thanks, but no thanks, Michael. You're not my type."

His eyes flashed and I got the impression he saw my words as a challenge. I turned and headed toward the building entrance.

"It's Damien, by the way," he called after me.

The next day, he was there again, and if I hadn't been so shocked that he was approaching me after the day before, I'd have gotten up and walked away. I wish I had gotten up and walked away—and never eaten lunch there again.

"I told you, you're not my type," I said as he neared me.

"You did," he replied smoothly, a hint of amusement in his voice. "But you're definitely mine."

I rolled my eyes dramatically.

"So, Renata, what exactly is it that you think isn't your type?"

My heart stalled. "How the hell do you know my name?"

"Lucky guess," he said. "Now I know your name."

"Lucky guess?" I asked. "Renata isn't a common name. It's not like Sarah or Elizabeth or Nicole or something."

"I'm good with names," he said with a shrug. In spite of my intuitive wariness, I felt a thread of kinship with the stranger who was now sitting next to me again. Maybe there was more to him than I thought. "Unlike you," he added.

"I'm great with names," I snapped, defensive.

"If you say so," he replied. "But your track record is zero for one right now."

"No, it's not!"

"How isn't it? My name's Damien, and you called me Michael yesterday."

"That's not my entire track record."

"But how would I know that? The only frame of reference I have is that you botched my name."

I opened my mouth, but couldn't figure out something to say. He was an asshole and aggravating, but I didn't like that he thought I was bad at something I was actually good at.

"I'll tell you what," he said, taking another bite of his wrap—the same thing he'd eaten the day before. He chewed slowly, his eyes scanning the people going about their day in front of us. "You can prove it to me. I'll point people out, and if you can guess their names, I'll believe you and won't question your name-guessing ability again."

"Done," I said. "I will."

"Wait," he said. "That's one-sided. If you get their names wrong..." He grinned at me. "We go on a date."

"No," I retorted. "Absolutely not."

"I mean, it's not going to happen anyway, right? Because you're so good with names? If you are—as you say you are—you shouldn't care what I would get if you lose this bet because you'll win, right?" He cocked an eyebrow at me.

"Fine," I ground out after a short hesitation. I didn't like that he so obviously didn't think I could do it. And I felt more need than ever to prove to him that I was good with names after he'd somehow guessed mine. Who the hell thinks Renata when they look at someone? How did he do that?

It was only the first of countless times I would wonder how he knew something, just as I still wonder how he found five random people off the street and brought them over only for me to get every single name wrong.

SIXTEEN

October came and I still had yet to write a single word of something I'd consider *writing*, despite journaling daily. In fact, I looked forward to journaling almost as much as I looked forward to spending time with Chad. Occasionally, I wrote about him or work or my struggles writing, but mostly I wrote about Damien. It had inadvertently become the story of our relationship, and I couldn't stop. I wrote about the good and the bad and used the page to try to unravel things I'd never been able to unravel before; sometimes it worked, and sometimes it didn't. But it was helpful overall. I was relaxing even more into the relationship I had with Chad and was beginning to think about Damien less and less outside of journaling. I still had that feeling I was being watched, but it was getting easier to ignore. I was sure it was paranoia on my part; I'd always been prone to it when it came to Damien.

Chad's thirty-third birthday was in three days, and Caroline, Fern, and I had a big surprise planned for him. I'd found an indoor plant expo near a mountain range with world-class hiking trails. While it was most famed for its spring foliage, pictures showed it should also be beautiful in mid-October. When I'd approached Fern and Caroline with the idea, wanting to know if Chad had ever been there before, they'd told me no and been enthusiastic about it. Because of work, I was planning for it to be a very long day trip—it was a six-hour drive away—but Fern insisted on making a multi-day trip of it, with her and Caroline joining for part of it. She gave me five days off and somehow worked it out with Chad's boss for him to be off as well. He would have to find someone to teach one of his classes, but that was it. Fern and Caroline were going to come for two of the four nights, but that was the most they could both be gone from the café since there was only one manager and we were still short on cashiers.

Chad knew we were doing something—we'd had to tell him so he could plan for coverage of the baking class he taught—but he had no idea what it was. He was alternately impatient and content to savor the anticipation. I, however, was exceedingly nervous. I wanted him to like what was planned, yes, but I was also nervous about spending so much time with him. Being around each other around the clock could change things; parts of people you've never seen can come out when you spend so much time together, and in the past, that wasn't a good thing. I couldn't imagine there was anything about Chad that was alarming, but what if after so much time with me, he wasn't as interested?

It had happened before, in a way. Damien had been both more and less interested in me once we were living together, as contradictory as that sounded. He wanted me there all the time, was jealous of every moment I spent outside our shared apartment that wasn't with him, but he also spent less time with me and paid less attention to me when we *were* together, his focus always on crossfit or work or other people.

But Chad wasn't Damien.

The other thing that had me nervous was that we'd be sharing a room. We hadn't yet spent a night together—we hadn't even done more than make out, though I'd thought about it many times. I'd told him I wanted to move slow, and we were doing just that. I wanted to do more, but I was also afraid to. Most of my memories of sex weren't of some mutually pleasurable experience. I'd recently begun to realize through my journaling that sex with Damien had been another way to control me, an obligation I had that proved my devotion. It hadn't begun that way; passionate affection had contorted into something manipulative and dark. Nothing with Damien had been over time the way it was at the beginning. And I was afraid of that transformation happening with Chad. That fear had kept our clothes on and ensured I slept in my own bed, alone, every night.

"What are you packing?" Caroline asked me, pulling me from my thoughts. We were eating lunch together after work, which we did a few days a week—usually when Chad was working. Seeing him had gotten more complicated after classes commenced because, on baking days, he worked a morning shift and we could spend time together after his shift was over, but on teaching days, he worked in the afternoon and evening, so if I was working that day, we didn't see each other at all, except the two times he'd baked a dessert and picked me up to have it with him before bed.

"No idea," I said. "You?"

"Probably half my wardrobe," she laughed. "The weather is supposed to be warm during the day but cool in the mornings and evenings. Obviously, we'll need some jeans and cute tops, a few sweaters. Definitely a few dresses for dinner. *All* the sexy lingerie."

She waggled her eyebrows and I laughed. "I can handle that."

"You looked homeless when I met you—I'm afraid to know what you think qualifies as sexy lingerie."

We both laughed. "Let me clarify—any undergarments I have would be an insult to the word to call them lingerie. But I can handle everything else, thanks to you."

"Oh my god, Renata!" she exclaimed, her shoulders falling. "You don't own *any* pretty underwear?"

My face heated. "I haven't needed to. I mean, Chad and I haven't... you know..."

"Forget about Chad," she said, waving her hand dismissively. "You should own pretty underwear and bras for *yourself*. I mean... I feel better about myself, like I'm attractive and worth something when I dress myself well. When I wear something lacy, I feel sexy. Fern thinks I am, whatever I've got on, but it's not about her—it's about me. How do you feel attractive and sexy and glamorous and worth it if you don't do things like that for yourself?"

I don't, I realized.

"Okay, finish up, woman," she said, her eyes narrowed on me. "We're going shopping again."

An hour later, we walked into *Veronica's*, a store devoted to women's lingerie, ranging from subtly sexy to naughty—at least, that was the label used in that section of the shop. I was intensely self-conscious, even with Caroline's bubbly chatter as she collected different things for me to try on: bras, panties, bodysuits, nightgowns, pajama sets, chemises, and more. I wouldn't have grabbed more than two, maybe three, things in that whole store to try, but Caroline was a fan of trying just about everything to allow yourself to be pleasantly surprised.

It was uncomfortable even touching the items at first; the soft, stretchy lace and silky satin felt like they belonged to a different world than the one I inhabited. But something almost magical happened as I continued to try things on; my attitude began to shift. My shoulders stopped hunching over my chest and moved back, and I noticed the way different items highlighted my abs or accentuated the curve of my hip. Shifting around to look in the mirror and feeling the way the sensuous material moved over my skin made me feel feminine in a way I never had. I'd been brought up to prize intellect and kindness over looks, then given years of my life to a man who prized looks above all but always found me lacking. This was the first time I felt that I was more than all of that. More than intellect and kindness and more than looks—I could value all three in their own way. Instead of feeling shallow to like the way I looked in these sexy pieces, I felt empowered. It gave me a spark of confidence. When I finished going through the pile Caroline had picked out, I went back to the first items, trying on again those I'd tried before I found appreciation for what I was doing.

"So?" Caroline asked as soon as I cracked open the fitting room door.

I grinned, biting the corner of my lip in a frail attempt to curb it. I felt like I was glowing.

She returned my grin. "See?"

"Yeah," I muttered with a small nod.

"Chad's going to love this."

"You don't even know what I'm getting yet."

"It doesn't matter what you're getting," she said. "You feel sexy right now, and *that* looks good on you."

After shopping with Caroline, I went home and took the tags off all my new lingerie—that word still felt weird to use for something I owned. But lingerie was defined as all intimate apparel for women, so that's technically what it was. I went for a quick run, showered, dressed in some of my new *lingerie*, journaled, and then it was time to go. I was meeting up with Fern, Caroline, and a few of their friends for a girls' night out—my third with this group. I didn't know where we were going yet, but I was sure we'd have a good time; I always had fun with them.

I'd typically have worn jeans with a t-shirt, but felt an urge to wear something nicer on top of my new undergarments—not for anyone else, but for myself. I pulled on a knee-length flounce skirt in teal and a rich cream buttoned v-neck blouse that I tucked in. I completed the outfit with a pair of sheer tights and surprisingly comfortable ankle boots Caroline had talked me into buying after we'd left the lingerie shop. I stood in front of the mirror and looked myself over from head to toe. My internal dialogue was much more complimentary than usual. My eyes were drawn to the definition in my calves, which was accentuated by the shoes, but in place of embarrassment, I realized I looked strong in a sexy kind of way. My shoulders were soft and rounded, my arms were defined to show the shape of my triceps and biceps. But rather than thinking my shoulders were carrying extra fat and my arms were too muscular and masculine, I thought they carried a feminine curvature that was enticing.

Screw Damien, I thought. *Strong can be sexy. It* is *sexy.*

Fifteen minutes later, I was smushed into the backseat of a car with Fern and Caroline. Their friend, Elsa, was driving, and another friend, Ruth, was in the front seat. As the four friends chatted, I was content to listen. Everyone took turns deciding what to do for girls' night, and Ruth had chosen a bar with live music by a band called The Mids.

"Chad's going to be so jealous," Fern said. "He loves The Mids."

"What kind of music do they play?" I asked.

"Kind of a fusion of soul and blues and pop," Ruth answered.

"Huh. That sounds like a strange combo."

"You've heard what Chad listens to when he's baking, right?" Fern asked. "That's James Gillespie—it's the same kind of music. The Mids have a very similar sound."

I shivered lightly. The artist Fern was referring to had become a favorite of mine. His music was bass-heavy and hypnotic and emotional and sexy. I enjoyed listening to it for its own sake, and I especially enjoyed watching Chad bake to it; his movements with the dough seemed to coordinate with the music, and it gave me flutters in my belly.

The band was setting up to play just as we found a table—the last one in the bar. The curved booth could comfortably fit eight people based on how much space was left after our group of five was seated. We ordered drinks and appetizers, and before long, conversation had mostly tapered off because The Mids had taken the stage. The entire bar was packed, large groups of people standing around small bar tables and some even just squeezing between tables. I'd never been somewhere that busy before, and I had a twinge of anxiety; it would be difficult to get through all the people to leave. Not that there was a foreseeable reason to need to leave without warning, but it would have set me at ease to have a clear and easy exit available.

I eyed the margarita in front of me; I'd ordered it, but hadn't touched it yet. Not a drop of alcohol had passed my lips since the day I'd found the rohypnol in the kitchen cabinet nearly eighteen months earlier. More than anything right then, I wanted to relax and have a drink with friends like everyone else was doing, but just the thought made me panicky; I hadn't watched it being made, let alone made it myself to know for sure what was in it. Even if something *was* in my drink, I was safe—I trusted Fern and Caroline—but my body didn't agree with my mind, and every time I wrapped my fingers around the glass, I began to shake and felt sick.

My palms flattened on the table with pressure in an attempt to stop the trembling before anyone noticed. I didn't realize someone had approached me, my attention focused on the stage ahead and to my right, until something touched me. I jumped at the same time the touch registered as familiar: Chad was running his index finger down the back of my left hand.

I looked into his eyes, my insides in chaos. I was excited to see him, especially since I hadn't seen him in a few days because of our schedules, and that part of me wanted to jump up into his arms. But the other part was instantly on guard—why was he there? How the hell had he known where I was? It was something Damien had done a lot, seemingly magically appearing anywhere I was. He attributed it to coincidence, but something about it had always unsettled me, even before he confessed to tracking my movements out of concern for my safety.

Somewhat belatedly, I stood, and his arms wrapped around me, hugging me with just the right amount of pressure to where I felt he was happy to see me without the hug being uncomfortable or painful. When we pulled apart, he used his fingertips to brush my hair back over my shoulder and kiss my temple.

"Everything okay?" he shouted into my ear. Even so, it was hard to hear him.

I shifted so he'd be able to hear me and instead of answering his question, asked him one of my own. "What are you doing here?"

He tipped his head toward the table. "Fern texted me that The Mids were playing here, so we left the pool hall to watch them play. She didn't say you guys were going to be here." He placed a small kiss to the top of my ear lobe. "I'm glad you are, though. It's a nice surprise. I missed you."

Most of my anxiety melted away and I leaned my head into him. I'd missed him, too. We listened to the rest of the song this way, his arm around my back, his fingertips strumming up and down my spine. The song ended, and in the brief pause after the applause before the next song began, Chad turned toward the table. "Can we join you guys? There's nowhere else to sit."

There were scattered waves and greetings as my group squeezed together to accommodate the four men. Once everyone was seated, the next song was coming through the speakers, but Chad shouted over it to his friends. "Guys—this is my girlfriend, Renata."

They reached out their hands and introduced themselves as I shook each one, barely able to hear them, before everyone's attention turned to the talented band performing.

I never did touch my drink, yet I felt intoxicated as the evening wore on. The band was every bit as hypnotic and talented as James Gillespie, but it was even more powerful to listen to live, to feel the bass thumping through my body with a distinct pulse. With Chad there, I was able to relax more than I had before, the density of the crowd less worrisome with him by my side. My body was buzzing from his fingertips skimming up and down my bare arm and the intense expression on his face as he watched and listened to the band. It was clear he connected profoundly to the music, and it felt intimate to watch him enjoying it.

The band played until nearly midnight, well past when I normally was in bed; at least I wasn't opening at the café the next morning. As people finished their drinks and paid their tabs, we worked out how to carpool everyone home with the cars available, and I ended up leaving with Chad.

"Your friends seem nice," I said once we were en route to my apartment. "I mean, as much as I could tell."

"They are," he agreed. "We've all worked together at different places for over ten years."

"Wow." The only person I'd ever had in my life who I'd known for that long was Connie. Now, there was no one. The longest I'd known someone in my life now was five months, and those someones were Chad, his sister, and Caroline.

"They were excited to meet you," he said.

"Really?"

"Yeah, although I told them if they said or did anything stupid when they met you, I'd be sure to embarrass the hell out of them by sharing things they'd prefer to let fade from memory." He chuckled. "So they behaved. But they wanted to meet the person who takes up all my spare time now."

"I was surprised you introduced me as Renata."

"Rena is for me," he said. "You're *my* Rena—not theirs."

His joy. I blushed and bit my lip trying to keep a neutral countenance.

"You seem different tonight," Chad observed.

"Good different or bad different?" I asked.

"Good different. You're radiant."

My blush deepened. "I feel different," I confessed, almost to myself.

"Good different or bad different?" he repeated my words, grinning.

"Definitely good." I paused and he waited for me to elaborate. "Caroline helped me to understand something about myself, that's all."

"Well, whatever she helped you to understand, I'm glad. You seem happier."

I pulled my teeth off my lip and allowed my smile to spread. I couldn't remember ever feeling as good as I did right then.

The rest of the drive occurred in silence. I stole glances at him every few seconds, unable to stop myself, and often caught him looking over at me. Each time, my lips pulled wider and the gripping tension in the car grew. By the time he'd parked in a visitor spot at my apartment, I felt downright giddy.

Chad's absence when he got out of the car gave me an opportunity to breathe and try to clear my mind, which felt muddled by all my feelings and the sensations in my body. He came around the car and opened my door, reaching a hand to me as I stepped out. Once on my feet, he pushed the door closed, then lifted my hand and rested it on his shoulder. An arm slipped around me, his flattened palm pressing lightly into my back. With his other hand, he raked his fingertips gently along my jaw, pulling me toward him until our lips were touching. The kiss was soft and sweet, and when he pulled away, I wanted more. I leaned forward, pulling him toward me. This time, the kiss was different. It was heavy and sensual and left me with a profound wanting in my body.

"Oh, god, Rena," he groaned after pulling back and dropping his head to the crook of my neck.

My feet as we walked, hand-in-hand, felt as if they floated above the ground. As we neared my door, I felt an urge to ask him to come inside, but hesitated. Not only had we not spent the night together, but he'd never been inside my apartment before. I'd wanted to keep that space as my own, a place where I always felt safe, but tonight I felt almost desperate for him—everything about him. His kiss, his touch, his voice, his calm, the way he made me feel safe and cherished, the way he made me want him and the way he wanted me.

At my front door, I looked up at him and his eyes were so dark, the gray-blue only a narrow ring, and the realization that it was because of how I made him feel sent a shockwave through me; my breath caught. He swallowed and looked away, his own breath coming out in a rushed, ragged exhale.

"Rena," he said, his voice low and mesmerizing. His eyes shifted around, scanning the hall, the ceiling, the wall, not settling until they returned to mine. He swallowed again. "I want to kiss the hell out of you."

I sucked in a lungful of air.

"Then I want to do more than kiss you—a hell of a lot more."

The air I'd sucked in refused to leave and my whole body began to buzz.

"I want that so badly I can't really think straight right now."

His eyes darted around again, and I began to feel dizzy.

"I think..." His eyes returned to mine, and his fingers tucked my hair behind my ear, then trailed along my jaw and down the side of my neck, barely a whisper on my skin. "I *think* you feel the same way, but... God, I want you." He inhaled deeply and let it out. "I don't want to read you wrong because I can't think clearly. I need you to tell me if I'm wrong and you don't want the same thing right now. I don't want to mess things up with you."

Every reason I had to keep him out of my apartment, every reason I had for not having sex with him, was now buried far below my intense desire for him. I'd never have guessed that someone saying they wanted me to tell them if I wanted sex or not would be so... well, sexy.

But it was.

It was the sexiest thing that had ever happened to me.

"You're not wrong," I breathed out, my heart hammering into my chest.

"Thank god," he said on an exhale. His mouth met mine and he indeed kissed the hell out of me up against my apartment door.

When he pulled away enough for me to turn around to unlock the door, he swept my hair over my shoulder and pressed his lips into the crook of my neck from behind. I fumbled, missing the keyhole several times before my door finally opened. I pushed it closed after us, and by the time I locked it, Chad's mouth was on mine again, his hands skimming up my thighs under my skirt. My skin broke into goosebumps and I shivered. My fingers grasped at the buttons on his shirt, which I pushed off over his shoulders once I managed to pop out the last one. His fingers were also unsteady, and slower than mine as they worked the buttons on the front of my blouse. The buildup of anticipation was dizzying; my head spun.

He pulled me against him, his bare chest against my bra-covered torso, and I felt *his* body shiver this time. His hands moved lightly across the skin on my back from my shoulder blades down to my mid back, then my lower back, moving from my spine outward toward my hips. I was so used to his touch when I was fully clothed that it took a moment for me to remember his hands were touching badly scarred skin. That alone was enough to make me stiffen and want to push his hands away, but then I remembered that I'd lied to him about the source of those scars and my entire body went rigid.

He immediately pulled back, his hands continuing to tenderly caress my deformed skin. The area between his brows was creased. He was worried about me, having no idea that he'd been lied to. He touched his lips to my temple.

"What is it, Rena?" he asked softly.

I opened my mouth, but I didn't know what to say.

"Was I too pushy?" he asked.

I shook my head, shocked that he thought he was pushy. I'd been with someone who was pushy, and Chad was nothing like that. "No."

He didn't respond, and I knew he was waiting for me to say something more. I pulled away and crossed my arms over my chest. The crease in his forehead became more pronounced and he bent, picking up our shirts, handing me mine.

"Rena," he said, his voice trailing off. His eyes scanned the wall as he tried to sort through things in his mind.

"I'm sorry," I said. "It's—"

"No, Rena, please," he interrupted me, reaching out and running a finger down my hand, which was finishing the last button on my blouse. "You don't need to do that. You don't have to explain to me why you changed your mind. If I did something wrong, I want to know, but otherwise, you don't owe me any kind of an explanation." His lips just barely pulled up at the corners. "You're allowed to change your mind, you know."

I looked away. "You didn't do anything wrong." *I did.* I wanted to tell him the truth and opened my mouth to do so, but the words got stuck inside. They wouldn't come out.

He lifted my hand and brushed his lips over my knuckles. "I should probably go," he said. "It's late anyway."

I nodded, almost absently, and walked to the door, opening it and stepping aside. Chad examined my face, his forehead still creased with worry as he gave me a small smile. He tucked my hair behind my ear, his fingers running through the length of the strands.

"Goodnight, Rena."

"Goodnight."

SEVENTEEN

I laid awake most of the night, then stayed in bed half the day, trying to figure out how I could tell Chad the truth about Damien without ruining his trust in me. I wished I'd never lied, but I couldn't undo the past. The damage was done, and I was afraid he would walk away from me. Not that I could blame him—I wouldn't trust someone who'd lied to me, either.

I usually began my days off with a run, but I simply didn't have the energy after getting so little sleep. Instead, I wandered around my apartment for a while, restless, before sitting down with my plant that Chad had named Potty—because it was a potted plant, he'd said, laughing, before asking if I got his terrible play on words. I gingerly fingered each leaf, amazed at how well it was growing. I couldn't believe how many leaves had grown already. Chad assured me I was doing a beautiful job of caring for it every time I sent him photos. Watching it grow made me want to try another plant soon; I liked having something alive inside my apartment with me.

Chad once told me about an experiment in which identical plants were cared for exactly the same way with one exception: one group was talked to in a loving way while the other group was berated and criticized. The plants that received love prospered, while the others shriveled and began to die. What would happen to Potty if I told it lies the way I had to Chad? What if it never found out—would it continue to live a happy, prosperous existence or would it somehow know and begin to die?

Could I keep these secrets from Chad? Could I continue to lie the way I would inevitably have to over time because of the lies I'd already told? I couldn't imagine a future with him if I did, and more than just about anything, I wanted a future that included him. It had only been a few months, but I was undeniably in love with him. But how could a person lie to someone they loved? There was no way to answer that question, and yet I was doing it every day I continued to let him believe things that weren't true.

Carefully, I returned the plant to its spot and checked the clock. It was early afternoon. Chad would be getting off work soon. I glanced at the unanswered messages on my phone from him—two from the night before and several from earlier in the morning. I hadn't even read them yet. I knew more would come in soon, and that he'd be worried since I never left his messages unanswered. Leaving my phone on the kitchen counter, I grabbed a small tote and dropped in my journal, a pencil, and a pencil sharpener, swapped my pajamas for jeans and a café sweatshirt, and set out for the preserve.

I wanted to be alone with my thoughts and headed straight for the same secluded clearing where Chad and I had now picnicked a number of times. The air was cool, but the tree branches had lost about half of their leaves, and just enough sun filtered through to keep me from getting too cold. I closed my eyes and listened to the breeze rustling the dry leaves, remembering so many other times I'd done that before when I was growing up.

I missed my dad every day, but some days were harder than others, and this was one of them. If he were alive, he'd know what to do. Hell, if he were alive, I probably wouldn't have the past I did to even lie about; I'd never have ended up with someone like Damien. My dad was probably turning over in his grave knowing I'd gotten myself into a relationship like the one I'd had before. But even if I had somehow done it while he was alive, he'd know what to do now.

"What do I do, Dad?" I asked the air. "I've screwed up and I don't know how to fix it. I don't know if it's something that *can* be fixed. I don't know if what I've done is forgivable."

Tears slipped down my cheeks and I dropped my head to my knees. Then I heard him, his voice faint but exactly how I'd heard it the last time he'd said the words to me: "Follow your heart, Renata."

But what was my heart telling me to do? I picked up my pencil, opened my journal, and decided to see if I could figure it out on the page.

I'm trying to take Dad's advice and follow my heart, but I can't figure out what that means. I don't want to lie to Chad anymore, but I don't want to tell him the truth, either. I think I have to, though. The lies will always be sitting between us if I don't. I don't know if I can tell him when I can see his face, his expressive eyes. I don't know if I can handle the pain and betrayal I'd see there. Maybe I should write him a letter.

~~Dear Chad,~~

~~I'm a liar.~~

~~Dear Chad,~~

~~I've been lying to you for months.~~

That all sucks. He wouldn't read past the first sentence, and I don't blame him. And I don't feel right calling myself a liar, even though I obviously am because I've been lying to him. Maybe I should start at the beginning—start with the first lie I ever told...

Dear Chad,

The first time I remember ever telling a serious lie in my life was about six years ago. I was twenty-three years, one month, and sixteen days old. The person I lied to was my best friend, Connie. We'd been best friends since kindergarten, and she knew I was lying right away. I had no practice at it, so I sucked. I'd get better at it over the years, but I'll get to that in a minute—first, it's important that I tell you what I lied about.

I was a little over two years into my last relationship with a man named Damien. We were engaged and lived together. I'd lost my job that day and locked myself in the bathroom while I was crying so he wouldn't see me. He didn't want me to work, so he would have been angry with me for being upset about losing my job. He was angrier that I had locked him out of the bathroom, though. He broke through the door and punched me in the face. I had a broken nose, shattered cheekbone, and needed eight stitches. My face was so swollen and hurt so much by the time I got to the doctor's office that I only bobbed my head in agreement when Damien told them I'd slipped on the shower curtain and hit my face on the faucet when I fell. It was almost the same story he'd told me right after it happened, except that he'd told me I hit my face on the side of the tub and didn't remember because I had a concussion.

He was good at that—convincing me my memory was faulty. And despite knowing deep down that it wasn't true, I'd believed him. Like I said, he was really convincing. I believed it even after I left him... I believed it up until I was writing down everything that happened in our relationship and the truth became apparent. But that's not why I'm writing you this letter.

Like I said before, that was the first time I ever lied. Connie didn't even ask me what happened—she knew. She'd always known he would do something like that to me eventually, even if I hadn't believed her. Or, rather, I did, but Damien convinced me she was just jealous and trying to split us up.

The first time I lied to YOU—the very first time—was on my birthday. We were in the kitchen and you asked me if I was okay. I told you I was.

I wasn't.

You'd said something that set off a memory—a flashback—of Damien saying those same words ("Try me.") to me. I wanted to go out with my former coworkers to socialize and maybe find a way to get my job back. Damien didn't want me to get my job back, and he thought I would cheat on him with the men there. He always thought I would cheat on him with everyone. When I tried to leave, he grabbed me and flung me across the room before physically blocking the door.

When you asked me the next day if I was okay in the café and I said I was, I lied then, too. I was scared about our date, scared that you would end up like Damien—he hadn't been that way at first, either.

But the first big lie I told you was a few hours after that, in your apartment after I'd thrown up in your kitchen. I told you about my dad dying in a car accident when I was fifteen (which is true), and you asked me if that's where the scars on my back had come from. I said yes. You asked if that's what I had flashbacks about. I said yes.

They were both lies. I do have flashbacks sometimes to that car accident; I just never have with you.

The flashback in your kitchen that made me so sick to my stomach that I threw up... god, this is hard, even just writing it down. I haven't gotten to this part in my journaling about Damien yet, so I've never written it, and I've never told anyone about it before, either.

It was about two years ago. It was the day I woke up with a splitting headache and black hole in my memory after only two glasses of champagne. I hurt between my legs and had many bruises I had no memory of getting. It was far from the first time I'd woken this way, hours and hours after I normally woke up. But this time, Damien was still asleep or passed out—probably the latter since he'd been pretty intoxicated when he got home the night before. He must have been so drunk he forgot to hide what he'd done, and I found it when I went to the kitchen for a glass of water.

Rohypnol. The date rape drug.

He'd been drugging me for years when I wasn't willing to give him what he wanted from me.

I'd like to say I walked right out, but I didn't. I had no friends left—I'd turned my back on all of them at Damien's insistence. I didn't have a job. I hadn't even been out of the apartment for nearly three weeks because Damien wouldn't let me leave, afraid I was cheating on him. I had money my dad had left me and that I got from his life insurance policy, but Damien had talked me into putting it into a joint account, which he then put restrictions on so I couldn't access it. It took me months before I could get to it. He controlled everything; I was completely dependent on him.

When I confronted him about the Rohypnol the day I finally did leave him, he nearly convinced me that I'd imagined what I'd found and that I would end up alone and living on the streets if I left him. He was so, so good at convincing me of whatever it was he wanted me to believe. He had a way of making me question my sanity and believe him over my own memory, over what I could clearly see.

The other lie... the scars on my back. Damien and I were at a cabin for the weekend four years into our relationship, and I'd made the mistake of smiling at our waiter at dinner when I thanked him after he set down my food. I knew better, but sometimes I forgot. Damien didn't say anything until we'd gotten back to the cabin and were sitting outside with a roaring fire in the firepit; in fact, he'd acted like he was in an unusually mellow mood, but I should have known he wasn't by how much wine he ordered. I didn't realize there was a pattern until I saw it all on paper, but there was. He served me drink after drink when he was angry. I'd be tipsy—sometimes even drunk—and then he'd unleash his anger. I always ended up hurt, and he blamed it on me, on my clumsiness from drinking.

But I was only tipsy this time when he kicked off his line of questioning. I knew that no matter what I said it would be the wrong answer, that he'd find a way to twist my words to make it look like I'd said something awful. He was convinced I'd wanted to sleep with the waiter. He told me I'd screw him right then if it wasn't true. But my scalp was on fire from him pulling on my hair to make me look at him while he was interrogating me, and I wouldn't do it.

I'd never told him no so firmly before. Well, I had, and he'd ignored me. But this time I fought against him. He was furious. He told me I was his fiancée and that he supported me and that I had no right to keep from him something he was entitled to. I tried to push him away from me and he grabbed my hair and yanked. I stumbled, and that's when he shoved me. I fell backward into the firepit.

I was in the hospital for weeks, and you saw what it looks like now—at least some of it. I think he actually felt bad for that one. He didn't try to force me to have sex that violently ever again. It was only a few months later I had my first experience with complete memory loss of the night before; I think drugging me was his solution to make sure I was never hospitalized again.

You told me at one point that you were worried I had an eating disorder, and I got upset and accused you of seeing me as a project. That part was true, but it was only part of the truth. This is the rest of it.

I don't know if I have an eating disorder. Does it qualify if it's driven by PTSD? At least I think that's what it really is. I never had a body-image problem growing up. My dad was big on valuing things that matter like kindness and strength and honesty. Looks wasn't one of them. And I was an athlete, so I was strong, and I liked my muscular physique. But Damien didn't. He said I looked masculine and didn't want me to run. It caused problems between us every time I did, and over time, I stopped entirely, especially when Damien became ever more suspicious anytime I left the apartment without him.

But then he said I wasn't thin enough, that I was too "puffy." He encouraged me to stop eating breakfast, next to skip other meals, then gave me a strict diet to follow comprised only of foods that wouldn't "stick." He monitored my weight and my measurements, saying he wanted me to be healthy and the most attractive me I could be. He compared me to runway models and pointed out where I could improve to look more like them. Everything he drilled into my head has stuck in some capacity, despite my efforts to eradicate everything from my years with him. You said I seemed uncomfortable around food sometimes and you're right. I am. I always liked food, but now it's almost an enemy, too. Sometimes. Not all the time.

I don't want to lie to you anymore. I want to tell you everything because I don't want dishonesty to be a part of us. I've never felt about someone the way I feel about you... I thought I loved Damien, but I know now that I didn't. Not really.

Something my dad always told me, at least once a week since I can remember, was to follow my heart. That if I listened, it would guide me and would never lead me astray. I couldn't hear it for a long time after he died because I'd buried it under grief and loneliness. But I'm starting to hear it again these days, and it spoke loudly from the very first time I saw you. It practically shouted at me even before I knew Fern was your sister and I thought you guys were dating. It's loud and clear anytime I even think about you. It tells me I've found the one I was always meant to find.

I probably shouldn't even tell you that—it probably makes things worse to read those words after finding out how much you've been lied to. However, I also don't know that I'll ever find the courage to give this letter to you. Or let you read it, I guess, since it's in my journal, and only savages rip pages from a book. And whatever else I may be, I'm not a savage.

I haven't told you yet because I'm afraid that once I say the words, everything will hurt that much worse when you find out what I've done and walk away. And if you're reading this, I know you're about to do just that. I want you to know that I understand and I don't blame you. Honesty is important, and any relationship with a hope of survival needs trust. I've not given you the first and in the process destroyed any hope of the second. But I can't let you walk away without telling you this first because you deserve to know: I love you.

P.S. I never told you what your name means. Chad means protector and Connelly means love, friendship and loyalty; together, loving and loyal protector. I think it's perfect for you.

EIGHTEEN

By the time I was done writing, there were graphite smudges and the paper was wet and puckered, ruined by my tears. I wasn't sure I'd find the courage to give it to Chad, but I felt like a weight had been lifted just from getting the words out and was glad I'd written it anyway. It needed to come out. And maybe having done so on paper would give me the courage I needed to tell him in person.

Maybe.

The sun had moved beyond the clearing to a lower spot in the sky, and the air was cold in the shade. I packed up my journal and pencil and headed back toward my apartment. Rushing inside as I always did when I was alone now, unable to get rid of the feeling of being watched, I practically ran into Caroline before I saw her standing in front of my building.

"Renata!" she exclaimed in obvious relief, giving me a quick hug. "You're okay!"

I drew back. "Of course I'm okay." I averted my gaze so maybe she wouldn't notice that I'd been crying. "Why wouldn't I be?"

"Chad called me, asking if I'd heard from you. He said something happened last night and that he hadn't heard from you since. That you weren't answering your calls or text messages. So I tried, and I couldn't reach you either. We were worried something happened to you. He said you seem nervous sometimes and your eyes dart around like you're looking for someone. He's a bit of a wreck, Renata. He's beating himself up for never asking you what was spooking you."

I stared at her, forgetting I wanted to keep my eyes from view, trying to take in everything she'd said.

"Well," I said, swallowing. "You can see I'm fine. I was in the preserve and left my phone here."

"Since last night?" she asked incredulously.

"I'll text him," I said, avoiding responding to her question and opening the entrance door. Caroline followed me. I cocked an eyebrow at her.

She shrugged. "You kinda look like shit, and I'm more worried now than I was before. Honestly, I figured your battery died or something and Chad was just overreacting because he can be a little overprotective and he's crazy about you. But now I think he was right to be concerned."

I didn't have the energy to argue or try to assure her that I was fine. I wasn't really fine. I mean, I was, but I also wasn't. And I was too tired to try to convince her otherwise. I sighed and started up the stairs.

When we walked inside, Caroline stopped and spent a minute looking around; Chad wasn't the only person who'd never been in my apartment before I'd let him in the night before.

"Aw, it's Potty," she said, pointing to my plant.

I half-smiled. "Yeah."

"That's such an awful name."

I chuckled this time. "I know. But Chad was too cute to say no to."

Caroline plopped down on my sofa and pulled a pillow over her lap, then looked up expectantly. I looked back at her blankly.

"Spill it, woman," she said, patting the sofa cushion next to her.

I sat, dropping my bag onto the coffee table.

"Actually, hold on," she said, holding up a finger. She pulled her phone from her back pocket. "I'm going to let Chad know I found you, so he can stop worrying, and tell him your phone isn't working."

"Please don't tell him that," I rushed out. "I don't want another lie between us," I added, voice shaky.

Caroline's eyes darted to me, then back down to her screen. A second later, she set her phone down and looked at me again. "I told him I found you and that you'll text him later after I leave."

"Thank you," I said.

"But you have to explain what you mean by 'another lie between us.'"

Caroline's eyes were slightly narrowed and her eyebrows in a wavy line from furrowing her brow. She was in a tough position; she cared about both of us. I sighed, and with it came another round of tears. I sobbed into my palms, and Caroline shifted over to wrap her arms around me, rubbing a hand up and down my back.

"Talk to me, Renata," she soothed when my sobs tapered off. "Did Chad do something to you? I love him dearly, but that won't protect him if he did something to you. He said something happened last night—is this because of whatever that was?"

I took a deep breath and let it out at a slow and controlled pace, my jaw still trembling. I was so tired of carrying all this by myself. I wanted to be able to talk to someone about it, to hear another person tell me I wasn't crazy, that what happened with Damien was as bad as it felt to me. I wanted to have someone I didn't have to hide anything from. Dad told me to follow my heart... well, my heart was telling me to trust Caroline. I reached into my bag and pulled out my journal.

"Here," I said, handing it to her. "I'm going to take a shower."

I took the longest shower of my life. My body remained under the water until it ran cold, and then I donned sweats—the baggiest ones I could find in my closet—and had another cry in the privacy of my bedroom. I wasn't even sure what I was crying about... over Damien, over Chad, over my anxiety at letting Caroline read things about me no one else knew? Probably all of them.

It was close to two hours later when I came out of my bedroom, and I half-expected to find Caroline gone. But far from gone, she was at the stove heating up some leftover soup Chad had made a few days earlier and sent home with me, humming quietly to herself.

"Hey, woman," she called. "Feel any better?"

I smiled weakly, then looked from her to the journal. No way she'd read all of it—there wasn't enough time and she was way too perky.

"I read really fast," she said, having noticed my eye movements. "I learned to speed read my freshman year of college so I'd have more time to paint."

"So you read it all?" I squeaked out.

"I think so," she replied. "The last thing is the letter to Chad?"

"Yes," I responded, my bafflement making it almost sound like a question.

"Then yes, I did."

I slid onto a barstool at the counter. "And?"

"You want to know my thoughts?" she asked, half-turning from the stove. "Like, all of them? Because I have a lot. And I should remind you that I double-majored in psychology. It's also okay if you don't, I swear."

"I mean... I think so."

"About Damien or about Chad?"

It was so strange to hear Damien's name coming from her that I just stared at her for a minute. The last time I'd really talked to anyone about him had been with Connie, and that was so many years ago.

"Both, I think."

She sighed. "Damien's a motherfucker who should rot in hell for eternity."

My jaw fell open. I'd never heard Caroline use a tone of such hatred and violence.

"He knew exactly what he was doing from the instant you first met him. Everything he did was calculated to manipulate you and make you question yourself and rely solely on him. He emotionally, verbally, physically, and sexually abused you and made you think it was your fault or that it didn't happen." She took a breath—everything had come out in a single one so far—then continued. "He likely has a few different personality disorders and he preyed on you, Renata, because you were vulnerable and trusting. Absolutely nothing that happened with him was your fault. Not only that, but there is absolutely no reason on Earth for you to be ashamed of or carry guilt for what that asshole did. You aren't stupid now—and you weren't then. He was just really skilled at what he was doing." Another breath. "And—" She stopped abruptly, her voice cracking, and she cast her eyes up toward the ceiling. "Sorry," she said, clearing her throat. "You are the absolute bravest, strongest person I've ever met, Renata. Many people never escape what you did."

She turned off the stove and walked over to me. It wasn't until then that I realized I had tears sliding down my cheeks. After a brief pause, she wrapped her arms around me. And that's when I basically lost my mind... at least that's what it felt like. I was crying—practically sobbing again—but I was also laughing. There was nothing actually funny about any of what was happening, and yet I couldn't stop the laughter. When Caroline pulled away, I spoke.

"I'm not crazy," I wheezed out, holding my sides and laugh-crying even more. "Oh my god, I'm not crazy."

"Oh, Renata... No. You're not. And you never were."

Eventually my laughs subsided, and my tears mostly dried up, only an occasional lonely drop slipping out, and I was left feeling more drained than I ever had in my life. I felt empty and sad and also somehow lighter.

Caroline set down two steaming bowls of soup in front of us. "Eat up," she said. Then, after she'd swallowed her first spoonful, "Oh, man, this is good."

"Isn't it? You should have tasted it when it was fresh. Believe it or not, it was even better."

"You're lucky to have someone as talented as Chad wanting to cook for you all the time, you know that?"

A small smile curved my lips and my face warmed. "Yeah, I do." The smile faded. He wasn't going to want to once he knew I'd been lying to him. I lowered my spoonful of soup back to my bowl, any hint of an appetite having now vanished.

"You have to eat, woman," Caroline said after swallowing another spoonful. "We'll talk about Chad after."

"I can't. I feel sick."

"Everything will be okay, Renata. I promise. But you have to eat. It'll help."

While we finished eating, Caroline told me about work that day, what regulars asked after me and some new faces that had come in. It was a nice distraction and I managed to finish most of my bowl of soup. When I hadn't taken another spoonful in a while, Caroline reached over for my bowl.

"Leave it," I said. "I'll clean up later."

"I've got it," she said, grabbing my bowl anyway.

"You don't have to do that."

"I know that, but I want to. It's been a long time since anyone has taken care of you, Renata. Let me do this small thing for you."

We settled onto the sofa when she came back, Caroline sitting sideways and facing me, and me with my knees pulled up to my chest, my arms around my legs.

"Okay, Chad," Caroline said.

"Yeah."

"You have to tell him everything."

I turned my head to face away from her and rested it on my knees as I stared at the wall. "I know. But I can't."

"Renata," she said in a voice filled with sympathy, "he's not going to blame you for anything that happened with Damien. Chad's not like that. He's going to feel the same way I do: like hunting that piece of shit down and hurting him for the things he did to you."

"I lied to him Caroline. He even asked me about my last relationship, and I told him it ended because we just weren't compatible. I let him believe I'd never really been hurt before."

"Yeah, and you lied to him a bunch of other times, too. I read the letter, remember? But none of that really matters. You were—rightfully so—afraid. He'll understand and he won't hold that against you."

"But his last girlfriend lied to him. Even if he forgives me, he'll never trust me again. And I'm so afraid of losing him. But I also can't keep lying to him. Last night..." I exhaled slowly, then inhaled again, trying to make the words leave my mouth. "What happened last night is that we were half-dressed and going to have sex for the first time, and I freaked out because I knew he wouldn't have been there about to do that with me if he knew how dishonest I was. I couldn't do it. I... I love him, Caroline. I really do. And I couldn't do that to him."

"He loves you, too," she said.

"If he really does, he won't when he finds out what I've done. The why doesn't matter—I still lied to his face. More than once."

A long silence stretched between us, my words hanging in the air.

"You have to trust me," Caroline said. "I've known Chad a long time. It's going to hurt him, but he'll forgive you. And he'll trust you again."

"I do trust you, but I'm afraid you're wrong. I have to tell him anyway. I know that. I can't even read his messages to me because of the guilt I have. I'm just so scared, you know?" My voice cracked. "I never expected to find someone after Damien, let alone someone like Chad. And now I've ruined it. As wrong as he was about a lot of things, Damien was right about *that*—I sabotage myself all the time."

"I don't buy it," Caroline retorted. "From what I read, you never once sabotaged yourself. Not once. *He* sabotaged you and made you think it was your own fault. But it wasn't, Renata—it *never* was." I could hear and feel her shifting around on the sofa, then she spoke again, gently this time. "I think you should find a therapist, Renata. This isn't something you can or even should try to face and unravel and heal from on your own. Everything you thought you knew for years was a carefully crafted deception, and he systematically, one by one, removed everything and everyone you cared about from your life and made you think it was your fault or that they were bad people. That's a serious mindfuck, honey. And I'm here for you whenever you need someone, but I can't help you the way someone trained could. And you deserve to heal, Renata. Don't let him keep controlling you from afar."

I nodded, a tear slipping from the corner of my eye, trailing down over the bridge of my nose, then across my other cheek. Control from afar was definitely how it felt a lot of the time. "Okay."

"I can help you find someone. I can ask my old therapist for recommendations. She was great for me, but I don't think she'd be a good fit for you. But I'll talk to her."

"Thank you. For everything."

"Oh, honey, it's what you do when you care about someone."

After Caroline left, I faced my phone and the myriad voice and text messages from Chad. I had a twinge of anxiety over how many there were, remembering Damien calling and texting nonstop anytime I wasn't with him until I answered. But Chad was nothing like Damien, and I reminded myself that it wasn't strange for him to worry because my lack of response was uncharacteristic—it hadn't happened once in the four months since he'd had my phone number and we'd been dating. His worry was normal and understandable.

I didn't respond to anything he'd sent since the night before, simply apologizing for my silence and telling him we needed to talk. He responded immediately that he was on his way. I felt panicked—I wasn't ready. But I would never be ready. I forwarded a screenshot of the text exchange to Caroline. She responded quickly, assuring me that I was doing the right thing and that everything would be okay.

Back and forth across my living room I paced, watching the clock. The seconds ticked by so sluggishly, and yet it felt like no time at all had passed when I heard a knock at my door. I peered through the peephole and saw Chad looking more anxious than I'd ever seen him.

He stood still, his brow furrowed as he studied me when I unlocked the door and opened it.

"How did you get in the building?" I asked.

"Someone heading out held the door open," he said quietly, gesturing toward the front of the building. "Can I come in?"

I wish people would stop doing that—they could let in someone crazy.

I stepped back and swung the door wide as he crossed over the threshold. There was no going back now. I closed the door behind him, then locked it as I always did. My hands were shaking and I felt sick, like I might throw up the soup I'd eaten.

I turned and crossed my arms over my chest, staring at the floor between us. I needed to speak, but the words were stuck again. Chad reached out and ran a single finger over mine, which were tightly grasping my bicep. I let out the breath I realized I'd been holding.

"Chad. There's something you should know."

I raised my eyes to his and my breath stalled. There was so much emotion in them, the gray-blue stormy and the brown so wide and bright. I'd never seen his pupils so small before. I looked away—I couldn't do it. I thought I could, but I couldn't. I was about to wreck him, regardless, but it would be better this way than if he knew I'd lied to him; that would destroy him in an entirely different way... he'd maybe never trust anyone again.

He tucked my hair behind my ear, and I started crying, leaning into his touch for a second before stepping out of his reach.

"I can't do this," I said, my voice barely above a whisper.

"Rena—"

"No. Please."

"Is it because of last night? I'm sorry, Rena, I didn't mean to push you, I won't—"

"No, Chad. It's not you. It's... it's me."

He huffed out a breath, and when I glanced toward him, his cheeks were wet. "Relationship-ending words," he said under his breath. "You're breaking up with me. Why?"

"I told you," I cried. "It's me."

"I don't believe that," he replied, his voice watery. "Please tell me what I did—what I can *do* to fix this, Rena. Please."

I gave a sad shake of my head. "There's nothing."

He now paced in front of me, five steps in one direction, turn, five steps in the other direction, turn. After several passes, he stopped and faced me. Whatever he was going to say, I knew it was going to make things harder, so I spoke first.

"It's over, Chad." I sniffled loudly and cleared my throat. "I need you to leave." I unlocked my door and held it open. I felt like scum for breaking his heart, then kicking him out the way I was, but it was better than the alternative. "Please leave now." I needed him to go before I completely broke down.

"Rena... my Rena," he whispered, stopping when he reached me, still two steps from being out of my apartment and into the hallway. His voice wavered, and I knew he was hurting. His hand, shaky, reached toward mine and I pulled it out of the way.

"Don't," I said. "Please," I added more mildly when I realized how harsh I sounded.

His head bobbed up and down a few times, then he took those remaining two steps, and I closed the door. It was done—over.

NINETEEN

After I'd asked him not to text me anymore, the messages Chad was sending every minute or so since he'd left—asking me if we could talk, asking me to explain, to tell him what happened, asking me not to do this—slowed before stopping altogether. Caroline called, but I didn't answer; I texted her instead, explaining to her the best I could why I'd done what I did. I was emotionally wrung out. I didn't have what I needed to have a conversation with her.

Eventually, sleep found me, the pull of exhaustion overpowering my racing mind. When my alarm went off for work the next morning, however, I felt like shit. I felt almost hungover, nauseous and with a severe headache, and still had dark circles under my eyes. I was nervous that Chad would be waiting at the café when I arrived, but he wasn't. I walked in and avoided the office, not wanting to face Fern after breaking up with her brother. Caroline was out front already and stopped stocking the self-serve area when she saw me.

"I just couldn't," I said. "I know how hard it must have been for him to trust me, and I couldn't hurt him that way. It would have destroyed him, Caroline."

"Renata," she said, with a sigh. "He's already destroyed."

"I know," I replied quietly.

"No, like he's more destroyed than I've ever seen him. He thinks it's his fault, that he did something wrong. He came straight to our apartment from yours last night, and Renata... he's a mess. He wanted to come this morning to see if he could talk to you, but I told him that would just make things worse. I don't know if that was the right thing to do, though."

"It was," I said softly, beginning to pull down chairs.

"I don't know if I agree with you," she said a minute later.

After the chairs were down, I hesitated before going to the back to get my cash drawer. I was afraid of how Fern might react to seeing me. I turned to Caroline.

"Is Fern... I mean, is she...?"

"Is she pissed off at you?"

"Yeah."

"A bit, yeah, she is. But she's not going to say anything here—this is work. She just doesn't understand, and her brother is in a lot of pain."

"You didn't tell her?"

Caroline drew back in surprise. "Of course not. It's not my place to tell your story unless you want me to. I think you should, though, and I think you should also tell Chad. What you're afraid of isn't going to happen."

I gave a nod of my head, acknowledging that I was listening, then took a deep breath and turned toward the office. Fern's expression was hard and guarded in a way I'd never seen it before—the closest had been on my birthday when they thought for a minute that I had a problem with homosexuality. But Caroline had been right; Fern didn't say anything about Chad.

The day crawled by despite how busy we were, and I was relieved when it was finally time to clock out. When I took my cash drawer back to the office, I told Fern that if she needed more coverage, I could work—I wouldn't need the five days off anymore. She thanked me stiffly and said she'd let me know if that happened. I headed back to my apartment, half expecting to see Chad there waiting even though I knew Caroline had told him not to do that. He wasn't, though.

After a shower to wash off work, I crawled into bed and cried myself to sleep, knowing Chad, Fern, and Caroline would soon be on their way on the trip I'd planned for Chad's birthday. I wouldn't be there to see his reaction, something that made my heart ache, but I hoped he loved it all the same. I hoped they all enjoyed it. And I hoped the days he spent hiking would help him begin to forget about me.

I continued to journal over the next few days, filling in more of my story with Damien as I'd been doing since I bought the journal, but I also picked up *Heal Your Heart, Heal Your Art* again. I couldn't explain it, but I just felt like I wasn't done with it yet. I started from the first page and read through like I had the first time, even completing the exercises again. This time, I was shocked to find my responses were different.

When I read the question about my earliest experience with criticism related to my creative endeavor, rather than my mind scouring my childhood and coming up empty again, I thought of the first time I showed Damien one of my work pieces for the journal before I turned it in.

"I finished my piece today," I said when Damien and I sat down for dinner. It had taken me longer to complete than normal. Damien knew I'd been stressed about missing my deadline.

"That's great, babe. Did you turn it in?"

"Not yet—I just finished it before we sat down. I've already edited it a few times, but I want to do one final read-through on the copy I just printed to catch anything I missed."

"I can do that for you," he said.

"You don't have to do that."

"You think I wouldn't do a good job?"

"No, that's not what I meant. I just know you have enough on your own plate."

"Babe, I wouldn't have offered if I couldn't handle it."

I wasn't nervous about turning my work in, but having Damien scrutinize it had me sweating. He'd read my pieces after they'd been submitted for a while, and he always gave in-depth criticism and suggestions for doing things better the next time. For some reason, though, having him do that before I turned it in was giving me a lot of anxiety. "Okay."

We finished dinner and Damien suggested I clean up the kitchen while he read my piece. It was a short story about dealing with grief after losing a parent. I could see with a little hindsight some of the ways I'd not done that in a healthy manner after losing my dad and saw an opportunity through fiction to reach others in the same situation. Normally, my pieces were entirely fun fiction, but this one was rooted in my real life.

When I finished the dishes, I found Damien in the living room, still reading. As I watched, he finished and set the pages face down on the table.

"When's your deadline?" he asked.

I scrunched my face, not understanding why that mattered—the piece was finished. "Next Wednesday."

"Hm," he said, staring at me as if he was trying to decide something.

"Why?" I asked when he didn't speak. My nervousness was now on full blast.

"Well... are you sure you want me to tell you?"

"Of course," I replied. I wasn't someone who couldn't handle criticism; constructive feedback helped me to improve. It was absolutely necessary if I didn't want to stagnate in my writing career.

"I'm not going to sugarcoat it, Renata, because I respect you too much to do that to you. It's... you can't turn that in."

"Wh-what?" My stomach dropped. I'd expected he was going to suggest rewriting a sentence or two, or that I might need to expand or cut some content somewhere, at most.

"It's no good, babe."

"I... I don't understand."

"First, your main character's name is Evin."

"Yes..."

"That's a boy's name. You can't give that to a girl."

"Anyone can have any name, Damien, but that's a girl's name anyway. That's why it's spelled with an 'i' and I chose it because it means strong and fighter. And Evin is both of those things, she just doesn't realize it."

"Well, and that's another thing. She's just... she's abrasive and weak and seriously unlikeable."

"That's harsh to say about someone who's trying to process grief over losing their father," I said, on the defensive. It felt like a personal attack since I'd written Evin to be so much like myself.

"Look, I'm not arguing with you about that. I'm just saying that, as a reader, this is what I think about your story and your main character. You don't have to listen to anything I think, I just thought you'd want to know before you turn this in and they reject it, and you have even less time to figure out how to fix this so it'll be something they'll publish. Because I'm telling you, babe, they're not gonna publish this."

He watched me steadily, and as the seconds ticked past, I felt more confused. I felt like his feedback was ill-founded and not reflective of our readers, but Damien was also one of the smartest people I'd ever met. And he wouldn't tell me that if he didn't think it. He was trying to look out for my best interest. I was just hurt because I didn't want to hear it. But I needed to be able to suck it up and do what was required.

"What do you think it needs to be publishable?" I asked, unable to keep eye contact. It felt like I was betraying myself. I'd never felt that way when receiving feedback before and wasn't sure what my problem was.

He spent the next ten minutes tearing my story apart and telling me what he thought I'd have to do to fix it. I hated every suggestion. Every single one. They grated on me like sandpaper on my skin, each one feeling like it was tearing apart the foundation of what made the piece unique and relatable and authentic. When I told him that, he said I could make the changes needed and turn in something worthwhile or I could let my ego get in the way of my success. I gritted my teeth and made his changes.

And when the piece was rejected, he said it was because I didn't make the changes well enough. He instructed me again on what needed fixed, and in trying to restructure to his satisfaction, I missed my deadline—they re-ran an old piece and told me to come up with something different for the next month's publication. I never did find out if the additional changes Damien suggested would have been accepted or if my original would have been.

"Oh my god," I breathed out loud, my hands shaking. The book had slipped from my fingers and was sitting on the floor. All this time I'd been searching for something in my childhood... had it been more recent? Had it begun with Damien?

I leapt off the sofa and booted up my neglected laptop. *Come on, come on, come on*, I chanted in my mind, impatiently waiting for it to load the desktop. As soon as it did, I opened up my online file storage; thank god I'd always used that for work stuff so I could work remotely. Damien had encouraged me to delete everything I'd ever written off my hard drive after I was fired, but I didn't touch my digital file storage I used for work. And because I'd written it for work and I'd always been particular about saving copies of every draft just in case I ever needed to revert back to a previous version, there were copies of everything I'd written for the journal in there.

I found the file easily enough, but got stuck staring at the file name. I was afraid to open it and find out I was wrong, that it hadn't been Damien, that he'd actually been right and it was just me losing my talent. But I was also afraid to open it and discover it *had* been Damien, that I'd been blaming myself for so many years when he'd manipulated me into thinking that way. That I'd been struggling because of him, even after I left him.

Even so, I took a deep breath and opened the file. When I was done reading it, I read it again. Then I sat and cried for a long time. I was fairly certain I knew in my heart the truth about my writing, but I had to know for sure. I opened a new email, attached the file, and wrote a quick letter to one of my old coworkers and friends—the one Damien had accused of trying to sleep with me. He'd also been my editor at the publication. I hadn't spoken to him in years—not since the night I stood him and my other coworkers up for dinner when Damien wouldn't let me leave the apartment—and I had no idea if he would even open my email, but I hoped he did.

After clicking send, I couldn't sit still. I paced my apartment for a while, then tossed on sweats and my running shoes and headed for the preserve. I ran for hours, covering every trail in the preserve several times. My body was exhausted, but it was what I'd needed: to get out the anxious energy that felt like it was gradually poisoning me.

I didn't expect a response from Jeb for at least a few days, if I ever got one at all, but couldn't help glancing at my inbox anyway.

My heart skipped when I saw there was an email from him already. My hand trembled violently as I clicked to open it. My message to him had been short, apologizing for the sudden email after so many years of silence, and for never having shown up that day for dinner, and lastly asking him if he could find some time to read the attached; I wanted to know if that version would have been published or rejected all those years ago.

Renata,

It's good to hear from you! It's been a long time. And no need to apologize for missing dinner—we all figured there must have been… extenuating circumstances and just hoped all was okay when we never heard from you again. I'm glad to know you're well.

In response to your question, I wouldn't have hesitated to publish this. It's what the piece should have been and what I expected from you—what you submitted, however, was writing I'd never seen from you. Whatever happened back then with the writing you turned in starting with this piece, it looks like you've sorted things out—this is fantastic.

We now take freelance submissions and publish up to three pieces each month, assuming we have enough that are up to our standards. I encourage you to submit to it (link below). Someone else leads that part of the journal, but I'm sure Sarah would publish this—I would if it was up to me.

It really was nice to hear from you. If you're still in the area, we should grab coffee or lunch and catch up sometime; I'm interested to hear what you're up to nowadays.

All the best, Renata.
Jeb

I did the laugh-crying thing I'd done when Caroline was in my apartment a few days earlier, relieved and angry and devastated all at once. I was sure it wouldn't be that simple to get my words to return, though it was one hell of a start. But the thought of how much of myself I'd lost because of Damien, how stupid I felt that I'd never realized what he was doing to me, was excruciating. At the same time, I had a kind of hope I'd been missing. I wanted desperately to tell Chad, but he wouldn't understand since he didn't know about Damien. I just wanted to share my relief and happiness that I'd never really lost my ability the way I'd thought.

I opened the photo app on my phone and opened a picture of Chad so his smile filled my screen. His face was soft and there was pronounced crinkling at the corners of his eyes, which had just the tiniest sliver of brown ringing his pupils—a sliver that lasted only seconds after I snapped the picture before we were kissing. He'd looked the happiest I'd ever seen him, and I'd insisted on taking a picture of him that way even though we were in the middle of kneading dough. It seemed to turn him on that I'd stopped amidst his protests to wash my hands and pull out my phone just to take a photo of him. The bread had suffered from the impromptu make out session on the counter, and so had our clothes, which ended up covered in flour, but it had been worth it.

My thumb smoothed over his cheek on the screen and my eyes welled up. I missed him more than I'd have thought possible.

"I miss you," I whispered, my tears spilling over. "I wish you were here." I wiped my face with the back of my arm. "I think... I had an epiphany today. I realized or discovered or... I don't know, I'm so hyped up and tired at the same time that I can't even think clearly right now, but the bottom line is that... I'm not a shitty writer after all. I never was, it seems. And while I've lost my words, I think I know how to get them back now. I'm so excited but I'm also really sad. It's so bittersweet to finally understand what happened." My jaw trembled and I breathed deeply for a minute, trying to calm down. "I love you, Chad. And I'm so sorry for everything."

TWENTY

Day four of my five days off work that were supposed to be spent on an incredible trip with my even more incredible boyfriend had arrived. It sucked to be not working and have so much time to think about the *reason* I wasn't. I'd already gone for a run and showered, but the inside of my apartment was making me crazy. All I could think about was Chad the night he came in the first time and the way he'd touched me... then the devastation on his face when I broke up with him the next day.

I'd actually slept the night before—slept well, that is. The email from Jeb and all the implications from it was like a catharsis, and I'd not only fallen asleep quickly, but had mostly stayed asleep with only mildly disturbing dreams. But my more rested state was bringing on more intense regret over how I'd handled things with Chad. I'd already regretted ever lying to him, but now I was regretting having broken up with him and wishing I'd come clean about the lies I'd told. I vacillated between conviction I'd done the right thing and certainty that I hadn't. And it was driving me nuts.

Caroline was supposed to come over that evening; she was going to fill me in on the trip and Chad's birthday, and I was going to tell her what I'd discovered about my writing. But that was hours away and I couldn't just sit around until then. To get some relief, I decided to take my journal and head to the preserve. It was a fairly warm day in contrast to the chilliness of the last few days, so I tossed on some sweats, grabbed my journal and a pencil and sharpener, and swung my door open.

I nearly screamed, I was so startled to find someone on the other side.

"I didn't mean to startle you. I was getting ready to knock." Chad glanced down, then back up after taking a breath. When he did, there was a steely set to his eyes and jaw. "We need to talk, Rena. I can't... we just need to talk, okay?"

I stared at him, my eyes glassy. I hadn't expected to see him again, aside from the pictures in my phone or the occasional, uncomfortable encounter at the café.

"Let me in? Please?"

I swallowed and stepped back before I really thought about what I was doing. Letting him in was actually a terrible idea, but now it was too late.

"Wh-what are you doing here? I mean... you're not even supposed to be home until tomorrow."

"And what? I was supposed to stay in the hotel you booked for *us* and do the hikes you'd planned for *us* without you?" He huffed, staring at the far wall. "No, Rena. I don't even know why I stayed there as long as I did. Hell, I don't know why I even went without you."

"It wasn't about me," I said. "It was about *you*—for your birthday."

"But it was your idea. You planned it all. And before I even knew what it was, I wanted to do it because I'd be doing it with you. But I was there alone. Without you. It sucked, Rena. You should have been there with me."

He began to pace, lost in thought, then stopped abruptly in front of me, his eyes piercing through mine.

"I've run through every minute since I met you, Rena. Every second we've spent together, every word we've spoken, looking for something to help me understand what happened, and I can't find anything. I can't. And I realized that something didn't make sense. The change in your attitude about our relationship was too sudden. I know you cared about me, Rena. I'm sure of it. Just as I'm sure you still do. And everything changed the night I was here, right after I took your shirt off. And it dawned on me this morning that you have PTSD. We've talked about it. And you told me the scars on your back were from the car accident when you were fifteen. The only thing that makes sense is that taking your shirt off triggered your PTSD. I looked it up and that kind of thing happens. And the only thing I can figure is that you think your PTSD makes you broken or something—

that's apparently common for people with PTSD—and that's why you broke up with me. But, Rena..." he reached out and tucked my hair behind my ear, his hand lingering on my jaw. "You're not broken. You're not. You have PTSD, but that doesn't make you broken."

My jaw trembled as I got lost in the emotion I saw in his eyes, and he lifted his other arm so both hands cradled my face, his thumbs moving gently over my cheeks. His eyes turned glassy.

"Rena... my Rena... I love you. I. Love. You."

I broke down hearing him tell me he loved me for the first time, and when he pulled me into his arms, I clung to him tightly, whispering through the tears into his neck that I loved him, too. He lifted me and carried me over to the sofa where he sat with me curled on his lap and crying into his chest. His arms formed a solid wall between me and the reality that I would have to tell him that he loved a liar. But I had to do it. I owed him that much. I could see that not knowing why I'd broken up with him was torturing him.

As soon as I felt I was able, I sat up, clearing my face of moisture, then went to the bathroom for a tissue. Without a word, Chad watched as I returned with a glass of water for each of us, which I set down on the coffee table. When I sat, I clasped my hands in my lap and tried to figure out how to start. After a time, he reached over and ran a finger over my hand. I looked up and gave him a soft smile.

"I love it when you do that," I murmured. "I always have."

He mirrored my expression and continued to move his finger leisurely up and down the back of my hand.

"I need to tell you something," I said, not sure how I was speaking over the nausea I felt. "But I don't know how." I swallowed and raised my eyes to his. "It's going to hurt you. A lot. I thought it would hurt you less if I broke up with you, but now I'm not so sure and I think you need to know. When I told you it was me, not you, I meant it. It wasn't just a cop-out breakup line. This is all about me and something I did."

"Rena, we've all done things we regret. I would never judge you for that."

"I know," I replied softly. "This is different, though." I wanted to tell him using words while I was looking into his eyes, but it was too much—I couldn't do it. "I need you to read something."

I stood and retrieved my journal, clutching it tightly as I sat back down.

"Your journal?" Chad asked, eying it.

"Y-yes," I stammered, uncertain about what I was doing. But whatever happened as a result, it felt more right than breaking up with him had. "At least part of it. Maybe all of it. I'll let you decide. I'm okay with you reading as much of it as you decide to. But there's somewhere you should start."

He reached out a hand.

I continued to clutch the journal. "But, I don't think you should read it here." I wasn't sure if that was because I thought it would be easier on *him* or because I thought it would be easier on *me* for him to be away from me while he read it.

"Unless you tell me to, I'm not leaving, Rena."

"Okay." I wasn't entirely surprised by his response. "I'm not going to tell you to leave, because I don't want that. But I don't think I should be here while you read this. I don't think I even *can*. I'm going to tell you where to start, and then I'm going to go for a walk. I'll give you enough time to read it all, if that's what you want. And it's okay if you change your mind and you want to leave."

"I won't."

"It's okay if you do," I said again.

I flipped open the journal to the page with my letter to him and walked out my door, not sure if it would be the last time I ever saw him, but feeling in my heart that I was doing the right thing this time, however it turned out.

I wandered the trails at the preserve for a while before settling in my favorite clearing. I'd brought my phone so I could keep track of time and decided to text Caroline.

You won't believe what happened. Chad's in my apartment. Right now.

What??? Then why are you texting me?!

I'm not there, I'm at the preserve.

You have some explaining to do, woman!

He came back early and came straight to my apartment. I decided to tell him, but I was too much of a coward to do it, so I gave him my journal, but I couldn't stay there while he was reading it.

You're not a coward, Renata. What you're doing takes a lot of courage.

I feel like one. He deserves for me to tell him to his face that I've been lying to him.

You're not. And you're telling him. It's not fair to expect more from yourself after what you've been through.

Okay. I'll try to remind myself of that.

So I'm guessing our plans are off for tonight. I'd join you now while you're waiting if I could.

No, I don't think so. I don't expect Chad will still be there when I get back.

He will. You'll see. And we'll catch up later. Unless you want to tell me what your other news is?

I just figured something out, something big, from my time with Damien. But I don't want to talk about it over text.

That's great! I can't wait to hear about it. Why don't you text me later if you're right and Chad is gone and I'll come over? Otherwise, update me later tonight or tomorrow on how things go with him.

Okay, I'm sure I'll be seeing you in a few hours, so don't make other plans just yet.

Don't worry – if I do, I'll make sure I can cancel if needed.

Thank you. :)

I set my phone down next to me and laid back with my knees up and hands resting on my belly. One of my favorite things about the preserve aside from feeling my dad there was that it was a place Damien had never been; there was nothing about the preserve tainted by a memory from my time with him. It had upset me when we were dating and he refused to visit my hometown or let me do so alone, but now I was glad he'd done that. All I had now were memories of Dad and memories with Chad. All good memories.

My fingers twitched; I had an urge to write. What, I didn't even know. Just something. Anything. I wanted to smell the cedar and graphite of freshly sharpened pencil and feel the texture of a toothy page under my hand. I wanted to just let whatever words came to mind flow and be as surprised as a stranger might at what I'd written when I was done.

I allowed my thoughts to drift far back in time to when things like that happened with frequency, and I could feel the excited high that came with it for a fleeting moment. But in that fleeting moment, I found my conviction. It would happen again. I wasn't sure when, but I knew it would happen. I just needed to not give up and that was something I could do.

My mind continued to drift, finding snatches of memories where I'd had an idea about a story but had never gotten around to writing the idea down and tried to make a mental note to come back to it when I had pencil and paper. I completely lost track of time and had no idea how long it had been when I heard someone on the path leading into my hidden clearing. I sat up, noticing the sun was much nearer the horizon, and glanced at my phone. It had been hours since I'd left Chad with my journal. Even if he'd decided to read it all, he would have had enough time. With a sigh, I looked up from my phone and my heart skipped. It was Chad I'd heard on the path.

He gave me the saddest half-smile I'd ever seen around bloodshot eyes. He'd obviously been crying. "I thought I might find you here."

I watched him as he walked up and sat down next to me. He reached down and pulled up a few blades of mostly dead grass before examining them briefly and tossing them aside.

"I read it all," he said quietly, breaking the suffocating silence a few minutes later.

My stomach turned and my heart raced.

"I'm still... processing, I guess." He inhaled and exhaled with deliberate slowness. I got the impression he was trying to keep his emotions under control. "Honesty and trust are a really big deal to me. You already know that, and you know why. And... you lied to me. I trusted you and you lied to me." His voice cracked on the last word. "But every time I feel this wave of... I don't know... anger, I guess? Betrayal? I think about why and it feels like I'm splitting apart. I can't blame you for not trusting me enough then, Rena. I can't. And I don't. You didn't know yet if you could trust me or not. I don't like that you lied to me, but I can't be upset with you for doing it, either." He paused, wiping the moisture from his face. "This is really fucking hard," he muttered.

I looked up at him and he was staring at the sky. Then he turned and our eyes connected. It destroyed me to see the pain he was carrying, but I couldn't look away.

"Rena..." he breathed out, his voice shaky.

He raised a trembling hand and touched my cheek more delicately than he ever had before. His thumb slid up and smoothed over a small area near the corner of my eye. There was a thin scar there from when Damien had punched me in the bathroom—it was where I'd had stitches.

"You deflected when I asked you about this before. It's from *him*, isn't it?" he asked, his voice so soft, it was nearly lost before it reached me.

I gave a small nod.

His face crumpled and then I was in his arms. His chest shuddered against me as he cried and held me tight against him. I wrapped my arms around his waist and clung to him. The way it felt to be in his arms again was indescribable, and I was afraid of what would happen when it ended. He was upset about what Damien had done to me, but that didn't mean he'd be able to trust me. It didn't mean we could have a relationship.

After a while, he pulled back, my face between his hands. He used his palms to smooth my hair back and cupped my cheeks before pressing his lips into my forehead. He pressed them against my eyes next, then every inch of skin on my face, kiss by kiss.

"I love you, Rena," he whispered against my lips, pressing our foreheads together. "God, I love you. And I'm so sorry any of that happened to you. I wish I could go back in time and protect you. I hate that I can't. If you can just trust me, I promise I'll never hurt you."

I swallowed around the lump in my throat. "The question is if *you* can ever trust *me* again."

"No, it's not," he said, pulling back and looking into my eyes with urgency. His sparkled with intensity. "Because if you trust me, you're telling me you won't lie to me ever again. And because I understand why you did, if you tell me you won't do it again, I'll trust *you*."

I didn't even have to think about it; if I hadn't already trusted him enough to tell him everything, I would have right then with how he'd reacted to what he'd learned so far.

"I trust you. Completely."

He pulled me into his chest again. "I trust you, too. Without a doubt."

We ended up there in each other's arms on the grass until it was nearly dark. We probably would have stayed there until eternity except that it was getting really cold and I was shivering nonstop. I wished futilely that I had a coat on or a blanket or something. I wanted to stay where I was until the stars filled the sky overhead.

Maybe one day.

We walked back to my apartment with our hands clasped tightly together, and they were still like that when we walked through the door.

"Can I cook for you?" he asked.

"I don't have anything here."

"That's okay. We can go to my apartment if that's alright with you."

"Yeah." I smiled. "Okay. Just give me a minute."

I first wanted to get changed out of the sweats I'd been living in the last few days. I tossed on a pair of jeans and a sweater and emerged from my room a few minutes later. Chad was sitting on the sofa, holding my journal. It was closed, but he was staring at the cover and his eyes were moist. There was a painful stab of guilt through my chest.

"I'm ready," I said barely above a whisper.

He startled and turned away from me, clearing his throat and quickly wiping his eyes as he pushed to his feet. When he turned back to me, he was smiling, but the pain was still in his eyes. He was trying to hide it from me. "Alright. Let's go."

Chad made stir-fry for dinner, and while I wasn't very hungry, I did actually feel much better after eating. After dinner, we put on *Star Wars* and I settled into the comfort of Chad's arms. Within minutes, exhaustion descended and I dozed off. Chad woke me briefly sometime later and told me he'd take me home if that's what I wanted, but that he wanted me to stay. I agreed, too tired to contemplate going home before going back to sleep, and changed into a t-shirt and sweatpants of his. I crawled under his covers and was asleep by the time my head hit the pillow.

TWENTY-ONE

I woke with a start, my heart pounding. I bolted upright and noticed around my headache that I was alone. My eyes scanned the room for answers, and I replayed my memory of the night before. We'd eaten dinner and then I'd suddenly felt so sleepy I couldn't keep my eyes open. There was a sickening feeling in the pit of my stomach. But I remembered, almost like it had been a dream, Chad waking me and asking me to stay before giving me clothes to change into. I'd crawled into his bed, then... I remembered nothing else until seconds earlier when I woke.

This can't be happening again.

With shaky hands, I flung off the blankets and was relieved to see I was wearing the same clothes I vaguely remembered changing into the night before. I shifted around, then stood; nothing hurt—not between my legs or anywhere else. On the nightstand was an alarm clock next to my neatly folded clothes; it read seven thirty. In the morning. I hadn't slept the day away. I did have a headache, but this one was dull—the same headache I'd had every morning for several days, a result of crying so much the day before. It wasn't the kind of headache I'd always had after Damien had drugged me. Even so, I was scared something I had no memory of had happened. I'd never have spent the night there if I hadn't been so deliriously tired the night before.

In the bathroom, I splashed cold water on my face and brushed my teeth using a brand new toothbrush that was sitting on the counter. Using my fingers, I combed through my hair, then changed into my jeans and sweater from the day before. I felt more confident now that nothing more than I remembered had occurred, but the fear wasn't entirely gone.

I followed a mouth-watering aroma toward the kitchen to find Chad baking. The oven was already occupied with what appeared to be a pie, though the air didn't smell sweet. James Gillespie played in the background, and I could hear the deep hum of Chad's voice singing along as he scattered flour everywhere. It always amused me that he was so neat and organized, but not at all bothered by the almighty floury mess he made when he was baking.

"Hi," I said, feeling awkward and a little uncomfortable as I tucked hair from my face behind my ear.

He looked up and smiled, his eyes warming. "Good morning, my Rena."

I couldn't help smiling back even as I dropped eye contact. "Last night... did anything happen?"

When I glanced up, afraid of his response, his smile faltered and understanding and sadness passed over his features. "No," he said in a soft voice. He swallowed, and his eyes shifted to look more playful—more reminiscent of his usual self. "Except you sleeping through one of the greatest movies of all time."

I huffed out a soft breath, feeling intensely relieved by both his assurance that nothing happened and the return of his playful demeanor. "Obviously, it wasn't that great if it couldn't hold my attention," I teased.

He grinned, his eyes on the counter where his hands were pressing the dough into a small pie dish. "Challenge accepted. I guarantee you'll like it the next time we watch it." He turned and grabbed a bowl from the counter behind him and brought it over, whisking the contents. Opening the oven, he swapped out the pie dish he'd been working with for the larger one in the oven.

"Empty pie crust?" I asked, perplexed.

His lips quirked on one side. "I'm making quiche. You partially bake the crust—it's called par baking—before you add the filling and it keeps the crust from getting soggy." He poured in most of what was in the bowl and returned the pie dish to the oven. It still amazed me that he rarely used timers. I couldn't make anything without a timer, but he apparently had one built in.

Without a pause, he stepped over to the main sink and washed his hands. While rinsing, he looked back over his shoulder. "Coffee?"

"Yes, please."

He tipped his head toward the far end of the island where there were bar stools tucked under the countertop. I'd spent hours sitting there over the last several months, watching him manipulating dough and cooking for us. He often wanted me in the kitchen with him, eager to teach me, and I was just as eager to learn; less because I wanted to be able to cook or bake better and more because I loved the sexy flirtiness of it all and the way his eyes lit up when he was explaining things to me.

"I just need to clean up while the water's heating," he said. "Get comfortable."

I sat and watched him move around the kitchen, expertly cleaning up the mess. Within minutes, his kitchen was pristine again. The only thing other than the heavenly aroma from the oven to indicate any baking had been done there was a smudge of flour across Chad's jaw. When he walked over with my coffee that he'd just made using a pour-over method, I reached up and rubbed my palm across the area to clear it. The brown around his pupils shrank. My breath hitched when I watched it happen. He swallowed, then turned and walked back to the oven, pulling out the small pie dish. The crust looked exactly like it had on the first one when he pulled it out. He poured in the rest of the egg filling, popped it back in the oven, and cleaned the bowl and whisk. When he was done, he turned around and leaned back against the sink, his eyes on me.

"I was thinking we could spend the day together," he said.

My chest warmed. "I'd like that."

"Have you ever been apple picking before?"

I shook my head.

The corners of his mouth pulled wide. "It's fun. There's an orchard a little over an hour away. There won't be a lot left—it's near the end of apple season—but there should be enough for us to make an apple crumble for dessert tonight."

I agreed and he hopped in the shower while the quiche was cooking. I was acutely aware that he was naked on the other side of the apartment and my body was flushed; I wished I had another shirt so I could take off my sweater. When he came out in jeans and a gray-blue long-sleeved Henley, his eyes scanned me, then he smirked. It was as if he could see exactly what I'd been thinking about. My face leapt into flames, and I glanced away. He stopped behind me and pulled my hair back over my shoulder, lightly kissing my cheek before heading over to the oven to pull out the quiche.

After we ate, he drove me home and waited while I showered and dressed, again in jeans and a sweater—a different sweater this time and with a t-shirt underneath. I flipped my head and fluffed my hair, pulled on some comfortable lace-up boots, and walked into the living room feeling unexpectedly nervous. We'd done things like this before—we'd dated for months—but everything felt different now. I kept waiting for him to look at me differently or say he didn't actually want to do this thing between us after all.

"You're beautiful, Rena," he said, his eyes roving over me.

I blushed and bit the corner of my lip trying not to smile, but it didn't work. No one had ever said that to me in a way that made me feel it the way I did when Chad said it. It didn't feel like a compliment coming from him; it felt like an observation—one I believed when he was the one making it.

He lifted my hand and kissed the back of it, then slipped his fingers between mine. "Ready?"

I looked up at the warm, loving expression on his face. "Ready."

"Red apples or green?" Chad asked when we exited the highway. We were only a few miles from the orchard.

"Red. You?"

"Depends on what it's for. Honeycrisp or Gala?"

"Honeycrisp or what?"

"Gala."

"Those are types of apples?"

He laughed, glancing sideways at me. "Do you even eat apples at all?"

My face heated and I giggled. "Yes, I do. They're great snacks."

"Well, what kind do you buy?"

"I dunno... they're red-ish."

He gave me a faux glare. "There are dozens and dozens of types of apples, and they all have a different flavor and different texture—

some are crisp, some are soft, some are sweet, some are tangy. And the flavor intensifies the more ripe it is."

"Dozens? Really?"

He glanced over at me, his eyes narrowed. "I can't believe I have a girlfriend who has so little appreciation for the flavor nuances of different types of apples."

I bit my cheeks, trying not to laugh.

"We're going to remedy this today. You're going to get an apple education. And you better pay attention because there'll be a test at the end."

I giggled. "Understood, Chef."

"*Red-ish*," he griped playfully, shaking his head. "What about peaches?"

"There are different types of peaches?" I asked, barely keeping in my laugh. I had no idea what the different types were, but I knew there were actually different types.

He gave me a faux glare. "Plums?"

"A plum isn't a plum?"

He groaned and I burst out laughing.

"I do know there are different types of flours," I said. "Doesn't that count for something?"

He chuckled, pulling off the paved road onto a gravel road that led up a large hill to the parking area for the orchard.

"It amazes me you know so much about different kinds of foods," I mused aloud.

"Of course—I have to. It's one of the three things you need to be successful in a kitchen."

"Three things? So, three things for success in life and now three things for success in the kitchen."

"Yeah. Most things in life can be boiled down to three basic tenets or requirements. For the kitchen, baking or otherwise, it's knowing your ingredients, knowing your cookware and utensils, and being willing to try again when you inevitably fail."

He parked and we walked up and got a bag for apples and a map. An older woman wearing a bright orange t-shirt advertising the orchard gave us a quick rundown of which apples were ready for picking and also indicated we could pick pumpkins, winter squash, and some late blooming sunflowers. I perked up at the mention of sunflowers. I'd seen sunflower fields on television and always thought it would be so magical to walk through one. Despite them being my favorite flower, I'd never been to one. Before I said anything, though, we were being directed to the far corner of the small building in which they sold homemade butters and jams where we could grab these long sticks with what looked like little baskets on the end.

"What are these?" I asked when we stopped and Chad grabbed one.

His eyes danced. "Are you ready for this? It's complex and technical. It's called an apple picker."

I laughed.

"No, seriously," he said.

"You're not kidding?"

His head moved side to side as he laughed. "No. It really is called an apple picker."

I searched my memory but couldn't recall if I'd read that in the dictionary before. I'd have to check my dictionary when I got home. Chad slid our hands together and we set off toward the first section of apple trees.

"We'll just grab a few of each type," he said as we approached. "I personally prefer to use different kinds of apples for most apple desserts because it gives more depth of flavor and texture. Some dishes you don't want to do that, but for most it elevates it. A little age and bruising is okay, too, because it'll add more flavor." He walked up to a branch and used his hand to tug daintily on an apple. "See how this one isn't coming off yet? It's not ready." He tried a few more until one popped off into his hand almost as soon as he touched it. "This one is perfect. See how it came off with very little coaxing?"

I gave a nod and reached up, tugging the same way he had.

"Perfect."

We moved from tree to tree until we had a handful of perfectly ripe apples from the first section, then moved on to the next open section. When we arrived, the trees were mostly bare, with only a few dozen apples left on the branches.

"These are the Honeycrisp," Chad said. "It's really a bit past the season for them, which is why there aren't very many left on the trees." He pulled an apple out of the bag he carried after finding a ripe one off one of the trees and held them out, one in each hand. "The other one is a Jonagold. You see they look similar, but they're not the same. The Honeycrisp is a little more red and is a more squat, round apple. Also, the reds are a bit different. See how the Jonagold is brighter and the Honeycrisp is a darker shade of red?"

I scrutinized them and thought I could see the differences he pointed out; however, I wasn't sure I could tell them apart once he put both of them into the bag.

"The Jonagold is interesting because it's a hybrid of Jonathan and Golden Delicious apples and inherits their respective sweet and tart qualities." He looked up at me. "What?" he asked.

I beamed back at him—I couldn't help it. He was so passionate and animated. It was like a switch got flipped on inside him when he talked about certain things like plants and baking and cooking... and apples, apparently. His eyes glowed and there was an intensity and seriousness he didn't usually have. It was mesmerizing and beautiful. It reminded me of how I felt about writing and words and the preserve. I felt honored to witness him excited the way he was.

His brow furrowed and I laughed, leaning up onto my toes so I could kiss his cheek.

"You're bored," he said.

"Not at all. I was just thinking that I love seeing you like this."

"You mean you always wanted to be able to tell a Honeycrisp and Jonagold apart?" he asked, his lips pulling up on one side sheepishly.

I laughed again. "No. Definitely not. But I could listen to you tell me the differences between apples all day long because you're so excited about it. That's what I love seeing."

The brown in his eyes disappeared and I thought he might kiss me, but he didn't. Instead, the corners of his mouth twitched, then he turned to check the apples higher in the tree with the apple picker.

It took us a few hours to get through the entire orchard; it was nearing lunchtime. Chad said he had one more section for us and I agreed, walking hand-in-hand with him and just taking in the orchard around us. It was rather picturesque and peaceful, even with how many people were now there to pick their own apples. We meandered along and I wasn't paying any attention to where we were headed, simply present with the areas we were passing, so it was a surprise when Chad slowed and I shifted to look ahead of us and saw row after row of lush greenery dotted with yellow.

The sunflower field.

I squealed and my hands shot up to cover my mouth. I wasn't sure where that sound had come from. But I couldn't help it; the field looked just like it did in the movies. "Holy shit," I breathed out. "It's amazing."

"Isn't it?" Chad asked, his fingertips pressing into my lower back. "Plants are incredible."

I nodded in lazy agreement, my eyes still roaming the field. "Especially sunflowers."

"Come on—let's go pick some," Chad said, starting forward.

I walked with him, oohing and aahing like a little kid at the towering plants with these beautiful yellow flowers atop dark green stalks. It felt like walking through a movie set or even a book... a book... there was a stirring of an idea in my mind and I wished I had a notebook and pencil with me. I needed to start keeping one on me at all times. I drummed my fingers on the outside of my leg to release the energy from wanting to write.

Chad ran a finger down my wrist and hand, concealed worry on his face. "Everything okay?"

I turned to him, grinning broadly. "Yes. This place makes me want to write, and I don't have anything to write with or on, that's all."

His expression relaxed, and I turned back to the field around us. We wandered around for a while until we'd cut a few sunflowers, then headed back toward where we'd entered so we could pay for them as well as the apples we'd picked. Chad also grabbed a loaf of homemade artisan bread, a few different cheeses, and some sparkling waters. There was live music playing, and we settled somewhere we could still hear it, but where it was quiet enough we could hear each other, too. Chad emptied the paper bag of the bread, cheese, and waters, then smoothed the bag down on the grass. Next, he dug around in the apple bag and pulled out five apples; we'd collected five different types—all but one that looked almost identical to one another—so I could only assume it was one of each.

After laying them out, he gave me a review of which was which, pointing out the identifying characteristics, which were almost impossibly subtle to me. Next, he pulled out a pocket knife and opened the blade. I watched in silence as he used the knife to cut slices of cheese, bread, and, lastly, apple—a few slices from each type. When he was done, he smiled at me, then launched into an explanation of the flavors of the different cheeses and apples and how they would go together, as well as how the bread would impact the overall flavor. After he was satisfied with the information he'd provided, it was time for a taste test.

He told me to choose an apple slice to start and I did. He picked up one of the same type and we both took a bite. He explained what I should be tasting and noticing about the flavor and texture, and then he selected one of the cheeses and broke it into smaller pieces, carefully placing one on each of our half-eaten apple slices. Finally, this was done again with a small bit of bread. The process was repeated for each apple type, and I did actually notice the differences Chad pointed out. After the instruction was over, we munched on the remaining cheese, apples, and some of the bread, sipping on our sparkling water, which tickled my tongue deliciously. It had always been my favorite thing about champagne and other sparkling wines, but it was nice knowing this contained no alcohol.

"So," Chad asked, collecting the remains from our little picnic, "now that you've had a private lesson in apples, which was your favorite?"

I bit the corner of my lip, holding back my grin. "The red-ish one." I barely got the words out before I was laughing.

Chad's eyes sparkled and I could tell by the way the corners of his mouth twitched that he was trying not to laugh. "You are the worst student I've ever had," he said. "You're unteachable."

"Maybe it's a teacher problem," I suggested, giggling.

He snorted, but as he watched me trying and failing to deadpan at him, his expression shifted. The brown ring in his eyes gradually disappeared, and his mouth curved softly, that intensity he sometimes had creeping back into his gaze. I could feel his focus on me and knew there could be a building on fire right behind me and he likely wouldn't notice unless I was in danger.

"You're different," he murmured, tucking my hair behind my ear, then caressing my cheek.

"In what way?" I breathed out. His sudden seriousness coupled with that tender touch he had set my heart racing and my body warming.

"You seem freer. It's... beautiful." His thumb smoothed over my skin. "I'm under your spell, Rena."

My cheek heated under his hand. Right then I wished we weren't in an orchard, at least not one with other people. More than ever, I wanted to finish what we'd started the night I'd invited him into my apartment before I pushed him away.

And I wanted to tell him he'd gotten it wrong because it was *I* who was under *his* spell.

TWENTY-TWO

Chad and I stopped by the grocery store on the way back to grab some produce for dinner after apple picking, and it felt so comfortably domestic to be there with him. He kept a grocery basket on one arm, his other hand tightly holding mine. There were moments I tensed up when another man walked past and looked at me, and my eyes darted to Chad to gauge his reaction, but he didn't seem to care. Maybe he didn't even notice. The only thing he did was grin at me and kiss my temple or the back of my hand from time to time and tease me about my lack of knowledge about produce varieties. It was so different from how Damien had been. And while I'd gotten somewhat used to being out in public with Chad, the last few days had brought everything from Damien to the surface and I was getting nervous about things I hadn't in a while.

"Your apartment or mine?" Chad asked after loading groceries into his car. "If we're going to yours, I need to stop by mine to grab some stuff."

"Yours." Mine had nothing he needed to cook, and while I wouldn't mind him bringing what he needed, I kind of liked being in his apartment. Mine was small and sparse and held a lot of sadness. I could feel it when I walked in. I was proud of it, because I'd managed to get it after leaving Damien when he'd convinced me I couldn't, and it had become my safe haven since then, but it felt like I'd just stepped into a new chapter of my life after baring everything to Chad.

When we got back to his apartment, we unloaded the groceries together and got to work on dinner. He taught me to make Chicken à la King over buttermilk biscuits. After we ate and cleaned up together, it was time to make the apple crumble that inspired our trip to the orchard. We used all five types of apples for it.

Chad had taught me how to properly use a chef's knife, but I wasn't nearly as fast as he was, so he did the majority of the prep work, just as he had for dinner. We pulled out the ingredients for the crumble once the apples were in the baking dish, and I got to work measuring things out as Chad listed them off. While I was mixing with my hands, Chad hunched over to see the consistency, and I huffed out a breath intended to blow back errant strands of hair from my ponytail out of my face. Unfortunately, my breath didn't go up as much as it should have because I was more focused on what my hands were doing, and flour puffed into the air, coating Chad's face.

I straightened, but before an apology had a chance to cross my lips, I was laughing; there was flour stuck in the hair on one side of his face.

"I didn't mean to do that," I said, wheezing. "Here." I reached up, but forgot to wipe my hand first and just smeared more flour on his face. I let out another peal of laughter.

"I think you're doing this on purpose," he said, his eyes dancing, not at all bothered by the flour on his face.

"I'm not, I swear," I said between laughs.

"I think you are—and I think it's because you think I look ridiculous this way."

Still struggling to keep my giggling to a minimum, I replied. "You kind of do look ridiculous right now, that's true. But not always—usually, it's kind of... sexy."

The air charged as soon as the last word was out of my mouth.

"Sexy, huh?" he asked, quirking an eyebrow.

"Yeah," I muttered, my cheeks heating.

He stepped closer to me so that we were only a few inches apart. "You know what *I* think is sexy?"

I responded with a headshake, my words completely gone.

"Well," he said, drawing the word out, his eyes lingering on my lips. "Aside from seeing you having fun and laughing so much..." He paused, lifting my right hand. Using his hands, he delicately brushed the flour and bits of dough off my skin, then carefully turned my hand so the edge was visible. He ran a single finger along the skin on the outside of my palm, then the outside of my little finger. "This is usually stained gray from your pencil, especially right after you've been writing."

I couldn't believe what he'd just said. That was one of those things Damien had hated to the extreme. He'd said it was childish. I was conscious of that staining on my hands and was always embarrassed when I didn't get it all off. Of course Chad had noticed... but it didn't bother him?

His finger traced along the inside edge of my thumb. "Here, too." Down the thumb-side of my index finger. "And here."

I could feel his touch reverberating through my entire body, and my breathing became shallow. He looked up and I nearly combusted when I saw only a thin ring of dark gray in his eyes.

"It's so damn sexy."

I was stuck in his gaze—I couldn't look away or move or breathe. All I could do was chant in my mind for him to kiss me because I wanted to be kissing him more than I wanted anything else right then. He turned and scooped up the crumble, dropping it onto the apples, then returned to me, close enough I could feel his body heat.

"Do you want to eat this?" he asked, his voice low and hypnotic, matching the tone and quality of the James Gillespie song in the background.

I nodded even though all I wanted right then was to be kissed.

He picked up the baking dish and slid it into the oven.

"Was it ready?" I asked, embarrassed by my disjointed breathing.

"It's ready enough," he replied in that same voice.

He then quickly set a timer. It was the first time I'd seen him use a timer when there was only one thing he was cooking. By the time he turned back around to me, his apron was off and he tossed it carelessly on the counter, his eyes on me. I stood stock still, watching him, feeling his desire across the shrinking space between us as he stepped toward me. Reaching behind me, he plucked the tie of my apron and lifted it over my head, tossing it to lie with his own.

And then I got the kiss I wanted; he was kissing the hell out of me again. I cradled his head and held him to me, and his hands touched my back, my shoulders, my neck, my jaw. We were leaving a trail of flour all over each other, a roadmap of our passion.

"Rena..." he panted out, reaching under my legs and lifting me onto the counter; I was sitting in the flour left after he had scooped up the crumble topping. I giggled, the sound absorbed by his mouth. He pulled back as he reached over his head to pull his shirt off.

"What's funny?" he asked, then kissed me again before allowing me to speak. He gently tugged my ponytail from my hair as I spoke.

"The flour," I rushed out on an exhale. "It's everywhere."

He smirked and kissed me again, his fingers combing through my hair. "I'll deal with it later."

I sighed, my eyes closing.

"Besides, you said you find it sexy," he added between kisses he was trailing down the side of my neck.

I laughed, but it ended abruptly when he sucked lightly just below my ear. "Flour on *you* is sexy," I breathed. "Seeing you in your element is sexy. Watching you knead and shape dough, your hands and fingers strong yet also gentle and precise is sexy."

His mouth was even hotter when he kissed me this time, his hands cradling my face. The way he kissed me was like he couldn't get enough, and that made me feel so powerful and desirable. My hands skimmed down his sides and grasped his hips lightly, then slid back up to rest on his chest. With him standing between my legs the way he was, holding me to him and kissing me with so much desire and urgency, his large hands on my face, I felt small.

But this wasn't how I'd always felt small with Damien. With him, I'd felt small and weak. Even at the beginning, his strength had been such a show for him that I was always acutely aware that if I ever needed to stop him, I wouldn't be able to. His desire had overruled any change in mine, any time I tried to push away met with being pulled closer in a way I couldn't counter.

I wasn't afraid right now, though. I felt small and delicate in Chad's hands, but still powerful. I felt that if I pulled away even a fraction of an inch, he would notice and stop whatever he was doing. With him, I felt cherished and respected and feminine in a way I never had, and because of it, for the first time in my life, I liked feeling small. In fact, it made me want him even more.

A light pressure against him was all it took. He stepped back, putting space between us, his fingertips skimming up my back, his eyes as dark as I'd ever seen them, but with a slight questioning crease between them. I watched his muscular bare chest moving up and down as he breathed, saw the bulge of his erection in his jeans. There was no doubt he wanted me.

But his want for me wasn't overriding what I was communicating, what *I* may or may not have wanted. And *that* was the reason I felt powerful. And that feeling simply fueled my own desire, as did the next words he spoke as he kept one hand skimming my back and used the other to tuck my hair behind my ear again.

"I want to make love to you, Rena. I want to show you physically how I feel about you. I want to feel your body against my body, your skin against my skin. But I only want that if you want it, too. Whatever you want is what I want. I promise."

I turned my head and kissed his palm. "I want everything you said," I whispered.

He stilled for a second and I could tell my words were sinking in. Then he was kissing me, sliding his hands along my thighs, cupping them under my knees and lifting. I wrapped my legs around his hips, and with his arms snug around my waist, he lifted me from the counter. He carried me to his bedroom and lowered us onto his bed.

"The flour," I panted out; I was covered in it, so his pristine bed was now, too.

"I don't care," he breathed against my mouth.

For a while, every time either of us started to remove any clothing on ourselves or each other, we got distracted by the erotic tangling of our tongues. Then Chad pushed up over me, his chest heaving, and stared into my eyes.

"I've never wanted someone the way I want you right now," he rasped out.

My whole body clenched. "Me, neither."

"Let's savor it."

He bent his head and kissed me more leisurely this time, his mouth just as hot but the slower pace somehow more intoxicating. He peeled my shirt off, one inch at a time, then took a few seconds to let his eyes roam over me. I felt grateful in a whole new way that Caroline had taken me shopping for lingerie. Chad trailed a single fingertip down the side of my neck, then between my breasts, over my stomach, until he reached the waistband of my jeans. It was the same way he touched my hand, except he was touching parts of me he never had before. If I'd thought I loved it when he touched my hand, there wasn't a word to describe how I felt about him doing the same thing on my body.

His finger circled my belly button, then whispered up and along the curve on the underside of my breasts, his finger gliding over the soft, stretchy lace of my bra cups. Without warning, he stopped and rested his palm on my chest.

"Breathe, Rena," he said, his voice soft and his eyes watching me carefully.

I hadn't realized until he said something that I'd forgotten how to.

"Are you okay?" he checked in, remaining still.

I moved my head in short, vigorous bursts. "Oh my god, yes."

He resumed his single finger exploration of my body, this time unbuttoning and unzipping my jeans once he reached them with an excruciating slowness. The speed with which he had removed my shirt felt like a sprint compared to how slowly he peeled off my jeans; I could barely handle the anticipation. I thought I might go crazy.

In the background, I heard a new song start; his shuffle of James Gillespie was still playing on the integrated speakers throughout his apartment. This song, however, was one of my favorites.

"I love this one," I said, lifting a finger and pointing toward the ceiling.

"You do?" he asked.

"Yeah." It had the most hypnotic and sexy beat of any of the artist's other songs.

He finished pulling my jeans off over my feet and walked over to a small control panel on the wall. A second later, the volume of the music increased. I could feel the beat pulsing through my body in time with my desire. Chad's lips pulled up on one side as he stepped back toward the bed while unbuttoning and unzipping his own pants. He watched me watching him as he pushed them and the waistband of his boxer briefs down over his hips, over his thighs, until they fell to the floor at his feet.

He stepped out of his puddle of clothing and set a leg on the bed, his palm running from my ankle toward my hip as he crawled over me. I felt like I was going to combust until all of a sudden, I felt nothing.

Absolutely nothing.

TWENTY-THREE

"You're mine, Renata," Damien whispered into my ear before taking the lobe between his teeth with almost enough pressure to hurt.

His hand was moving in rhythmic circles between my legs. I gave a small nod, then there was a sharp pain on my earlobe; he'd bitten down.

"Say it, Renata," he whispered again in that same weirdly magnetic voice he always used when he wanted something. His hand was still moving over my clitoris.

"I'm yours," I whispered.

"Whose?" he asked louder, his teeth starting to tighten down again.

"Yours, Damien."

His tongue caressed the area he'd bitten, then he moved his hand from stimulating me and shoved my legs open, driving hard into me. I yelped; I hadn't been ready for that and it hurt. He began to move in and out of me quickly.

"All this is mine, Renata," he said, his jaw clenched this time. "No one else will ever have you."

I knew I was supposed to repeat what he was saying. "It's all yours, Damien. No one else will ever have me."

"Never, Renata, do you hear me? You belong to me, and no one else. You always will."

He was slamming into me and every movement was painful. Bruises would inevitably follow. I pushed against his hips.

"Damien, you're hurting me—I want to stop," I pleaded.

He grabbed my hands and pinned them in one of his above my head without stopping or even easing up.

"I'd kill for you, Renata. And I will if anyone ever touches you."

"Damien—"

"Say it! Tell me you understand."

"I understand," I replied, fighting back tears.

"The words, Renata."

"I belong to you, and I always will. No one will ever touch me or you'll kill them."

"And you," he added.

I swallowed my fear as my body and mind went numb. He was passionate, he was jealous... but he wouldn't really hurt anyone... let alone kill someone. He was exaggerating. He had to be.

It wasn't the first time he'd made me repeat that I was his and only his—he made me do that every time we had sex, and several times a day outside the bedroom. It *was* the first time he'd threatened me, though. And it was the first time I explicitly told him to stop and that he was hurting me... the first time he ignored me, pinning me down and continuing anyway.

"Stop!" I shouted, eyes screwed shut.

"Rena." It was Chad's voice, and I opened my eyes. "I'm not touching you."

He wasn't. He had been when my memory reared its ugly head, but he wasn't now. He was sitting on the bed, easily over a foot of space between us, not touching me anywhere, his face holding a mixture of worry and sadness. I watched his face as he studied me, the crease between his eyes becoming more pronounced. I didn't know what he was thinking; *I* was trying to shake off feeling like Damien was there, ready to hurt me, hearing his whispered threats.

"What's happening? With you, I mean? It's the PTSD again, isn't it?" he asked as he reached down and pulled a blanket over me, his movements as gentle as his voice.

I exhaled, releasing some tension now that I was covered. It was uncomfortable laying there practically naked with what was happening. I dropped my chin in affirmation, my eyes shifting away. Of all times for a flashback...

He slid down in the bed so he was lying on his side, facing me. He reached out a hand and ran a finger faintly along the back of my hand. "This is okay?" he asked.

The contact felt grounding. It was familiar and so uniquely Chad that it provided a clear separation from everything Damien had been and done. It was like a reminder I was safe now. I swallowed. "Yes. It helps."

Chad gave a small nod and I knew he was committing that small fact to memory. His finger continued to trek back and forth across the skin on my hand and I let my eyes close. I could still see images of Damien behind my eyelids, but there was a battle between that and Chad's touch, and the way that touch made me feel. It was as if the two were dueling each other... and Chad's touch was winning. I wasn't with Damien anymore—I hadn't been in a long time. He couldn't hurt me anymore. His threats had been simply that—threats. If he was going to do something to me or come after me like he'd sworn he would, it would have happened already.

"Tell me?" Chad asked.

I gave a jerky nod, inhaling and exhaling at a slow, deliberate rate a few times before telling him about how Damien used to threaten me. I kept my eyes closed, not wanting to see the impact of my words. These were words I had but didn't want, and now I'd given them to Chad, who surely didn't want them, either.

"Your body changed, your energy, I guess," he said, his finger still moving on my hand. "Your eyes closed and you kind of went limp and tense at the same time. I could tell you weren't here anymore."

I swallowed again. "I went numb. I used to go numb a lot. He..." I took another slow inhale and exhale. "He hurt me during sex... often. Sometimes worse than other times. If I told him to stop, he pinned me down. Going numb helped."

Chad muttered something I couldn't understand; I was fairly certain there were a number of expletives included, however. "Can you look at me?" he asked after a beat.

Doing so would make the fact that I'd just told him about sex with Damien real, but I managed to do it anyway. His eyes were clear and carrying sadness. He lifted a hand and smoothed it over the side of my face like he did when I had hair there, then tenderly flattened his palm to my cheek. "You're safe with me, Rena."

I nodded, my eyes flooding. I felt what he said in every fiber of my being.

His thumb smoothed over my cheekbone. "I don't care what he said he'd do to you—it won't happen. If he ever tried, I'd stop him. I won't let him hurt you, Rena. That bastard will never lay a hand on you or rape you again."

My heart stalled when he said "rape" and my eyes slid away again. That was an uncomfortable word. "That word's a bit strong," I said quietly.

"Strong or not, it's the correct word," he replied gently, still cupping my cheek.

"I mean..." My mind raced. How was that possible? "Even if I didn't want to, I was engaged to him..."

"Rena," he began, his voice cracking. He took and released a slow, deep breath. "It doesn't matter if he was a stranger or you were married to him... he forced you to have sex when you didn't want to. That's rape." He swallowed loudly. "I'm so sorry, Rena."

Rape... the word was rolling around in my mind. It wasn't one I'd ever used for what Damien did. I'd always thought about it in terms of forcing me to have sex when I told him no or tried to stop him, or having sex with me when I was unconscious, but had never even thought that word because he was first my boyfriend, then my fiancé.

"He told me that being in a relationship meant I owed my body to him," I whispered, my eyes screwed tightly closed again, filled with a mix of anger and shame. "I didn't know any better... I didn't have anyone to talk to about it. I just thought... he was forcing me to do something I didn't want to, but that it was *my* fault."

"It wasn't your fault," he said, his voice thin with strain. "He lied to you, Rena. You don't owe your body to anyone. Ever. For any reason. He told you that to justify raping you."

Again, that word. It was hard to swallow. I saw what he was saying, but it was different to think about it applied to myself. Me? A victim of rape? Not just domestic abuse, but... rape? "Oh, god, how did I let that happen to me?" I muttered, forgetting for an instant that I wasn't alone.

"You didn't," Chad replied, his thumb again moving across my cheek and bringing me back to the present with him. "You didn't 'let' anything happen to you... he did those things to you. And none of it is your fault. It never was."

I tried to digest and process his words, but it was a lot to take in.

"I will never do those things to you, Rena. I promise you. I would never hurt you during sex, and I will always stop when you tell me to. *Always*. I won't say I'd stop even if I wanted to keep going because the thing is, I don't even want to touch you when *you* don't want me to."

If ever there was someone telling the truth, it was Chad right then. Before he'd said the words, he'd demonstrated the truth of them. I hadn't even needed to stop him, because he'd already done so. He was so observant, he noticed before I could communicate it that I wasn't present anymore... and he cared enough to stop what he was doing.

I pressed his hand against my face as I leaned into it, then turned and kissed his palm. My tears slipped out and slid down my temples as I turned back and looked up at the expression on Chad's face: adoration. He used a thumb to wipe away some of the tears, then bent and kissed the others gently from my temple. I flung my arms around him and squeezed him tight to me, overflowing with gratitude to have someone like him in my life. His arms slipped around me and held me just as tightly against him.

"I love you, my Rena," he whispered into my ear, before kissing my temple again.

I turned my head and touched our lips together. When the kiss ended, I did it again. And again. Chad pulled back, studying my eyes for a second. His were shifting again. The brown had appeared but now it was slipping away again. If I'd had his hazel eyes, the same thing would have been happening. He must have seen that because *he* kissed *me* this time, his tongue sweeping against my tongue.

"Tell me," he said between kisses, "if anything changes."

"I will," I breathed into his mouth.

The energy this time was different as our desire ratcheted up quickly. It was deeper and desperate, not in a hurried way, but more that I felt a need to be physically closer to him, to get as close as humanly possible. Judging by the way his hands moved over my body, the way they grasped and squeezed, firm but tender, much like when he was making pastries, he felt the same. I still wore my bra and panties, and even when removing those, we didn't allow much space to come between us—only as much as strictly necessary to get them off.

Once I was as naked as he was, we slowed for a minute, holding each other with our bodies stretched out on our sides, face to face, and touching from our foreheads to our toes. My skin broke out in goosebumps and Chad shivered. His kiss was slow and hypnotic and my leg slid up along his, hooking over his hip. His hand wrapped around my hip and held me against him. I rolled to my back, but Chad didn't follow, pulling his mouth from mine.

"You're in control, Rena," he whispered. "You tell me what you want."

In lieu of words, I grasped the back of his bicep and tugged lightly.

"You want me on top of you?" he asked.

"Yes," I breathed. I wanted that small but powerful feeling again.

He kissed me while he shifted until his body covered mine, keeping some of his weight on his elbows, which rested on the mattress above my shoulders. His weight rolled slightly to his left and he lifted his right hand to trace my facial features with a whisper-soft touch of his fingertips. My eyebrows and cheekbones. The bridge of my nose. The outer contour of my lips. When his fingers moved to trace along my hairline, he leaned down and tenderly kissed my forehead. When he did, my body broke out into goosebumps again and the smell of his skin—like leather and cedar and a hint of bread dough—filled my nostrils. I moaned softly against his throat and his body tensed, and then his lips were on mine again, kissing me in that same slow, intensely wanting way they had earlier.

I could feel his erection hardening between us, and it occurred to me that he was waiting on me to initiate going any further. My hands skimmed his sides and he trembled, his body growing heavier on top of me. I began shifting against him, my hips moving of their own volition, and Chad groaned into my mouth with a hot puff of breath.

"Tell me what you want," his lips brushed against my cheek, his breath heavy in my ear.

The thought of saying out loud what I wanted right then made me nervous; I'd never done something like that before. I felt it would be weird or ruin the moment. But at the same time, the idea of having control over what happened between us turned me on even more. I took a deep breath and spoke, my lips brushing his ear.

"I want to make love with you." I paused when his body tensed and his breathing hitched and stuttered out. "You said before you wanted to do a hell of a lot more than kiss me, that you wanted to show me physically how you feel about me."

"Mm-hm." The sound of his reply vibrated all the way to the tips of my toes.

"I want that," I whispered. "I want you to do that." My belly fluttered with the words all out.

Chad cradled my face with the hand that had traced my features. "You have to tell me if anything changes or if you go numb again."

I couldn't imagine the observant man speaking to me wouldn't notice before I'd have a chance to tell him if it did happen again, but agreed anyway. "Okay."

"Promise me." He kissed my cheek. "And I promise to bring you back if it happens."

"I promise." I pressed a hard kiss to his mouth, opening my eyes when he pulled back.

His hand feathered over my cheek, his eyes following his hand. "I love you, Rena," he said, his voice husky and heavy.

"I love you, Chad."

With our mouths connected, he rested his weight back down on both arms and his hips lifted. My hands pushed subtly against his back as he situated himself between my legs and began to press inside me. I hadn't thought it possible, but the numbness returned; a split second of amazing sensation, then nothing.

"Chad," I whispered, desperately not wanting to, and not really needing to—he'd already stopped.

"I know," he soothed.

Without pulling out or moving any further inside me, he shifted his weight to his left again and began to trace my face like he had before, interspersed with soft, tender kisses. As soon as shame began to well up inside me, it seeped away, no match for the loving attention he was giving me. And after some time ticked past, the numbness also faded away, leaving me breathless at what I felt.

"I'm here," I said, my voice soft.

His hand flattened against the side of my face, and then we were kissing again. And as we kissed, he surged forward until there was nowhere else to go. I could feel *everything* and it was almost a sensation overload, especially once he began to move in and out of me. I didn't know if it was him, or if it was feeling like I was in control of what was happening to me, or both, but sex had never felt like this before. It was emotional—a few tears slipped from the corners of my eyes—and physical and so intense. Soon, I was lost in the movement of our bodies, the sound of our labored breaths to the backdrop of James Gillespie, and Chad's whispered words of love against my skin.

Our breathing wasn't quite back to normal yet when the kitchen timer went off. I sighed and Chad grinned at me.

"Don't go anywhere," he said with a kiss, hopping up after disentangling our limbs.

I watched him walk from his bedroom, naked, my cheeks burning as I did. It felt strange lying there nude, only a sheet over me, but I stayed and waited for Chad to return, closing my eyes and replaying what had just transpired in my mind.

"Is that grin coming from what I think it is?" Chad's voice broke into my replay.

I'd been so engrossed in my thoughts I hadn't even heard his footsteps approaching. I opened my eyes and bit the side of my lip to keep from smiling so obviously. He slipped under the sheet and shifted until he was wrapped around me again, my back to his chest. I could feel his heartbeat against my shoulder and the steadiness of it was comforting.

"So," he said, a hint of amusement in his voice. "I've never walked around my kitchen naked before." He kissed the back of my head. "I kind of like it. I might do it more often. Maybe I'll even start baking naked."

I laughed. "You'd hurt yourself if you were all exposed like that."

"Hm. You might be right. Fine—I'll wear an apron."

"Just an apron?" I asked, snorting as I pictured him in nothing but an apron moving around the kitchen and kneading dough.

"Just an apron," he confirmed.

"If you tried to do something that ridiculous, I wouldn't wear anything under *my* apron, either."

His erection became more noticeable against the small of my back. "If you did that, I might not end up baking anything. I might end up accidentally trying to make bread on your body instead."

I sucked in a breath at the thought of his hands moving over my body the way they did with dough, the way they had been only moments earlier. Chad heard and chuckled, then a hand slid over my hip and squeezed the fleshy area where my hip curved below my butt and into my thigh. He shifted, faintly pushing against my shoulder until I was on my belly.

"Is this okay?" he asked, his palm resting on my shoulder. "Being on your belly?"

I hesitated; it was fine right then, but that's because there was a sheet covering my back.

Chad kissed my shoulder. "What is it, my Rena?"

My body shuddered pleasantly at the feel of his lips on my skin. "My back," I whispered, my eyes closed as I tried to focus on the sensations from his touch rather than the fear of him seeing my disfigured skin.

He kissed my shoulder again. The sheet gradually moved down my back until it came to a stop just below my hips. Chad's fingertips brushed from my shoulders down to the sheet and back. Over and over and over, tracing the contours of my scars, my shoulder blades, my sides. My heart continued to race, the fear that was driving it giving way to arousal.

"You're beautiful, Rena," he murmured, his lips at the small of my back.

He pressed them gently against me, the sheet traveling down my legs, and soon he was settled near my feet. His hands smoothed up and down my calves a few times, unhurried. His languid touch made me feel so alive, setting off a clenching deep inside as my body remembered him touching me as we made love not long before. Pinching gentle handfuls of my calf, he moved toward my knee, then started over near my ankle. It was both relaxing and arousing. I had a flash of watching him pinch together the corners of turnovers using the same motion.

My breath was loud.

His hands continued the pinching movement above my knees.

My breath got louder.

He began to knead the curves of my butt like bread dough.

I stopped breathing altogether.

Chad's hands moved to my hips and stilled. "Breathe, Rena."

In the silence of my paused respiration, I could hear *his* breath; it sounded like mine had just before my lungs forgot what they were supposed to be doing, harsh and uneven. I let air back in but kept it quiet so I could hear his breathing, then rolled over onto my back and watched him for several seconds. The rise and fall of his chest, the expansion and contraction of his abdomen. The continued darkening of his eyes until there was little of his iris left at all. Most fascinating, however, was that as I watched him, my own want for him increased. And as that desire built inside me, I could see it growing in him. He was so aware of what was happening inside *me* by observing the tiniest changes in my body, and my desire was directly fueling his. He'd made me feel powerful before, but it was nothing compared to how I felt with this new realization.

TWENTY-FOUR

Chad pulled into a parking space behind the café early the next morning. I'd spent the night at his apartment again, and we'd gotten up insanely early so he could take me home to get ready for work. He'd insisted on making me breakfast while I showered and dressed, but when we went to part ways, we couldn't, so he drove me to work so we could have a few more minutes together. Now we'd arrived and I didn't want to get out of the car, didn't want to let go of his hand.

"I'll walk you in," he said, kissing my hand before letting it go to get out of the car.

"You don't have to do that," I replied as I shut his car door behind me.

He tucked my hair behind my ear and my breath hitched. How I still felt this want for him after we'd made love most of the night, I didn't know. I'd never felt like that before. I was exhausted, but felt giddy and like I was soaring above the ground. His body leaned lightly into mine and he cupped my face with one hand. Then we were kissing and touching against the side of his car in the dark parking lot.

"We have to get to work," he said, pulling back, then leaning in and kissing me again. "Seriously." Another kiss.

"Yup." Yet another. "We do. Or we'll be late."

Another still. "We can't be late," he agreed.

Five minutes later, we managed to pull apart and walk toward the back door into the café, hand-in-hand. But we didn't make it inside before we were all over each other again. And that's how Caroline found us a few minutes later, making out against the wall beside the back door.

"I was going to ask how things went, but I can see the answer for myself," she said, smirking when Chad and I startled.

"Sorry," I giggled, my face on fire.

"I'm not," Chad said, his hands squeezing my sides.

Caroline laughed. "I'll see you inside, Renata."

Chad cradled my face as the door shut behind Caroline. "I don't want to be away from you." He kissed my nose.

"Me, neither," I breathed out.

"This is real, isn't it?" he asked. "I didn't go to sleep alone in the hotel in Hilderstown and I'm about to wake up and find out everything since has just been a dream?"

My body felt like it was melting at his words. He was so straightforward and forthcoming about his thoughts and feelings and it gave me a thrill.

"If it *is* a dream, I never want to wake up from it," I replied.

He pressed his mouth firmly against mine for an extended kiss. "Same." One more. "Okay, go. I have to go, too."

"Okay," I agreed reluctantly. Right then I wished neither of us had jobs. I just wanted to go back to his apartment and crawl back into his arms under his sheets and fall back asleep with him so I could wake up with him again.

"I'll call you later."

I sighed. I wanted to see him later. And I knew he wanted to see me, too. But I had plans with Caroline to catch up since we hadn't a couple of days earlier. Besides, Chad and I could both use some sleep.

I walked over to the door and opened it, taking a step inside before looking back over my shoulder. Chad was standing there, his hands in his pockets, watching me with a big, lopsided grin on his face. I bit the side of my lip, trying not to smile any wider than I already was, and let the door close behind me with a sigh. I called out a greeting toward the office, nervous about seeing Fern since she'd been upset with me the last time I'd seen her—and that was before they went on a trip to watch Chad imploding with misery when he should have been enjoying his birthday, all because of me. I honestly wasn't sure how she would feel that Chad and I were back together now. I couldn't blame her if she wasn't happy about it. And I didn't know how much she knew about why I'd broken up with him to begin with; I'd given Caroline permission to tell Fern about Damien, but I didn't know if she'd ever ended up doing so.

After greeting James, the only baker we had that already worked there before I was hired, I headed toward the front so I could help Caroline get things ready.

"Hey, James. Hi, sis," Chad's voice rushed out, and I turned to see Fern outside the office as Chad grinned and barreled past her.

"What are you doing?" I asked, giggling.

He reached me and pulled me into his arms, kissing me soundly. Then he tucked my escape artist hair behind my ear and lightly touched his lips to my cheekbone. "I forgot something."

"What?" I asked.

"To tell you that I love you—madly, I love you. Deeply, I love you. More than anyone else has ever loved another person in the history of mankind, I love you." He dropped a kiss to my lips. "I love you." Another. "I love you, my Rena."

"Oh, god, I love you, too."

There was a throat clear behind him.

"Don't worry, sis," he said, lips smirking and eyes dancing as he continued to look at me. "I'm going. I won't keep distracting your employee." He winked at me. "Today, anyway."

I glanced over his shoulder to catch Fern rolling her eyes, but I didn't think she looked angry. She looked a little guarded, but her expression was soft as she watched her brother.

Chad kissed me one more time, then turned.

"What are you doing here?" Fern asked him. "Shouldn't you be at work soon?"

"That's correct," Chad replied cheerily. He slipped an arm around Fern's shoulders and squeezed her into his side.

"You're probably gonna be late, Chad," she chastised.

He laughed, the sound so carefree. "Maybe. But it would be a first—who's really going to get mad?" He gave her a peck on her cheek and another shoulder squeeze, then headed toward the back door. "Have a great day, everyone!" he called, then disappeared through the door.

I realized a little later that I was still standing there watching the back door, and a blush roared across my face, especially when I saw that Fern was still standing near the office, eying me contemplatively.

Caroline and I headed to a nearby restaurant after our shift to get lunch. We'd chosen the place because they had three-season outdoor seating thanks to large heaters, so we were able to dine al fresco on the sunny, but very chilly October day. The café had been slammed all day, so we hadn't had a chance to catch up at all during work, but that was okay with me. If it had been slow, I probably would have gone crazy thinking about Chad.

My phone buzzed as we were sitting, and I waited until the waiter was done telling us the specials before looking down. It was a message from Chad telling me he missed me terribly already and asking if it was really all that important for us to have jobs.

I giggled, firing off a quick text telling him I missed him, too, and that if we didn't have jobs, we wouldn't be able to afford groceries and he wouldn't be able to cook for me anymore. With a contented sigh, I slid the phone back into my purse and found Caroline watching me with a smirk.

I blushed and looked away, biting at my lip as I tried to stop grinning.

"You look hot right now, Renata," Caroline said.

I released a short laugh at the unexpected comment. "What?"

She shrugged, still smirking. "Happiness is just bursting out of you. That's an attractive thing. No wonder Chad couldn't keep his hands off you long enough to let you come in to work this morning."

I laughed and looked down at the menu without saying anything. The waiter returned just as I'd made my decision about what to eat, and we both ordered, then Caroline went to the bathroom. As soon as she left, I pulled my phone out of my purse to see if Chad had responded yet. He had.

Hm, good point. Where did you and Caroline end up going for lunch?

Ronaldo's.

They have nice outdoor seating.

That's why we're here. :)

What did you order?

Cedar plank salmon with green beans and rice pilaf.

You'll like it, but mine's better. ;)

I believe it. Everything you do is better.

Everything, huh?

Especially the way you make dough.

Are you talking about dough right now?

;)

I can't wait to make dough with you again.

I let out my breath in a rush, my heart thumping wonderfully in my chest, and looked up. Caroline was nearly back to the table, that same smirk on her face, and I dropped my phone back into my purse.

"Okay," she said as soon as her butt hit her chair. "I want to hear *everything*."

I sat up straight and let out a sigh, looking her straight in the eye. "You were right. I should have believed you to begin with."

"You decided that on your own?"

"No. As you know, he just showed up at my apartment the day you and I were supposed to hang out."

"I'd told him not to do that, by the way."

"Well, he didn't listen. And I'm glad he didn't. He told me we had to talk, and I decided that even if he walked away from me, I wanted him to know the truth, so I gave him my journal, like I said. I lost track of time in the preserve and he found me there a few hours later. He wasn't mad at me."

"I knew he wouldn't be." She thanked the waiter who was setting down our drinks, then resumed our conversation. "That's just not the kind of person Chad is."

"I know. I was just scared. But now he knows and things are better than they were between us."

She laughed. "I could see that this morning."

I blushed and bit my lip. "Sorry you saw that."

She held up her hands, palms facing me. "Didn't bother me in the least, Renata. I was happy to see you guys back together. You're both happier that way."

I bobbed my head in agreement. "Yeah, I think so, too."

"So, what else? What happened after he found you in the preserve?"

Over the next hour and a half, I filled her in on everything that had happened in the last two days, up to the point where Chad and I slept together. I eyed her, nervous, because I'd never talked about my sex life with anyone before; I would have with Connie early in my relationship with Damien, but she'd hated him from the very beginning. But I wanted to ask Caroline a question—as my friend and because of her background studying psychology.

"Spill it," she said with a small laugh. "Whatever it is, spit it out. I guarantee if you're going to tell me you had sex with Chad, it's not going to phase me."

I bit my lip, my face heating up. "I wouldn't expect it to." I glanced away. "We did have sex last night."

"I figured, based on how you guys were acting this morning."

"But that's not it." I looked up at her, a fluttering in my chest. I was more nervous than I expected.

"What is it, honey?" she asked, her eyes softening toward the center.

My eyes drifted to the table. "Chad... he..." I glanced up at her quickly, then back down again. "You read my journal. You know that Damien drugged me and had sex—"

Caroline made a low noise in her throat, but didn't say anything.

"—with me while I was unconscious. You know that he tried to force me to have sex with him the night he pushed me into the fire. But he used to do that a lot—force me to have sex, that is. He would hurt me, and if I told him no or tried to stop him, he pinned me down." My eyes darted around the immediate vicinity, confirming we were still relatively alone and no one could hear us talking. "But we were engaged. He was my boyfriend first, then he was my fiancé when this was all happening. And I didn't leave him." I paused, swallowing the sour taste in my mouth. "Chad said Damien raped me."

My eyes sought hers as soon as the last word was out, looking for I didn't even know what. Did I want her to confirm? To disagree? I wasn't sure. Either was going to be a lot to process. If she confirmed, that completely changed so much of the narrative I'd fed myself for years, including taking blame for what happened. But if she didn't, it meant it *was* my fault all those violent things had happened to me.

Her eyes searched mine, then her eyebrows lifted. "Oh," she said. "Oh." Her eyes glassed, but no tears spilled over. "Chad's right, Renata," she said sympathetically. "Damien raped you. Repeatedly. It doesn't matter that you were engaged or that you didn't leave him for so long—that doesn't change that what he was doing was rape." She paused. "I didn't know you didn't realize that. I'm sorry."

"Why are you sorry?"

"Because I would have told you when you let me read your journal so you didn't spend another day thinking what he did to you was okay."

My head moved sluggishly up and down, but I didn't know how to respond. After a minute or so, I changed the subject and asked Caroline about the birthday trip, and she filled me in on what I'd missed out on.

"Fern probably hates me," I said after she told me how miserable Chad had been.

"She doesn't hate you," Caroline said. "But she's wary. She likes you, Renata, and she liked you and Chad dating because she'd never seen Chad so happy before, but he was completely destroyed by what happened, and now she's scared you'll leave him again and he'll end up in pieces."

"She told you that?"

Caroline nodded. "We talked about it yesterday. Originally, Chad was supposed to stop at our place for dinner when he got back to town. When he cancelled, he told Fern he was with you and that you guys had mended things between you. She wasn't too happy about it at first, but I told her about Damien—not all of it, just enough. I know you said it was okay, but it doesn't feel right to talk about your past that way. She understands, and she hates what happened to you, but she's worried it will get between you guys again and that Chad won't recover if you hurt him like that a second time."

It all made sense, and I understood where Fern was coming from. I couldn't promise it wouldn't come between us in the future, either, even if I didn't see how it possibly could—I wasn't hiding anything from Chad anymore. I refused to. And that was the only reason it came between us in the first place.

"I think it helped to see you two together this morning in the kitchen, though. She could see how happy you both were, and she's a sucker for sappy displays of affection like that. Not to mention that Chad's good mood always puts her into a good mood, too."

"I don't blame her, you know. I'd be furious if someone else hurt him the way I did."

"I know. And that's part of why we all love you so much."

I beamed. "I love you guys, too."

She winked. "Of course you do—what's not to love?"

"What else?" Caroline asked as we meandered down the street. There was a new bookstore a few blocks away that we hadn't been to yet and we were headed there. While Caroline didn't have a deep abiding love of bookstores the way I did, it had kind of become our thing to explore them together. "You said you had some other news before Chad showed up."

"I do," I said, letting out a sharp breath. "I um... I guess I had an epiphany. I went back through my *Heal Your Heart, Heal Your Art* book again, redoing the exercises, and this time a new memory surfaced."

"Really?"

"Yeah. But this wasn't from my childhood. It was from Damien. He, bit by bit, eroded my self-confidence, talked me into second-guessing everything I did, ditching perfectly good writing until everything I turned in was rejected, and soon I couldn't write anything at all. When he told me I must not have been meant to be a writer after all, I believed him because I thought I'd lost what little talent I had. I completely missed that it was something he constructed. He never wanted me to work—he was jealous of my job early on, and once we were living together, he began trying to talk me into quitting and just staying home while he supported us. And while he talked me into a lot of things, I didn't budge on that."

I sniffled, pulling a tissue from my purse and blowing my nose. I wiped away the tears from my cheeks. "Sorry. It's a bit emotional."

"Renata, don't apologize for getting upset."

I glanced at her gratefully. "I realized it was all his doing. He'd done it on purpose, planting doubt and convincing me my writing was terrible, urging me to change it until what I turned in was inferior. He wanted me to get fired. I knew he was happy when I did, but I realized the other day he'd orchestrated it."

"What a worthless son of a bitch," Caroline bit out.

I hmphed. "And that's putting it nicely, I think. Anyway, that was my writing trauma right there. I couldn't find it in my childhood memories because it wasn't there. It was with Damien. That means I can figure out how to unravel the damage he did to my psyche. And I already started." I paused and looked over at her. "You'll be proud of me for this. I dug out the very first article Damien talked me into overhauling to the point it was rejected by my editor. I found my original draft and reached out to my old editor, asking him if that version would have been rejected or not all those years ago."

"I *am* proud of you, Renata," Caroline said, reaching out to briefly rest a hand on my arm. "That was really brave."

"Thank you. It was unbelievably nerve-wracking, but I *had* to know."

"Have you heard back from him yet?"

"Yep. He emailed me back in less than a day, Caroline—just a few hours. I couldn't believe it. I half expected he'd ignore my email after the way I just disappeared on everyone and having been fired."

"And...?"

"He said he would have accepted it. And he told me I should submit it. They have a freelance section now and he thinks they'd want to publish it there."

"Oh my god, Renata, that's amazing!"

"Yeah? I mean, I think so, but it's not like before when I was on staff or anything."

"Woman—who cares?" she shouted so loudly some other people on the sidewalk looked at us. "On staff or freelance, it's still getting published. This is cause for celebration!"

"Well, not yet," I laughed. My chest felt full, and it felt I was standing taller. She was right; published was published. "They have to accept it first—it's a different editorial staff and they could disagree with Jeb's opinion."

"They'll accept it. You submitted it right away, right?"

I shook my head. "No. I wasn't sure—"

"Sure about what? Submit it!"

"I guess I'm afraid it would be rejected," I said quietly. It was the first I'd admitted it, even to myself. "It was great to get some validation from Jeb, but that's a big deal to submit it for the journal. The journal that fired me, remember."

She waved her hand like none of what I'd just said mattered. "It'll be accepted—trust me."

"You haven't even read it yet."

"Well, send it to me, then. *After* you submit it."

"Okay."

"Like today, woman."

"*Okay.*" I shook my head again. "I will. I don't know about today, but I'll do it. I promise."

"Good. Now let's talk about how we're going to celebrate."

I laughed. "Caroline, seriously—"

"Renata, this is a big deal for a lot of different reasons. And you're my friend; I want to celebrate the shit out of this with you. Which means we need to start planning. I need you to tell me the date you'll get notified that they accepted it because we'll do it then. We can go out, or we could do it at our place. Chad's place is nicer and much bigger, but he hates hosting parties because of all the mess..."

I half-listened as Caroline chattered on with barely a breath the rest of the way to the bookstore, planning all the details for the party to celebrate me getting an article published that I hadn't even submitted yet. I couldn't help grinning. I was so lucky to have a friend like her.

TWENTY-FIVE

It took two weeks after my promise to Caroline before I mustered up the courage to submit my piece to the freelance section of the journal. By then, I'd also written a second piece, this one about friendship and the loss of important friendships in your life, but how they can still sustain you because of what you once shared together. It was about Connie, of course.

I thought about her often. I always had, but it happened even more often now. As I got closer with my new friends, especially Caroline, I couldn't help but think about the last time I'd had a close friendship and miss Connie. I'd even Googled her online and found that she was running a nonprofit to help victims of domestic abuse. I considered reaching out to her via the contact information for her nonprofit, but I couldn't imagine she'd ever want to hear from me again. I was content to know she was doing well, and from what I could find online, she appeared to be happy—married to the man she was dating when we last spoke, and they now had two toddlers.

After Chad read the piece about friendships while we were snuggled on his sofa, he encouraged me to write her a letter, even if I never intended to give it to her.

"You never know what might happen," he said.

Thinking of the letter I'd written to him that had saved our relationship, I agreed. He grabbed some paper off his printer while I pulled out the pencil I kept in my purse. I usually had a notebook on me, but I'd been so rushed that morning that I'd forgotten it when I left my apartment. Making a mental note to get a notebook to just keep at Chad's since I spent so much time there anyway, I began my letter to Connie.

Dear Connie,

I looked you up on the internet recently. Ha, who ever thought I'd say something like that about you? But I did. You seem happy. I'm smiling as I write this because that makes me happy if you are. I always thought you and Dave would last. And kids! Wow! They're beautiful, it's just hard to think of you as a mom. I still remember us sneaking out at night to ride our bikes to the lake and talk for hours—we never thought we'd grow up and have kids one day, did we?

I left Damien. Thirteen months ago. And this is the first I've been able to consider talking to you, even if it's just on paper that I'll never send. You were right—about everything. I know you know that, but I want to tell you that I know it, too. The embarrassing part is that deep down I knew it back then. I knew I should have stayed away from him. I still don't entirely understand why I didn't. Every internal alarm sounded from the very first time I met him. I think I ignored the message because I was feeling something after so long of feeling nothing. Except grief, that is.

I didn't mean anything I said to you the last time we talked to each other... or the times leading up to that day. I was repeating what Damien had drilled into me, but I hated myself with every word. I knew it was wrong, and yet I did it anyway because I thought he loved me, and I thought his love was what I wanted. What I needed. And because I was confused. I was always confused then—Damien made sure of it. I didn't know which way was up or what was my own idea or one Damien had suggested, what was my fault or his. You always saw through his bullshit, but I wasn't able to—at least not enough to walk away from him before he could really hurt me.

And he did really hurt me, Connie. I know this news won't surprise you, and you maybe don't even care anymore. I'm not even sure why I'm telling you this. But he did. That fight we had the day I claimed I slipped and fell in the bathroom? You were right—I didn't slip. Damien punched me. He was out of his mind with jealousy, and I don't know if he actually meant to or not that time. But he did. He told me that he didn't, and he was so damn convincing that I doubted my memory of what happened. That was only the first time. By the time I managed to leave him, my body was regularly covered in bruises. He regularly drugged and raped me. God, that's the first time I've put it that way and it sounds so horrible. I mean, that's what it was—but it's hard to think of it as rape. He was my fiancé, and I didn't fight him—I couldn't. Of course, I had fought him before he was drugging me, but he was stronger than me and it was futile. Damien always got what he wanted. Even so, the word rape is a hard one. It makes me uncomfortable. But Chad and Caroline are adamant about using that word for what he did to me.

Caroline's my closest friend. I met her earlier this year and we clicked right away. It reminds me of how you and I met and were best friends five minutes later. I think you'd like her—she reminds me of you in some ways. Chad... he's my boyfriend. And I know what you're probably thinking, but Chad's different. I've never met someone like him. You'd like him—you'd like him a lot. I'm sure of it. He's gentle and kind and thoughtful and funny. He's not controlling or jealous or violent. He's a baker—a really good one. That's actually how I met him. I got a job, the first one since I was fired from the journal, though I recently submitted a piece to the same journal and am hoping to work there again one day. I was so nervous to apply to this new job because I hadn't worked in so long and Damien had convinced me I was unemployable, but I did it anyway. You'd have been so proud of me. I went in and I did my best to hold my head high and have confidence in my ability to learn whatever I needed to. You always thought I was smart... maybe you were right. It's a café and I still work there. The owner is Chad's sister, Fern, who I think you'd like, too. She's Caroline's girlfriend. Caroline also works there, and Chad used to when I started.

He really is amazing, Connie. I wish you could meet him. I'd say he's way out of my league, but I know that would irritate you, so I won't. You really were always my staunchest defender. Thank you for that. If you hadn't been, I don't think I'd have ever found the strength to leave

Damien… or thought I was worth enough to deserve something better than the life I had with him. He worked hard to make sure I didn't think I deserved anything except what I had, what he did to me, but something in me refused to die completely and it's because of you. Thank you for loving me like you did until I turned my back on you.

It's a good thing I'm not actually going to give this to you. I've been writing for pages and am just now getting around to apologizing. I'm sorry for that, too, but nothing like the remorse I have for the things I said to you. For turning my back on our life-long friendship. I'm so, so sorry, Connie. More than sorry, but the English language doesn't have a better word to convey the depths of despairing regret and pain I feel, so sorry it is. I would ask your forgiveness, but I don't deserve that. Damien was abusing me, but that doesn't excuse me from my own actions. Just know that I would take it all back in a second if I could.

I miss you.

Thank you for always being there for me and loving me even when I was screwing up.

Love you, Cons.

I was home, getting ready for Chad to pick me up so we could head over to Fern and Caroline's. I'd just found out hours ago that both of my pieces had been accepted and would be published in the following month's edition of the journal. I still couldn't believe it; I buzzed with excitement. I hadn't wanted to have a party to celebrate it, but now I didn't mind that Caroline had insisted. Not much could bother me right then. I was too elated by the news. I'd received a second email ten minutes after the first, this one from Jeb, congratulating me on the acceptance and expressing a desire for me to continue to submit. I was thrilled, ecstatic, terrified. Again, I needed a word like bittersweet to describe this strange mix of emotions. Perhaps I could find a word in another language and use that. I should start looking when I couldn't find an appropriate word in English.

There was a knock on the door and I walked over to swing it open. As soon as I did, Chad engulfed me in his arms, lifting me off my feet and spinning me around.

"Congratulations, Rena! I'm so proud of you," he said into the hair over my ear. "I knew you could do it."

And he had. From the second I told him about what had happened, he'd had unwavering faith in my success. Much like Caroline, he'd spoken as if it were already a done deal. Turned out they'd been right; even so, I was still in shock about that after so many years of thinking I couldn't write anymore.

"Thank you," I said, hugging him back tightly. "I still can't believe it."

He set me down and cradled my face after tucking some hair back. "You will. In time, you'll know how amazing and talented you are." He kissed me with tenderness. "Because you really are, my Rena."

I smiled, biting the corner of my lip to try to rein it in. "Thank you," I whispered, giving his sides a squeeze.

He groaned and stepped back. "We don't have time for that—Caroline will kill me if we're late. She's got everything planned down to the minute we arrive."

"Oh god," I laughed. "I'm kind of scared."

He chuckled. "It's gonna be great, actually."

Chad spent the evening attached to my hip, introducing me to people I already knew, keeping everyone in stitches.

There was: "Hey—thanks for coming. Have you met my brilliant writer girlfriend, Renata? She's a brilliant writer. And she's my girlfriend."

And: "Don't forget to congratulate this amazing woman right here, the reason we're celebrating. Did you know she's the most talented writer in this hemisphere? It's one lucky man who gets to date her... oh, wait, that's me! I'm that lucky man."

Also: "May I present Renata Hayden, writer extraordinaire? You can save your applause for later. And, please, curb your jealousy that she's *my* date and not *yours*."

Within two hours of arriving, my sides were hurting, I'd cried a few times from laughing at his antics, and I had a permanent blush on my face. I felt heavily intoxicated, drunk on excitement and pride and feeling loved; no alcohol required. Caroline had managed to round up pretty much every person I'd so much as met since I'd gotten the job at the café for the celebration, and they all appeared to be genuinely excited for me. As the night wore on, I began to feel more confident in my ability to continue to write pieces that would be published.

After going to the bathroom at one point, I snuck into the kitchen and grabbed a seltzer from the fridge. Almost everyone there was at least tipsy except for Chad and me—we'd stuck to seltzer, as usual. We'd been there for hours, and I was exhausted. I'd worked the opening shift at the café that morning, then had the excitement from my submissions being accepted, so adding three and a half hours at a party on top of that was taking a toll.

The seltzer was cold and refreshing on my throat, which was dry from chatting for hours, and I closed my eyes, savoring the way the bubbles cascaded over my tongue and listening to the mixture of music and voices coming from the living and dining rooms. My eyelids lifted at a soft touch to the back of my hand—a soft, *familiar* touch. Chad's touch when he was running a single finger over my skin. I turned and smiled at him. His eyes, a thin brown ring just visible, danced and the corners of his lips twitched.

"I've got another one," he said.

"Oh, god, no," I laughed. "Please. We don't need another introduction line."

He chuckled. "Alright, I'll save it for the next party."

"Hopefully you'll forget it by then."

He lifted his eyebrows playfully. "I won't."

He trailed his finger delicately, leisurely up my forearm. When he reached the crease of my elbow, I shivered and broke out into goosebumps, my breath catching.

"Ready to go?" he asked, his voice low and seductive. The brown ring was gone.

"Yes. But I promised Caroline we'd stay until at least nine."

He lifted my hair over my shoulder away from my neck and kissed below my ear. "It's close enough," he said, his lips brushing my skin. "Let's go say bye and head out."

I sighed, smiling. "Okay, sounds good."

We found Caroline and Fern at the dining table in a heated game of Skip-Bo with several other party-goers.

"Don't go!" Caroline pleaded, hugging me. "It's so early still!"

Before I could reply, Chad did. "We can't stay out too late; we have to make a lot of dough still. We'll be up half the night at least."

Holding my breath and squeezing his hand, I tried desperately to keep a straight face at him using his new favorite euphemism for sex.

"Dough for what?" someone asked.

I lost it and exploded into laughter after that question. Caroline's face scrunched up for a second like I was crazy, and I tried to come up with a reason for my uncontrollable laughter, but every time I tried to speak, I laughed. I knew my face was red as a beet because it was on fire. Chad managed to keep a neutral face, yet I could see in his eyes and the twitching at the corners of his mouth that he was struggling not to laugh, too. I didn't even hear what he said in response to the question because I was laughing so hard.

"Please excuse my girlfriend here. Apparently her wild writing success has gone to her head or something," he said, setting off a new spurt of laughter in me. "Rena, dear, making dough is something I take very seriously, and you should, too."

Stemmed glass to her lips, Caroline's eyebrows shot up and white wine sprayed from her mouth. Luckily, she'd thrown up a hand and kept most of it from getting all over the table; instead, the majority ended up on her shirt.

"Seriously," Fern said in a voice between amusement and annoyance, "what the hell has gotten into you two?"

"Right?" Chad chimed in. "I just don't get it. Making dough isn't something to laugh at."

I caught Caroline's eye and we both dissolved into a fresh round of giggles until we were out of breath. We tried to compose ourselves, but failed each time we looked at each other, spurred on by Chad's expression of mock annoyance and confusion. Eventually, play resumed at the table, and Chad and I left. The second the door to their apartment was closed behind us, I broke into laughter again, now joined by Chad's rumbling chuckle.

"I can't believe you," I said, shaking my head.

He smirked and shrugged, obviously pleased with himself.

"I can't believe you did that, or that you managed to keep a straight face."

"That was hard, actually," he said. "Especially when Gary asked what the dough was for. But when I really almost lost it was when Fern was staring you and Caroline down while you were laughing. *That* was hilarious. I almost told her why you guys were losing it, but it's going to be so much more fun when she figures it out in like a year and remembers all the times she thought I was actually talking about baking."

"She's going to be so aggravated with you."

"And grossed out. It'll be great."

"You guys have an interesting relationship."

"Maybe. But it's ours, and we love it."

"I do, too," I said.

And I meant it; I loved the dynamic between Chad and Fern. If I'd had a sibling, I'd have wanted a relationship like theirs.

When we got back to Chad's apartment for the night—where we spent most nights together—there were three wrapped gifts on his coffee table.

"You didn't have to do that," I said when I saw them.

"Do what? Who said those are for you?"

I stared at him for a second, realizing I'd made an assumption.

"I was kidding, Rena love."

"Ooh," I said, distracted from the presents. "Rena love. I like that."

"Yeah?" he asked, his fingertips sliding up my arm and giving me goosebumps again.

"Yeah." I shivered.

"Okay," he said and kissed my cheek. "Now open your presents so we can make some dough, Rena love."

I laughed and lifted the smallest gift from the stack after sitting on the sofa; it was small enough that it fit in my hand.

"Open that one last."

I set it down and lifted the next one. I had a hunch what it was because it was shaped the same as the box of pencils he'd given me months earlier. When I opened it, I discovered I was both right and wrong. It was indeed a box of my favorite pencils, Blackwing 602s. But these were different because they were sunflower yellow-orange, my favorite color, and personalized with "Renata Hayden, Writer Extraordinaire." The largest present was a new notebook, which was a darker yellow-orange and had perfectly toothy paper, just the way I liked it for writing.

"You hate writing on your computer," Chad said. "So I thought you could use this for writing your first drafts of your pieces for the journal."

"You're the most thoughtful person on the planet, you know that?" I asked, leaning into him for a hug. I pulled back and gave him a hard kiss. "Thank you."

His finger moved along my hand. "I'm really proud of you, you know. I know I said a lot of stupid shit tonight for fun, but I *am* proud of you. I really do think you're amazing, Rena, and that you're an incredibly talented writer. And I seriously feel so lucky every day that I have you in my life."

I sniffled and stared up at the ceiling, willing my eyes to dry up. "Also the most romantic," I added. "And just so you know, I thank the universe all the time for having met you, too. I'm not glad I went through the things I have in my life, but I'm glad they led me to you."

We kissed for several minutes, and Chad pulled away just as he was about to peel my shirt off. "One more present first," he said, breathing hard.

"I can open it tomorrow," I replied, my breath as harsh as his.

He shook his head and placed the small box in my palm. "I can't wait that long. I've been wanting to give this to you for a while. It's not related to your writing, but I thought it was as good a time as any to give it to you. Mainly just because I couldn't wait any longer."

I narrowed my eyes at him, now intensely curious about what was in the box. I'd assumed it was something to do with writing after opening the pencils—maybe a pencil sharpener or something—but now I had no idea. Inside the wrapping paper was a small box, like a jewelry box, but for a necklace rather than a ring. Had he gotten me jewelry?

"Open it, please," he said with a nervous laugh. "You're just staring at it and it's killing me."

"Okay, okay. I was trying to guess first, but I'll just open it."

I lifted the lid of the box and my heart skipped. It wasn't jewelry. It was a key. My eyes shot to Chad's.

"It's the key to my apartment, Rena love. I know you have your apartment, and I'm not asking you to get rid of it or anything—you can decide and let me know when you feel ready to take that step for us to live together—but I want you to be able to come and go here whenever you want. It was my apartment before, but now it's home because of you. And my home is your home, Rena."

My heart stalled. Had anyone ever said something so beautiful to me before? I didn't think so. "Chad..." I said with my exhale. I wanted to tell him that I loved him, but that seemed so inadequate for how I felt. It was more like he'd become a part of me and filled in my cracks and missing pieces, making me whole and solid in a way I'd never been before. "I... more than love you... I *everything* you."

"I everything you, too, my Rena," he rumbled out, his voice huskier than I'd ever heard it.

He grasped behind my head and pulled me to him, kissing me hard. My arms wove around his neck and held him close, kissing him back just as fervently. His hands moved down and yanked off my blouse, then his own shirt. I loved watching his chest heaving, knowing I was doing that to him. He stood, grabbing my hand and tugging me to my feet and then behind him toward his bedroom. I followed, my heart beating out of my chest. This was the most assertive he'd been since that first time I'd gone numb, and it sent hormones raging through my bloodstream. His confidence and assertiveness about what he wanted was one of my favorite things about him, but it had been missing in the bedroom because of me... because of what Damien had done to me. But it had been a month since the first time we'd had sex, and nearly two weeks since the last time I'd gone numb.

He stopped inside the bedroom door and turned to me, his eyes scanning me for signs I wasn't okay. I stepped up against him, pressing against the hardness in his pants as I rested my hands over his bare chest.

"I'm good," I said, kissing the base of his throat. "And I *will* be good." I kissed him again, sucking gently this time and he groaned, his fingertips flexing harder into my hips.

"Rena..." he breathed out. His voice wavered with his struggle.

"Don't hold back," I whispered against the spot I'd just kissed, shifting against him. We both sucked in sharp breaths at the friction. "Please. That's what I want. You, as you are, unconcerned about me."

"But—"

"I'm good," I repeated, sucking lightly at the skin on his neck, knowing it drove him to the brink of madness. "At least, I *will* be once you stop holding back."

His chest rumbled with a sound akin to a low growl, and his fingers dug yet further into my hips. His body trembled. The want between us was so thick it was hard to breathe. I kissed his neck again, touching his skin with my tongue.

That did it. He clutched my head between his hands and crushed his mouth to mine. My fingers, frantic, fumbled to unbutton and unzip his jeans, and he turned to sit me on the bed. Faster than I'd have thought possible, my remaining clothes joined his on the floor, and he pushed me back further onto the mattress.

My heart skipped and thudded with anticipation; I had no idea what to expect, and for once, that thrilled me. He kissed me with passionate abandon, and I rocked my hips against him. His hand grasped my hip tightly, his other pushing under my chin to expose my throat. He kissed and sucked down the front of my neck and groaned. Shifting, he pushed inside me, moving quick and strong. His arms wound under me to grasp my shoulders from behind and hold me in place as he buried his face in my neck and moved deeply into me, grunting with effort against my skin with each thrust. There was no hesitation, the movements so much stronger than ever before, and it was exquisite, like at the top of each thrust was a merging between us.

I could feel my body building toward something I'd never experienced before, originating somewhere far inside me rather than between my legs; it felt my entire body was involved. My legs locked around his hips and small sounds I'd never made before escaped my throat with each movement.

"Oh, god, Rena," Chad ground out against the crook of my neck. Somehow his movements intensified in strength and frequency.

"Chad," I breathed out. I wasn't even sure what to say and couldn't speak, but I wanted him to know how I felt right then. But just then something inside exploded and I couldn't breathe, my whole body tightening and streaks of light flashing behind my eyelids. A strangled whimpering sound left my lips, and Chad made that growling sound deep in his chest again, pushing hard inside me until he stiffened.

I gasped in air, my body floating back down to earth, Chad doing the same, his body heavily resting on top of me. My body was vibrating everywhere and I could feel the rapid beating of his heart against my chest. He raised his head from the crook of my neck and dropped kisses all over my face between hot, moist bursts of breath.

"Are you okay?" he asked, a hint of worry in his voice.

I nodded rapidly, trying to form words. "Yes. God yes." A small giggle escaped. "Never better."

His hips thrust forward, pushing me up against his hands again, and then he kissed me hard. "Good, because we're not done yet."

Everything in my body clenched at his words, another pulse of ecstasy rippling through me. He rolled me over and moved behind me, his hands hot against my hips as he raised them up from the mattress. He pushed inside me again, and all the air rushed from my lungs. His mouth pressed against my spine as he moved, and it was almost too much, the contrast between the tenderness of his kiss and the power of his thrusting. It, like what had just transpired between us, was everything that was Chad; he was confident and full of conviction and assertive and tender and gentle and loving all at the same time. And now, for the first time, he was making love to me in the same way he loved me every other moment of the day.

It was late and I was sleepily draped across Chad's chest after making love. His heart beat steadily under my cheek and his fingertips skimmed over the scarred skin on my lower back. We'd been that way for a while, and I would soon doze off if he kept it up.

"I want to kill him," he said softly, his voice rumbling into my ear through his chest. I knew immediately he was talking about Damien. "Sometimes I have that thought and I know it's just anger. But sometimes I think I actually would if I saw him, and that scares me."

I swallowed, unsure how to respond. Sometimes I felt the same way, but I also didn't want Chad to be holding onto anger, let alone for something that had happened to *me*. "It's in the past," I said, pressing my palm into his chest like he did to me sometimes.

"I feel your skin and I try to imagine the kind of pain he caused you, but I can't, because I've never experienced something like the things he did to you. And it tears me apart because I want to take that away from you so it never happened."

"At least I'm stronger because of it."

"You shouldn't have to be."

"I know. But I am. I've thought about getting a tattoo over those scars. I always wanted a phoenix tattoo because of my name and losing both of my parents the way I did, but I never got one. I've thought about doing it on my back and having the scars incorporated into the tattoo for the ashes and the phoenix is rising out of them."

"That sounds beautiful."

"I think so, too. I'd never actually do it, though."

"Why not?"

"The same reason I never got one on my arm like I wanted: I'd look trashy."

"What makes you think that?"

I opened my mouth and froze for a second. "Damien," I whispered.

"Rena love... there's no such thing as trashy. People aren't trash—they're people. If you want a tattoo, I think you should get one."

"You wouldn't mind?"

"Why would I mind? You know I have tattoos."

He was right; I did. One of them was also a phoenix; he and Fern had gotten them together after their parents had died and after her battle with anorexia. Fern's was on her thigh and Chad's was on his forearm and bicep. I loved that tattoo of his, loved watching it move as his muscles worked when he was baking and when he was touching me.

I was quiet for a long time, thinking about how Damien had brainwashed me. I'd loved tattoos when I was younger, and my dad had even had several. I was planning to get one after graduating college, but just hadn't gotten around to it yet when I met Damien. Every negative thought I had about getting a tattoo had begun after that.

"This... what he's done to you psychologically... I want to hurt him."

"It's okay," I soothed. "It's not happening anymore."

"No, Rena, it's not okay," he said. His voice was still soft, his touch still gentle. "It will never be okay that you had to survive the things you did."

TWENTY-SIX

I was waiting for Chad to pick me up from my apartment. I'd just finished doing some light cleaning, watering Potty, and packing a suitcase. We, along with Fern and Caroline, had rented a cabin near some mountains for Thanksgiving, and we were supposed to be on the road soon. We'd be spending the better part of a week there, and we wouldn't be the only ones. Caroline's parents and brother were coming, as were several cousins Chad and Fern had, their partners and children, and a few out of town friends who didn't have family to spend the holiday with. They apparently rented a block of cabins every year for the holiday. I was eager to leave but Chad was running late. Which was unusual—Chad was always early or right on time. I decided to text him.

Everything okay? Do you need me to meet you at your place?

Yes, all fine, just waiting on Caroline; she decided after I got here that she needed to do more packing. :|

Sounds like Caroline! Do you want me to drive over there? I think I can leave my car in their visitor area for up to a week.

No, she's just about done now. We'll be there in twenty minutes or so.

I'll wait for you out front.

Impatient, are we?

No, just excited.

Ah – I see. You're antsy to go make dough in the woods ;)

I giggled and bit my lip. Seeing his words sent desire rippling through me. I couldn't wait to have his hands on me again. The way he touched me turned me on, yes, but it was more than that. I felt safe and powerful and feminine and cherished every time he touched me, even the simplest touches, like when he greeted me with a fingertip on the back of my hand.

Now I had sexual energy on top of the excitement and anxiety I already had over the trip and couldn't sit still. It would be another ten minutes or so before they arrived, and I decided to head down and wait outside. Maybe the cold, fresh air would cool me down; it was always awkward and a little embarrassing when there was sexual tension crackling between Chad and me when we were around other people. At least for me—Chad couldn't care less.

All in all, the four of us were close, and I was very much looking forward to our five days away, despite being nervous about meeting all these people who'd known them longer and who were really important to them. I wanted to make a good impression and be accepted into their friend-slash-family group. Especially as Chad's girlfriend. Surely they'd be making comparisons between his ex and me—how could they not?—and I just hoped I didn't fall short in their eyes.

I stepped outside into the bitter cold air and draped my coat over my suitcase. Despite the temperature outside, my body was still on fire after Chad's text message. I leaned against the low retaining wall outside the building and sighed contentedly, closing my eyes and listening to the rustle of leaves in the breeze. I was glad that, even though it wasn't a very nice building or in a very nice part of town, my apartment was close enough to the preserve that I could hear it when I stepped outside if there was even a moderate breeze.

The hair on the back of my neck prickled and I forced myself to keep breathing. I'd been feeling that way for months and nothing had happened. I was sure at this point that it was just me. But I was also rarely out front alone because Chad always came to the building to get me and walked me up when he brought me home. Sometimes, when I was running and he was off work, he even accompanied me to the preserve. He didn't like running that much, but he would run for a bit with me, then walk around while I finished, at which point we'd meet up to go back to my apartment together.

Easy, Renata. You're safe. Words I needed to speak to myself less often, but that I'd practically chanted as soon as I woke every day for months after I left Damien. The frequency had tapered off and now I almost never needed them—at least not to say to myself. Chad was so attuned to me that he noticed before I did when I was getting anxious or scared, and his touch communicated the words to me. His finger moving down my hand, his fingertips on my lower back, his palm over my heart or cupping my cheek. Those were touches that told me he was there and I was safe and reminded me to breathe. I could have used his touch right then to ground me. My words in my mind weren't helping at all; I needed Chad.

I heard footsteps nearby and opened my eyes... then froze.

"It's too cold not to be wearing your coat, babe," Damien said.

He stood in front of me, looking the same as he always had: clean-cut, polished, put together. Handsome. Charming. His voice had that same magnetic quality, too. My stomach turned.

"Wh-why are you here?" I stammered out. I felt dizzy and like my body was lit with electric wires.

"For you, of course." He gestured between us, stepping closer. "For us."

I jumped to my feet and stepped away from him. "There is no 'us,' Damien. There hasn't been in—"

"Over a year, Renata. Over a year. I never would have let you go if I'd known you'd be gone that long."

He pulled his hand out of his coat pocket and I jumped back.

"Still jumpy, I see. You always were."

No, I wasn't—you made me that way.

"I'm not going to hurt you, babe. I love you. I just have your ring for you." He held out my old engagement ring.

"I don't want it," I gritted out. I was furious—not only that he was trying to put his engagement ring back on my finger, but also because I *hated* that ring and everything it stood for. I hated it as soon as he bought it because of what he did with my mother's ring.

"Don't be petty, Renata. It's yours. What am *I* gonna do with it?"

"I don't care what the hell you do with it!" I shouted.

He stared at me. His face barely changed its pleasant expression except for the hardening of his eyes. I recognized that hardening and I knew what it meant. He was about to lose his temper. I eyed my purse sitting next to my suitcase, which had my keys to get into my apartment building in the pocket. Because I'd backed up, it was now closer to Damien than it was to me. There was no way I could get to it before him. I began edging away, mentally mapping a route away from him in the preserve—one with plenty of turns so I could disappear without being seen. I might be able to make it to the hidden clearing before he could catch me.

Maybe.

"Are you thinking about running, Renata?" He tsked in disappointment. "You aren't fast enough to outrun me, babe, remember?"

I froze, staring at him, my stomach bottoming out at what I suddenly understood. "That's why you made me stop running," I whispered. "I always thought it was because of the way I looked, because that's what you said, but it was because you needed me weak and slow."

"There you go again, babe, making me out to be something I'm not. I didn't make you stop running. You chose to do that. You *chose* to give it up for us. Remember? You wanted to look sexy for me and we never had enough time together, so you decided to stop. I never made you do that, or anything else. That was your own decision. I pointed out that running took a lot of time and that it was what made your legs so muscular, but I didn't decide you should stop running. You did. Remember? You even got into a fight with Connie about it because she thought you were being stupid, because she didn't understand how much we loved each other. You do remember that, don't you?"

I smashed my fingertips into the space between my eyes; my head was spinning and I felt like I was sinking underwater. I *did* remember that fight with Connie. I remembered telling her I didn't like running that much anymore, that I wanted to be with Damien more, that I wanted to have a sexier, more feminine physique. I did say all those things. But they hadn't come from me.

"No, Damien, that's not right. I stopped because you made me stop. You made me feel like running was hurting you, and hurting our relationship, and like if I didn't stop it was because I wasn't committed enough to you."

"Renata, I didn't make you feel anything. That's how you felt all on your own. I simply made observations."

I shook my head. "No, Damien, that's not how—"

"You even threw out all your cross-country medals because you said it was part of your old life, and that you were starting a new life with me and you didn't need them anymore."

Again, it was true. But it wasn't because I wanted to. It was because Damien told me I was too stuck in the past from before my dad died and that I needed to purge things from that time in my life so I could move on and just focus on my new life with him.

"And—"

"Stop!" I shouted, knowing the interruption would make him angrier. "Just... stop."

Tears hot on my cheeks, I covered my face with my hands in a bid to hide what was happening. Doing so was a big mistake. Damien's steel grip circled my wrists.

"Don't touch me," I growled as he forced my hands down and held them between us, my disgust muffled by my tears. I tried to pull away, but it was futile—he was so much stronger than I was.

"Oh, babe, I hate seeing you like this. If you hadn't left, this wouldn't be happening right now. But I still love you and I forgive you. We'll just put this period in our lives behind us and pretend it never happened. I'm willing to do that for you. But you can't ever do something like this again. If you do, I'm liable to lose my mind and do something crazy to get you back. I could end up hurting you by accident, or that pathetic asshole who thinks he could ever love you like I do."

"Get the fuck away from me, you bastard!"

Damien glanced around us as if he were looking at the trees and the sky, just taking the day in, but I knew better now. He was looking for people. And I knew there were none. He turned back to face me and his grip on my wrists tightened. I ground my teeth together, refusing to show how much he was hurting me; it felt my hands would separate from my arms. He wrapped my arms behind me and pulled down hard. Pain shot through my shoulders, the sockets straining, and it forced my back to arch. He hovered barely an inch over my face.

"Don't talk to me like that, Renata," he said. He sounded calm, but I knew it was an act. "I'm already pissed off that you left, and it took me so long to find you. And I'm even more pissed off that when I did, you were having a fling with some lowlife baker. A kitchen worker, Renata? It's insulting that you'd try to replace me with someone who couldn't hack it in a *real* job. How the hell do you think he'll support you, huh? Because we both know you couldn't keep a job if your life depended on it, so that little café job you have isn't going to last. What then? That money you stole from me won't last forever."

"I didn't steal a damn thing from you. That was *my* money from my dad."

"No, Renata, that was *my* money, because I spent more than that on you after you became unemployed and couldn't support yourself anymore."

"I hate you."

He pulled down harder on my arms, and his eyes flashed angrily before falling to roam over me. The way he was holding me left my breasts pushed into the air and my throat exposed. I felt disgusting, like there was slime dumped on me as his gaze raked my body.

"You're dressed for attention again, babe. If it's attention you want, it's attention you'll get."

He smashed his mouth to mine and I tried to turn away, but at the angle he had me pinned, I couldn't. I could feel my teeth cutting into my lips as I fought to keep them closed.

"Rena?" Chad's voice rang out through the air.

He was coming up from behind Damien and wouldn't be able to see that I was being held in place; he maybe couldn't even see it was me there at all. Damien pulled back and released my hands, his eyes flashing. He spun before I'd found my voice.

"The fling," he said.

"He is *not* a fling, you asshole," I said, rubbing my wrists and moving carefully around Damien. I wasn't sure if he would let me or not and wanted to be ready in case he reached out for me again. With every step further from Damien and closer to Chad, more relief flooded through me.

"Who the hell is this?" Chad asked. However, by the look on his face, he already knew.

I hesitated. If I admitted it, I was afraid of what might happen after what he'd told me the night of my celebration party, that he might do something to Damien that came with serious, legal consequences.

"H-he's no one," I stammered. "Let's go."

"No one, Renata? That's not a very nice thing to say about the man you're engaged to."

"I am *not* engaged to you," I bit out.

"Then why are you wearing my ring?" he asked, raising his eyebrows innocently.

I looked down and my old engagement ring was on my finger. I'd noticed him putting it on me when he had my arms pinned, but had forgotten in my focus on tracking his modd and trying to edge away. I pulled it off and threw it at him.

"Rena—" Chad started.

"Rena is such a cheapening of her name. *Renata* is my—"

"I'm not your anything, Damien!" I screamed.

The instant his name was out of my mouth, I could feel the energy in the air tense further, Chad having confirmation of who I was arguing with.

"*Damien.*" Chad's face scrunched in some combo of disgust and rage I'd never seen on him before. He moved toward Damien but halted when I grabbed his arm.

"Please," I whispered. "Please, Chad. Let's just go, okay? Please let's go. He wants to make you mad."

Chad's eyes moved to Damien for a second before returning to me. He appeared undecided.

"I'm the one who should be mad, Renata. You broke your promises to me, babe."

"She's not your babe," Chad ground out, his body tensed and hard, all his focus now on Damien. "You're pathetic. You think it makes you strong to manipulate women? To prey on them and control their lives? You think beating up a woman makes you strong? You're nothing but a weak, worthless piece of shit."

I rested my palms against Chad's chest, hoping desperately it would calm him down. I could feel his anger ramping up with every word he spat at Damien, just as I could feel Damien's rage building behind me at being insulted.

Chad glanced down at me, and his face softened slightly. He wrapped an arm around me, holding me to him protectively.

"*I'm* worthless and pathetic?" Damien said. "*You're* the one who can't hack it in a real job that doesn't leave you smelling like shit every day. No one respects someone like you. Is that why you're going after the used property of another man? She—"

"Fuck you," Chad growled, his arm around me tightening at the used property comment. The words made vomit track up my throat. Damien's jaw clenched—he didn't like being interrupted—but Chad continued. "Nothing you say will make you any more of a man. I pity you for thinking it will."

Damien was talking again, but I couldn't hear him anymore. My heart was hammering so hard it was the only sound in my ears. But something in Chad had shifted; he'd gone from ready to fight Damien to determinedly ignoring him, his eyes steady on me. He grabbed my suitcase and turned our backs to Damien, his arm still firmly around me as he steered us toward the parking lot.

When we got to Chad's SUV, he opened the back and loaded in my suitcase while Fern and Caroline fired off questions asking what took so long and if we were okay. I couldn't have spoken if I wanted to, and Chad ignored them, providing only a curt, "Not now." With the back of the car closed, Chad pulled me into his arms. I huddled against his chest, wanting to shrink down and hide away from everything that had just happened. Then, my entire body began to tremble and all the fear that had taken a backseat during the encounter washed over me. I pushed back, hunching over and dry-heaving. Chad's hand rested on my back with a gentle pressure and he spoke to me in a soothing murmur. I couldn't understand anything he was saying though; I could only hear the hum of his voice. When the nausea passed, I broke down, sobbing in the parking lot. Chad leaned back against the car and held me until I began to shiver uncontrollably from the cold. Out of nowhere, I was frozen to the bone.

"We have to get inside, Rena love," he murmured against the top of my head.

I straightened up, wiping my face with my palms and taking a shaky breath. Chad pushed my hair from my face, then held my cheeks gently between his hands, his thumbs smoothing rhythmically over my skin. He touched his lips to my forehead, holding them there for several seconds.

"Are you okay?" he asked.

"Yeah. I'm okay," I replied quietly.

"Are you sure?"

"I mean..." I looked into his eyes, his beautiful, hazel eyes that were clear and softened with worry and sadness. "I'm not, but I am."

"What can I do right now?"

"This," I whispered. "You're doing it."

TWENTY-SEVEN

We spent hours at the police station before we ever made it out of Amestown. Despite my promises to go after we got back to town—I didn't want to make everyone late—Chad, Fern, and Caroline had all refused to leave until it was done. Before they even knew everything that happened, they agreed that if Damien was there, I needed to go to the police right away.

I'd clung to Chad's hand for dear life the entire time we were there. I stuttered and clammed up, then cried, over and over, trying to explain why I needed a restraining order against Damien when I had no proof he'd ever done anything to me. Even the things I had to go to the hospital for, there was some story that excused Damien from all blame that was given to the doctors and nurses. There was no reason for anyone to believe me, and I was acutely aware of that fact the entire time. However, we'd been lucky.

There were two police officers who listened. One, maybe ten years older, who was obviously bored, but the other one, who looked easily thirty or forty years older, listened attentively. When I was finished speaking, he said they could request an emergency protective order that would be effective immediately, but it would only last for a few days. He explained and wrote down instructions for how to file for a permanent protective order, what the stages were to obtaining it, and the timing for each. Lastly, he wrote down a phone number and handed it to me, looking me steadily in the eye.

"If you need any help with filing or this asshole comes back or you just don't feel safe, you can call me. I don't care if you just need someone to walk you to your car. I always have this cell on me."

"Thank you," I said. "This is..." I teared up and my voice cracked. I couldn't believe he'd taken everything I said at face value, that he believed me without knowing me, without any proof. "Thank you."

He reached out and patted my hand, giving me a sad, kind smile. Chad shook his hand and thanked him, and we were, at long last, en route to the mountains for our holiday getaway.

Much as I had in the police station, I clung to Chad's hand as we headed out of our cabin toward the much larger one a few cabins down. Because of the detour to the police station, we'd barely had time to unpack the car and freshen up after several hours on the road before it was time for dinner. On the drive, they'd explained to me that dinner was always in the largest cabin the first night and on Thanksgiving, and that otherwise it rotated by cabin. Our cabin, which consisted of the four of us as well as Caroline's parents and brother, would be feeding everyone on the last night. I'd received a rundown of everyone who was going to be there, what they looked like, and how they fit into the picture—if they were family or friend and of who—as well as key tidbits to know about them. By the time we were walking out of the cabin, though, I remembered very little of what they'd said; it was just a jumble of names I didn't know. I was afraid of messing up and calling someone by the wrong name and offending them, or getting someone's job mixed up with someone else's, or any other number of things. I didn't want to upset anyone or embarrass myself or anyone else.

On the front porch, Chad pulled me to a stop, facing me, and placed his palm on my chest. "Breathe, Rena love," he murmured, then kissed my forehead.

I took a deep breath. We were supposed to go eat, but I felt sick. And exhausted. I just wanted to be back in Chad's apartment wrapped up in his arms on the sofa and to forget about meeting all these new people... and forget about having encountered Damien only hours earlier.

He studied my face, his forehead creased. "We don't have to go. I can go grab us some food and bring it back here or we can ask Fern or Caroline to, but we don't have to go over there. We can stay here. What do you want to do?"

His offer sounded amazing, but I didn't want to have everyone's first impression of me be that I was needy and kept Chad from his family and friends; it was bad enough I'd caused Chad, Fern, and Caroline to be late arriving. "We can go."

"I know we *can*. But what do you *want* to do?"

I looked away and my eyes flooded. "I want to go back to yesterday and have packed then and spent the night with you so I wouldn't have seen Damien today."

His fingertips brushed my cheek as he tucked my hair behind my ear. "He'd have found you either way, I'm afraid."

"I know. But at least it maybe would have been after this trip so I wasn't causing so many issues for you guys."

"You're not causing issues, Rena."

"You guys coming or what?" Fern shouted with her hands cupped around her mouth; she and Caroline were almost to the big cabin.

I looked up at Chad and gave him a nod, but he looked over at Fern and shouted, "No—bring us some food when you come back."

Fern flashed two thumbs up, then turned to head up the driveway to the big cabin with Caroline.

"Chad—it's okay, really," I said quickly.

"Rena love," he said, cupping my cheek. "I can tell it's not. And it's okay that it's not. It's okay to ask for what you need. And what you need is to not be in a big crowd of rowdy strangers for the next few hours."

We ended up changing our clothes and going for a hike behind the cabins. For a while we walked in silence, hand-in-hand, and the physical activity in the crisp, cold air was refreshing. There were patches of snow that hadn't melted yet from a snowfall a few days earlier that dotted the otherwise brown, red, and burnt orange landscape; it was rather picturesque, and the quiet beauty helped dissolve the anxiety that had been ramped up since that morning.

"Why did you lie to me about who he was?" Chad asked after we'd been walking for a half hour or so.

I swallowed and my anxiety flared right back up. "I was afraid of what you might do if you realized it was him after what you told me the other week."

"You're concerned about his safety?"

"No, it's not that. I'm worried about you doing something that could get you arrested or worse."

He was quiet for a minute or two, then let out a loud breath. "I wanted to. I saw red when I heard his name and realized who was standing there. I wanted to hurt him, Rena. I wanted to hurt him so bad. But you grabbed my arm, and when I looked at you, I could see my future in your eyes. I could see us growing old together. And I realized in that instant that I'd be giving up the ability to have that future with you if I killed him. I couldn't do it. Maybe that makes me weak. I don't know. But I couldn't do it."

"I think it makes you strong to be able to stop yourself, not weak."

"Maybe. Though when he called you his used property, I almost lost it. I had to keep my eyes on *you* because if I looked up at *him*, I would have gone after him and I wouldn't have stopped until... I don't know if I would have killed him or not, but maybe." He sighed. "Why did you have his ring on?"

Anger flared through my chest thinking about that ring. "He tried to give it to me and I wouldn't take it, I told him I didn't want it and I didn't care what he did with it. He... I knew better than to let my guard down at all, but he said these things and I couldn't think clearly and then I started crying and when I did, he grabbed me. He held my wrists behind me and forced it on my finger while he was holding me there and threatening me. I forgot until he said something." I swallowed again. "I hate that fucking ring," I snapped. "I *hate* it. I never wanted it. I had..." my voice cracked and tears made their way down my cheeks. "I had my mother's engagement ring that I wore on my right hand. I never took it off. It was all I had from her, since she died when I was a baby. My dad wasn't there to give it to someone to use to propose to me or anything, but I always wanted that to be my engagement ring if I got married one day. And if I didn't, and I didn't have kids, I was going to pass it down to Connie's kids, assuming she had some."

"Let me guess," Chad said, his voice hard, when I went silent. "Damien didn't care."

"Worse—it pissed him off. He thought it was the most ridiculous thing he'd ever heard, and when I told him I was serious, he got mad.

I told him I wouldn't marry someone who didn't want me to use my mother's ring. He convinced me that I was being unfair and not allowing him to show me he loved me the way he wanted to. He tried to convince me to get rid of the ring when he had me get rid of everything else from my past, but I wouldn't. Eventually, we agreed that he could get it resized for me so that I could wear it on my middle finger on my right hand; he said that would make it seem less like an engagement ring, which doesn't make any sense for so many reasons, but he was always so convincing. He even offered to take it to the jeweler's for me. I never saw it again. He said the jeweler lost it, but I know they didn't. He probably threw it away. I don't know. But every time I looked at that hideous engagement ring, all I could think about was my mother's ring that I should have been wearing. I hated it."

"What did it look like?"

"Which one?"

"Your mom's."

"It was simple and small. It was rose gold with a thin rounded band and a single small square diamond in the middle, with two tiny diamonds on each side set into the band, like a triangle pointing away from the central diamond. It had a matching wedding band that had the same triangles, with three tiny diamonds like the ones on the sides where the large central diamond would have been, but it was lost when the house was packed up after my dad died. The engagement ring was engraved on the inside of the band with the date my parents met—the date my dad said he fell in love with her."

"That sounds beautiful, Rena."

"It was," I agreed, sniffling. My thoughts wandered, running back through the encounter with Damien. "He knows things about you," I said. "I didn't tell him anything, but he knew what you looked like, and he knows you're a baker."

I could feel Chad tense beside me. "I'm not surprised. He found you outside your apartment."

"And he knows I work at the café."

"You said you didn't live in Amestown before, right?"

"That's right. I mean, I grew up in Amestown before my dad died, in the neighborhood on the north side of the preserve, but not since. I was living in Sutterton before I moved here, about eight months before I started working at the café. Damien knew I grew up here, but that's it. He didn't like me talking about my life before him."

"What a bastard," Chad muttered. I was fairly certain there wasn't a name he hadn't called Damien at this point.

We returned to the cabin in silence, each of us lost in our thoughts. We found two plates of food covered in foil on the table and a scribbled note about what was happening at which cabin for the evening in case we decided to venture out. Chad read the note, then suggested I take a shower while he got a fire going.

With my hair in a messy bun on the top of my head, I stood in the hot water for a long time, letting it beat the feeling of filth off me that I hadn't been able to shake since seeing Damien. When I emerged at last, I was more tired than anything else. Chad was sitting on the sofa, lost in thought, and I watched him, thinking about how different he and Damien were, wishing I'd met him first.

Chad looked up when I walked over and smiled at me, this one reaching his eyes like usual. I loved watching his eyes when he looked at me—they revealed so much. My favorite were moments like this, when his thoughts had been elsewhere and then he looked at me. I could see the softening of his features, the light wrinkling near his temples, the slight shift in how much of the brown in his eyes was exposed, making them appear to be changing color. I'd never seen his eyes do quite the same thing with anyone else. The closest was Fern; his expression also softened when he looked at her, and even when he looked at Caroline. I knew that change was when he felt love toward whoever he was looking at, one of those subconscious tells he had no idea happened. But that was what I loved about it; it wasn't intentional, but a reaction to seeing me.

Love was his reaction to seeing me.

I snuggled into the comforting warmth of his side and he wrapped the arm he'd lifted around me. We shifted until we were comfortably lounging, and he lifted a hand and kissed my palm. As he was setting it back down on his chest, however, he paused before lifting it again, holding it close to his face.

"Oh, Rena," he whispered, his fingertips running faintly over my wrists. I'd seen in the shower that they were both bruising. "Does it hurt?"

I sighed. "Yeah. It's sore on both of my wrists. But it'll be fine in a few days. The bruises will last a couple of weeks, but it should only really hurt for a few days—definitely less than a week."

He carefully kissed my bruised skin. "I hate that you know that," he whispered.

Chad replaced my hand on his chest, then reached behind us and flipped off the lamp so the only light was coming from the fireplace. I let out a sigh and my body relaxed into his.

"I'm scared. I know he won't just leave me alone after today."

"I know," he replied just as softly as I'd spoken. "We'll go together to get the protective order on Monday when the General District Court is open again."

"We both have to work on Monday."

"I'm taking the day off. I already called Randy while you were in the shower and explained things to him. And Fern won't expect you to work until this is taken care of."

I nodded against his chest and his fingers skimmed along the length of my spine. "I'm afraid he's going to hurt you, too," I added. "When we were together, he used to tell me he'd kill anyone who ever touched me."

"I remember you telling me."

"And when I left him, he threatened to kill me and anyone who came near me if I did. I'm scared he's actually going to do it."

Chad's chest rose and fell under me after having stalled and tensed.

"I won't let that happen," he said. "I promise."

I didn't know how he could promise something like that, but I realized that I believed him. I nodded again and pressed a kiss to his chest, feeling sleepy. "I love you," I murmured against him, my eyes closed.

His arm tightened ever-so-slightly around me. "I love you, too, my Rena."

TWENTY-EIGHT

Chad and I were the first to rise the next morning. He made us coffee, which we shared together under a blanket on the front porch in the stillness of the bitterly cold air. It had snowed the night before, and everything was dusted in white, disturbed only by animal tracks; deer, rabbits, and foxes, Chad said. After finishing our coffee, we walked in to find Fern awake and getting herself a cup of coffee.

"Good morning," she said in a hushed voice. She was smiling, but she looked tired.

"Late night?" Chad asked.

"Yeah." She yawned, stretching. "Skip-Bo tournament took half the night." She let out a small laugh.

"Who won?"

"Who do you think?"

"He shouldn't be allowed to play," Chad said with a chuckle. Then he turned to me. "Our cousin, Adam, always wins at Skip-Bo. *Always*."

"Even when he's drunk," Fern added. "And he was totally sloshed last night. So annoying. But Caroline made him sweat a bit. She's gotten really good." She looked at me and tilted her head. "You're good at it, too. You might be able to beat him."

"Uh-uh." There was no way I wanted to usurp their cousin's title.

"You have to try, Renata," Fern persisted. "It's crap that he wins every year. We can have another tournament this week and you can play in this one. Someone needs to beat him. He's more arrogant than ever."

I laughed, shaking my head again. "No, thank you. I don't want to meddle in your family's dynamics."

"It's all in good fun. Adam's a sore loser, but he'd eventually forgive you for beating him." Fern winked. "Besides, you're part of this family now, too."

My chest warmed at the thought of being considered part of their family, and I glanced at Chad to gauge his reaction to what Fern had said.

He shrugged at me. "It's all true. She just forgot to mention that Adam is a bit of a dick."

Fern rolled her eyes at Chad, then yawned again and held up her coffee mug. "I have a feeling I'm going to need a constant stream of this stuff today. But you guys look pretty well rested. What did you do yesterday?"

We told her we'd gone for a walk, then hung out by the fire before eating the food she'd left for us and going to bed early.

"I was really tired after yesterday," I said.

Fern's brow creased. "I can imagine. How are you feeling this morning?"

I took the time to check in with myself before answering her. How *was* I feeling? I still felt a bit drained—sleep interrupted by nightmares would do that—but nothing like the day before. The coziness of the cabin and being there with them filled me with a sense of warmth and safety, and made what happened with Damien feel far away. Especially after having Chad's gentle calm to soothe and reassure me after each nightmare the night before.

"Pretty good," I said, smiling.

"That's good," Fern replied. Then she smirked. "Because everyone's dying to meet you, and I expect they'll all be coming over here looking for breakfast over the next couple of hours in part so they can."

My heart rate picked up and I glanced up at Chad again for reassurance. He provided it in the form of a smile and fingertips on my lower back.

"I guess we should start cooking, then," he said.

By the time Chad and I had pulled out the ingredients for biscuits, bacon, and eggs, Caroline and her family were up, and we went through a round of introductions. It was striking how much alike Caroline, her mother, and her brother were; not only did they look almost identical, but they had the same mannerisms and friendly, effusive personalities. Her father was quieter, an observer, but appeared to dote on his wife and children, and to also adore Fern and Chad. I imagined that's how my parents would have been if they were alive; not the exact personalities, but the affection and love they obviously had for each other and the people their children loved. Rather than being more nervous, meeting them set me at ease. It felt like I fit seamlessly into the group in our cabin, Caroline's family greeting me with hugs and accepting me into their fold with warmth.

"Breathe, Rena love," Chad whispered into my ear before kissing my cheek.

I let out the breath I hadn't realized I'd been holding. It wasn't that I was upset; it's that I felt so wonderful right then that I was having a difficult time not crying over the food I was making. I looked at him with gratitude, but he was back to focusing on the biscuit dough. I was at the stove working on the bacon and eggs.

When he glanced up and caught my eye, I mouthed "thank you."

He mouthed back "I love you."

"I love you, too," I mouthed in return.

"You guys are so cute," Caroline said, reaching next to me for the coffee pot to pour herself another cup.

"You're welcome," Chad said.

I snorted and Caroline rolled her eyes. "I said you guys, as in both of you together," she said.

"Yup, and that's because of what I'm bringing to the table," Chad replied. "And that's all the cute."

"I mean, look at him, can you blame the guy?" Caroline's brother called out.

"Don't encourage him, Brandon," Caroline retorted.

"Brothers gotta look out for each other, right?" Chad asked.

"That's right, brother," Brandon called out.

"You both know you aren't actually brothers, don't you?" Caroline asked.

"We're not?" Chad and Brandon said at the same time, affecting a tone of shock.

"Oh, lord, it's going to be a long day," Fern chimed in, rolling her eyes.

"Bacon's about to burn, Rena," Chad called out.

I startled from my near-trance of watching and listening to everyone interact to realize my bacon was, in fact, in danger of burning. Chad's back was to the stove; it was like he had a sixth sense when it came to food; he always knew when it was ready.

"How do you *do* that?" I mumbled.

"I'm just that good," Chad responded.

I laughed. I hadn't thought he could hear me. When I looked over at him, he was watching me and winked. I bit my cheeks and his eyes darkened. My heart and my body reacted to the way he was looking at me and I let my eyes fall. When I did, they landed on his hands skillfully working the biscuit dough into a consistent thickness. I watched as they lowered a biscuit cutter into the dough, then lifted the round disc off the counter. His fingers deftly popped the disc out and placed it on a cookie sheet. I knew what it was like for his fingers to touch my body in that way. I lifted my gaze and it collided with his again. His eyes were darker still, and the corners of his mouth were twitching.

"Eggs," he said, tilting his head toward the stove.

I turned back to what I was supposed to be doing after taking a second to think about how sexy it was when he did that, and the time it took made the eggs overcook. "Shit, shit, shit," I mumbled, rushing to get them out of the pan before they cooked any more. Too late—I couldn't serve them.

As I set the pan back down on the stove—sans eggs—Chad stepped up beside me.

"I'll eat those," he said, tilting his head toward the plateful of overcooked eggs. "Just set them aside for me—don't throw them out."

"But they're overcooked," I said. "You said eggs are one of the worst things to overcook."

"They are," he agreed, "but these are going to be the best overcooked eggs I've ever had."

I deadpanned at him.

"You know why?"

"Why?"

"Because I know they were overcooked because you were distracted thinking about my hands on you."

My face flamed and I glanced around, hoping no one was within hearing distance. He cupped my face, turning me to face him, then kissed me.

"I was thinking about the same thing," he said. He turned and walked back to the other counter where he was making biscuits. "By the way," he said casually, smirking, "you've got some flour on your face."

I hadn't even noticed he'd touched me with his flour and dough covered hands, but sure enough, I could see in my reflection in the microwave door that there was flour on my cheek. I used my apron to wipe it off, laughing, then turned back to the stove to start another batch of eggs and turn the bacon.

Once people from the other cabins began to arrive, the flow didn't stop. Our cabin was overflowing, people filling their plates with food and holding them to eat wherever they could find space to stand. Overall, they were a rowdy, playful group and I got the impression that they loved having someone new there, a rare attraction. Caroline had whispered into my ear after shooing people away from the kitchen when she was making more coffee, assuring them they'd get to meet me later, that they liked having something new to talk about.

After what felt like days, it was thankfully time to stop cooking. Chad had finished baking a while earlier and hung out cooking eggs and bacon with me. It didn't require two people, but I was grateful that he'd stuck around and that he hadn't insisted I go out and mingle. Just the number of people alone for me to meet was intimidating. When the last of the bacon and eggs came off the stove, I wished I could go outside for a while to cool off and clear my mind before meeting everyone. Breakfast had been chaos, but we couldn't put it off any longer.

I was acutely aware of everyone's eyes watching us interact as Chad reached his arms around me to untie my apron and pull it off, pressing a kiss to my lips as he did. His eyes were dancing and he was noticeably giddy.

"Ready?" he murmured as he folded my apron and set it on the counter.

"As ready as I'm going to be," I replied.

"They're all going to love you," he said, running a finger down my hand. "And even if they didn't, it doesn't matter, because *I* do."

I blushed and bit the corner of my lip, trying not to grin like an idiot. He bent and kissed the crook of my neck, then turned, an arm around my waist, and stepped us toward the living and dining area. Some people were eating, some chatting, but it felt that all eyes were on us, waiting.

"Finally!" a woman shouted, and laughter—including Chad's—rippled through the room.

"Everyone," he said when the laughter had quieted down. "I'd like you to meet Renata, my talented, famous—"

I groaned.

"—gorgeous, amazingly brilliant writer—"

A few whistles rang out from somewhere and the blush I already had turned into flames engulfing my face.

"*—girlfriend*," Chad finished, chuckling. "Besides, she's way out of your league."

"Mine or Josh's?" someone shouted, sending a wave of laughter through the crowd.

"Both of you," he replied.

"What about yours?" the same person called out.

Chad laughed. "Oh, *definitely*."

I shook my head, laughing, but I was also ready to be done with being on display.

"Famous, huh?" someone said from my right.

I turned, shaking my head again. "No, I'm not famous. Chad is completely making things up."

"No, I'm not," Chad chimed in. "You're published."

"He's got a point," the man who's name I didn't know yet said.

"I'm not published like... J.K. Rowling or Colleen Hoover or something. I've got a few short stories in a journal."

The man shrugged. "I think that counts."

"See, Rena?" Chad said, the corners of his mouth twitching again. "I told you you're famous. And Josh agrees, so it must be true."

Josh held out his hand and I took it. "Nice to meet you... Renata? Rena? Which is it?"

"Renata," I replied.

"Rena is just for me," Chad added, wriggling his eyebrows.

Josh chuckled and leaned around me; he and Chad embraced. "Good to see you, man," he said. "And thanks for breakfast. Those biscuits were the best yet."

Chad winked. "Rena and I are *really* good at making dough together."

My eyes widened in shock; I couldn't believe he'd just said that here of all places. I burst out laughing.

Josh's eyebrows drew in and he smiled, then looked at Chad with an expression that clearly said, "what's with her?"

Chad shrugged, his lips really twitching now. "I don't know, every time I talk about making dough with her, this happens. It might be some obscure medical condition where she has to laugh every time she hears that phrase."

I could barely breathe because I was laughing so hard, and Chad's affected nonchalant exterior broke; he began laughing with the last word he spoke. Josh looked a little confused but didn't seem to be bothered by it.

Josh looked at Chad. "She's going to fit right in here."

"That's high praise coming from him," Chad whispered into my ear as Josh responded to a question from someone else. "He gets along with just about everyone, but he doesn't actually *like* most people. He hated Lilith right away."

Over the next hour, I met everyone except Adam, the cousin who always won at Skip-Bo. He was apparently sleeping off his hangover from the night before. I was ready for bed by lunchtime, but I did feel much better about being there. Everyone was laid back and cheerful like Chad, Fern, and Caroline were, and I felt welcomed by all of them. Several asked me how I was doing or commented that they were sorry about my ex, and I discovered that Fern had shared with everyone the full reason we'd been late and that Chad and I hadn't joined in the night before. I wasn't sure what to think when I first realized that, but became more comfortable with the idea as the day wore on.

I was accustomed to keeping things like that to myself—it had been necessary for so many years, both from Damien and from my grief over losing my father, that it was strange to be so open about it. But within this group, it became apparent that everyone was open about their lives—there didn't seem to really be any secrets. And what I noticed was that it meant that there were more people to give support and encouragement to those who needed it, whether about a lost job or failed relationship or illness or anything else, as well as more people to celebrate milestones and successes. After being alone for so long, because I was definitely alone during those years with Damien, it was a novel and wonderful thing to witness. They weren't all related by blood, and yet were certainly one large family. And I was honored they were welcoming me to become a part of it.

I stayed back with Caroline and Brandon to clean up when everyone else headed over to the lodge. There was ice-skating, cornhole, and Kubb tournaments all day, and the family unit was going en masse. I could have gone, but I needed some time away from the crowd to kind of reset. Chad offered to stay back to help as well, but Fern and I convinced him to go and spend time with his family since he'd missed out the evening before. It made me nervous when he left; it was the first he hadn't been within arm's reach, basically, since the encounter with Damien. Realistically, I was safe; there was no way Damien had followed us to the cabin. But my body and my mind were having a hard time believing it.

"So, what did you think?" Caroline asked. I was washing dishes, she was drying them, and her brother was alternating between putting them away and cleaning up the rest of the cabin.

"Of what?" I asked.

She gestured generally around the cabin. "Of everyone."

"Oh! I mean... it was a lot, but everyone was really nice. And accepting."

She smiled. "They like you."

I laughed. "They just met me—how can they already like me?"

She shrugged. "I dunno. *I* liked you as soon as I met you."

I blushed. "Same." I set down the frying pan I'd just rinsed for her to dry. "Was it like that with Lilith, too?"

Caroline's face instantly transformed into an expression of disgust and hatred. "Lilith was a bitch."

I laughed.

"It's true," Brandon chimed in.

"Why's that funny?" Caroline asked.

"Her name means demon or monster."

Caroline and Brandon's laughter joined mine.

"I'm serious," I said, chuckling. "I looked it up the first time I heard Chad use her name."

"She has a thing for the meanings of names," Caroline said to Brandon.

"What's my name mean?" he asked.

"Prince or brave," I replied.

Brandon beamed, an impish gleam in his eye. "I'm a brave prince!"

Caroline groaned. "Why did you have to tell him that? That's all we're going to hear for the rest of the trip."

I rolled my eyes, still smiling, until my thoughts drifted back to Lilith. "So people didn't like her?"

"Good god, no," Caroline laughed. "She was too stuck up. She only came here once. She hated it here because there wasn't enough to do, it was too rustic, the smoke from the fire made everything smell bad, she didn't like babies and the kids were newborns then, it was weird to play games like Skip-Bo and she'd ruin her boots if she played Kubb or cornhole, everyone was too loud and laughed too much... I think that's a pretty good summary. It's a good thing she didn't want to come back because everyone would have revolted if she had."

"She was also weird about Fern and Caroline," Brandon added.

"She was weird about everything," Caroline said.

"Yeah, but I could tell she had a problem with you guys, I don't care what she said. I still can't believe Chad didn't see it."

"He did," I said. They both turned to me with brows raised, and I wondered if I shouldn't have said anything. "He told me they fought all the time about you guys, and that he always knew in his heart that she thought there was something wrong with your relationship. And when they broke up, she made some comment that confirmed it. He still feels really bad that he didn't trust his gut about that and break up with her sooner."

"Chad's so sweet," Caroline said.

Brandon came up behind her and put her in a headlock. "What about your brother?" he laughed. "*I'm* a sweet, brave prince."

"Real sweet, putting me in a headlock," she gritted out.

She set down the plate in her hands with a deliberate slowness, then moved so quickly I couldn't even see what she did before she was out of the headlock and her brother had his arm pinned behind his back.

"Ow," he said, but he was grinning.

"Do it," Caroline said. When he shook his head, she pulled up more on his arm.

"Don't break it," Brandon laughed.

"Then tap."

She pulled a little harder before Brandon tapped her side. She smirked and let go of his arm.

"You've still got it, sis."

"Of course I do," she said, turning back to drying dishes.

I looked back and forth between them, shocked at what I had just witnessed. I wasn't even sure what it was.

Caroline glanced at me, then tipped her head toward her brother. "He used to wrestle. And he thought it was funny to pretend like I was a drilling dummy, so I learned to wrestle, too, so I could take him."

I laughed, shaking my head. I'd had no idea that Caroline could wrestle. She was so girly, I never would have guessed. I loved that unexpected tidbit of knowledge about her. "That's so cool."

"Thanks," she said with a smile.

Brandon draped his arm around Caroline's shoulders. "She used to be really good, too. She won silver in all her events in worlds two years in a row in high school. She could beat *anyone*. Except me, of course," he added, flashing a cheesy grin.

Caroline rolled her eyes. "The only reason you ever won was because I didn't want to really hurt you and you were too stupid to tap."

He shrugged, giving Caroline's shoulder a squeeze. "I still won."

She shrugged his arm off and elbowed him in the gut. "Whatever."

Brandon crossed his arms and leaned against the counter. "What about you, Renata? You have any brothers or sisters?"

"No, I was an only child."

"Oh, the peace if I'd been an only child," Brandon said.

Caroline barked out a laugh. "Ha! Right. You'd have been bored to death without someone to torture incessantly."

"It's not torture if you love it."

"Do something useful and put this away," Caroline said, handing him the small pile of plates she'd just finished drying.

She looked at me and rolled her eyes. I laughed and handed her the next dish. I would have loved to have a sibling relationship like she and Brandon had, but I was happy that I at least had this.

"Are you ready or need me to explain anything again?" Chad asked, his hand smoothing up and down my jacket-clad back.

He'd just finished giving me a rundown of how to play Kubb so I could join. Based on the quick explanation he'd given me, the game was fairly straightforward. Even so, I would have been content to stand and watch, but no one else was having it. Apparently, I was expected to participate in everything.

"I think I'm good. I'm sure I can figure it out if there's anything I missed."

"Okay, let's play," he said, leaning down and giving me a quick kiss.

There were a few nuances I'd missed, but everyone was quick to explain what I needed to know, and they were all friendly about it. There was only one person who gave the impression of being unhappy out there; the only face I hadn't seen before. It had to be Adam. Not that I could blame him, if he was hungover—he must have felt like shit.

Hours passed, and soon everyone was heading back to the cabins for dinner. Caroline had driven us down, but Chad and I opted, along with several others from the group, to walk the mile back. It was cold, but the air was refreshing. As everyone split into their separate groups to start back, Chad was engrossed in conversation with Josh, and I trailed a little behind to take in the trees and have a moment to myself. Lost in thought, I jumped a little when Adam walked up, scowl still in place.

"So you're the girlfriend everyone's talking about," he said.

I tensed; scorn and hatred oozed from him, but I'd never met him before and didn't understand why he'd feel that way.

"Um... I guess. I'm Renata." I held out my hand. "You must be Adam."

He stared at me, ignoring my hand.

"So, Renata, what are you doing with Chad?"

My head drew back. "Excuse me?"

"What's your angle?"

"What?" I asked, my voice faltering. "I don't understand."

"I heard about your ex. Crazy guy, right? What kind of crazy? What things did he do to you? I'm curious."

I felt sick. I didn't understand what was happening or how to respond. I glanced toward Chad, who was a short ways in front of us, but we were the last two in our group by a decent enough gap that no one else heard our conversation. I wanted to run from Adam or call to Chad, but felt ridiculous for that. I was fairly certain Adam was the cousin they'd told me had gone through a rough divorce recently, but Chad was the only one who'd said he was a dick. Maybe I was overreacting. Maybe I was too sensitive about Damien. Regardless, I wasn't sure I wanted to talk to this stranger about it, especially when he gave me the impression before I'd even responded that he wouldn't believe me.

"He... I..." I swallowed, tears pricking the backs of my eyes. "I don't want to talk about it."

"Don't want to talk about it or you're trying to remember what story you spun so you don't get caught in a lie?"

My mouth dropped open and I gaped at him. He stared back at me, his eyebrows raised like he was waiting for me to respond, his eyes burning with anger.

"Leave me alone," I said through clenched teeth, the first tears spilling over. *Chad was right, this guy's an asshole!*

I turned away, intending to jog back up to Chad, but Adam reached an arm out and grabbed my wrist. He wasn't squeezing hard, but the bruises from Damien were painfully tender and I yelped.

"Adam—what the hell are you doing?" someone called out.

He let go of my wrist. "Leave Chad the hell alone," he said, just loud enough for me to hear.

I cradled my wrist, watching as he strode off, still trying to figure out what I'd done to him.

"Rena?" Chad called. I turned away from watching Adam disappear back toward the lodge to find Chad jogging toward me. "What happened? Mark said Adam grabbed you?"

I swallowed and tried to stop crying. "He just grabbed my wrist," I said in a thin voice. "It wasn't that hard, it's just that I'm already sore."

"Adam!" Chad shouted, his body tense. Adam ignored him, and Chad shouted his name again, louder this time. Again, Adam ignored him.

"Chad, please," I said. "Let it go."

He looked down at me, his jaw softening. "I won't go after him right now, but I'm not letting it go, Rena. He had no right to touch you. Was that all he did?"

I wasn't sure if I should share the things Adam said to me or not. "Yeah. And he was asking me questions about Damien."

Chad kissed my forehead. "I'm sorry, Rena. I should have known he wasn't in a good frame of mind. He just went through a nasty divorce—his ex-wife, Kali, was crazy and ruined his reputation and got him disbarred and took all his money. But that doesn't make it okay for him to be an asshole to you."

I gave an absent nod. I could understand not being yourself when you're going through something like a divorce or dealing with someone like it sounded like Kali was. Which made sense since her name meant goddess of destruction. But that still didn't explain why he was attacking me, because that's exactly what it felt like—a personal attack. All I could do was hope we didn't cross paths again.

When we got back to the cabin, everyone showered and changed for dinner. By the time we were heading over, I'd mostly shaken off what had happened with Adam and only felt slightly nervous about running into him again. At least this time, Chad would be right there with me. When we got inside, Chad took our coats to one of the bedrooms while I said hello to people and waited for him where I was. My eyes moved around the cabin, shocked at how many people were in such a small space, then I froze when they landed on Adam. He was standing across the living room from where I stood, glaring at me. All at once, that same sick feeling returned in my stomach, and I was too hot in my sweater. I didn't have a shirt underneath, so I couldn't take it off, but I pushed my sleeves up to my elbows.

That sufficed long enough for me to manage to swallow a few bites of food. Chad noticed I wasn't eating much and that v appeared between his brows. I smiled to reassure him, and the v deepened. He could read me too well—I could never fool him. It was too much, knowing he was worried about me on top of knowing that Adam was there somewhere—I'd refused to look around anymore because of how much it unsettled me every time I saw him glaring—and I needed to get some fresh air and cool off.

Chad followed me to the porch where I drank in the cold air, relishing the feel of it on my bare forearms and my face. He ran a finger down the back of my hand that was grasping the porch railing. "What is it, Rena love?"

I gave a shake of my head. The last thing I wanted was to be the source of problems in his family.

He tucked my hair that had escaped my braid behind my ears and cupped my cheeks, his thumbs smoothing back and forth. "It's okay to not be okay."

"I know."

"Is my family bothering you?"

"God, no," I replied, shaking my head. "I love your family. Everyone's so nice and welcoming."

"Except Adam. It's him, isn't it?"

"Chad, it's okay."

There was a crunch of gravel as someone approached and we looked up. Chad tensed just as I registered it was Adam coming toward us, accompanied by three other family members.

"Adam," Chad growled out, starting down the porch stairs. "What the hell is your problem?"

Adam grunted, glaring at me, then looking to Chad. The front door opened and Fern walked out, calling for Chad. She stopped short when she saw Chad storming toward Adam.

"Not again," she grumbled, crossing her arms over her chest. "Guys, knock it off," she called out.

They both ignored her. Adam had stopped walking and Chad came to a stop in front of him. "I said, what the hell's your problem?"

"There's always something with those two," Fern said to me, rolling her eyes. "What are they pissed off at each other about now?"

"Me," I breathed out, wishing the porch boards would give out and I could disappear.

"What's my problem?" Adam asked, his jaw ticking. "My problem is *her*. Why the hell is she here?"

"Her name is Renata, and she's here with me because she's my girlfriend, not that it's any—"

"But why is she here?" Adam shouted over Chad. "Why, man? She says her ex was abusive and controlling, but who knows if any of that is true. What's the real reason she left him, huh? Did she clean him out? And you're next, man, and you're too stupid—"

"She's not Kali!"

"I didn't think Kali was like that either until it happened. I'm telling you, you can't trust her."

Fern tugged on my arm. "You should go inside, Renata," she said calmly despite the fire I could see in her eyes when I looked at her; she was angry. "You don't need to be out here for this."

Even so, I couldn't move. I imagined I looked much like the other family members who were standing nearby, silent and still watching. "This is my fault," I whispered.

Fern replied, but I didn't hear her; I was stuck on what Chad was doing; he was pointing at me.

"Look at her, asshole. Look. At. Her. From all the way over here you can see the bruises on her wrists—"

"I barely touched her!" Adam roared. "Whatever she said—"

"Shut up!" Chad shouted. Fern stepped down the porch toward them. "Just shut up for once and listen! Look at her and tell me if you can see the bruising."

"I don't believe—"

"Do you see it or not?"

Adam glared at Chad, then looked at me. "Yes," he said through gritted teeth.

"Her ex that you seem to think is a victim did that to her in front of her apartment building yesterday. He tracked her down, showed up at her apartment, hurt and threatened her. That's why we were late yesterday, because we were talking to the police about getting a protective order against him."

"You can't even know that's true, she could be—"

"I was there, Adam." They stared at each other, and Fern stepped up next to Chad, her arms crossed over her chest again. Chad shot her a glance, then looked back to Adam. "She's not Kali, man. If anything, her ex is the one like Kali, except so much worse; he actually did all the things Kali said you did... and then some."

Adam's glare faltered slightly as it shifted between Chad and me several times.

"Chad's right," Fern said. "She's not Kali, Adam. I know Kali screwed you over and she—"

"Fuck Kali," Adam said.

"—destroyed you, and that you just don't want to see that happen to Chad or anyone else, but you're wrong about Renata. Kali is still screwing with you, Adam, because she's turning you into an asshole."

"He's always been an asshole," Chad retorted.

"Shut up, Chad," Fern said. "You're not helping."

"Yeah, shut up, Chad," Adam said.

There was silence for a beat, then Chad said. "You owe Renata an apology. And you never should have touched her—don't do it again."

He turned and headed toward the porch. I was barely breathing and everything was spinning around me. I was no longer hot, now freezing and shaking. I was trying and failing to process everything I'd just witnessed.

When he stopped in front of me, I wasn't sure what to expect; I'd never heard Chad the way he was toward Adam except the day before with Damien. He was furious. But when he looked at me, all I could see was worry and love.

"I'm sorry. I shouldn't have done that in front of you."

I stared at my feet. "It's okay. I'm sorry I caused problems between you guys."

"You didn't." He kissed my forehead and pulled me into his arms, letting out a sigh. "It's not your fault when someone doesn't believe you—that's on them."

TWENTY-NINE

Adam didn't apologize, but he left me alone after the confrontation with Chad the night before Thanksgiving. Thanksgiving day flew by in a flurry of activity, each cabin preparing several dishes to contribute for dinner, and I spent most of the day helping Chad bake. The dinner itself was a monstrous affair with an unbelievable amount of food, guaranteeing we'd have leftovers for at least two days—the best part, according to Fern.

The day after Thanksgiving was much warmer than the other days had been, and we had another Kubb tournament, this one private for our group, and we did it in a field close to our cabins. Everyone was outside with lawn chairs set up in a circle around the playing area, and team members switched out at will. I now had the hang of the game, and while I wasn't great at it, I wasn't terrible either, and it was a lot of fun.

It was so warm after lunchtime that I was too hot. As I stood behind our baseline and pulled my sweatshirt off, my t-shirt underneath got caught and I didn't realize it until my shirts were halfway up my back and I felt the cold air on my bare skin. Embarrassed, I quickly reached up and pulled the hem of my t-shirt down. It was bad enough to have accidentally bared some skin I wouldn't normally, but it was even worse because most of that skin was badly scarred. I'd gotten comfortable with Chad seeing and touching my lower back, but I cringed knowing I'd just bared it to at least a dozen other people.

I could feel the heat in my cheeks as I walked over to hang my sweatshirt on the camp chair Chad and I were sharing next to Caroline. Unfortunately, Adam was standing over there as well. *Great.* It would be fine; he'd been leaving me alone, there was no reason for him to do something now. I hung my sweatshirt over the chair and smiled at Caroline as she cheered for someone on our team who'd just knocked over a skull.

"What happened to your back?" Adam asked.

I froze, staring at him, having forgotten how to breathe. He was scowling, but his voice hadn't sounded as angry as it had the last time he'd spoken to me.

Caroline looked between us, then answered for me. "Her ex happened."

For some reason, Caroline responding reminded my lungs how to function again and I sucked in a breath, turning and rushing back onto the field. I didn't want to hear Adam make some comment about how he didn't believe that. It was bad enough living with such an extensive and permanent reminder of what I'd been through *without* having to talk about it with someone who didn't believe me.

My mini-encounter with Adam soon faded to the back of my mind when it was my turn to throw again, and the rest of the afternoon passed without incident. That evening, everyone was heading into a tiny town about twenty minutes away for beer and live music, so we all ate a bit early to leave plenty of time to get ready. I stood in the bedroom, staring at the outfit I'd gotten with Caroline with this outing in mind. I'd liked it, and she'd assured me it was perfect for the occasion, but I was suddenly unsure. I wasn't even sure why I was having so much doubt; it wasn't often I worried about my clothes anymore. Chad had a way of making my insecurities disappear when I was with him, as if he were gradually unraveling the damage sustained over my years with Damien. At this rate, by the time a therapist had an opening, I wouldn't need one anymore.

Chad finished dressing and looked at me, then down at the clothes I had laid out. "It's perfect, Rena."

I smiled shyly, then changed into the outfit. It was a maroon fitted sweater dress with a low cowl neck and half sleeves. It fell mid-thigh, and I was wearing it with black tights and black ankle boots.

"You look incredible, Rena love," Chad said softly, his eyes taking me in.

"Thank you," I replied. I looked down. "Is it too short?"

Chad scanned over me. "No. But if you're not comfortable in it, you can wear something else. You don't even have to dress up if you don't want to."

I knew that, too, but I *did* want to. I wanted to look nice, and feel like I looked nice, for myself and for Chad.

"If you're sure it's okay and it isn't too short or revealing..."

"It's neither of those things. But you *are* missing something."

I glanced down at my outfit.

"A necklace, I think," Chad said.

I scrunched up my face and looked at him. What the hell was he talking about? He'd never commented on my lack of jewelry before, and I *never* wore any—I didn't even own any. Which Chad knew.

He slipped his hand into his pocket and pulled out a flat, square box. "I've been waiting for an occasion to give this to you."

He stepped up behind me and swept my hair over my left shoulder before lowering a necklace in front of me and clasping it behind my neck. It was all rose gold, a delicate chain with a circular pendant that had a phoenix cutout inside. It was gorgeous. He dropped a kiss to the curve of my neck.

"I chose rose gold because it's less common and looks delicate, but it's actually really strong—the strongest of the golds. The phoenix is a cutout so your skin shows through... making you the phoenix."

Tears welled in my eyes, and I tilted my head back against him to stop them from falling.

"Do you like it?" he asked.

"I love it," I whispered, my hands fingering the charm. "It's beautiful."

"Like you," he said.

I shook my head and rolled my eyes.

He kissed the crook of my neck again. "I wasn't being corny that time."

My breath caught and desire swept through me for the first time since the morning we'd left Amestown. I turned to face him, and Chad's fingertips whispered languidly down my spine as we stared into each other's eyes. We were watching each other's pupils change—literally watching each other getting turned on. Which just intensified the feelings.

"Let's go!" Caroline shouted from the other side of the door. "Chad! Renata! It's time to leave!"

Chad smirked and I grinned, biting the corner of my lip to contain it. He slipped his fingers through mine, kissing my lips soft and slow before we joined the rest of our carpool group to head to The Azure Fiddle.

The venue was fairly small, very crowded, extremely loud, and at least half the crowd was our group. But the band was talented and Chad was by my side. As usual, we were drinking seltzers, along with the other drivers from our group, while everyone else was drinking local beers and getting louder and rowdier.

My relaxed enjoyment hid behind a surge of anxiety when I realized I had to use the bathroom. Sitting on a bench with Chad, his arm around me and holding me close, I was in a bubble of safety. But having to get up meant weaving through a tightly-packed crowd. What if Damien was in that crowd somewhere? He'd found me in Amestown... What if he'd followed us here, too? Chad noticed me scanning the crowd anxiously and leaned over, speaking directly into my ear so I could hear him over the cacophony of sound.

"What's wrong?"

My face flamed and I turned to reply into his ear. "I have to pee."

He tipped his head down. "I'll go with you. I could go, too."

My shoulders dropped a few inches. I was embarrassed that I'd become so dependent on Chad's presence to feel safe. At the same time, I could hear Caroline's voice in my head telling me not to be too hard on myself because it had only been a few days since we saw Damien, and we didn't even have a protective order yet. Once that was in place and some time had passed since he'd shown up, I would surely relax a bit and stop depending so much on Chad. I just needed to be patient.

Chad led the way to the back corner where the bathrooms were, our hands linked, and we got into our respective lines. When I came out, I scanned for Chad, my heart already speeding up because I hadn't seen him immediately. Which made sense; the hallway was narrow and barely fit the people waiting in line to get in—it would have been inconsiderate for anyone else to hang out back there. I stepped back toward the main room until I reached the end of the hallway and looked around for him, but there were so many people it was impossible.

"Wanna get some fresh air?" Chad's voice asked in my ear, then I felt his fingertips on my lower back. "It's hot as hell in here."

I nodded in agreement. I was hot, too—I had been since shortly after we'd arrived. With how many people were inside, the temperature had been steadily climbing. Chad led the way again and we stepped out into the dark, crisp air outside the building. The Azure Fiddle was on the corner, and we walked just around to the side to get away from the group hanging out next to the entrance doors.

"I was melting in there," Chad said, leaning back against the brick wall. "I don't remember it ever getting that hot before."

"I was, too," I said. "This dress is way too warm."

"You *could* just take it off," he said, his mouth twitching.

I laughed. "Right."

"Well, you could if we left everyone here and headed back to the cabin."

"We can't do that."

"Of course we could," he replied, wriggling is eyebrows.

"And what would we tell everyone we ditched to find another ride back?"

"That it was imperative we get back to make some dough."

I tried not to, I even bit my cheeks, but I giggled.

"Really, Rena, I don't understand why you keep laughing about making dough. It's something I take very seriously."

I giggled harder.

"Making dough is a skill that requires a lot of practice—*a lot*—to be good at it and I intend to be the best dough-maker you've ever met."

Gasping for breath, my sides began to ache.

"In fact, I don't know why I call myself a baker. Anyone can bake—you just toss the dough in the oven. The part that matters is making the dough. I think I'm going to change my title to Master Dough Maker."

His ability to continue his euphemism with a straight face broke down and his laughter joined mine as we stood on the side of the building laughing hysterically. And every time we caught each other's eye as our laughter began to taper off, we were laughing all over again.

He snagged my hips and pulled me into him, his fingers kneading my flesh. "How's this?" he asked.

"Definitely need more practice," I giggled.

"I was thinking the same thing," he said, his voice low.

His fingers crawled further back on my hips to the curves just below my lower back and my breath hitched. Based on the pressure from his fingers as they kneaded my backside, I knew if there had been enough light, his eyes would be dark with only a thin ring of gray-blue. I knew mine would also be dark, and that watching them darken would make Chad's darken even more.

"I love that sound," he murmured, using pressure from his fingers to press my body against his. His hands stopped kneading, one circling my waist, anchoring me to him, the other tucking my hair behind my ear and then caressing my face. "It makes me feel so... I don't know the word, but like I'm on top of the world, when something I say or some way I touch you takes your breath away."

"Exhilarated," I breathed out.

"Yeah," he breathed in agreement. "But also strong, and honored almost. Except those words are too tame." His eyes searched mine. "What does it feel like to you when that happens?"

I inhaled and exhaled slowly, closing my eyes. "My heart trips a little, but not painfully, more like a flutter, and this warmth that's almost like electricity spreads in an instant from my chest to the top of my head and the tips of my fingers and toes. My body feels more alive and awake and buzzes with a heightened awareness of everything—your breath, your expression, your touch."

"What else?"

"It makes me want you, but it feels more like a need, and not just in a physical way, but just because I want to be as close to you in every way as possible."

"What things do that to you?"

I could feel a crackling warmth over my décolletage, and that very same breath hitch occurred again. "That," I breathed out, my chest rising and falling more rapidly. Chad's hand touched the skin it had been hovering over and I shivered.

"You could feel me before I touched you?" he asked. He sounded intensely curious.

"Yeah, I could."

"What did it feel like?"

"A warmth that crackled kind of like a fire does. Like a touch, but gentler."

"I wonder if I can feel you, too."

"Close your eyes," I said, opening mine.

His eyelids lowered and I raised a hand near his face. Little by little, I brought it closer without actually touching him. When I was a few millimeters away, his whole body trembled, then relaxed. He opened his eyes with a lazy smile.

"That's incredible. I wonder how that's possible and what it means."

I shrugged and returned his smile, feeling a little self-conscious for some reason. "I don't know. But I like it."

"Me, too. I want to try it other places on our bodies when we're alone."

The thought of that sent a wave of desire through me and I saw it reflected in Chad's eyes. He wrapped me up in his arms and kissed me, his mouth soft and slow and seductive. We kissed for several minutes before pulling apart and agreeing we should probably head back inside before we got too carried away. I slipped my fingers between Chad's, and he tugged me into his side, kissing my temple.

"I love you, my Rena. Madly."

We turned the corner of the building, and I bit the corner of my lip, glancing up at him. His eyes appeared even darker in the shadow between light posts. He grinned back and kissed my cheek, giving my hand a squeeze.

"I was wondering how long you guys would be making out over there."

I stopped short, my heart pounding. Adam was standing in the next shadow between lights, leaning against the wall along the front of the building with a beer in his hands.

Chad tensed. "Fuck off, Adam."

Adam scowled. "I was wondering because I was waiting to talk to you."

"I'm not talking to you until you've apologized to Rena."

"What the hell do you think I'm trying to do?" Adam bit out.

My heart was racing. Chad's thumb smoothed back and forth soothingly across my hand. Adam ran a hand through his hair, then took a long drink from his beer. We waited. He took another drink.

Adam looked over, glaring at Chad. "I was wrong," he said.

Chad breathed in sharply. "Don't tell *me* that. Tell *her* that. I'm used to you pulling some bullshit—I don't need you to finally admit to me something I already know. You've never admitted being wrong to me before, so why start now?"

"Fuck you, Chad," Adam growled. "I'm not the only one who fucks up around here."

"I didn't say you were—I've screwed up before, too. But this isn't about you and me, this is about the shit you said to Rena, the shit you accused her of."

Adam's jaw ticked and he stared at the ground, taking another swig of beer. "I'm sorry," he said. "I was wrong about you." He looked up at *me* this time and I could barely breathe. "Your story from before you met Chad is a lot like Kali's and she's a lying bitch. I made an assumption I shouldn't have."

For a second, the anger and pugnaciousness in his expression slipped and I could see how much pain he was in. My heart ached for him. I could, in a way, understand what Kali had put him through more than anyone in his family... just as he could understand what Damien had put me through more than even Chad could.

"I'm sorry for what she did to you," I said quietly, my eyes filling with moisture. "No one should be accused of things that aren't true."

Adam looked back to the ground and took another drink of beer. His eyes stayed trained down, but more looking through the sidewalk—not at it, exactly—and when he spoke, his voice had changed. It was missing the hard edge. "I felt like I was crazy since I met her. At first it was small things, small enough that I just figured it was me. And it spread to other things so gradually, I barely noticed. Until one day, it was like I was in the middle of a fucking tornado in my mind. I went to a neurologist because I thought maybe I had a tumor or something wrong with my brain. I just felt like I was going crazy, and Kali... she was so damn convincing."

He looked up and my mouth pulled into a thin line in sympathy. I understood exactly what he was saying. "So was Damien. I could be wearing a red shirt, and he could convince me it was white and that I was arguing about what color it was to embarrass him in front of his friends or something until I ended up apologizing."

Chad's fingers tightened noticeably where they were intertwined with mine. When Adam laughed, they tightened more and I gave his hand a squeeze. Adam wasn't laughing *at* me.

"God, he and Kali would be perfect for each other."

"I don't wish Damien on anyone," I said. "As awful as Kali sounds, I don't think anyone deserves the kinds of things Damien did to me... emotionally or physically."

Adam's eyes stared at me. "No. You're right. No one deserves to be abused." He tipped up his beer and finished it, then pushed away from the wall. He headed toward the entrance, pausing in front of us. "I'm sorry you were, and that I thought you were lying. People thought I was lying when I said I didn't do the things Kali accused me of and it fucking sucked. I shouldn't have done that to you."

And then Adam disappeared inside.

The next day, everyone ended up at our cabin for breakfast like they had every morning, looking for more of Chad's biscuits. As usual, I helped him in the kitchen and the time flew as people flowed in and out of our cabin. We were beginning to clean up, with only a few stragglers left chatting over biscuits with jam and coffee, when Adam walked in. I paused in wiping the counter where Chad had just scraped off all the flour and dough pieces from making biscuits, unsure what to expect.

"Good morning," Adam said to the room. "Is there any breakfast left?"

Chad looked over at him and tilted his head toward the table, his face tight. He was still really angry with Adam, and was also having trouble understanding why *I* wasn't. It was hard to explain... Adam had been an asshole, but I understood why. And he'd apologized. And the night before, I felt a kind of kinship with him because we both understood what it was like to be intentionally confused by someone.

"There's fresh coffee, too, if you'd like some," I added, pointing toward the coffee pot.

"Thanks," Adam mumbled, then walked over, grabbed a mug from the cabinet and poured a cup of coffee. Silently, he sat down and filled a plate with most of the remaining eggs and sausage, and two biscuits.

"Hey, Adam," Brandon called from the living room. "Skip-Bo tourney after the hike?"

"If you wanna lose again, sure," Adam replied.

"No, I've got it this time. You're gonna lose that undefeated title once and for all."

"Whatever helps you sleep at night, Brandon."

"I'm gonna shower real quick," Chad said, giving me a kiss on the temple. "I got flour everywhere today."

I laughed, brushing my hand over his hair where there was a clump of that flour. "Yeah, you did."

"You good?" he asked, glancing toward Adam.

"Yeah," I said, following his eyes. Brandon and a few others were still there, too. And I didn't think Adam would harass me anymore. "Go ahead."

He disappeared toward the bathroom and I took my time cleaning up the rest of the kitchen. I didn't mind gathering and washing dishes because it allowed my mind to wander and kept my hands busy. I was especially grateful when, within a minute or two of Chad heading to the bathroom, everyone else left except Adam.

"You bake, too?" Adam asked after a few minutes.

I gave a headshake. "No, I just help Chad sometimes. I'm a writer."

"What kinds of things do you write?"

"Mostly short stories."

"Published?"

I nodded. "Yeah. In a journal."

"That's cool," he said. An awkward silence fell before he spoke again. "Do you... have trouble trusting people now? You know, after your ex?"

I set down the dish I was washing in the sink and rinsed my hands, then turned around. Adam was watching me, an earnestness in his expression. "Yeah. It's not quite as bad as it was, but I get suspicious really easily. Chad, Fern, and Caroline are the only people I really trust, and even with them, I sometimes have doubts."

"How long's it been since you left him?"

"Fourteen months."

"It's been about that long for me, too, though our divorce wasn't finalized until this summer. Do you ever have moments where you think it's so crazy you must be imagining what happened to you?"

I nodded again. "Yeah. I hate when that happens. I feel so weak and am afraid if he ever found me when I was having those doubts that I'd wake up to find myself back where I was before I left him." I exhaled sharply. It was scary, but it also felt good to admit that out loud. It was a fear I'd never voiced before. I'd almost told Chad many times, but I didn't know if he could understand how I could love him and still be afraid that Damien could manipulate me into returning to him.

Adam laughed. "I thought I was the only one who felt that way. I hate her and I never want to see her again, but sometimes I think she could convince me to take her back, that I was wrong to leave her. Even after everything she put me through."

"You're not alone in that," I said.

Adam stood up and brought his plate into the kitchen. I stepped aside and he put it in the sink, then refilled his coffee cup. He leaned back against the counter in front of the coffee pot and crossed his ankles. I wasn't sure what to say, so I turned back to the sink to wash the last few dishes.

"I'll wash my own shit if you leave it," he said.

"I don't mind," I replied.

"I feel pathetic," he said quietly a minute later. "And trying to explain what she did made it even worse. No one believes a man could be the victim. She had no proof of anything she accused me of since it never happened, but no one cared. It was her word against mine and people believed her because she was a woman and I was a man."

"I don't think you're pathetic," I said. "But I understand why you feel that way. I did for a long time, too. I still do sometimes. Chad and Caroline are helping me a lot with that. Before Damien, I was independent and driven. But I was also in a bad place emotionally—I had been since my dad died in a car accident when I was fifteen. My dad was everything to me—my mom died when I was a baby. Damien must have sensed that or something, and at first, he filled in what was missing, but then he used that to manipulate me."

Adam looked toward the floor. "My mom died of cancer about a year before I met Kali. I wasn't over it yet. Kali soothed the pain I felt from losing my mom."

"She knew that, Adam. Just as Damien knew exactly what he was doing to me. It's hard to believe at first, but it gets easier after a while."

He sighed. "Yeah, I've read about it. I did a lot of research trying to find something that would tell me that I wasn't crazy."

I laughed this time. "I did the same thing. Did it help you?"

He shrugged. "Some. Talking to you is *more* helpful, though."

"Same."

He looked up and actually smiled. It was small, but it was a smile. I smiled back. It felt like something had been lifted from my shoulders—something small, but heavy enough to be noticeable.

THIRTY

It took a while to find a new routine after the trip since neither Chad nor I was comfortable with me being alone outside one of our apartments, even once the final protective order with a no contact provision was granted and served to Damien. It was unlikely, I knew, that he would break the order, since he was sitting there in court when they told him that doing so would lead to arrest and criminal charges, and that would immediately ruin his career and social standing that he cherished so much. However, I'd at one point thought it was unlikely he would try to find me in Amestown... and I'd been wrong. Chad, on the other hand, was simply unwilling to even take a chance that Damien would ignore the order and come after me again. The logistics became more and more challenging and, ultimately, we decided that I would move in with Chad, at least for a while, which I did over the few weeks he wasn't teaching around Christmas.

At first, living together was amazing. There was never a question of having to get clothes from one place or the other or whether or not we'd be able to see each other since we called the same place home. We existed for a time in a euphoric bubble of love that obscured the challenges we faced because of our fear of Damien.

After I moved in and we created yet another new routine, I began to miss being able to step outside and go for a run through the preserve. I already wasn't running as often as I needed to train for the marathon, since Chad wasn't always able to go with me and I didn't venture out alone, but I also hadn't been to the preserve at all since I'd moved in with him. After two months, it was almost unbearable. I missed the peace I felt there, and I missed feeling my dad's presence.

I'd also started therapy and my session times sometimes conflicted with Chad's schedule. He took off when he could, but as understanding as Randy, his boss, was, he was starting to get aggravated with Chad. It wasn't fair to disrupt him so much, but he wouldn't consider me going on my own. And while I would have, I was scared to, and let him continue to rearrange his life to assuage our mutual fears.

The only thing that had been going well was my writing career. As long as I was using a pencil and paper, I'd hit a groove and had no shortage of words anymore. And every piece I'd submitted to the freelance department of *Including The Kitchen Sink* had been accepted. Even so, I got nervous after every submission as I waited to hear back. Crossing my fingers, I opened my email account to see if my latest piece had been accepted, but in lieu of having an email from the freelance submissions mailbox, I had an email from Jeb.

> Renata,
>
> You've been busy! I was glad when you submitted the piece you shared with me and wasn't surprised when it was accepted. I've been tracking your submissions, and your knack for writing poignant and moving short stories has only improved with each piece.
>
> We've recently re-evaluated the contents and organization of the journal and have decided that expanding to include a permanent short-story section once again is in the best interest of the journal. The only thing that remains is to find the right voice to have on staff to write that section.
>
> And that brings me to why I'm reaching out. We would like to offer you that position. It would be much like the position you had previously, and you would report to me like you did before, and the position will be remote with no

in-office time required. Salary and benefits have also changed and the details are included in the contract offer attached.

If you accept, your latest submission to the freelance department would be the first piece published in the new section, and your first new piece would be due to me in three weeks. The publication and production schedules are also attached to this email.

Please review the attached contract terms and let me know your decision by next Friday. If you have any questions in the meantime, please don't hesitate to email or call me.

I'm looking forward to the opportunity to work with you again.

Jeb

I stared at the screen for several minutes, then re-read the email. Then re-read it again. I had to fight the urge to reply with a "yes" in all caps without even having read the contract. It was what I'd wanted. I'd been checking weekly to see if they had any staff writer openings, but there had been none for me to apply to.

I picked up my phone to text Chad the news, but saw that he would be home soon and decided to wait. While waiting, I opened the contract and encountered another shock. The salary offer was higher than expected—*much* higher. A quick Google search revealed it fell into the competitive average for *experienced* staff writers for professional writing publications. *Experienced? Me?* I couldn't believe it. I returned to the contract and learned that they now offered a 401k matching program and pension plan in addition to full healthcare benefits and a professional development allowance that was triple what it was when I last worked there. They also provided educational assistance, and more. Benefits I'd never even dreamed of. I was still laughing at how many there were when Chad came through the front door.

"Hi, Rena love."

I looked up from my computer that I had set up at the kitchen island as he walked into the kitchen. The grin on my face was so wide my cheeks ached and I was practically bouncing in my seat with excitement. The warm expression Chad always wore when he got home morphed into an answering grin and a slight questioning lowering of his brow.

"You're in an exceptionally good mood today," he mused, bending to kiss the crook of my neck.

I giggled and bit the corner of my lip as I noticed my vision was a bit blurred; I was so excited I was teary. Chad rested his hand against my chest.

"Breathe, Rena," he laughed.

I giggled again and shook my head, trying to get my thoughts to stop racing.

"What is it?" he asked.

"I... Jeb... I got a job offer from the journal!"

"A job offer?"

"Yes! Jeb, he emailed me—my pieces I've been submitting—they want to do a regular section for them. They want me on staff!"

"Rena, that's amazing!" Chad exclaimed.

I squealed. "Look—read this." I turned my laptop so Chad could see the email from Jeb and watched as he read it. His eyes widened slightly, and by the time he was done, his smile was so wide it was splitting his face. "And look at the offer," I added, toggling to the contract so he could read that, too.

"Wow!" he said. "This is incredible! I'm so proud of you, Rena! We have to celebrate."

"I'm still in shock. I can't believe it, I mean, Jeb reached out to offer the job to me, it wasn't like I even applied because I didn't even know there was going to be a position available, you know? I just can't even believe my luck, I—"

"Rena love, it's not luck. Remember when I told you I knew it would happen? That you'd get your words back? It's the same thing with this: determination, intelligence, tenacity. You've got them all and that means you'll only ever be successful. This happened not because of luck, but because of your talent, and because you were brave enough to submit to the freelance department to begin with, and because you didn't give up when you lost your words. You did this, Rena. You. Luck has nothing to do with it. And I'm so damn proud of you for that."

My tears slipped from the corners of my eyes and I laughed. "I did it, Chad. I actually did it."

He tucked my hair behind my ear and caressed my cheek as he kissed me. "Of course you did, my Rena. I always knew you would."

We already had plans to meet Fern and Caroline for dinner the next night, and I decided to hold my news to share with them until then. Once we arrived, it was clear after one glance that the two of them had news to share with *us*. I knew Caroline was planning to propose to Fern—I'd helped her with planning how—but she was planning to do it in a few weeks on the anniversary of when she'd come to Amestown with Fern from California. Had she proposed early? I glanced down toward Fern's hands, but her jacket sleeves were covering them.

After exchanging hugs and greetings, we were shown to our table and removed our jackets. When doing so, light caught my eye from Caroline's hand, and when I looked over, there was a new ring on *her* finger... an engagement ring. I squealed and clapped my hand over my mouth, looking over to Fern's hand that I could now see also had a ring—the ring Caroline had picked out for her. A glance at Chad revealed he was clueless, and I bit my tongue so I wouldn't ruin the surprise. While he was the most observant person I'd ever met, Chad wasn't looking at Fern or Caroline or even me; he was anxiously scanning the restaurant. It's what he did whenever we were out of his apartment now: constantly checking the area for any sign of Damien.

We all sat and Fern's mouth pinched in the same way Chad's did when he was trying not to smile too broadly, her eyes practically dancing; it was the most I'd ever seen the two of them look alike. I bounced in my seat, waiting for Chad to notice and react as Fern and

Caroline picked up their water glasses with their left hands, but his eyes were everywhere but at our table.

I reached under the table and rubbed a hand on his thigh to get his attention. He corralled his intense scrutiny of our surroundings and covered my hand with his before picking it up and kissing it.

"Rena has some news," he said, still looking at me, beaming.

I moved my head sharply side to side and looked pointedly toward Fern and Caroline. Chad's eyebrows drew in comically. I looked at them again with my eyes wide. I could hear Caroline giggle next to me. Still wearing his confused expression, Chad turned his head toward Fern.

"No way!" he exclaimed after a beat. "Oh my god, congratulations you guys!"

Fern's grin broke free and she laughed, lifting Caroline's hand and kissing the back of it much like Chad had done to mine. "Took you long enough!"

"I wasn't paying attention," Chad replied. "Tell us everything!"

We got the story about how Fern had proposed to Caroline on the anniversary of the day they'd come clean to each other about their feelings for one another, which was the day before, and how Caroline had been planning to do the same but in a few weeks. They laughed and smiled and teared up, and it was beautiful listening to them tell the story together. They wanted to get married in October, seven months away—only a few days after Chad's thirty-fourth birthday.

"You've been mother and father to me since Mom and Dad died," Fern said to Chad, grabbing his hand. Both of them had tears in their eyes. "Would you walk me down the aisle?"

"I'd be honored to," Chad replied.

Caroline and I glanced at each other, wiping at our eyes, and she asked me to be a bridesmaid, which I agreed to immediately, touched that she'd asked me. We chatted through the rest of our meal about their ideas for the wedding, something I had a feeling we'd be doing a lot of over the next several months.

After the waiter had cleared our dinner plates and taken our dessert order, Chad kissed the back of my hand and reminded everyone, including me, that I also had news. Like Fern and Caroline,

I'd completely forgotten, swept up in the excitement of their new engagement.

Three sets of eyes were on me, and I felt a strange combination of giddy and nervous, but I took a deep breath and told them I had a salaried job offer from the journal.

"I didn't know you applied!" Caroline exclaimed. "I thought they didn't have any openings."

"They didn't," I replied. "Jeb sent me an email; they're creating a new section in the journal and want me to be the writer for it. They haven't posted the job opening yet."

"Renata—that's amazing," Fern said.

"I'm so excited for you!" Caroline squealed. "I mean, I'm sad because this means you'll be leaving the café, right? But mostly I'm excited."

I hadn't even thought that far ahead yet to consider that I wouldn't need my job at the café anymore. "Yeah, I guess I will so I can focus on my writing. I'll need to have finished pieces more frequently than I have been to meet the publication schedule." I looked at Fern. "I'm sorry."

"Don't be!" Fern replied. "That's how things are supposed to be. I never thought this was permanent for you."

"I'll stay as long as you need to find someone."

"I don't think that'll be long, actually. Miranda took the job part time, but she wanted full-time. If she still does, then I can take you off the schedule after next week. I'll talk to her on Monday."

I gave a tight smile, feeling a mixture of excitement and trepidation about this step in my career. Another combination that needed a word like bittersweet. We chatted through dessert about the offer I'd received and the position details, and too soon we were all putting on our coats to leave.

On the drive home after dinner, I chattered excitedly about Fern and Caroline's impending nuptials, revealing that I'd known Caroline was planning to propose but that I'd been sworn to secrecy. Chad said Fern had kept him in the dark about her plans, likely worried he couldn't keep a secret from me and it would end up getting back to Caroline.

"Well, can you?" I asked playfully as we neared his apartment door.

"I don't know. I haven't tried yet. Would you want me to be able to?"

I thought about that for a second. "I mean, it depends on what it's about, I suppose. If it was something like a marriage proposal, then yes, absolutely," I laughed, facing him as he hung our coats.

Chad closed the coat closet in the hall and wrapped one arm around my waist, the fingertips of his other hand whispering along my bare arm, hovering just above. He watched his fingertips and the goosebumps that spread across my skin. It was something he loved to do since we'd discovered our ability to feel each other without touching. He'd researched it when we got back from Thanksgiving and learned that some people were able to sense the physical presence of someone in the way we could when they were profoundly connected to one another.

"So you'd want a proposal to be a surprise?" he asked, his lips brushing my shoulder.

My whole body shivered, and I closed my eyes. "Yes," I whispered.

He dotted kisses from my shoulder down my arm, to the underside of my wrist, then my palm. "And how do you feel about marriage?" he asked, his voice low and hypnotic.

"Depends on who it's with," I said, giggling and opening my eyes. His were as dark as night; the brown was long gone.

He chuckled, using a hand to slowly start lowering my dress zipper while my fingers just as slowly began to undo buttons on his shirt.

"Oh yeah? And who might you consider it with?" he asked.

"Hm," I said, pretending to think hard about it. "Chris Hemsworth maybe," I giggled. The last movie Chad and I had watched together was *Thor: Love and Thunder*.

He snorted.

"Or how about Benny Valentino?" I said, naming the celebrity baker who had the most popular baking show in the country. He irritated Chad to no end because he said he was more show than talent.

"Benny Valentino?" he growled out.

Giggling like crazy, I replied, "Yeah—he's supposed to be the best baker in the country, right? So I'd always have something delicious to eat. No more of the mediocre stuff I put up with now."

He picked me up and tipped me over his shoulder. I thought he was taking me to the bedroom, but he didn't; instead, he veered toward the kitchen and set me on the counter. He turned his back to me and opened the fridge, pulling out the rest of the fruit tart he'd made me the night before to celebrate my new job.

"Close your eyes," he said in that low, seductive voice.

I leaned back on my hands, feeling my unzipped dress gaping in the back, and closed my eyes on the image of Chad with his shirt hanging open. I heard him in the silverware drawer before he stepped between my legs again.

"Open your mouth," he said, one hand on my thigh.

I opened my mouth.

He slid a fork between my lips, and I closed them. Once the fork left my mouth, there was an explosion of flavor on my tongue. His fruit tart was my absolute favorite. Even better than his carrot cake. I moaned softly, involuntarily, like I often did when eating his food because it was so good.

I heard him make a subtle sound of satisfaction and could imagine the smug look on his face he always had nowadays when I reacted to his food that way.

"You think Benny Valentino's sorry excuse for baking could make you moan like that?" he asked. "Open up."

He slid in another mouthful, and I moaned again. "No," I breathed out, opening my eyes. I wanted him to see them; I knew my pupils would be huge. When he looked up from getting another bite on the fork, he froze for a second, then tossed the fork onto the remainder of the tart.

After we'd made love in the kitchen, then in the shower after getting the rest of the fruit tart all over us, we curled up in bed together, my back to Chad's chest. He kissed the crook of my neck.

"I love you, my Rena."

"I love you, too, my Chad."

His arms tightened around me, and in a flash, his breath was slow and even. I was tired, but I was buzzing with excitement. The last two days had been filled with so much wonderful news for me and the people I cared about, filled with so much love and support and connection. It truly felt like I'd opened the book of my life onto a new chapter, and I couldn't wait to keep turning pages and find out what would happen next.

THIRTY-ONE

With my first assignment on staff turned in and accepted by Jeb, I felt like I was walking on air. Except that I was also feeling claustrophobic pent up in the apartment. While I relished all the time to focus on my writing since I'd left the café, it had come with an unexpected side effect: I never went *anywhere*. I would go days without leaving the confines of the apartment, and I was going stir crazy with the need for some fresh air. I was desperate to go running; I missed my daily runs more than ever, and I missed the preserve and my independence.

Chad and I had both been too afraid for me to go anywhere by myself for four and a half months now, but we hadn't seen Damien since the court date to finalize the permanent protective order. While it wasn't the same as when I'd lived with Damien and he didn't allow me to leave for weeks on end, it was beginning to feel that way. Surely Damien would have appeared by now if he was going to; I was more convinced than ever that he wasn't going to violate the protective order. And how much more of my life did I need to give up to Damien? It was no different, really, than everything else I talked about with my therapist: my eating habits, my appearance, my suspiciousness of beverages I didn't prepare myself. This fear that was keeping me confined was another way Damien was still controlling my life. And because of that control, I was already likely to miss out on running the marathon I was supposed to run this year, the marathon I would have run with my dad if he were alive. Running once a week at most wasn't enough to prepare for it.

Screw you, Damien. You've taken enough from me.

I changed into my running clothes and paused near the front door where I'd placed my picture of my dad and me that I'd kept on the wall next to the front door in my apartment before moving in with

Chad. My eyes watered as I stared at my dad's face; I felt mortified that it had taken me so many months to decide to take a stand against my fear and that, as a result, I was likely going to miss our marathon.

"I promise you I'll run it next year if I can't this year, Dad. And I promise to face my fears."

His face smiled back at me the way it always did in the photo, but it felt like he was telling me he was proud of me.

My confidence had mostly eroded by the time I reached the lobby of the building, and I considered turning back, but I remembered the promise I'd just made to my dad. My hands were shaky and my heart raced like I'd just finished a long run ending with a half-mile sprint, but I pushed through the doors into the fresh spring air. I paused, my eyes darting around frantically, but I didn't see Damien. With a controlled inhale and exhale that was not very effective at calming my nerves, I bounded off.

The preserve was about two miles from Chad's apartment, the entire route along busy streets. Even if I saw Damien, he wasn't likely to try anything; there were too many people around. I would run to the preserve and back; that way I could at least see it and smell it again, and four miles would probably be plenty for my first run in a while. Certain in the knowledge that nothing could happen to me along the street, my body relaxed into the run, the anxiety over possibly seeing Damien dissipating with each step. Before I knew it, I could see the preserve ahead of me.

My heartrate picked up at the sight of the trees, this time in anticipation, and after another half-block, I could smell it. I even closed my eyes for several steps to focus that sense. It smelled like peace and balance to me. My steps faltered when I spied my apartment building.

Breathe. I'm not going there right now, and Damien isn't there.

As I approached the entrance to the preserve where I'd planned to turn around and run back to Chad's, I had a surge of energy and optimism; I could easily run further. Maybe I would just go in to the first set of benches and turn around, just so I could see it again, just long enough for me to feel my dad's presence. I wouldn't go far, then I'd be back out where there were more people around and I'd be safer if I saw Damien.

My feet carried me along the entrance, then far into the preserve. I ran and ran and ran, my feet moving without any input from my mind, traveling the familiar pathways, and I felt more like myself than I had in a long time. The preserve was home for me, and I'd been sorely missing it for the last four and a half months. Eventually, I began to tire, and the preserve began to darken as the sun moved lower in the sky. From deep within the preserve, before the final three-mile trek back to Chad's apartment, I sat and stretched on the same bench I'd sat on nearly a year earlier when the writing conference flyer blew into my lap.

So much had changed in the last year; some changes I'd never expected, some I'd never dared to hope for. If I had anything to do with it, the next year would bring even more positive change to my life. And I did have something to do with it, I realized. Things didn't just happen to me by chance, aside from that flyer landing in my lap. But, really, that didn't either; I had first had the courage to leave Damien, to move back to my hometown, to start running again, despite being terrified he'd come after me. I'd swallowed my fear and reservations and applied for the job at the café, then I'd refused to let my fears control me and given Chad a chance. I'd attended the writing conference and put the work in to find my words again, and had been willing to face rejection again in order to give myself a chance at success by submitting pieces to the journal. I'd had a hand in every good thing that had happened to me over the last year.

With a renewed sense of self and optimism, realizing I was following my heart the way Dad had always made me promise I would, I rose and ran back to Chad's apartment, eager to share with him everything I'd realized and experienced since I'd decided to go for a run a few hours earlier.

When I returned to the apartment, however, Chad wasn't there. Normally he'd have been back by then from teaching, and I didn't remember him saying he had anything to stay late for, but most likely I'd forgotten or something had come up. I was disappointed, because I was excited to share with him about my afternoon, but figured he'd be home sooner or later. After downing two glasses of water in the kitchen, I hopped in the shower. Once I was dressed, I decided to call

Chad to find out what the plan was for the evening, then I'd call Caroline.

"Where are you?" he burst out, frantic, the second the call connected.

"At home," I said, baffled. "Where are *you*?"

"Looking for you!" he shouted.

"What? Why would—"

"You were gone, Rena!" he shouted again, his voice thin with anguish.

My stomach sank as I realized he'd come home and thought something had happened to me.

"I-I w-went for a r-run," I stammered out, my heart pounding against my chest. My whole body felt electric and poised for flight; it was just like I used to feel when Damien began one of his jealous interrogations.

"You left without me, Rena! I came home and you were gone and you didn't even have your phone. I freaked out, Rena. I thought... I thought he got in somehow or—"

"I'm sorry," I said quietly. "I'm sorry, Chad. I'm sorry. I'm so sorry."

"Jeez, Rena, I can't even... I'm on my way home. Don't go anywhere."

He hung up before I could reply. My hand floated down to my side and I stared at the phone, tears streaming down my cheeks. I felt like I'd done something horribly wrong, and, worse, that something horrible was about to happen to me. My breathing was erratic and I felt sick. Running to the bathroom, I threw up until nothing was coming out and I was just dry-heaving. Afterward, I paced the apartment, my arms tight around me, until I heard the door open. I froze where I was, halfway across the living room, and stared toward the entryway as Chad emerged.

His jaw was hard, the set of his face indicating anger, but his eyes were bloodshot and glassy and he looked like he was being tortured. I had no idea what to expect; he'd never looked at me like that before. Just as he'd never yelled at me the way he had on the phone. He stopped at the far end of the living room and just stared at me, breathing hard. Abruptly, he turned his head to the side and wiped his face; he was crying.

"Damn it, Rena," he ground out. "You scared the shit out of me!"

"I didn't mean to," I said, my voice small, staring through the floor in front of me and trying to shrink into myself.

"Why the hell did you go out without me? Without even *telling* me? And you didn't take your phone, so I couldn't even call you when I couldn't find you at home. What...? What were you *thinking*, Rena?"

"I..."

"There's a maniac out there who's threatened your life, for god's sake, and you went out *alone* without a way to even call for help?"

"I'm sorry. I'm so sorry." I sank down into the corner of the sofa and hugged my knees up to my chest. "I'm so, so sorry."

I was sobbing into my knees for a while before Chad spoke again. He'd stopped yelling, but his voice was missing that warmth he always had for me.

"I was going out of my mind. You have no idea what I went through when I came home and you were gone. The worst scenarios went through my mind all at once and I didn't even know where to start to find you. I was terrified, Rena—*terrified*. I love you so damn much and I thought something happened to you. Do you have any idea what that feels like?"

His voice cracked and I heard the sounds of him crying for a few minutes. I didn't say anything—I didn't know what *to* say. There were no words that could make things better, and if I said anything, it was likely I'd end up making things worse. It was best if I just stayed small and quiet until he wasn't angry anymore.

No more words were exchanged between us before Chad went to bed. I stayed in the living room, holding a book like I would if I were reading until I thought he was asleep, then cried until I dozed off for a while. But I woke with a start after only a few hours and was still awake when Chad got up for work. His eyes rested on me as he passed, and he looked like he had things he wanted to say, but he didn't. I listened to him in the kitchen making breakfast before he stood at the far end of the living room. I stared at his feet—I couldn't raise my eyes, but I could feel him looking at me and got the sense he was waiting for something. Eventually, he sighed.

"I'm sorry I yelled at you. I'm pissed off, but I shouldn't have yelled at you the way I did. I have to leave for work. No classes today, so I'll be home a little after three and we can talk about what happened yesterday. Don't leave the apartment while I'm gone."

His footsteps disappeared toward the entryway, the door closing behind him as he left. For the first hour or two, I didn't move. I stayed in the exact same spot, afraid to do anything, my mind spinning with ways I could possibly placate him when he came home. And then, in a flash, I realized I was acting like Chad was Damien... and that it was because he was acting like him. My mind flashed to the future, and I saw myself cowering at home, not having left in weeks, being physically restrained from leaving like Damien had done to me... except it wasn't Damien I saw. It was Chad.

I panicked.

I jumped up and paced for several minutes, my mind racing too quickly for any thoughts to take hold except one: I had to get out before it happened again.

In the bedroom, I thanked the universe that I hadn't cancelled my lease, insisting that moving in with Chad would be temporary, despite his offer for it to be permanent. It meant that I had somewhere to go, unlike when I first realized I would leave Damien. I threw everything of mine that was in Chad's apartment into trash bags and lugged them down to my car. Then I placed the key he'd given me in the hall on the entry table with a note.

I'm sorry. I can't do this.

After hauling my last bag back into my old apartment, I stood in the middle of the living room, surrounded by the trash bags of my belongings, and broke down. I felt so stupid for thinking I had begun a new chapter in my life when all I was doing was repeating one that had already been written. I felt betrayed that Chad was just like

Damien when I'd thought he was different. I felt cursed that not only had it happened before, but it was happening again with a man who owned my heart in a way Damien never had... in a way that I knew I'd never get it back. My chest felt like it was splitting open, as if someone were inside with a crowbar and prying my chest cavity apart. I hugged my knees and cried until I had no tears left to fall. Then, I stood up and began unpacking my bags.

I'd become used to Chad's apartment, so filled with light and plant life; mine was dark, with only one window, and no life since I'd forgotten to grab Potty before I rushed out of Chad's. And the fact that it hadn't been cleaned in months meant everything was coated in a thick layer of dust and made the space feel even more depressing. I was in the middle of cleaning when my phone rang with a call from Chad. I silenced the call, turned my phone off, then continued to clean. I wanted to be proud of myself for making a clean break with him, but all I felt was a sickening guilt like I was doing something wrong.

I'd felt guilt when I left Damien, too, I reminded myself. In time, it would pass. I would begin to see more similarities between Chad and Damien, and the guilt would fade away to be replaced by conviction that I'd done the right thing. But rather than making me feel better, I had doubts. There were things that would never be the same between Chad and Damien, no matter how much time passed for me to analyze their behaviors. Was that only because I'd left so early, and if I'd stayed longer, more of Damien's behaviors would have appeared in Chad? Or was it because Chad was actually different, and I was being unfair?

I thought back to the day before, to the way he'd yelled at me for leaving the apartment without him. How angry he'd been, the way he'd berated me like I was a child who'd disobeyed her parents. I remembered that morning, when he'd told me not to leave while he was gone. I also remembered when I'd promised myself the day I left Damien that I'd never stick around with someone who tried to control me in that way ever again. I was keeping my promise to myself.

My intercom buzzed twenty minutes later, and Chad's voice came through the speaker.

"Rena, it's Chad," he said, his voice frantic and watery. "If you're there, please let me in. We have to talk, Rena. Please."

My jaw trembled, but I stood still and didn't go to the intercom and push the button.

The intercom buzzed again. "Rena, please. Are you there? If you are, I'm begging you to let me in so we can talk. Your car is here... maybe you're in the preserve. I'll look there next. Please, Rena love."

I had thought I'd exhausted my reserve of tears, but my eyes proved me wrong; they were streaming down my cheeks now. They'd dried up, though, by the time Chad was buzzing the intercom again nearly two hours later.

"Rena, please. Please. Just let me know you're okay. Even if you won't talk to me, just tell me you're okay."

I turned on my phone and, ignoring every message he'd sent, I typed out my own, letting him know that I was okay and telling him to leave me alone. It was harsh, and the guilt I felt intensified when I sent it. I could imagine his face when he read it, but tried to eradicate that image from my mind. What I saw was the reaction of the person I thought he was, not the person he actually was.

I also had messages from Caroline asking me what the hell happened and imploring me to call her. Fern, I knew, probably hated me. I texted Caroline back and told her I wasn't up to talking, but agreed to having her come over in the morning since she was off.

I was shocked, and a little upset with Caroline for not giving me a heads up, when I opened the door to my apartment the next morning to find not only Caroline, but also a very angry-looking Fern. Caroline's mouth turned down as she glanced at me apologetically.

"Sorry," she mouthed.

They both walked in and followed me to the kitchen. Caroline sat at a stool at the counter, Fern stood next to her, and I stood on the other side of the counter. I felt outnumbered, like I was about to go to war, and had an urge to just walk out of my apartment and go hide in the preserve until I thought they would have left. I'd barely slept the night before and wasn't sure I had enough energy for what was bound to be a very confrontational visit from Fern.

Silence stretched out as I stared at the countertop, feeling two sets of eyes on me. I didn't know where to start and decided to just wait until one of them spoke first. That person was Fern.

"What the fuck, Renata?" she bit out. "We all trusted you after you did this to him before, but then you do it again?"

"I..." I shook my head, trying not to start crying again. I forced myself to control my breathing.

"You what?" Fern shouted.

"Fern, stop it," Caroline said in a low but strong voice. "You don't even know what happened yet."

"What happened is that she broke my brother's heart—*again*."

There was a flash of anger in my chest. "He broke *mine*."

The air charged and there was a long silence.

"How exactly did my brother break your heart?"

I stepped away from the kitchen and Fern began to protest until Caroline told her to just wait. She must have suspected what I was doing. I returned with my journal; I'd spent an hour writing in it before Caroline was supposed to arrive, trying to process what had happened with Chad, and what I'd done as a result. Trying to make sense of it all and find the conviction I needed if I wasn't going to go crazy thinking I'd made a mistake and ruined the best thing that had ever happened to me. Except that it couldn't be—the best thing to ever happen to someone couldn't involve controlling them and when they were allowed to leave their home.

I flipped the journal open to where I'd been writing that morning and set it down on the counter in front of Caroline. "It's here," I whispered, sniffling.

My tears hadn't spilled over yet, but they were close. I walked to the bathroom and blew my nose, then looked at myself in the mirror. I looked like shit; my eyes were red and puffy with dark circles, my mouth pulled into a tight frown. I'd seen myself like that before and never thought I would again. At the same time, this hurt in a way it hadn't when I'd left Damien. My eyes drifted down, landing on my phoenix necklace. I never took it off. My fingers touched the metal and it felt like my heart would explode. I couldn't wear it. Reaching behind my neck, I unclasped it, then tucked it away safely in a drawer in my bedroom.

When I returned to Caroline and Fern, I waited on my sofa; I didn't want to see their reactions as they read. But I heard them: muttered frustrations coming from Fern and sympathetic sounds from Caroline.

"Damn it, Chad!" Fern burst out without warning. I turned at her shout as she smacked the countertop. Her eyes were still glued to my journal.

When I heard them close the journal, I took a deep breath and walked into the kitchen, standing where I had before.

"Renata," Fern said, her voice more even than before, even if she was obviously frustrated. "There's something you need to understand about Chad. He can be a little overprotective when he cares about you and thinks you're in danger. He's not a controlling person, he really isn't. It's just, he gets stuck in feeling like he has to protect you but that everything's out of hand, and that anxiety comes out in trying to find control by controlling the things around him. You have to understand, Renata—we lost our parents and Chad felt so helpless. We both did. We loved them, we prayed for them, we maintained positivity for them, we made sure they did everything the doctors said to do, and they both died anyway. There was nothing we could have done, but it felt like we must have done something wrong or not done enough—especially for Chad. As the oldest, he always felt it was his responsibility to... to... to fix everything. But he couldn't fix that."

Fern paused and wiped under her eyes as Caroline rubbed her back.

"When my parents died, Chad took care of me. He became my legal guardian and he gave up so much to make sure I was well taken care of. He was my brother, but he was forced to be my parent, and he took that role seriously because he loved me. But it was hard for him because he was so scared something would happen to me that he couldn't control, just like with our parents, so he became overprotective. Especially when I was anorexic. You could call it controlling, and I did back then, but I prefer overprotective now. He imposed rules to keep me safe, but they infringed on the freedom I was used to having as a teen. We fought mercilessly, and the more I tried to get him to understand, the more he doubled down. Until he realized he'd kept me from going to my senior prom, that I'd missed out on an experience I could never re-do. That's when he saw what he'd been doing. Things got better after that, although from time to time something would happen that would send him back into overprotective mode until I pointed out to him that he was doing it again."

She stopped talking for a second and reached her hand across the counter toward me. "Renata, please look at me."

I looked up.

"He's not trying to control you. He's trying to protect you. He shouldn't do it like this at all, I know, but it's not because he *wants* to control you. You have to understand that these things are different. And you can work through this with him. He *will* see what he's doing and he'll do better, I promise you, but you have to give him a chance. You can't just turn your back on him like you did. I get why you did that, I really do—I can see how it feels like what you went through before, but I swear to you it's not."

I stared at her, not sure how to tell her that, while it may not be the same... it also was. To *me* it was. Controlling was controlling and that was something I could never do again.

"Renata, please... he loves you. He loves you with his whole heart—he gave it all to you. Don't do this to him."

"I'm not doing it *to him*," I replied. "I'm doing it *for me*."

"I know, and I understand now, but please think about what I said. Please think about giving him another chance because he's not like your ex." She paused. "I have to go—I have to get back to the café. Please think about it, Renata."

Caroline followed Fern to the door and they talked quietly before exchanging a kiss. Then Fern left and Caroline walked back to the kitchen, coming around to stand next to me at the counter.

"She hates me. And I don't know if I can blame her."

"She doesn't hate you," Caroline replied. "She's upset for her brother."

"I'm not trying to hurt him," I said, my voice breaking.

Caroline wrapped her arms around me. "I know," she soothed.

I cried into her shoulder for a long time while she smoothed a hand up and down my back. At length, I stepped back, wiping my face with my shirt.

"Believe it or not, I've cried so much I didn't think I had any tears left, but apparently I was wrong."

The corners of Caroline's mouth turned down, along with the corners of her eyes. "I'm sorry, honey."

"You probably hate me, too, for this mess."

"No," she said, shaking her head. "I hate Damien. Because if it weren't for him, this mess wouldn't exist."

"I can't do it again, Caroline," I said, my eyes somehow filling again. "I can't. I just can't. I don't know how to explain to you what it did to me the first time and I can't do it again. I love Chad, I love him so damn much it feels like I've lost part of myself, but I can't do this."

"I understand," she soothed. "You're doing what you need to for yourself, and that's what you should do."

"You don't think I'm doing the wrong thing?"

"Renata, honey, I can't say what the right or wrong thing is. Of course I don't want you hurting and I don't want Chad hurting because I love you both, but I can't say if you staying or going is the right thing to do because I don't know. I'm not you. Of course I wish you two could figure this out together because I know just how much you love each other, but only you know what's best for you. No one else."

I gave a small nod and hung my head. The problem was that I *didn't* actually know what was best for me, either.

The next morning, I forced myself to get out of bed, even though I didn't feel like it. Caroline had stayed with me most of the day before she had to leave and we'd talked a little more, but mostly watched movies in silence. I hadn't had the energy or the heart to hash things out any further. But just having her there had helped; when she'd left, it felt like I was being smothered by loneliness.

But now it was time to pick myself up and make myself do something; I knew that from when I'd left Damien. But apparently I was braver then. Now, the thought of leaving my apartment filled me with terror. I'd had so much courage just a few days earlier when I left Chad's, but now I felt so alone and afraid. I paced my apartment, filled with anger and frustration; if I couldn't make myself leave alone, then what the hell was the point in leaving Chad? If I was just going to stay indoors anyway, at least it would have been with him.

No, that's not true, because I have a choice now. I didn't before—that much was obvious by the way he blew up at me for leaving and ordered me not to leave without him.

I scrubbed my hands over my face and shouted unintelligibly into the otherwise silent space. Opening my eyes, I headed over to my table where I used to keep Potty only to find the spot empty before remembering that I'd rushed out and forgotten to grab my plant. *Damn it.* Now I had nothing for comfort, nothing to help me feel safe and grounded again. That was all I had left after leaving Chad, but now I didn't even have that.

And what would I do if Damien *did* come after me? What if all mine and Chad's fears were justified and Damien broke the protective order and showed up? What would I do?

What *could* I do?

Not much. I could run, but that would only work if I saw him first and had a strategy to get hidden before he caught up to me. I was getting faster but doubted I could outrun him yet. And it wouldn't matter how fast I could run if he got to me first. I looked longingly toward the wall on the other side of which I knew was the preserve. I wanted so badly to go running through the trails to clear my mind, but I felt paralyzed thinking about unlocking and walking through my apartment door.

I walked over to the door where I'd re-hung the picture of my dad and touched the frame.

"Dad? What do I do?" I asked tearily. "I think I messed up big time, but I'm not sure. Maybe I didn't, I don't know. But now I don't know what to do. I'm so afraid. I'm afraid of Damien coming back." I wiped my face with the hem of my t-shirt. "And I'm afraid I'm going to end up alone. I was building a family for myself and now I've just walked away from part of it... no one will accept me again."

My thoughts wandered back to all the wonderful people I'd met the previous Thanksgiving, how kind they'd been to me and the bond they'd all had with each other. I thought about how staying in our cabin was the most part of a family I'd felt since my dad had died, because Caroline's parents and brother had accepted me immediately as part of theirs. A memory of the camaraderie among them flashed through my mind, followed by the entertaining dynamic between Caroline and her brother, Brandon, and I couldn't help but smile remembering watching Caroline break his headlock and pin his arm behind him. It was so shocking because Brandon wasn't a small guy, and he wasn't going easy on her either. She looked so harmless, but she could take down anyone who tried to mess with her, that much was clear.

My breath caught and I stared at my dad in the photo. Of course he wore the exact same smile he always had in that photo because it could never change, and yet it was as if he was gently encouraging me, like he was trying to tell me something. And then it hit me... Caroline could easily defend herself.

Maybe she could teach me to do the same.

THIRTY-TWO

My breath was hard and heavy, but even and measured at the same time. It was getting harder to maintain that evenness, but I wouldn't have to for much longer; there were only a few more miles to the finish line. My legs burned and I wasn't sure I'd be able to walk afterward, but I was going to make it; I'd been training for this marathon intensely since leaving Chad five weeks earlier.

We spoke only once after I left him. It was about a week later, and he came to my apartment with Potty and wouldn't leave until he handed my plant to me. I'd been too nervous to let him in, so I'd walked down and stepped outside the building, staying close to the entrance. Whatever parts of my heart weren't already broken broke that day. I'd never seen Chad the way he was. His face was scruffy and his hair looked unwashed. His clothes looked like he hadn't taken them off in days. His eyes were bloodshot and there were dark, deep circles under his eyes. I'd nearly run to him and wrapped my arms around him and told him I was sorry.

But I hadn't.

He'd held out Potty awkwardly and I'd taken the plant, holding it with both hands so they'd both have something to do, then turned after a quick "thank you" to head back into the building.

"Rena, please—wait just a moment?" he asked, his voice scratchy like he hadn't used it in a while. He didn't just look like crap, he sounded like crap.

I paused and turned back around, keeping my eyes averted. Being so near him with the way things were was torture.

"Fern... she explained everything to me." He paused. "You know that already, because I left you messages telling you that. But she did—she told me I was doing it again, that overprotective thing, and I'm sorry, Rena. I really am sorry. And I promise I'll do better, but I need you to come back to me. I miss you so damn much, Rena. I don't know what to do with myself without you. Everything is so gray and meaningless since you left me. And you never gave me a chance to fix things. Please give me that chance."

"Chad, you... I can't go through what I did before again."

"What you did before? Are you comparing me to Damien?" he asked, his voice rising.

I ignored his question and continued. "The last time I gave a second chance, I ended up trapped for years. And I don't think I could survive going through that again."

"I'm not Damien!" he shouted. His face was hard with anger, but he also had tears on his cheeks. "I would never—I couldn't—I can't believe you think I'm like *him*!"

For a long time, there was silence between us. He gaped at me, and I tried desperately not to fall apart on the sidewalk as the feeling that I'd made a grave mistake—which had plagued me since I'd left—grew until it was screaming inside me. I couldn't be in a controlling relationship ever again, and yet, somehow, my heart was trying to tell me I'd done the wrong thing by leaving. How was that even possible? Nothing made sense anymore, and I was so confused.

"Tell me I'm wrong, Rena," he said with urgency. "Tell me you don't really think I'm like him."

I stared at him as all the ways he was the opposite of Damien passed through my mind, his tenderness and gentleness compared to Damien's roughness and violence, his encouragement of my dreams compared to Damien's feeling threatened by them, his admiration for my physical abilities compared to Damien's desire to control them, his quiet humility and Damien's loud ego. Everything about him was so different.

"You think I am," Chad whispered.

I heard him but I was still trapped by my swirling, confusing mess of thoughts.

"Damn it!" More tears spilled onto his cheeks. "I thought you knew me," he said through a clenched jaw, touching his chest with his hand. "I thought you *knew me*, Rena. But you don't if you think I'm anything like that bastard. And that means I don't know *you* as well as I thought I did, either."

With that, he'd turned and walked away from me and never tried to contact me again.

In the weeks since that happened, I hadn't found any more clarity regarding whether or not I'd done the right thing, despite devoting a lot of therapy time to it. My therapist kept insisting I was focused on the wrong part of what happened, but I didn't understand how there was any other part; did I destroy the man I loved for no reason or was I right that staying would have ended the way it did with Damien? However, time was bringing a dullness to the pain of missing him.

Caroline told me things about him from time to time; I never asked, and sometimes I stopped her because it hurt too much to hear about him. Other times, I listened like my life depended on it, desperate for any information about him. In this way, I learned that she and Fern talked Chad into seeing a therapist to process their parents' deaths. Fern had seen someone when she was struggling with anorexia, her way of coping with their loss, but Chad hadn't been able to afford for both of them to go back then and also thought he needed to be "stronger" than that so he could take care of Fern. But he was seeing someone now. I also learned that he was recently promoted and received a grant to study at the world-famous Petite Académie in France for six weeks in the fall to learn new techniques to bring back and impart to his students.

I thought often about what life might have been like for us if I hadn't left him or if I'd gone to him the way I wanted to the day he'd brought Potty to my apartment or if I'd called him and told him I was sorry, that I knew he wasn't like Damien, one of the hundreds, maybe even thousands, of times I'd wanted to. Then I used those thoughts to start writing a short story series for the journal, where each publication was another version of what might have been, but it was written in such a way that the reader wouldn't know which version was what really happened for the characters. I hadn't been sure what Jeb would think, but he loved the idea when I pitched it to him, which I was relieved about since it was all I'd been able to write about.

Aside from training, writing, and therapy, I'd been having frequent lessons from Caroline in self-defense. I was the strongest I'd ever been, but my body still flooded with fear whenever I left my apartment alone, which was most of the time. To help with that, her brother was going to start coming to Amestown a couple of days per week so I could practice with him; we thought having a man—especially one so much stronger than me—to practice with would help build my confidence. I'd been surprised when he'd been so willing to give up his free time for someone he barely knew, but he'd insisted once Caroline asked him and explained why. I'd been next to her while she talked to him on speakerphone and heard the disgust and anger in his voice in relation to Damien.

My legs felt like half ton tree trunks and protested strongly as my feet continued to pound the pavement, but I pushed through it; the finish line was up ahead, and I thought I could make out Caroline in the mass of people lining either side of the road. I'd told her she didn't have to come, but she'd laughed at me.

"And you don't have to go to my art showings, either," she'd replied, rolling her eyes.

I'd smiled, accepting her response. She knew there was no way I'd ever miss one of her art showings; she was my best friend, and I was going to support her no matter what. I supposed that was her way of telling me that went both ways.

Each step was excruciating. I'd trained hard, but it was a lot to put my body through to run this far considering the shape I was in five weeks earlier.

"You're almost there, Renata," I heard my dad's voice in my ear. "I'm proud of you."

A lump raised in my throat and I tried to swallow it down, pushing even harder, picking up the pace until I was in a dead sprint for the last hundred yards or so. When I crossed the line, I collapsed into Caroline's arms. My legs were wobbly and most of my weight hung on her as I sobbed, drenching her with my sweat and tears as she squeezed me tight, first squealing with excitement, then telling me how proud she was of me.

"You did it!" She shouted again when I raised my face.

I smiled through my tears, my head bobbing up and down. "I did it," I whispered.

She squealed again. "You're amazing!" she shouted. "You ran twenty-six freaking miles, Renata. Twenty-six!"

I bit the corner of my lip. "Twenty-six point two, actually."

She laughed and hugged me again. "I'm so freaking proud of you," she said. "And I know your dad is, too."

The lump that was receding returned, and I nodded into her shoulder. "I think so, too," I mumbled against her. Then I started laughing. At first, it was a small giggle, but then grew until I was doubled over. My body felt like it was going to keel over... but I also felt amazing. I'd done it. I'd run the race I'd promised my dad I would run, the race he and I were supposed to run together. So many years ago, I'd given up hope of ever doing it because of Damien taking running away from me, but here I was. At the finish line. And I'd done it *despite* every way Damien nearly took it away from me, both when I was with him, and afterward by making me so afraid to be out alone.

"Fuck Damien," I said aloud.

"Yeah," Caroline agreed. "Fuck Damien."

I did it, Dad, I thought, feeling the weight of grief on my shoulders becoming lighter, like I was beginning to shed some of that pain from losing him. *I kept my promise to you. I'm keeping all my promises to you. I didn't think I could, but I did. You always knew I could, didn't you? Thank you for believing in me, Dad.*

Through controlled breathing, I tried to dispel the nerves I always had before beginning a session with Caroline and Brandon. We'd done this many times by now, yet I still got nervous about practicing with Brandon. He was goofy and sweet and as kind as Caroline, and we'd agreed that we felt like a big sibling group when we were together, but he was still much larger and stronger than me and took our training practice very seriously. His playful demeanor fell away when it was time for us to start, and he became aggressive. It was the whole point of practicing with him, but that didn't change how it made me feel.

"Ready, Renata?" Brandon asked, his eyes boring into me.

I stared back at him, wondering if doing this on my birthday was a bad idea. It always took a lot out of me, not just physically, but emotionally, and while it was still morning, Caroline had planned out the evening for my birthday, starting with dinner with friends at a restaurant I hadn't been to yet. But I supposed this was also part of the point, because Damien could show up anytime—not just when I was most prepared.

"Ready," I replied, my stomach fluttering with nerves. Brandon had said he'd be going hard today.

The word was barely off my lips when he rushed me. I almost didn't see him swinging in time to stick out an arm and sidestep so he stumbled forward instead of making contact. I managed, but he was faster to recover than I was, and he was now behind me with an arm around my neck. All knowledge of who it was and that he wouldn't actually hurt me was gone, as it always was within a few seconds of starting, my body's survival responses taking over. Which, again, was the point—to train my survival responses.

Panic was choking me, but I knew I couldn't let it take over. Keeping it just below the surface, I remembered what to do next and reached behind my head for his hand, grabbing it with both of mine and yanking forward with all my strength. The purpose was to get it out and trapped under my elbow so I could then work to break the hold of his arm that was wrapped around my neck. But I couldn't get his hand to move this time—his hold was too strong. My face was feeling tingly from lack of oxygen, but there was another way. I squatted down, trying to sit into the air, making myself heavier, and he was forced to bend with me, meaning he was hunched over my back now. With everything I had left in me, I rammed my hips up and continued to tuck forward, and his body flipped over my back, dislodging his choke on me.

I stumbled backward, gasping in air, trying to shake off how disoriented I was from the lack of oxygen.

"Great, Renata," I heard Caroline's voice as if from far away.

Brandon was on his feet, barreling toward me again. This time when he swung, I sidestepped and he stumbled enough that I could turn and back away, but I was now at the tree line in the clearing and couldn't get any further away. It was a mistake I shouldn't have made; I always needed to be aware of my surroundings. I could hear Caroline coaching me, but was too focused on Brandon to actually make out anything she was saying. He was already heading toward me again, and I wasn't sure yet what to do. He reached out to grab me and I grabbed his arm, pulling him in as he came, pushing him to the side, then stepping sideways to run.

I wasn't fast enough, and he had my back again, and then I was in another choke, this one using only a single arm. My panic rose and I froze.

"Break it, Renata!" Brandon shouted at me as the edges of my vision became fuzzy. "You know how to do this!"

I heard him and tried to search my mind, but my mind was blank, and I was paralyzed.

"Break it!" he shouted again into my ear. "Don't let him win!"

Him... I instantly imagined it was Damien holding me in this choke. *Don't let him win... don't let him win.* I knew he would if I didn't do something. Gritting my teeth, my vision narrowing, I fought to regain control over my body.

Renata, do you hear me?

You belong to me. You always will.

If you ever leave me, I'll kill you.

"Break it, damn it!" Brandon's voice pierced through the fog of Damien's words.

Something within me snapped and I jumped up, bucking my legs forward and landing in a crouch that forced Damien down with me, loosening his hold so that I could duck out of it. As I stood, I grabbed his arm and twisted it up high behind his back. Damien shot to his full height trying to outrun the pain, but it was too late. My jaw clenched and I pulled up with all my might.

"You got me," Brandon said loudly, tapping my leg with his other hand.

"Don't break Brandon's arm!" Caroline shouted.

I cocked my head to the side, feeling like I was coming out of a trance, and let go of Brandon, quickly stepping back a few feet.

Brandon turned, beaming at me. Then Caroline was there next to him, also beaming. I was proud, but adrenaline and residual fear had me trembling, my eyes flooding with tears. Unsteady, my legs quaked beneath me and my breath came in bursts. Caroline and Brandon both descended on me at once, engulfing me in a giant hug.

"You did it, Renata," Brandon said. "I gave you everything and you did it."

I wasn't sure whose shoulder it was that my forehead was resting against, but I didn't care right then. "That was so intense," I whispered tearily.

"I told you I wasn't going to go easy anymore," Brandon replied.

He had, but I hadn't expected it to be as intense as it was. Typically, we did one thing at a time with a short reset between. He'd never immediately jumped into the next thing before. It was more realistic, but it was also terrifying.

He chuckled. "You almost broke my arm, Renata," he said, sounding amused and pleased. It reminded me of Thanksgiving when Caroline almost broke his arm because he didn't want to tap. "You could have—and you would have if you pulled just a little harder. I was afraid for a minute you were going to."

We all pulled apart, Brandon and Caroline each keeping an arm around me. I wiped my eyes and laughed. "I was. Instead of you, I saw Damien after you told me not to let him win. I wanted to break his arm. And I was going to. It wasn't until Caroline shouted at me that I remembered it was you, not him."

Brandon chuckled again, patting my back and ruffling my hair like I often saw him do to Caroline. "Proud of you, Renata. We'll keep practicing, but that loser doesn't stand a chance if he tries to mess with you again."

Hours later, I was getting ready for my birthday celebration. I was still in a bit of shock and feeling drained from the training session, which had run an hour by the time we called it quits, but excited nonetheless for whatever craziness Caroline had planned. All I knew was that it was starting at Underwood, a restaurant a few towns over. She and Brandon were picking me up soon, but I was already ready to go and sitting on my sofa, my thoughts wandering.

Caroline had told me this was the restaurant she'd wanted to take me to the year before... which had never happened because Chad had insisted on cooking for me instead. The first time he'd ever cooked dinner for me, before I knew he liked me or that he wasn't dating Fern. I shook my head, remembering learning that they were siblings and how embarrassed I was that night. The rest of the night replayed through my mind like a movie reel, my body feeling all the same excitement and nervousness I'd had then.

My eyes darted over to my bookshelf along the far wall, settling on my copy of *The Dictionary of Lost Words*, the birthday present Chad had given me. The first gift he'd ever given me. As with every time I looked at it, my heart ached.

I missed him.

I missed him so much.

My eyes flooded and I huffed out a breath. This was why I tried to avoid thinking about him—because it always made me cry. But it was hard not to when I was sitting alone in my apartment the way I was. I wondered if the same thing happened to him. Did he feel the same ripping sensation through his chest when he thought of me that I felt when I thought of him? Did he ache to hear my voice and feel my touch the way I ached for those things from him? Did he feel this certainty that he'd never love again the way he'd loved me like I knew I'd never love again the way I'd loved him?

There was no way to know... and there was no point in even wondering about it. However he did or didn't feel, our time together was over. And while it had ended so abruptly and painfully, our relationship up to that point had been characterized by anything but pain. No matter what, he'd done things for me I never could have done for myself and helped me grow in ways no one else ever could have. I was better for having been with him, and even knowing in the end I'd have to leave because he was beginning to control me, I was fairly certain I wouldn't do anything differently; what we had while it lasted was worth the pain that came later. Because now, in the wake of that pain, I was coming out of it stronger than I'd ever been, physically and emotionally.

I felt like I was being born again almost. Painfully, with many scars, but rising up from the destruction again, much like my name indicated. Like the phoenix. I actually felt like the phoenix I'd always admired. Rising, I walked to my bedroom and opened my top dresser drawer, reaching in and pulling out the small box I'd decided to use for the necklace Chad had given me. I hadn't even looked at it since I'd taken it off right after I left him.

I lifted it by the clasp from the box and held it in front of me, watching the phoenix pendant swaying, the light catching the rose gold and making it look almost like it was flaming. It hurt to hold something Chad had given me when we were together and I thought there was nothing that could ever come between us, but I also felt worthy of it in a way I hadn't before. I used to wear it and hope it could give me that feeling of strength. Now, I had that feeling and the necklace felt more like a symbol of that strength. Using my other hand, I fingered the pendant and felt a painful, wonderful surge of emotion in my chest. I'd been destroyed, but I was still here, and I wasn't going to be destroyed again.

On impulse, I clasped the necklace around my neck and rested my hand over the pendant, feeling the metal pressing into my skin in the outline of the phoenix. Lifting my hand I looked down and saw my skin coming through the cutout and remembered Chad's words about how he'd selected that pendant because it made me the phoenix. I *was*, I realized. And this necklace would remind me of that if I ever forgot.

As well as my tattoo, because I knew it was time to get it. I was ready, and I felt deserving. I would start searching for the right tattoo artist the next day. My chest was buoyed with pride and excitement, and I rested my palm over the pendant again, pressing it against my chest. I closed my eyes and could see Chad's face behind my eyelids, smiling at me with love after he'd clasped the necklace around my neck the first time.

"Thank you," I whispered.

THIRTY-THREE

Six weeks after my birthday found me feeling stronger than ever. I still practiced with Brandon and Caroline a few days a week, and I was getting better. Brandon had to work hard every session, and rarely did he come out on top anymore. The biggest improvement, however, was in my mental ability to handle what we were doing. I still felt emotional at the end, still sometimes got a little shaky, but I didn't break down anymore like I used to every time. As a result, my fear when I left my apartment was minimal. It was always there, but it never controlled me anymore.

It was girls' night and Caroline's turn to drive. I finished getting ready in shorts, a sleeveless blouse, and sandals, and checked my phone. They'd be there soon to pick me up for an evening of mini-golf, Fern's choice this time. I shot Caroline a text telling her not to park because I'd wait for them out front and headed out the door. When I opened my front door and stepped out, I was digging in my purse for my keys and didn't notice I wasn't alone. As my door clicked shut, the hair on my neck rose and I froze. Before I had a chance to turn, I was pushed against my door from behind by another body.

"Renata," Damien said.

My purse slipped from my hands to the floor, and I forced a slow breath as the panic flooded my bloodstream. "You're not supposed to be within five hundred feet of me, Damien," I said, my voice not quite as steady as I'd hoped, giving away my fear. "Let alone touching me."

His hand ran down my side and grasped my hip. Vomit tracked up my throat and I had to swallow hard to keep it down.

"I've missed you, babe."

I clenched my jaw. "Get off me, Damien."

To my surprise, he stepped back and I turned, feeling disoriented. I hadn't expected him to do what I asked; that was unusual. My eyes scanned my surroundings; we were alone in the hallway. I looked back to Damien; he looked the same as he always did.

"You aren't supposed to be anywhere near me. If you leave right now and don't come near me again, I won't report this," I said. "You know if I do, you'll be arrested and it'll ruin your reputation." I hoped that reminder would be enough to make him leave.

He held his hands up in a conciliatory gesture. "Nothing to report, babe. I just wanted to talk."

"There's nothing for us to talk about. Ever," I bit out. My mind was racing to figure out what was going on; he'd never been so complacent before. It was unsettling and threw me off. I had no idea what to expect now.

"I wanted to apologize," he said.

I could feel some of my guard lowering. Apologize? He'd never once apologized to me for anything real. I eyed him warily, but didn't say anything.

"I'm sorry I let things come to this between us," he said. "I know I had a role in you leaving me."

"What?" I sputtered, my thought spoken aloud.

He inched closer. I went to move, but my back was against my door. "I realized I made some mistakes with you."

"Ha! That's an understatement."

He bowed his head forward in acknowledgement. "Perhaps. But I've learned from my mistakes."

Suddenly, I realized he'd been slyly shifting closer this whole time and was now very close to me. My heart hammered in my chest, my guard rising again as I cursed myself for letting it down.

"I won't make them again. This time, I'll do things a bit differently."

The contrition was an act—he was furious. With him only inches away, I could clearly see the fire raging in his eyes. But I was frozen as he leaned forward, grabbing my wrists and pinning them back against the door, then lowered his face next to mine to whisper into my ear.

"You're coming home with me, Renata. And this time, I'll make sure you never leave again—you won't even want to."

My eyes were glassy, and I wasn't really breathing, my body rigid.

"Because the things that'll happen if you do..." He rubbed his nose along mine, then kissed my cheek. My stomach heaved. He pulled back a little and his eyes raked over me, flashing and staring below my throat at my phoenix necklace. His grip on my wrists tightened and his jaw set. I knew what would happen next if I didn't stop him because he'd done things like that before; he was going to rip it off me. The thought of him taking something else of mine was enough for my anger to overtake my panic and my body unfroze.

With a growl, I rammed my knee upward into his groin, and in the second after when his grip on my wrists loosened, I yanked with all my might, freeing myself. Ducking and turning, I flipped out from in front of him and ran for the stairwell. Because I'd hurt him, I had a pretty good head start, but it wasn't enough; he caught up to me by the time I'd made it through the front door to my building. Obviously there had been people around to let Damien in, but of course there was no one around now to see what was happening.

Damien seized my arm from behind, but this was something I'd practiced with Brandon; I knew what to do. I turned with him as he pulled, then continued to turn, lifting my arm, bending my elbow, then slamming it down, breaking his grip. I knew I couldn't just run, though—he'd catch me again—so I grabbed his arm as I stepped around behind him and pulled with all my might.

He groaned in pain, but I didn't let up. I knew I was close to breaking his arm and I didn't care. I wanted to, even. But I didn't want to be like him and hurt someone intentionally, so gritted my teeth and forced myself to stop and just hold him where he was.

"Leave me the fuck alone," I ground out.

"Renata," he growled.

"Or I swear to god I'll break your arm," I added.

I pulled a little higher and he grunted and stiffened in pain.

"It's not so nice being on the receiving end, is it?" I asked, all the anger I'd ever felt toward him rushing through me at once. "To feel weak and helpless? To know if you don't do what I say, then I will fucking hurt you?"

"You're crazy," he bit out.

I laughed. "If I am, it's because you made me that way, you asshole. And I *will* hurt you if you ever come near me again. You don't scare me anymore, Damien."

I let go and shoved him, backing up several steps and wondering if I should have broken his arm to make sure he couldn't turn around and come after me again. He looked at me with disgust and rage, his hands balled into fists; he was deciding if he wanted to try me. My weight shifted on my feet and my arms readied themselves; I was prepared. Whatever he did, I'd counter it. There was a long, tense moment while he stared at me with narrowed eyes.

"You're not worth it," he said. "You never were. You were always pathetic. I can't believe I wasted time on you."

His words tried to sting, but then I realized he'd never have been saying them if I was actually pathetic, because that was what he preyed on. He was saying that now because I'd stood up to him and come out on top. *He* was the pathetic one. I released a hmph of breath in contempt.

"Renata!"

It was Caroline's frantic voice and I could hear her footsteps, but I didn't dare glance away from Damien for even a second in case he changed his mind. I held an arm out to my side and Caroline reached me as Damien turned and walked away, rolling his shoulder like he was in pain.

"Is that Damien?" Caroline asked as he disappeared toward the parking lot.

I let out a breath I hadn't realized I'd been holding and turned, collapsing into her arms. "Yes," I mumbled against her shoulder.

"Oh my god," she said, her arms tightening around me. "I wanted to get here faster—I could see something happening, but the traffic." I pulled back and she gestured down the street where I could see her car heading toward us behind a long line of cars, Fern behind the wheel. "I jumped out and ran down here as fast as I could."

I chuckled. "I scared him off," I said. "I actually scared Damien away." My chuckle deepened until I was bent over, my hands on my knees as I laughed. "I scared Damien," I wheezed.

Caroline stood next to me, rubbing my back while I lost my mind for a few minutes. When I finally had control over myself again, I stood up and looked Caroline in the eyes. "Thank you," I said. The words couldn't begin to describe my gratitude for her and everything she and her brother had done for me. What they'd given me meant I was standing there and Damien had walked away of his own volition. I knew he'd never be back this time.

Her eyes became glassy and she flung her arms around me. "I'm so glad you're okay."

Everyone else went out as planned, but Caroline hung back with me, insisting on being there while I talked to the police. I pulled out the card I'd been given the year before by the kind officer I'd spoken to in advance of getting the protective order and relayed to him everything that had happened. He listened, asking a few questions here and there. When we were done, he told me I should be proud of myself and I teared up.

I was.

After that call, I cried a little more sitting on my sofa with Caroline before we called her brother to tell him what happened and so I could thank him. He insisted on coming out the next day to celebrate, though it felt like an odd thing to celebrate. Caroline agreed for me, and I had to shake my head; she always wanted an excuse for a celebration.

By the time my emotions had settled down from the call with Brandon, I felt wrecked. I was bone-tired—more tired than I'd ever felt in my life. I could barely fathom getting off my sofa to go to bed, let alone going out to join our friends for minigolf.

"Do you mind if I just drop you off?" I asked, turning to Caroline. "I'm exhausted."

"I'll just have Fern pick me up later," she said, shrugging and reaching for the remote. "We can watch movies instead."

"I might fall asleep," I warned.

She settled back into the corner of the sofa, pulling her feet up to get comfortable, and powered the tv on. "Totally fine with me." She reached over and grabbed a pillow she'd tossed on the floor when we first sat down, situating it on her lap. She looked at me and patted it.

I sighed contentedly and laid down, resting my head on the pillow and stretching out on the sofa. There were definitely benefits to being short and this was one of them. I could comfortably lay on even small sofas. She rested an arm on my shoulder and started searching for a movie. I was asleep before she'd chosen one.

THIRTY-FOUR

Because I'd spent so much time researching and meeting tattoo artists before selecting one to do my phoenix tattoo, I didn't walk into the tattoo parlor until late August, but I didn't care. I was excited and proud of myself for doing something I wanted despite my fear of what other people would say to me. The only thing that might have made the experience better would have been if I was sharing it with Chad. But at least I had my best friend.

I squeezed Caroline's hand as we walked in the front doors to an office building of sorts, grateful she'd been willing to devote an entire day to supporting me. I was sure the tattoo was something I wanted to do, but I was also terrified; I'd never gotten a tattoo before. Because my tattoo artist, Oscar, and I worked together on the design for weeks, everything was ready to go when I arrived.

Within minutes, I was lying practically topless with my chest against the tattoo chair and Oscar was ready to begin. It was a decent-sized tattoo, but we were aiming to do it all in one sitting; I wanted to have it finished before Caroline and Fern's wedding since the bridesmaid dress I would be wearing was backless.

The first touch of the tattoo gun on my back was excruciating. There was the pain of what Oscar was doing, but there was also the pain from what happened to give me the scars I had. In an instant, I was back then, years before, in that argument with Damien about whether or not I'd wanted to cheat on him with our waiter from dinner. I was again fighting against him while he tried to force me to have sex with him, and falling backward into the flames when he pushed me. It was slowed down in my mind, and I could see in his eyes clearly that the push was deliberate. Maybe he hadn't intended for me to fall into the firepit... maybe he had. But he'd had no qualms about pushing me. It was no accident. And firepit or not, he never should have done it.

As the tattoo gun inched over my skin, I felt the literally skin-searing pain from the flames and the coals in the firepit melting the skin across my back. It was the worst pain I'd ever felt. I could hear myself screaming as if it were coming from somewhere else, then rolling off the firepit, my clothes on fire. I could remember how the momentum from leaving the firepit kept me rolling for several seconds, and then I blacked out. The next thing I remembered was coming to in the hospital.

I was groggy and bandaged and confused. It all felt like such a bad dream. Damien was there, holding my hand, and looked so relieved when my eyes found his, but I was confused because all I could remember was arguing and him pushing me. I tried to pull my hand back from him, but I was weak and he was holding tight. I was more scared of him than I'd ever been.

"Renata... you're going to be okay. You're going to be okay, babe."

Tears were now silently falling down my face.

"It's okay, babe," Damien said, moving his other hand so mine was clasped between both of his. "It's going to be okay. I'm going to help you so this doesn't happen again."

Again, I tried to pull my hand from his, but he wouldn't let me. I didn't understand what he meant by help me. My memory was foggy, but I knew he was the reason I was there.

"I'll monitor all of your drinks, Renata, and I won't let you drink so much anymore. I wish I had last week—then you wouldn't have stumbled into the fire when we were arguing. I'm so sorry, babe, that I didn't and now you're hurt."

Last week? I'd been out for a week? And he was saying I was drunk and fell into the fire myself? But I remembered him pushing me, then everything faded into nothingness only seconds later. I looked at him, at the way he was watching me so intensely, listened to him continue to talk about my problem with drinking having gotten out of hand and... my memory of the night it happened began to change until I wasn't sure what was real and what wasn't anymore. I realized right then that this *was the most scared of him I'd ever been, even more so than only seconds before, because he was able to influence my memories with his words.*

That was the first time I was sure of what he was doing. Still, he would later manage to convince me I was imagining things. It wasn't until I found the Rohypnol and took photos of it, so I could prove it to myself even after he'd spun a tale so convincing that I'd dreamt it, that I remembered that day in the hospital when I'd realized what he did to my mind.

All of this surged to the surface as Oscar outlined my phoenix and filled in the smoke and ash. For a while, I could even smell my burning skin again and had to keep my eyes open and trained on Caroline, who sat next to me with my hand in hers, to know that I wasn't on fire again.

We took a break after the black work was done, and while Oscar ate lunch, I carefully used the bathroom before returning to the chair and crying. I cried because of all the pain I'd been through because of Damien, but I also cried with relief because I was free. The tattoo was painful, but it was something I was choosing. Because I was now free to make my own choices. Damien was gone from my life. And while he could return at any time, no matter how unlikely, I was confident I could defend and protect myself. The protective order helped too, as long as I made sure to renew it every two years when it expired, but I didn't have to rely on that. I was safe and free.

And independent. I didn't depend on Damien for food or shelter or clothing, and I didn't depend on Chad to feel safe. I depended on myself for everything, and while I still missed Chad, I didn't need him, I realized. For a while, I'd thought I did. But I didn't. And before he'd become overprotective, he'd helped me to realize that. Thinking about Chad right then after all those memories of Damien during the worst experience in my life presented as stark a contrast as you could get between the two men. It was the first time in a long time that I'd mentally compared them, having given up long ago on trying to figure out exactly how much like Damien Chad was to determine if

I'd done the right thing when I left him. And with the distance time had provided, both with Damien and with Chad, I found I had a new clarity. I looked at Caroline, my eyes opening wide. Her eyebrows drew in.

"Chad's nothing like Damien."

She shook her head.

"He never was."

"No, he wasn't," she replied softly.

This was the conviction I'd been looking for before. And in the same breath as I was mentally berating myself for having made a mistake by leaving him, I realized it had to be that way. I'd needed to put myself first. If I hadn't done that—if I'd stayed to work through Chad's overprotectiveness as Fern had urged me to do—at some point, he would have stopped trying to control me. Chad and I would have worked through things in time. However, I also would never have known that I could put myself first. So much of my mental growth over the last several months had begun with leaving Chad.

When I'd left Damien, I'd done it out of instinct... I'd left in order to save my life. I'd known I would die if I stayed. I was already almost dead inside, and sooner or later he would have gone too far in his anger and gone from hurting me to killing me. The only things I knew were that I didn't want to die and that I would if I stayed, and animal survival instinct kicked in and took over until I was out of town.

But when I left Chad, it was different. I left so that I could have a life worth living. I'd never believed Chad would use violence against me the way Damien had; I wasn't afraid for my life. I was afraid of never being happy again, of never having a *reason* to be happy again outside of another person. And that was an enormous difference I hadn't noticed until now, while I was lying on the tattoo chair waiting for Oscar to finish his lunch.

It was another instance in which one emotion wasn't enough; it was bittersweet in the truest, richest way. I hated that things had to happen the way they did, but I wouldn't change what I had done. I needed to do it. I was lonely sometimes. I missed Chad every day and was confident I'd never be able to love again the way I loved him. Sometimes I was afraid and wished there was someone there to give me comfort. But I was gradually building a life that I wanted to be in, living it consistent with the whispers of my heart, like I'd promised my dad I would. It had been a long time since my heart was so loud and clear and I could listen to it without hesitation, but I'd learned how to do that again in the months I'd been alone.

THIRTY-FIVE

Excitement and anxiety warred for prominence as I flew north for Caroline and Fern's wedding; excitement over my best friend getting married and anxiety over knowing I was going to see Chad, and not just once because we were both going to be in the rehearsal in a matter of hours. I checked the time: four hours to be exact. I'd brought my laptop and my notebook to try to work on my final pieces in my short story series, but I couldn't get my mind to settle. I might as well have left everything at home.

My imagination ran wild again, cooking up various possibilities for how seeing each other might go and I got dizzy. *Breathe, Rena*, I reminded myself. But instead of my own voice in my head, I heard Chad's and could feel his hand pressing over my heart. That made breathing even harder. If I thought I could come up with a convincing reason to miss the wedding without hurting Caroline's feelings, I would. And even if I couldn't, she'd understand if I backed out—she knew how nervous I was about seeing Chad for the first time in six months—but that wasn't fair to her. She was my friend, and I loved her and wanted to be there to celebrate her.

Two nights. One half day, one full day, then I'd be leaving the next morning. It would be over. With any luck, we could manage to not fully cross paths. It was unlikely, but possible. And possible was all I had to hold on to so I didn't vomit into a paper bag sitting in coach on a plane. While I wasn't looking for a passenger of the year award, I'd rather not throw up in front of a bunch of strangers, let alone in such a confined space.

I tucked my hair behind my ear for what felt like the fiftieth time in the last few minutes and had a flash of Chad doing the same thing. He used to tuck my hair behind my ear so often.

Damn it. Stop thinking about Chad, Renata. Get your shit together because you're going to see him in a little less than four hours and you need to be able to function.

I forced myself to think about my new long-term writing projects instead. At Jeb's suggestion, I was collecting my short stories—my new ones as well as the ones I'd written years ago—into a short story collection that would be published late the next year. He'd encouraged me to pitch the idea to a publishing house during open submissions, and I'd ended up with a book contract.

My other writing project was even more personal; the idea was born after I joined a support group for other women who were victims of domestic abuse. I'd realized they were all as desperate for knowing they weren't alone as I was, and I decided to take my experiences with Damien and the ways in which he still impacted my life and write a book about it. My hope was that, in reading my story, other survivors would know they weren't alone, and they could be shown how we could end up so trapped, how the abuse could be so well hidden. I hadn't pitched it anywhere yet because I had no idea how long it would take me, but I was working on it a little bit at a time. And, one day, I hoped it would help a lot of people feel seen and find the courage to break free.

At long last, the plane landed, and thirty minutes later, I was en route to the lodge on the premises where the ceremony was going to take place. I texted Caroline to let her know I was almost there, and she asked me to come to the rehearsal early, as soon as I was checked in. I got my stuff unpacked, took a quick shower to clean off the plane trip, and put on the dress Caroline had helped me pick out for the rehearsal dinner. I flipped my head over and fluffed my hair, then pinched my cheeks to give them some color. Looking in the mirror, I rolled my eyes at myself; Chad probably wouldn't even look my direction, which was what I was hoping for anyway, and I wasn't in the market for a boyfriend—so who the hell was I trying to impress?

It didn't really matter who I was or wasn't trying to impress, I realized; *I* liked the way I looked. I liked my hair having a little more volume and my cheeks having a little more color. I liked the way the knee-length dress highlighted the curve of my muscles—I was proud of being strong and liked looking as strong as I knew I was. I liked the way I felt in my comfortable lace lingerie, and I liked the way my dress looked over it. It didn't matter what anyone else thought because I wasn't really doing any of it for them anyway.

When I walked into the room labeled "The Petite Ballroom," there were a handful of people from the wedding party already there even with another hour before the rehearsal was supposed to start. Caroline was near the center of the room with Fern, and they were talking animatedly to a woman I suspected was responsible for the flowers and decorations based on the bits of conversation I could hear. Standing behind that woman was someone I'd never seen who appeared to be waiting his turn to talk to them.

"Renata!"

I turned at the exclamation and beamed at Caroline's mom. After leaving my purse on a table near the door, I reached her and the rest of the group and exchanged quick hugs and greetings; they were all faces I remembered from Thanksgiving. The last person I greeted was Adam. There was an awkward pause when I got to him because I wasn't sure how to interact with him, but he grinned and leaned forward for a hug, so I hugged him back. When he pulled away, he kept his hands on my elbows.

"It's good to see you, Renata," he said.

I smiled back. "It's good to see you, too," I said sincerely. "You seem really well, Adam." And he did. He wasn't scowling, for starters—he was still grinning actually. And he gave off a warm aura—not the chilly one he'd had before.

"You do, too," he said.

"I am. A lot has happened since Thanksgiving, and I'm in a different place than I was then."

"Good things, I'm guessing."

"Yeah... well, most. Not all, but most."

"That's good. It's been about the same for me. Thanks to *you*."

"Me?" I asked, my eyebrows curving in.

His grin turned sheepish. "Yeah. Talking to you made me realize I wasn't the only person who'd had a Kali in their lives. I ended up joining a support group shortly after Christmas so I could meet more people like me."

"You did? I joined one, too, but not until more recently. Has it been helpful for you?"

"Yeah. I felt stupid at first and didn't really want to keep going, but I was desperate and figured Chad was so pissed off at me he wouldn't give me your number if I asked for it. Since I couldn't talk to *you*, I kept going, and after a while, it really started to help."

"Adam... I would have talked to you as often as you wanted. It was really helpful for me, too. I'd never just talked about things with Damien that way before, to someone who had some level of understanding of what it was like for me, and it was a tremendous relief. It helped me get rid of the last of the doubt I had about wronging Damien by walking out on him the way I did. And I'd love to talk sometime if you still want to."

"Yeah, I'd like to, as long as it's not going to cause any issues between you and Chad."

My heart skipped and my eyes fell for the first time since we'd begun talking. "It won't—Chad and I aren't together anymore." There was a quiet pause. "I can give you my number and you can text me so I have yours—my phone is in my purse by the door."

"I'm sorry to hear that. I can imagine this wedding might be kind of awkward for you then. I'm here if you need to talk," Adam said. He checked his pocket, then laughed. "My phone is over there, too. We can exchange numbers later. I won't forget."

Caroline and Fern walked over just then, and I excused myself to say hello to them. Caroline gave me a bear hug, giggling and bouncing on her toes. Fern gave me a tight smile, the way she'd greeted me for months once she'd mostly forgiven me for breaking her brother's heart. I didn't think she'd ever fully forgive me, and while it hurt, I also understood.

"I can't believe it's happening," Caroline whispered, her eyes wide. "Like I literally can't. I'm pretty sure I'm dreaming right now and I'm going to wake up and be pissed because this has got to be the best dream I've ever had."

I laughed and gave her a playful pinch on her arm.

"Ow," she said, laughing.

"See? Not a dream," I said. "It just feels that way when our dreams come true sometimes."

She squealed and hugged me again.

The next thirty minutes or so passed quickly while Fern and Caroline fielded questions about how things would look, what was going to be served at the reception, exactly where everything was taking place, confirming what time we should be doing what, and on. There was an endless amount of information to be imparted.

Caroline was giving me a fifth excited hug when I knew he was there. It was like he had a powerful and unique air signature or something because I sensed him as soon as he walked in. My skin broke into goosebumps like it used to when he was about to touch me, and then I heard Fern confirm that he was behind me.

"Chad—you're finally here!"

He chuckled and the sound vibrated all the way to my toes. "I left Baldwin's house a little later than I meant to, then hit traffic. I told you I'd make it, though."

"Barely," she said, rolling her eyes.

Chad stepped up into my field of vision and hugged his sister. I watched, my eyes roving over every inch I could see, parched for the sight of him. I'd told myself I would avoid looking at him, and yet here I was staring. He looked good—*really* good. He was wearing dark pants and a white button-up with navy stripes, the sleeves rolled up to show his muscular baker's forearms. I saw his fingers on his sister's shoulder as he kissed her cheek, and I had a flash of him running his fingertip over my hand and sucked in a sharp breath.

A sharp enough breath that several heads turned toward me, including Chad's. I looked down immediately and told Caroline I needed to use the bathroom and would be right back. I rushed out without looking at anyone else and beelined to the closest bathroom where I splashed gallons of cold water on my face until I'd convinced my body that he wasn't actually there for me, that he wasn't touching me when I simply had a memory of it happening. I realized this was going to be so much harder than I thought and gave myself a pep talk. It was less than forty-eight hours left; I could do just about anything for forty-eight hours.

THIRTY-SIX

I managed to keep my eyes from looking at anything on Chad other than his shoes throughout the rehearsal, but it hadn't been easy. Especially because I could feel every time *his* eyes were on *me*. Thankfully, the rehearsal was over and we were heading to the rehearsal dinner. At least there, I should be able to sit in some way that meant I didn't have to face him until I'd been there long enough I could excuse myself without seeming rude or disinterested.

I grabbed my purse and was about to walk out the door when Adam's voice rang out.

"Renata—hang on!"

I stepped away from the doors so I wouldn't block anyone else from leaving and waited as Adam finished talking to the minister, then headed in my direction, stopping to grab his phone off the back table.

I smiled as he walked up next to me, as hard as it was this time because I was acutely aware that Chad was on the other side of the room, talking to Fern, his eyes on me every time I peeked in his direction.

Adam opened up his phone. "Okay, I'm ready. First, what's your last name?"

"Hayden."

"Mine's Connelly, like Fern and Chad. Our dads were brothers. Number?"

I recited my number and he recited it back, then tapped a few times. I felt my phone vibrate in my purse.

"Okay, I texted you so you have my number, too." He pulled open the door out of the room and held it for me to walk out. "After you," he said.

With an inhuman display of strength, I kept myself from looking back toward Chad one more time and walked out of the room, followed by Adam. We headed down a long hallway, followed by a short one, before entering the onsite restaurant. The back side of the restaurant had been cordoned off for our group and we made our way in. Several other friends and family members who weren't part of the rehearsal itself were also there, and Adam excused himself to go say hello. I figured I should follow him, but I needed a few minutes to collect myself first. As unobtrusively as possible to avoid attracting anyone's attention, I wove through the tables to the furthest one that appeared to have no one sitting at it. Perfect—a little solitude was much needed.

I sat down with my back to the rest of the room at the small square table for four and let out a sigh, but it was barely out before I could feel that Chad had entered the area. *Well, shit.* I'd hoped to have more time before he came in. At least I was sure he wouldn't be coming my way; he had too many people to catch up with, and that would keep him on the other side where everyone was milling about and socializing.

My heart sped up and goosebumps broke out over my body without warning; Chad was close. I hoped my senses were wrong and he wasn't actually there. Why would they be correct? What reason would he have to be anywhere near this side of the restaurant? Everyone else was at the other end.

"Seltzer?"

It *was* Chad. I forgot how to breathe. He pulled out the chair to my right and sat down, setting a bottle of San Pellegrino on the table near me. He had another one in his other hand, which he set down on his right.

"Unopened," he added.

I gave him a weak smile in thanks. I couldn't make eye contact, though. I held the bottle of seltzer with both hands, my trembling fingers toying with the label. It had been six months—why was his presence affecting me so severely? I reached up and tucked some hair behind my ear, then asked him if he was excited for the wedding at the exact same time he asked me how the trip up had been. I laughed nervously, still staring at the seltzer bottle. After an awkward silence, he spoke.

"Yes, for different reasons. You?"

It took a second for me to remember the question I'd asked him and realize he was answering it.

"Very. I'm happy for Fern and Caroline."

"I am, too. I love Caroline like a sister."

"Me, too." I smiled, a genuine smile for my friend, and glanced up.

Whoops. I should *not* have done that. His eyes were more beautiful than I'd remembered, that golden brown that bled into gray-blue, and they were intensely focused on me, as if we were the only people in the world. A touch to my hand—a single fingertip tapping once—sent a shockwave through my body.

"Breathe, Rena," he said, his voice as soft as his expression.

I inhaled sharply and cleared my throat, looking away and scrambling for something to fill the stretching silence. "I saw that James Gillespie was at Amestown Pavilion a few months ago. Did you get a chance to see him?"

Chad didn't answer right away, allowing a few breaths to pass first. "I had a chance, but I chose not to go. I stopped listening to him a long time ago because I couldn't do it without thinking about us."

My heart slammed into my chest and my body flooded with hormones. We'd made love to James Gillespie dozens of times, which meant that's what Chad was thinking about.

"I'm sorry," I said.

"It's okay—"

"No," I interrupted. "I mean, I'm sorry but I can't do this. I can't sit here and make small talk with you."

I waited for him to get up and walk away, but he didn't.

"You're still angry with me," he said evenly.

"No." I swallowed. "This is just... more than I can do."

"I didn't finish answering your question earlier. You asked if I was excited and I said yes, but I didn't tell you why. I'm excited for Fern and Caroline, of course, but that's not the reason I've been counting down the days. *That's* because I knew you'd be here."

My eyes filled and I cursed under my breath. He couldn't say things like that. I reached down to grab my purse and saw Adam approaching. I glanced between him and Chad and hoped they'd resolved their issues from Thanksgiving. Chad stood and the men shook hands; things were still a bit tense between them, mostly coming from Chad. Adam sat to my left and Chad to my right, and I wondered if it would be rude if I stood up and just walked off. Adam asked Chad how he'd been and he said good. Adam said he heard from Fern that Chad had gotten a grant to study in France and Chad said it was true, but didn't elaborate. Then Chad asked Adam how he'd been, albeit grudgingly.

"I've been good," Adam replied. "You and Renata talked some sense into me at Thanksgiving, and I'm a lot better than I was with all the Kali bullshit. I'm sorry I was such a dick." Adam turned to face me. "Thank you."

I blushed; I hadn't really done anything.

"I wanted to ask you something about your support group, actually," Adam said.

We talked for a while about how our respective support groups were set up, the pros and cons, and what we'd found most helpful about them. I glanced over at Chad every now and then, not wanting to exclude him exactly, and he was focused on our conversation; he was listening intently.

After twenty minutes or so, Adam excused himself to get another drink and catch up with other people, giving me a kiss on the cheek before he left. I glanced at Chad, nervous, which made no sense—Chad and I weren't even friends anymore, not to mention that Adam had kissed my cheek the way all their relatives kissed each other's cheeks.

"Friends or... more than friends?" Chad asked.

"Who?"

He tipped his head toward Adam.

I snorted. "Friends."

He nodded, then didn't say anything else, his eyes moving over my face. I could feel a blush creep up and looked away.

"Dating or single?" he asked.

"You're really interested in my relationship status," I said under my breath.

"I am," he said.

Again, my breath caught. I'd forgotten how direct and straightforward he was.

"I'm single," he added. "On purpose."

"Same." My voice was barely audible.

His face broke into a relieved grin, which made no sense considering what lay between us. I could feel his eyes resting on me while I feigned interested in the San Pellegrino bottle that was again between my hands.

"You're wearing your necklace," he said.

My hand immediately went to my chest and touched my phoenix pendant… the one he'd given me. I'd been afraid of him seeing it and almost left it at home, but I hadn't taken it off since I'd clasped it around my neck on my birthday months earlier. I would have felt too naked without it.

When I didn't respond, he said, "I heard you ran your marathon. Your dad would be proud of you."

Tears pricked the back of my eyes, and I met Chad's gaze, smiling. "Thank you."

"You're welcome. I also like your new short story series."

"You've read them?" I balked. I'd never considered he might read them—it would be obvious they revolved around him.

"Of course," he replied. "I've read everything you've ever written—at least everything that's been published."

I swallowed; I'd had no idea he was still reading my work after I left him.

"They're really good, Rena."

"Thank you."

He looked away, over my shoulder toward the rest of the group, his eyes distant. When he looked back, there was a resolve there now, though the slight glassiness told me he was nervous.

"I have something for you."

"Chad—"

"Rena—it's yours. It's not mine. I should have given it to you a long time ago—I've had it for almost two months. I just, I didn't want to mail it or give it to Caroline to give to you because I didn't want something to happen to it, but I wasn't sure how you'd react if I called you or came by your apartment, and I didn't want you to think I was stalking you or something, or show up unwanted like him..." He sighed. "I didn't want to cross any boundaries. Anyway, that's why I didn't give it to you sooner."

He reached into his right-hand pocket and pulled something out. He held his hand out and I opened mine, palm up on the table. Very carefully, he placed a small off-white folded square of cotton on my palm. I glanced up at him, my eyebrows curving to the center. He gave me a soft smile and tipped his head toward my hand. I looked down to my palm, then took the small square delicately between my fingers. I had no idea what it was, but Chad had been very gentle with it, so I would be, too. I set the cotton on the table and carefully unfolded the corners, spread them apart, then gasped.

I looked up at Chad, my eyes wide. "How?" My eyes returned to the table and my shaking fingers lifted a ring that looked eerily like my mother's engagement ring. I peered inside the band and saw the inscription. My cheeks were suddenly damp. "I don't understand," I said, my voice watery. "How did you get this?"

"After we got back from Thanksgiving, I began calling pawn shops, starting with the area you'd lived in with Damien." He couldn't keep the distaste from his mouth when he said Damien's name. "I didn't find it, but I asked every shop I called to please call me if something like I described showed up. I got a lot of calls, but none of those rings had the inscription, and none of them were actually rose gold, either. But about two months ago, it turned up. Originally, I was... well, it doesn't matter right now. I found it, and it's yours. It's as beautiful as you described it to be, Rena."

I slipped the ring onto the ring finger of my right hand where I used to wear it, and a painful wave of emotion moved up through my chest. I'd never thought I'd see it again, this last piece of my parents. "I don't know how to repay you," I whispered.

Chad ran a finger down the back of my hand. "There's nothing to repay, Rena. It belongs to *you*. I'm just happy I was able to find it for you. And that I got to see your face when you saw it."

"I thought you hated me," I said after pulling out a tissue from my purse and drying my face.

"I was really angry with you for a while. I'd never been angrier in my life. I couldn't believe you thought I was like your ex, that there was even a chance of it. But I realized a few things when Caroline told me you'd run your marathon. First, I realized that I'd been keeping you from doing things you loved, things that meant a lot to you, because I was scared and being an idiot. If you'd stayed, you'd never have run because you weren't able to train the way you needed. Second, I realized that while I'm nothing like Damien, there was something similar between us because he also kept you from doing things you loved. Third, I realized that you'd chosen yourself. I hated that it wasn't with me, but... I'm proud of you, Rena. I'm really proud of you. And I could never hate you; you can't hate someone you love."

I tried to make my lungs expand and contract, but they refused. Chad was sitting next to me, six months after I'd walked out on him, and he'd basically said he loved me. It was so unexpected, my body didn't know how to process his words.

"Breathe, Rena," he said softly, resting his entire hand over mine.

I wasn't sure if I loved or hated right then that he could tell when I wasn't breathing by looking at me. I also wasn't sure if I was okay with what he'd just said to me, and I couldn't think there, like that. I needed to get away from everyone and try to figure out what the hell I was feeling, try to make some sense of it all. I grabbed my purse and stood up.

"I have—I'm sorry—I can't—" I stopped abruptly, unable to find my words, turned, and walked away.

I could feel his eyes on me but had no idea if he said anything or tried to stop me or if he was still sitting there—I heard nothing and the edges of my vision were darkening. I avoided meeting anyone's eye as I rushed past, trying not to be noticed as I slipped out of the back room and jogging once I got out of the restaurant until I found a bathroom down the hall toward where the rehearsal had taken place. It was empty, thank god.

I sat down on a toilet in a stall and fell apart like I hadn't in a long time. All over again, the pain of leaving Chad washed over me, just as fresh as the day I'd done it. Grief came in waves, I knew that from losing my dad, but this one felt like a tsunami and had come on without warning. But then I had a flash of anger that he was saying things like that to me; it wasn't fair. It was like torture because I'd thrown it away. Anger was easier than the pain, so I latched onto it. My tears dried up and I came out of the stall and splashed cold water on my face. As I dried my hands, the paper towel caught and tore and I looked down.

My mother's ring. He'd found my mother's ring for me. My anger gradually softened into pain again, and I lowered my hand. Whether he found my mother's ring or not, he had no right to sit down and say the kinds of things he was when we hadn't spoken in six months, just assuming it would be welcome news. Or maybe he was getting back at me for hurting him by doing something he knew was going to hurt *me*. I didn't know, but regardless of his reason, it was bullshit, and I was going to tell him so if he said so much as another word to me.

With newfound resolve and a chest full of anger, I barreled out of the bathroom and smack into Chad standing along the wall a few feet away.

"Why are you here?" I shouted, feeling off-kilter that I'd just literally run into him. He opened his mouth to speak, but I cut him off. "I don't know what your purpose is, seeking me out when I was clearly trying to keep to myself, telling me shit like you're single and can't do things that make you think about us and that you're proud of me! We haven't so much as seen each other from across a room in six months and you think it's okay for you to just come up and start talking to me like we're friends or something?"

"Rena—"

"And what makes you think you have a right to touch me? Or follow me to the bathroom, for god's sake? What makes you think I want any of this? You said you wanted to see me, but I almost skipped my best friend's wedding so I *wouldn't* have to see *you*!"

"I'm—"

"And what in the hell is wrong with you after the way we left things between us to tell me you love me? Why would you say something like that to me?"

I was breathing hard, at least as hard as I had when I crossed the finish line in my marathon, and I was vaguely aware that my face was damp again. My whole body was shaking, and I felt nauseous. I'd wanted to scream at him until he left me alone, but now that I'd run out of steam, I was terrified he was going to do just that. I wanted him to leave, but I wanted him to stay at the same time. I wanted him to take back everything he'd said and hate me instead, but I also wanted him to say it all again. I was a mess of contradictory feelings and desires and emotions.

"I've had six months to think about what I lost," he said. "Six months to think about the reasons why and do everything I could to make sure I would never make a mistake like I did with you again with someone else. And in those six months, I realized there would never be a someone else because loving you was everything, Rena, and once you've had everything, you can't settle for less, and no one else could ever be more than less compared to you. It's been six months since I saw you in the flesh, but not a day has gone by that I haven't seen you in my memories and dreams."

I wrapped my arms around myself, trying to hold in the pain that pulsed inside my chest. Chad paused, then stepped forward and hesitantly raised an arm, tucking my hair behind my ear. A sob tore up my throat.

"And I didn't tell you I love you. I told you that you can't hate someone you love. I was *going* to tell you next that I love you—that I love you more than I did the last time I saw you, but you walked away before I had the chance. And I followed you because I know what I want, Rena, and it's you. And I'm not giving up without a fight. I see the way you look at me and I think you feel the same way I do. And the possibility of giving us a second chance is worth fighting for. *You* are worth fighting for, Rena love."

I looked up then at his endearment, tears streaming down my face. "Leaving you nearly killed me," I said. "And it still hurts... god it hurts."

"I know," he said, lifting a hand to my cheek and using his thumb to wipe away my tears.

I leaned my head into his touch and closed my eyes. It had been so long since I'd felt him touching me that way, and it brought on another wave of pain. It was wonderful and yet hurt so much. When I opened my eyes, his cheeks were also damp, and I realized it was hurting him as much as it was hurting me. That realization softened the pain a bit. I stepped back out of his touch, wiped my face, and sniffled loudly. Chad did the same.

"Are you hungry?" he asked.

I shook my head.

"Me, either," he said with a soft smile. "There are trails outside—wanna go for a walk?"

"Sure." Movement sounded nice.

We meandered side by side along the trails through the gardens outside the hotel in the dark, the only light from stake lights along the path and the moon over our heads, and talked about everything. We got caught up on each other's lives—what we didn't know courtesy of Caroline—from the last six months.

At one point, I realized we were holding hands, although I couldn't remember when exactly it had started. I didn't pull away; instead, I curled my fingers a little tighter around his, and he did the same to mine. I glanced up sideways at him and smiled, biting the corner of my lip to temper it. As we talked, it was like we fell back into rhythm together and things went from tense and awkward to relaxed and easy and natural. Me screaming at him in the hall outside the bathroom felt so far away.

Eventually, we both got messages from Fern and Caroline looking for us, and we decided we should head back. Dinner would be over, but people would still be around catching up.

Chad stopped just outside the restaurant entrance and gave my hand a small tug. "Wanna' just tell them we didn't feel well and order room service and watch a movie?"

"We shouldn't."

He shrugged. "Want to anyway?"

I didn't hesitate. "Yes."

We found a collection of older movies and ordered a variety of foods from room service, lamenting the poor quality and high prices, Chad telling me what they should have done differently to make the food more palatable. Most of the dishes were stacked on the nightstand next to me, and it was getting late, but I wasn't ready to leave yet, and Chad did nothing to indicate he was ready for me to go, either.

"One more? 'Breakfast Club'?" he asked, turning and raising his eyebrows.

"Never seen it," I said.

He rolled his eyes. "I still don't understand how you grew up when you did and never saw these."

I shrugged, smirking. "My dad and I spent time outside instead of watching crappy movies."

He deadpanned at me, a twitch at the corners of his mouth. "These are not crappy movies."

I shrugged again. "If you say so."

He narrowed his eyes. "I do. And you'll agree. You'll like this one a lot."

There was a knock at the door, room service bringing us more seltzer.

"Perfect timing," Chad said with an eyebrow wiggle.

I reached over to the nightstand and used a hand to lift the tray with all the dishes stacked and turned to hand it to Chad.

His eyes widened as he took the tray from me. He walked to the door and traded out the dirty dishes for our seltzer. When he shut the door, he walked back over, handing a seltzer bottle to me as he climbed back onto the bed next to me, again situated so we were touching from our shoulders to our feet.

He chuckled. "I can't believe you lifted that tray up one-handed," he said, gazing at me.

I blushed. "It wasn't that bad."

"That's a heavy tray, Rena," he laughed. "You're really strong."

My blush deepened and I looked down, my teeth sinking into my lip. "I guess."

"It's from the self-defense training, isn't it?" he asked, his voice more sobered.

My eyes darted up, my brows furrowed in. I hadn't told him about that yet.

"Caroline told me." He was running a finger down my hand. His eyes followed his finger. "I asked her about you every time I saw her," he said, his voice dropping. "I begged her to tell me everything. She didn't, but she did tell some things, including that she was teaching you self-defense."

I took in what he'd said, my heart racing from the sensation of his finger running over my hand. "She did. Brandon helped, too."

"He did?"

"Yeah. We thought it would help to have someone more like... Damien... for me to practice with."

Chad huffed. "I bet that didn't work out too well—Brandon may be the same size, but he's too much of a goof."

I sighed, thinking back over all the times I'd trained with Caroline's brother. "Actually, he wasn't. He took training with me really seriously. It was..." I tried to find words to explain how it felt when Brandon flipped into training mode. "He was aggressive when we trained."

Chad's finger stopped moving on my hand and I could feel his body stiffen. "What does that mean?"

I sighed again. "It means he came after me like he was an actual attacker."

"Did he hurt you?" Chad asked, a note of incredulity in his voice.

I flipped my hand over and slipped my fingers between his, hoping to soothe him. I was staring through the bed as I thought about the summer and everything that had happened. "Nothing serious."

Chad tensed. "So he did."

"I mean... he had to. It had to be realistic to be helpful, you know? But he never hurt me more than necessary and never really badly." I glanced up at him, but he was staring down at our hands, his face pained. "If he hadn't done that, I wouldn't have been able to face Damien again."

Chad's eyes darted up to mine, panicked and glassy, and the blood drained from his face. "Damien came back?"

I nodded, blinking back my own tears. "He did. He got into my building and was waiting for me outside my door when I left one day."

"Jesus Christ, Rena," he muttered, his tears on the brink of falling over.

"It's okay," I soothed. "Because of what Caroline and Brandon did for me, I was able to protect myself." I chuckled softly. "I almost broke his arm. I could have, and I wanted to, but I decided not to. I didn't want to stoop to his level and do something like that if I didn't absolutely have to, and I didn't. I'd already hurt him enough, and he decided I wasn't worth it and left on his own."

"Jesus Christ," he said again on a rushed exhale.

I smiled, but Chad grimaced and turned away, sniffling loudly and using his other hand to wipe under his eyes.

"The thought of him anywhere near you..." He let out a harsh breath. "It makes me feel sick."

I squeezed his hand. "Well you don't have to worry anymore because he won't be back. I can fight back now, and he needs someone weak."

"You're definitely not weak, Rena," Chad said, his voice thick with emotion. "You're the strongest person I've ever met."

We sat quietly for a few more minutes, then Chad began the movie. By the time it was over, I was snuggled into his side, my head on his chest, and he had an arm wrapped around my shoulders. But it was well after midnight, and we both had to be up relatively early the next morning. Reluctantly, we pulled apart and Chad walked me back to my hotel room, our hands glued together.

When we reached my door, an awkwardness fell between us. I wasn't sure what to do or how; it was still so new to be near him again. He faced me, holding both of my hands, then raised them and kissed the backs of them, one at a time. My breath hitched when he released my hands and skimmed his fingertips up my arms, over my shoulders, to cradle my face. He pressed a light, lingering kiss to my cheek.

"Goodnight, my Rena."

I looked down, again biting the corner of my lip to keep from grinning obscenely like I wanted to. His thumb gently touched that corner and pulled. I released my lip from my teeth, and the grin broke free.

"That's better," he murmured.

My whole body clenched, and I felt intoxicated. I had the urge to giggle, but managed to curb it. I raised my eyes to his, feeling the intensity of his attention wash over me as his eyes roved over my face.

"Goodnight, Chad."

THIRTY-SEVEN

It was really early the morning of the wedding, and I couldn't sleep even despite having been up so late; I was too excited about seeing Chad again after the night before. I had no idea what it all meant—we hadn't talked about *us* at all—but my heart was ecstatically happy with what was happening and that was enough for me. I went for a run through all the trails I'd walked the night before with Chad as well as the trails through the nearby woods that were vibrant with leaves changing color in preparation for the cooler season ahead. After showering, I pulled out my journal and wrote about the night before. When I was done, I felt even more settled about how the evening had unfolded and even more eager to see Chad again. However, I knew I wouldn't see him until the ceremony. I thought about texting him, but I didn't know if he had the same number as before, and I didn't want to distract him from his big day with his sister.

The time flew by once Caroline was up, with a flurry of activity getting her ready and putting final touches on everything else for the ceremony and the reception. Finally, it was time. I was paired to walk down the aisle with another of Fern's cousins and it felt surreal. It wasn't my wedding, but I could almost imagine it was. The bridesmaid dresses were an elegant maroon velvet that brushed the floor, while the top was actually comprised of two long velvet panels that wrapped up the front and crossed over the shoulders before wrapping around the waist to end with being tied in a bow in the back, resulting in an open back. It was the first anyone other than Caroline would see my tattoo... the first I'd ever intentionally shown my scars. And I was nervous about that, but the dress felt so beautiful on my body that my worries faded into the background.

From my spot on Caroline's side, I watched Chad walk Fern down the aisle, saw him brush aside tears after kissing her cheek. I watched Caroline walk down the aisle with her father, saw him also with tears as he kissed her cheek. I looked around and noticed that Chad and Caroline's father and I weren't the only ones in tears; nearly everyone was. There was so much love between everyone present that it was close to overwhelming. That's what relationships were supposed to be like, whether romantic or platonic or familial: full of love. There were no jealous looks or irritation or boredom. Everyone there obviously wanted to be there to celebrate two amazing women marrying each other. I was proud and honored and grateful to be part of this group, to have found a family of sorts after feeling so lost for so long after my father died.

I blinked and it was over; my best friend was now a married woman. I cried, several fat tears down my cheeks, seeing the love and happiness on Caroline and Fern's faces after they kissed, and then everyone was cheering. It was the most beautiful thing I'd ever seen, watching two people who loved each other pledge to spend the rest of their lives devoted to one another.

The guests filed away from their chairs to the tent for the reception while the wedding party remained for photos, which took the better part of an hour. Whenever I looked away from the camera, I found Chad observing me, his eyes warm and intense. And every time I blushed, the twitch in the corners of his mouth gave way to a grin. As soon as the photographer was done with everyone except Fern and Caroline, Chad was there, his fingertips pressing lightly against my bare back.

"This tattoo is gorgeous," he said. "I pictured what you described last night, but *this* is so much more than I imagined."

I smiled. "I like it, too."

"I *love* it, Rena. Really. It's perfect. And the artist did an incredible job."

I grinned. "I know. I took a long time to pick someone because I wanted to make sure it was done well."

"Your dress, it's like it's framing the tattoo. It's like a piece of art."

"Really? It's hard for me to see."

Chad held up a finger and pulled his phone from his pocket. "Turn around."

I obliged, turning to look over my shoulder at him. I watched him as he focused on the screen and moved this way and that, to get the right angle, I presumed. He looked up at one point, his eyes darkened, and I blushed and bit the corner of my lip. He walked over and held his phone in front of me.

"The last one is my favorite," he murmured.

I looked at the screen and felt I was looking at someone else. There was photo after photo—he'd taken dozens in the short minute I waited. My dress indeed framed my tattoo, but in the last one, his favorite, my face was turned over my shoulder, my eyelids cast down almost demurely. You could see the pink on my cheeks, and he'd snapped the picture while I was biting my lip. It looked like something from a magazine. I looked… exotic and beautiful.

"I hope you don't mind if I print that one and frame it," he said, pocketing his phone.

My teeth dug further into my lip as it got harder to keep my grin contained. I imagined a photo of me in a frame on his foyer table. "No, I don't mind."

We walked together, following the rest of the wedding party, to the reception tent, but we moved at a fraction of the pace, talking about the ceremony and how happy we were for his sister and Caroline.

"At one point, I didn't think this was something that could ever happen for Fern," he said. "People were so mean to her when she was younger. Where we grew up, people thought being gay was a sinful choice or some bullshit. It was awful. Fern was so depressed, especially once our parents died and it was just the two of us—against the world, it felt like at times. I didn't think there was any way she'd ever meet someone, and at the time, even if she had, she couldn't have gotten married because it wasn't legal. What kind of bullshit is that, telling my sister who she can and can't marry? Telling *anyone* that?"

I sighed. "I'm glad that changed. But it never should have been illegal to begin with."

"Yeah," he agreed. "I was scared when she went to college because we'd just gotten her anorexia under control and now she was going somewhere I couldn't follow her and protect her from a new wave of hatred toward her. I called her every day." He glanced sideways at me, his lips pulled up on one side. "That overprotective thing, of course. Which just made her mad. But then, when she came home for winter break, she talked nonstop about her new friend, Caroline. I'd never met her, but I was grateful for her. Fern was animated and happy again. Believe it or not, Caroline had a boyfriend at the time. She struggled to come to terms with being gay—she didn't do that until she moved here from LA. But I knew from the first time I met her that she would always be a part of Fern's life; I could see she adored Fern as much as Fern adored her. I've loved her since that day like my own family. I can't tell you what it's like to have been able to watch them marry each other today."

We came to a stop outside the reception tent without entering and turned. We could just see Fern and Caroline with the photographer and watched them as they finished. Even from such a distance, you could feel their happiness and love. I leaned my head onto Chad's shoulder, and he wrapped an arm around me.

"I want what they have," I said quietly.

"I've already found it," he replied in a voice just as soft, his thumb running and up and down the bare skin on my arm.

Warmth bloomed in my chest, spreading outward until my entire body was heated and buzzing, warding off the chill that had begun to set in from the cool autumn air. We stood that way, watching the newlyweds finish with the photographer and the three of them head our way. As they neared, I began to get nervous; Fern wasn't my biggest fan since I'd left Chad, and I didn't want to upset her on her wedding day.

"Maybe I should go ahead in," I said quietly.

Chad turned to look down at me, his eyes soft and sparkling with life, his brows drawn in.

"I don't want to upset anyone," I explained. "By being here with you."

He smiled and spoke gently. "Caroline's going to be thrilled. And my sister will, too, in her own time. But she won't be upset today. I promise."

I wasn't so sure. She may have forgiven me for leaving Chad six months ago, but that didn't mean she'd be okay with us potentially putting that relationship back together. As they approached, Caroline beamed at us between glances at Fern, but I scrutinized Fern. She was still beaming the way she had been, her eyes barely leaving Caroline, but worry clouded her eyes when she looked at Chad and me. Thankfully, she didn't seem angry.

We all entered the tent together and headed toward the wedding party tables. Chad's lips brushed my temple as we parted ways; we were sitting on opposite ends of the long table. Dinner was served less than ten minutes after we'd sat down, then it was time for toasts. Chad's speech was a version of what he'd told me, mixed with funny anecdotes about Fern as a little girl and concluding with Chad telling her that their parents, as happy and proud as they would have been, had nothing on how happy and proud *he* was.

Caroline's brother was next, and he had the room in near constant laughter as he regaled us with stories of their childhood together, ending with how, as her older brother, nothing made him happier than seeing her with someone who would always love and take care of her.

And with that, it was my turn. I'd thought I'd be okay with speaking in front of people, but I was shaking pretty severely and regretted that I'd agreed to speak. I stood up, however, and pushed through that fear, the way I'd been learning to the last months.

"I met Caroline over a year ago on my first day of work at Fern's café." In my periphery, I saw Caroline cover her face and heard her groan. "She looked at my clothes and asked me if I was homeless." Everyone laughed and I looked over and caught Caroline's eye. We grinned at each other. "It's true. And then she felt so bad for asking me that when I told her I wasn't, that she insisted on taking me shopping for new clothes." There was another round of laughter. "It wasn't the first time she'd balk at what I owned and insist we go shopping together." Another groan from Caroline and laughter from Fern. "It was never just shopping, though. Caroline was showing me how to care about myself again, because the reality was that I didn't know how to anymore." I turned to face Caroline. "You helped me learn to love myself again by showing me how." She mouthed "love you" to me and I mouthed it back.

"Fern I'd met a few days before Caroline. I'd walked into her café with no experience, apparently looking homeless." I paused while people laughed. "Fern looked at me for a minute, told me she liked unusual names, and hired me." A loud round of laughter, someone calling out that it sounded just like Fern. "I loved that she said that because I have a thing for names and their meanings. When I was growing up, my dad and I played this name game where we'd try to guess strangers' names based on what we observed about them, and it was shocking how accurate that could be. Of course, there are thousands and thousands of names, so sometimes we got it wrong, but if you looked up the meanings of the names, they'd be similar. My dad believed that our names—the meanings behind our names—in part shape the person we are, and my experience in life backs that up."

I turned toward Fern and smiled at her. "Your first name means new life or beginnings, humility, sincerity, and magic. Your last name means friendship and loyalty. From the moment I met you, I thought you couldn't have been more aptly named. You had this vibrancy and passion about you—you still do. And you certainly gave the woman standing here before you giving this speech the opportunity for a new beginning. From the first time I saw you and Caroline interact, I could tell you were close, that you were the best of friends and deeply loyal to one another. Of course, I also thought you were dating Chad." There was a loud ripple of laughter through the room, including from Fern. "We all make mistakes," I added. Fern nodded at me, smiling back.

I turned to Caroline. "*Your* first name means strong, free, and song of happiness, and I'm not sure there's ever been a more fitting name for someone. One of my first thoughts when I met you was how much you smiled." Caroline laughed, her face turning pink, and I saw Fern squeeze her hand as she chuckled. "You're the most positive, upbeat, joyful person I've ever known, Caroline, and it's infectious. It's one of my favorite things about you, aside from your ability to find excuses to go shopping, of course." I winked and continued, sobering. "Your last name means loyal protector, and it suits you perhaps even more than your first name. You're fiercely loyal to and protective of those you love, and loyalty and protectiveness is how I first knew you loved me." My eyes moved between Fern and Caroline for a breath. "You two women are two of the best humans on this planet, and you deserve every happiness to be had in life. And I have faith that you're going to find it all because you have each other. I love you both."

The guests cheered while Caroline, Fern, and I broke protocol and hugged each other tight. "We love you, too," Caroline whispered.

"I know," I whispered back. "And it's changed my life."

"Would you like to dance?" Chad's voice was in my ear, his finger running down the back of my hand.

I turned from where I'd been leaning against a wall, watching the dance floor fill in after the first dances were done. My eyes widened. "I had no idea you could dance."

He smirked. "I can't, really, but Fern made me take lessons this summer, so I can do a few things."

"Do you like it?"

"Dancing?"

"Yeah."

"I will with you."

His fingers laced through mine and he led me to the dance floor. We moved, somewhat clumsily at times since I couldn't dance very well, either, through the next several songs. Despite our obvious lack of talent, I was enjoying myself, and he appeared to be having fun as well. A while later, as a song neared its end, I asked if we should maybe dance with other people, too.

He said no.

So we kept dancing.

It had been maybe thirty minutes when some familiar sounds wafted through the speakers and my whole body came alive, buzzing from hair follicle to toes. It was a James Gillespie song. It was one of my favorites by the artist and the one we'd made love to most often because of the deeply hypnotic, sexy beat.

Chad's eyes closed for a second and I could feel his body tense. When his lids lifted, his eyes had performed their magic color-change; they were all gray-blue now and my breath caught. We moved slowly to the beat, the length of our bodies touching. Chad bent and pressed his lips into the crook of my neck, lingering.

"Breathe, Rena love," he coaxed against my skin.

"I can't," I whispered. It hurt and felt so wonderful that it was nearly paralyzing.

His palm skimmed over my bare back and my skin broke into goosebumps. I was breathing now, but it was coming in short bursts.

"Your pupils are growing," he observed. "You're thinking about the same thing I am... making dough."

He winked and I giggled, grateful he'd made the joke. It had lightened some of the smothering tension that was building between us. By silent agreement, we left the dance floor after the song was over and had nearly reached an unoccupied corner when we were stopped by Caroline.

"You're literally glowing," I said, giving her a hug.

She squeezed me back. "So are you."

I blushed. "You guys are about to leave, aren't you?"

She gave a quick head nod, then exchanged hugs with Chad.

"Welcome to the family, sis," he said.

She beamed back at him. "Thanks, bro."

His face fell. "Don't ever call me bro."

"Alright, bro," she said with a wink.

I laughed and Chad rolled his eyes.

"Have an absolute blast on your honeymoon," I said. "It's going to be amazing."

"I want to hear all about it when I get back, alright?" she said.

I drew back slightly in confusion. "Don't you mean you'll tell me all about it when you get back?"

"Nope," she said, scrunching her nose. "I said it right."

I replayed her words. "You want to hear all about what?" I asked, baffled.

Her eyes darted back and forth between Chad and me. My cheeks leapt into flames.

"Get out of here," I said, nudging her with my shoulder.

She lifted her eyebrows. "I'm going. I just wanted to tell you guys that I love you both to pieces and to thank you for everything you've done for us, for today and in general. All I wanted was to see you guys happy, and now my day is complete."

I blinked hard to keep from crying again when we exchanged final hugs, then she and Fern were off. Chad and I stood, hand in hand, watching as they left, and I rested my head on his shoulder. He glanced over toward the unoccupied corner we'd been headed to before looking toward the exit.

"Wanna' go?"

"Yes," I replied. Wherever he had in mind for us to go was more than good with me, because I wanted to be wherever he was.

The corners of his mouth twitched and his eyes danced. "Me, too."

With our hands firmly clasped together, we said goodbyes to a few people on the way out, but mostly just beelined for the exit. Once we stepped into the cold, fresh air, it felt like entering a whole new world, a whole new chapter. It was surreal to be there, stepping through the cold grass, the sun setting, my fingers intertwined with Chad's. I bit the corner of my lip and stole a sideways glance at Chad. He was already looking at me, his expression and smile soft. I blushed and looked away. He stopped walking and pulled me around to face him near the tree line. His hands cradled my face and his intense gaze roved over me while his thumbs smoothed over the skin on my cheeks.

"I've dreamed about this so many times," he said, his voice husky and emotional. "But my dreams have nothing on reality, Rena. God, when I touch you, I feel it everywhere in my body... *everywhere*. It's..." his voice cracked and trailed off.

I reached up and, trembling, took his face in my hands, wiping the moisture appearing below his eyes.

"I've missed you like I didn't know I could miss someone, Rena. I missed you so much that standing here with you in my arms again,

I *still* miss you. If you never left my side again for the rest of our lives, I think I'd still miss you until the day I died."

My head moved gently in affirmation because I understood. "I've missed you the same way. Looking at you right now hurts like I'm being torn apart from the inside."

Chad bent and our lips touched for the first time in six months. My heart alternately wouldn't beat, then beat furiously against my ribcage.

"Oh, god, Rena," he said on a shaky exhale. "It's almost too much."

I nodded. "And nowhere near enough."

"Not even close."

He slipped an arm around my waist when our lips met again, pulling our bodies together. In an instant, I wanted to be somewhere with more privacy. When he started kissing down the side of my neck, I found my voice.

"Let's go inside."

"My room or yours?" he asked, his lips still against my skin.

"Whichever's closer."

He left a quick kiss on my cheek, then turned, pulling me along with him. We moved quickly across the grass and into the building, and in what felt like an eternity and only a second at the same time, he was using his keycard to open his hotel room door. I bit the corner of my lip, my body clenching with anticipation as I waited. I followed him over the threshold, and then my back was against the door as it closed and he was kissing the hell out of me.

I wrapped my arms around his neck and clung to him as his mouth devoured mine, then moved down to the crook of my neck. I moaned and his body compressed me harder against the door. He lifted me by my hips and I wrapped my legs around him, kissing down the side of his neck and wishing I could remove his clothes from the back. His hips drove forward, his erection grinding between my legs, and I moaned again. Our hands were all over each other in a blur, then I was on my back on his bed and we were both naked.

He climbed over me and I pulled him closer by his hips, and then he was inside me. His hand cradled the top of my head as he moved harder and stronger. I registered briefly that we were those obnoxious hotel guests who had sex loudly as the bed pounded against the wall, but then the thought was gone because I was overtaken by sensation. I clutched him, my body tight and my lungs seizing as an orgasm ripped through me, Chad's following just after mine began.

His body was limp over mine as we both gasped for breath, and we stayed like that for at least a minute before he moved, shifting some weight into his elbows. Using one hand, he tenderly moved my hair from my face, then kissed my cheek. His eyes shone brightly as he stared into mine.

"Are you okay?" he asked.

I lowered then raised my chin, biting the corner of my lip again. "Definitely."

He chuckled, the sound rumbling in his chest and vibrating mine. "That was over faster than I intended."

I giggled. "I'm not complaining."

He kissed the corner of my lip where I always bit it, then pressed his mouth fully to mine. I could feel him twitch inside me as he lingered in the kiss and my body clenched. He lifted his mouth and kissed me again, this time our tongues softly touching. We kissed like this, slow and tender, for a while, and then he was moving his hips again, much slower than before.

"I want to take my time this time," he murmured against my lips, his breath hot where it broke across my face.

My breath hitched; that sounded amazing.

The morning found me wrapped in Chad's arms in his bed after spending much of the night making love. I wanted to stay where I was, to extend time so reality wouldn't set back in, but I had a plane to catch. At the door to his hotel room, however, we couldn't stop kissing each other. I ultimately pulled away, knowing if I didn't get a move on, I'd miss my flight. Chad walked me to my hotel room and we found ourselves in the same situation all over again.

"Can I just hang out while you get ready to go?" he asked, his eyes hopeful.

I smiled and he followed me inside. As the door closed, he pulled me into him again, cradling my face. "Do you have anything pressing to get back to?" he asked.

"I mean, I have a flight to catch," I laughed. "They won't hold that for me."

He smirked. "I meant at home, in Amestown."

"No."

"Then come back with me instead."

His eyes were studying mine as he waited, and I studied his back, realizing he was holding his breath. I smirked and placed my hand over his chest.

"Breathe, Chad."

He grinned sheepishly, sucking in air. "Drive back with me," he whispered. "Please."

I bit the corner of my lip. I wanted to. I desperately wanted to. "Okay. I'll drive back with you."

His breath rushed out and my skin pebbled with goosebumps. I'd had to wear my dress from the wedding back to my hotel room, and now Chad's hands were slowly pulling out the tie in the back. Memories of his hands on me the night before flooded my thoughts and my breathing shallowed. The straps were now unwrapped from my waist, and he lifted the heavy, sensuous velvet up over my shoulders. Within moments, we were both naked and panting again, this time against the back of my hotel room door.

When we were finally sated with each other—at least for a while—we showered together. Chad squeezed out my shampoo while I was under the stream of water, then used his fingertips to massage it into my scalp.

"We can take a few days to drive back," he said, his voice low and unhurried as he worked my hair into a lather. I moaned; it felt amazing. He chuckled. "We can stop anywhere you'd like. Is there anywhere along the east coast you want to visit? I'll take us there. And in a few days or a week at most, you'll be home."

"Don't you have to work?" I asked, resting my hands on his chest as he rinsed my hair. I wanted to bottle up the way I felt right then.

He shook his head. "No. I leave in ten days for France, and since I had the wedding, I just took all of it off."

My shoulders fell; I'd forgotten he was going to France. We'd just started something back up between us, whatever this thing was, and now he'd be gone for six weeks.

"Rena?" His arms circled my waist.

"Hm?" I looked up.

"Come with me. To France."

The only sound as his words sank in came from the shower water.

"I can't imagine being away from you again for six weeks." He touched his mouth to mine. "Come with me." He kissed my cheek. "Come to France with me, my Rena." He kissed my other cheek.

My mind swirled as he nuzzled into the curve of my neck, and I ran my hands up and down his back. I couldn't go to France on short notice like that.

But why not? You have a job you can do anywhere, you don't have any pets, you can afford the flight. Why not go?

Using my hands, I lifted his head and looked into his eyes—his beautiful, expressive eyes. He was eager and hopeful and full of so much love. I tried to hear my heart, but it was beating too erratically; I thought it would tell me to do it, though. Everything with Chad had felt right so far. Besides, it wasn't committing to move in or something like that. It was more like an extended vacation.

In France—Paris, one of the most romantic cities on Earth.

With the sweetest, sexiest, most wonderful man alive.

THIRTY-EIGHT

My eyes roved over the remaining boxes of my belongings in my living room, all that was left. It had been chaos in my small apartment for the last week, but now it was mostly empty rather than chaotic. I worried that I'd mislabeled some of my boxes and that items that were going into storage would contain things I needed and I'd be combing through boxes in a tiny storage unit to find my laptop charger or something.

After spending six weeks together in France, Chad and I felt stronger than ever, were more in love than ever. Even so, when Chad had asked on the flight back to the US nine months earlier, I hadn't wanted to move in together just yet. But now my lease was up and there was no reason to renew it; Chad and I were buying a house together. We hadn't really been planning to, but Chad, ever on the hunt for things that mattered to me, had been secretly keeping an eye on the real-estate market around the preserve, and a house on the opposite side from my apartment—the same neighborhood I'd grown up in—had gone up for sale. It was an average-sized, three-bedroom house with a small back yard, a huge kitchen, and a large front porch that faced the preserve; it was perfect. We were closing in seven weeks, and in the meantime, I was going to live with Chad in his apartment, which Fern and Caroline were buying from him.

In the spring, on the second anniversary of the day we'd met, Chad had taken me for a picnic lunch in the preserve and asked me to marry him, which explained why I'd found him talking to the picture of my dad I kept by my front door a week earlier. He'd apparently been telling my dad all the ways he loved me and would take care of me for the rest of our lives the way he would have before proposing if my dad had been alive. Knowing he did that just made me love him even more. As did him sliding my mom's ring off my right hand and onto my ring finger on my left hand when I said yes.

It was then that I realized we'd met on the same day my parents had, that the date inscription was for the same day, simply a different year. When I voiced that realization to Chad, he said he already knew, that when he was told the date of the inscription when the pawn shop had called, that was how he knew without a doubt he'd found my mother's ring.

My eyes found the ring on my left hand, and I just stood gazing at it for a time. *Engaged. I'm engaged. To Chad.* A pleasant energy enveloped me; I could feel my dad. It had started happening on occasion in places other than the preserve, and I closed my eyes, savoring the feeling of a warm embrace from my father that accompanied these moments.

"I'm so happy, Dad," I whispered. "This one's a good man. The best human alive. You'd adore him, I know you would. And I think you'd be proud of me for taking a chance and following my heart like you told me to."

I opened my eyes to find Chad leaning against the wall, wearing a soft smile, his eyes on me. I smiled back.

"I guarantee he'd be proud of you," he said.

My eyes turned watery. "I love you," I replied.

He smirked, the corners of his lips twitching. "Naturally. I'm the best human alive; how could you not?"

I snorted. "Never mind. I take it back."

He pushed off the wall. "You can't take it back—too late." He wrapped me up in his arms and kissed the crook of my neck, his fingertips pressing lightly into my lower back. His lips traveled up the side of my neck, then across my jaw, until he reached my mouth and our tongues explored each other for several minutes. "Wanna take a break to make some dough, future Mrs. Connelly?" he rumbled out against my cheek.

I laughed.

"I was serious," he said, though he was laughing, too.

"I'll tell you what—once we get the rest of these boxes out of here, as long as I have some energy left, we can make dough the rest of the day."

"Wait, really?" he asked, his eyes dancing.

I narrowed my eyes. Was I missing something? He usually acted this way when I hadn't considered my offer carefully enough. But I couldn't figure out what it was. "Yes, really," I replied sluggishly.

He grinned from ear to ear. "Why don't you carry Potty down and just relax out front while I do the rest. I don't want you to expend any unnecessary energy or anything. And I'll have this done before you know it."

I shrugged, shaking my head again, and grabbed Potty. "Deal."

He turned to pick up another box, humming "What You Do" by James Gillespie to himself. My body clenched and I bit the corner of my lip to keep from grinning back at him. He certainly knew me, that was for sure. If he kept humming *that* song in *that* rumbling voice, I'd make dough with him no matter how tired I was. I'd maybe make dough right there on my living room floor between boxes. And the smirk he wore, combined with his wink as I held the door open for him to pass through, told me he knew all of that, too.

After delivering the box and Potty into the back of Chad's SUV, I sat on the retaining wall in the front of my apartment building. As crappy as it was, I was going to miss it. I'd gone through a lot of transformation in my life while living there. My plan was to let Chad bring down one armload of boxes alone to make him think I'd actually be okay with sitting there and watching him work without helping him, then get back to it myself. I turned my face up toward the sunshine and closed my eyes. The air had already begun to cool for fall, but the sunshine was still warm, and it felt nice on my skin.

"Nata?"

I froze for a second. I knew that nickname. And I knew that voice... but it couldn't be the person it belonged to. Hesitantly, I opened my eyes and tilted my head down from the sky toward the voice, then gaped at the woman standing a few feet in front of me.

"Connie?" I stood up and almost flung myself around her like I would have done once upon a time, but it had been over seven years since we'd last spoken and we hadn't parted ways amicably. "Wh-what...?" I swallowed and sat back down, mostly because my legs felt unsteady. "What are you doing here?"

Her brows drew in and she looked uncertain. "The letter you sent me."

"Letter?"

She pulled some papers out of her purse and handed them to me. "You didn't write this? It's your handwriting."

I glanced down. It was the letter I'd written at Chad's apartment with no intention of ever sending to her. I'd assumed when I couldn't find it that he'd thrown it out by accident. Had he sent it to her? When? I looked back up.

"I did write this," I responded slowly, trying to choose the right words. "But I didn't send it. When did you get it?"

She rolled her eyes and I half-smiled. She had always been an eye-roller—she did it all the time. Apparently that hadn't changed.

"It arrived in the mailroom at my nonprofit close to two years ago. It was misplaced and just found recently. It landed on my desk last week."

I couldn't believe Chad had sent it—because it must have been him.

"I wasn't sure what to do with it at first; I didn't even know where you lived anymore and your number changed a long time ago—I discovered that when I tried to call you a few weeks after we last spoke and it wasn't your number anymore. I'm guessing Damien was responsible for that. But you said you were submitting a piece to the journal, and I decided to call just in case they could give me some information about you. I talked to Jeb. He told me you'd be here today moving, and I decided to come down and hope I'd catch you."

I beamed, my eyes watering. I couldn't believe Connie was standing in front of me and we were talking to each other. My lifetime best friend who I'd thought I'd pushed out of my life for good. "I'm so glad you did."

I heard footsteps and turned just as Chad reached us. I stood and his left hand rested against my back as he reached out his right hand toward Connie.

"Hi—I'm Chad, this amazingly talented writer's lucky fiancé."

I rolled my eyes, glad he'd toned down his comically lavish praise.

Connie reached out and shook his hand, her lips quirking in amusement. "I'm going to go out on a limb and guess that you're the one who sent Nata's letter to me. I'm Connie."

Chad's eyes widened and his mouth pulled into a wide grin. "Connie? This is perfect! I'm so glad you're here, I've heard so much about you from Rena."

Connie, still smiling, turned to me. "You were right—I *do* like him already."

"Rena love," Chad said, turning to me and kissing my cheek. "Why don't you guys go out or back to our place or something and catch up? I can finish here by myself."

"My car is full of stuff for the storage unit, too," I said.

"Just let me know where you end up and I'll come swap cars once mine is empty."

I considered taking him up on his offer. "Are you sure? It's a lot to do, and it's all *my* stuff, so I hate for you to have to do it all."

"Positive."

I smiled, biting the corner of my lip. "Okay."

Chad kissed the corner I was biting and I released it, smiling widely now.

"It was really nice to meet you," he said, turning back to Connie and smiling at her. His eyes sparkled—he was obviously excited. He held his hand out and they shook again. "Thank you for coming."

She raised a brow. "Thank you for sending me her letter." She turned to me. "Lake?"

I grinned. "Perfect."

We walked through the preserve to the small lake near the center, the same lake we used to sneak out and bike to when we were kids, catching each other up on the last years of our lives. Like when I'd done the same thing with Chad when Fern and Caroline got married, the longer we talked, the more natural and easy things felt. Despite the rift between us since Damien, it seemed our friendship had never really gone anywhere; we just needed to find it again.

"I'm assuming this is the same Chad you wrote about in your letter?" she asked at one point.

"Yeah. We did break up for a quite a while a few months after I wrote that to you, but don't worry—he didn't do anything wrong. Not really, anyway. Damien had shown up just before Thanksgiving outside my apartment, intending for me to leave with him. He basically threatened to kill me and Chad if I didn't go with him. I got a protective order against him, but Chad and I were really freaked out about him coming after me again and seriously hurting me this time. It caused a strain in our relationship. Chad got a little overprotective about me going out without him, and I freaked out, afraid he was turning into Damien, and I left him."

"Oh, Nata."

"Yeah. I know. It sucked. But it was the right thing to do. I *needed* to show myself I could do it, and I needed to learn how to feel safe alone again, which I couldn't do with Chad always with me. I did a lot of healing from what Damien did to me while Chad and I were apart, and he worked on his overprotective tendencies. I didn't think we'd ever even speak to each other again, but he wasn't giving up that easily, and we reconnected at his sister's wedding."

"His sister married your best friend... Caroline, right?"

"Yeah, that's right.

"So you guys are like a little family."

My heart warmed; it was true. "We are."

She gave me a soft smile, her eyes glassy. "I'm so happy for you, Nata. You've found what you were looking for. And I'm glad you escaped from Damien. I was so scared for you. And I felt so helpless because you couldn't see what was obvious to me, and I knew once we were estranged that if you ever did, you'd be trapped because he'd cut you off from everyone else. What Damien did to you is the reason I started my nonprofit. I wanted women who found themselves with men like Damien to know there was somewhere they could go where they could get help and support to leave them and start a new life. My hope was that, one day, if you needed it, it would help you. It was the only way I saw that I could do anything once Damien changed your number and I couldn't reach you at all anymore."

"Cons..." I said, my words disappearing.

She grabbed my hand and gave it a squeeze, her gaze on the lake.

"I love you, Nata," she said, again using her childhood nickname for me, which meant hope. "I had to do something, and that was all I could do."

"I can't believe you don't hate me after everything I did," I said with a soft laugh, despite there being nothing funny about what I was saying.

"Would you hate *me* if this was reversed?"

"Of course not," I said, shaking my head.

"Exactly."

We reminisced about childhood and our escapades at the lake and throughout the preserve for a long time before I realized it was getting close to dinnertime. "How long are you in town?" I asked as we headed back toward my apartment building.

"Until tomorrow morning."

"Come over for dinner. Chad's an *amazing* cook."

"I thought he was a baker?"

"He is, but everything he touches in the kitchen is to die for."

"You sure he wouldn't mind?"

I laughed. "He's probably silently begging me to invite you. He loves cooking, as well as anything that makes me happy, and having you over for dinner would definitely make me happy."

"He seems good for you, Nata."

"He is. He's a really good man, Cons—the *best* man, really."

"And he calls you Rena."

I nodded.

"Joy."

I nodded again.

"Does he know that's what it means?"

I grinned and nodded a third time. "Yep, he sure does. He looked it up himself when he realized names were important to me to make sure it was an okay name to call me. That was before we were really even dating."

"Oh my god, Nata," she said.

I laughed. "I know! I'm a lucky woman, I really am."

"Can I see your ring?" Connie asked after a while.

I held my left hand up.

"Nata! Is that your mom's ring?"

"It is."

"You *found* it? Damien didn't actually get rid of it?"

"He did get rid of it. I don't know what he did with it—probably chucked it in the dumpster outside our building. But someone found it, and I don't know how many times it changed hands, but it eventually made it into a pawn shop."

"How the hell did you manage to find the right pawn shop?"

"I didn't. Chad did. He called *all* of them in a hundred-mile radius of where I lived with Damien after I told him what Damien had done. He didn't even tell me he was doing it, he just gave me mom's ring one day when he found it."

"I think Dave could take some pointers from Chad," she said.

We both laughed and my cheeks ached. I'd dreamed about walking and talking with Connie about Chad, but I never thought it would actually happen. I pinched myself lightly and it hurt.

It was real.

Fern and Caroline joined us for dinner, and the five of us talked and laughed, trading stories, for hours. As I'd suspected, Connie got along wonderfully with Fern and Caroline. Chad was his normal goofy and romantic self, though there was an extra twinkle in his eye all evening and he couldn't stop grinning at Connie and me. Finally, it was late enough for everyone to head out. Connie and I exchanged phone numbers, and I got her home address so I could send her a wedding invitation, then I walked her to the door after saying goodnight to Fern and Caroline. We hugged each other tightly.

"It's so good to see you well and happy, Nata," she said, still holding tight. "It's everything I always wanted for you. It's all your dad ever wanted for you. He'd be so damn happy right now if he was here to see you."

I squeezed her.

"Is this Chad's doing?" she asked, gesturing up at the wall as we stepped apart.

Over the entryway table was a very large framed photo—the photo Chad had taken of me at Fern and Caroline's wedding and asked me if he could print and frame. My cheeks warmed and I nodded. "It's from Fern and Caroline's wedding."

She studied the photo, like she had when she first came in. "I love this picture of you," she said. "You look so happy. And that tattoo is amazing."

"Thank you."

"I like him," she said, turning to me. "I like him a lot. He might just be good enough for you."

I laughed, crying by now.

"I missed you so much, Cons. I'm so sorry for everything. I wish I could take it all back."

She stepped back and our hands hung clasped between us. "I missed you, too, Nata. And I know you are, but you shouldn't be. What Damien did to you wasn't your fault, and what happened between us was because of what Damien did. I don't blame you and I'm not angry—I never really was—not with *you*, anyway. And it's in the past for us. We can be a part of each other's lives again now, and I'd really like that. I'd like for you to know my kids and for them to know you."

"I'd love that."

We talked for another minute or two and then she was gone. But this time, I wasn't sad because I knew I'd be seeing much more of her from then on. When I turned, Chad was leaning against the wall at the far end of the entry hall, his arms and ankles crossed, wearing a small smile.

"I can't believe you sent her my letter. When I couldn't find it, I thought you'd accidentally thrown it away," I said, walking up and leaning into his chest.

He wrapped his arms around me and smoothed his hands up and down my back. "I was worried you'd be pissed at me for doing it, but I had to, Rena. From what you'd told me about her, I knew she wouldn't hold what happened against you—there was just no way. But you didn't believe that, so you were too afraid to send the letter. I knew when she got it she would find you. I thought I was wrong after a while, but, somehow, here she is two years later."

"She said it got lost in the mailroom and they just discovered it last week."

Chad chuckled. "Well, I'm glad they found it eventually."

"Me, too. And I'm glad you sent it."

He kissed the top of my head and sighed. I listened to the beat of his heart, steady like he was. Like he'd been since I met him. My life was perfect, it seemed. Though, at the same time I had that thought, a wave of fear washed over me.

"It feels like everything is too good to be true," I murmured into his chest. "I'm afraid something's going to happen."

"Nothing's going to happen, my Rena."

"You really think that? You think we'll make it for the long haul? That I won't somehow mess us up again like I did before?"

He used his hand to tilt my face toward his and looked into my eyes with that intensity and focus that made everything else disappear. He tucked my hair behind my ear, his hand lingering to cup my jaw, his thumb smoothing over my cheek.

"Without a doubt, we'll make it for the long haul." He paused, his eyes roaming my face. "I love you, Rena. From the second you walked into the kitchen at the café for your first day of work, I fell in love with you. Something in me recognized something in you and that was it, I was a goner, as they say. We've had a rocky road, and it may get rocky again in the future, but that doesn't mean we shouldn't be on it together. Besides, I've never had all three things with anyone else."

"All three things?" I asked, smirking a bit. Another set of three. It applied to success in life, in the kitchen, and—apparently—in love.

He nodded. "I believe there are three things you need for love to last, to survive anything thrown at it. One, you need to be *in* love. And I am definitely in love with you—I'm madly in love with you. Two, you need to love someone even when things are tough, through not just the moments it's easy, but the moments it may seem impossible—you need love that's deep, not shallow. And I've loved you every beautiful and painful moment that I've known you. Three, you need to be willing to take risks to keep your love alive and well, to go outside your comfort zone and do whatever it takes, even if it seems wild. I think I've already shown you that I'll do that, and I wouldn't hesitate to do it again and again and again if I had to—whatever needed doing in order to keep you."

My heart beat riotously against my ribcage, but Chad's demeanor was calming it. He pressed a hand against my chest over my heart and held mine over his. Now I could feel his steady, rhythmic heartbeat against my palm.

"That's how I know we're going to last, Rena love. Because I don't just love you, but I love you madly, deeply, wildly."

ACKNOWLEDGEMENTS

As I'm sitting down to write my acknowledgements for this book, it seems surreal that I'm here again. That I've written another book, am publishing another book. When I returned to my love of writing, I'd have laughed if someone told me I'd be writing the acknowledgements section for my sixth published book five years later. And yet here I am. Here you are. Here *we* are.

And I do mean "we." As much as writing is a solitary endeavor, it also isn't. Without readers, who would writers write for? And I want to thank you, my readers, first today. I feel so fortunate and practically overwhelmed with gratitude that you're there, that you're willing to give up some the most precious commodity we all have—time—to read the words I've written for you. For that, I'm eternally grateful.

Thank you, always, from every crevice within me, to my husband. You're my support, my cheerleader, my tether to reality. Without you, and the tumultuous, beautiful story of us, I'd be sorely lacking in inspiration. I love you most.

Melissa... what can I say that I haven't said so many times already? You rock and I'm fortunate to have you in my corner, always willing to read and give me the kind of feedback that helps me be a better writer, and tell stories better.

It takes a lot of moving parts from different places to get a book out there in the hands of a reader and I'm so thankful for all of mine: Murphy for my gorgeous covers and Jo for my beautiful ebook formatting, for starters. You guys are awesome and I love working with you. Seriously.

I want to thank my editor extraordinaire, Kayli, though those words don't come close to doing justice to the depth of gratitude I feel. No matter what I hand to you, you've got my back—emotionally and editorially. I know after every book we work on together that I'm becoming a better writer because of the time and care you invest into my manuscripts. As always, you've helped me ensure I'm telling my story the way it's meant to be told. You're the best—I couldn't do what I do without you.

Lastly, a thank you to Canaan Valley Resort and The Purple Fiddle in Thomas, West Virginia, for inspiring the location for Rena and Chad's Thanksgiving getaway and their night out for music.

ABOUT THE AUTHOR

Katherine Turner is an award-winning author and a life-long reader and writer. She grew up in foster care from the age of eight and is passionate about improving the world through literature, empathy, and understanding. In addition to writing books, Katherine blogs about mental health, trauma, and the need for compassion on her website www.kturnerwrites.com. She lives in northern Virginia with her husband and two children.

PLAYLIST

All songs are by artist James Gillespie

What You Do

Good Life

Beyond Today

Him.Her.

ICFTI

Dead In The Water

Hold Me Down

Rescue Me (Mahogany Sessions x IRIS)

Kerosene

Someday Sundays

Home

Lost

Foolish Love

BY KATHERINE TURNER

Fiction

End of Interludes

Madly, Deeply, Wildly

Life Imperfect Series

Finding Annie

Willow Wishes

Wildflower Promise

Non-Fiction

resilient: a memoir

moments of extraordinary courage

CPSIA information can be obtained
at www.ICGtesting.com
Printed in the USA
BVHW031911260523
664952BV00011B/240